THE FAMILY FORTUNA

THE FAMILY FORTUNA

Lindsay
Eagar

CANDLEWICK PRESS

First edition 2023

Library of Congress Catalog Card Number 2022915442
ISBN 978-0-7636-9235-3

22 23 24 25 26 27 LBM 10 9 8 7 6 5 4 3 2 1

Printed in Melrose Park, IL, USA

This book was typeset in Dante MT Pro, Colesberg Script, and Fortuna Serif.

Candlewick Press
99 Dover Street
Somerville, Massachusetts 02144

www.candlewick.com

For Kenneth,
my dove,
my sweet

A History

"**A**VITA, MY KITTEN," MY FATHER WOULD SAY, twirling a licorice root in that damned bone-white smile of his, "any girl can be beautiful. But it takes a special girl to be as ugly as you."

On sold-out nights he waxed magnanimous, the heat from hundreds of mouth-breathing patrons making his head swell beyond its usual juglike proportions. Despite its size, there was room for little in those meaty swirls of brain—my mama was allotted a tiny corner, as were my siblings and I, though we all knew our father's love for us ran only as deep as puddles. Compared to his beloved circus, we were inconsequential.

So when he pried his gaze away from the lusty white lights of the midway to look at my face and purr, "Yes, my angel, what a monster you are!" I swilled his words, drunk on his rare attention.

Every time he said this, it was like hearing it for the first time . . .

I was only a winkling, three or four years old. The sons of our grunts, the migrant workers my father paid in pennies and bitch beer, paraded a group of local kids through our village of parked wagons and took turns boosting one another up to peek through my window.

"Monster," they whispered, terrified, delighted.

"I saw her eat a live piglet once," one of the sons curated, the red Texan dirt smeared across his cheeks like a burn. "Held it by the tail and dangled it over her mouth, then chomped its head clean off."

When I glanced up, they shrieked and ran, laughing and rolling in the yucca.

My father insisted he punished the boys, yelled at the grunts to keep a tighter leash on their little bastards, but that's cow pie.

He saw the way those boys gawked at me, and a thrill shot through his stomach.

An opportunity.

Alone in the wagon, I climbed onto my sister's vanity and stared at the girl in the mirror. I lit a lamp, I looked, and I saw—

I saw the freckles of blood, dried into blackened scabs where barbed feathers grew from my shoulders and back. Mama plucked them out of me on Sundays like I was roast chicken dinner. A fresh garden of feathers had already started nosing up through my skin, which meant that tonight when I curled up in bed, my skin would itch like I had the scabies.

I saw the teeth that burst from my oddly formed mouth—two rows of black triangular razors, fragile as glass. A bearded lizard's smile.

I saw a pair of eyes that blinked when I blinked—no pupils, no color, not even when the sunshine hit them. Just holes, deep and dark as abandoned gold mines, hauntingly empty, like you might trip and fall into them if you stared too long.

I saw my beak.

Home was the Family Fortuna, traveling circus and midway, the pinnacle of tented spectacle in the southwestern states of the land of the free. And my father was Papa Fortuna, owner, ringmaster, and asshole extraordinaire.

Being raised in a circus was a very particular kind of life. By the time I could toddle, I'd seen stranger things than most adults could fathom.

Our needle man, for instance, who pushed wires and nails into his pasty, spongy flesh as though he were a pincushion. He was Uncle Myron to us even though we did not share blood. Papa expected his offspring to embrace all our fellow comrades in exhibition as family, nothing less.

Or the woman we hired in South Bend who grew snarls of hair on her face, her chest, and the tops of her knuckles—we called her La Loba and took money from customers who wanted to hear her howl and scratch for her long-dead lover.

Or Graciela, our adored grotesque, seven feet tall and heavy as a train car, who let her audiences watch while she ate a cake large enough to bury a pharaoh inside, then swirled around to a Strauss waltz, wiggling her cloudlike backside.

There were many other sights both dazzling and disturbing, sights that would make a priest's skin crawl.

But nothing was as unsettling as that little girl in the mirror. I'd glanced at my own reflection plenty of times with a toddler's fascination, but I had never truly looked until that day.

I looked not with my own peepers but through the

eyes of those boys who had ogled me. I looked, and I saw a monster.

It would be weeks before I had a nightmare about anything but myself.

Later that same evening, the screams and cackles of the boys still percussing in my ears, my father squatted on the porch steps of our wagon and pulled me onto his knee. He tucked a dahlia behind my ear the way I'd seen him do to his dancing girls from the kootchie tent.

"Gorgeous women make the world go 'round, my sweet," he said. "People will pay good money to see a pair of pretty ankles, pretty thighs, a flash of tit . . . anything a girl is willing to show for a buck. But you, Avita—in our line of work, you're worth a thousand whores."

And so my father spoiled me with presents and drowned me in compliments. He flattered my glossy black hair, my porcelain hands, my quiet nature, my non-hideous features, all to make me forget that my ugliness was his profit.

I was the baby of the Fortunas.

Luna, the oldest, was as tall and svelte as a flamingo, singularly stunning, with pale hair that she kept in a sharp bob swish-swishing along her jawline like those Parisian minxes in the magazines my father ordered for her. Some blondes slant golden, but Luna's hair was electric white against the glow of her waxen skin.

My father liked to say that the night he'd planted Luna into our mother, he'd drunk from a glass of water that had sat out all night on a table in a pool of moonlight. "Nine months later, out sprang our baby girl, moon tufts on her head," he'd brag, placing an arm across Luna's shoulders. Luna, who saved all her human affection for her audiences, remained statuesque, immovable.

My sister's hair fell across half her face in a curtain, and she glanced up at her crowds this way, sizing them up with one hooded, kohl-lined eye. This was how she viewed everyone— with only half of her—and she allowed only half of herself to be viewed. Her shows ended with her mostly nude, but even I, her own sibling, did not know much else about her.

She spent most of her daylight hours dozing in the wagon we shared. At night, however, inside the Tent of Wonder, my sister came alive with glitter and charm. Luna was the duchess of the kootchie tent, the red-hot queen of the circus nightlife. Other parents would be ashamed to have their daughter work as a glorified stripper, but my father himself sized Luna up for the Tent of Wonder when she turned twelve and her breasts became too big to fit inside the clown costumes.

As a child, my sister dreamed of walking the ropes. But Family Fortuna ropewalkers needed itty-bitty compact bullet bodies, and Luna's hips swept out like a guitar. "A body for enticing men to empty their wallets," my father told her, "not for high-wiring." And that was that.

When Papa was ringleading and Mama was busy showing her blue-ribbon piglets to prospective buyers, I would slip into the Tent of Wonder to watch my sister, watch her halt the respiratory systems of every male under the canvas, watch her gyrate her silk-clad body, bells jingling, tassels dangling. My fascination with her was familial pride but also curiosity. I made a study of the way she performed with the hint of a smile, which suggested she had all the mysteries of the universe laced under her corset and she'd share them with her audience . . . for the right price.

My big brother, Lorenzo—we called him Ren—was two feet shorter than I was. He was born with dwarfism, and when he emerged from my mother, bowlegged and big-noggined, my father danced a celebratory jig.

"What's a proper circus without a half-pint running around the ring?" he said, and dreamed up things for my brother to do: flaming gauntlets of fireworks for Ren to leapfrog over; hoops of silver metal for Ren to dive through dressed as a poodle; massive tigers for Ren to ride like a sultan, a creamy cape flowing behind him in the dust.

But Ren turned out to have a curve in his spine and a bubble in his lung, so my father folded up Ren's would-be spangles as mournfully as if his son were being measured for a casket and cut his imaginary losses. "He's useless to me, an utter failure!" he would cry, even when Mama hissed, "Shhh! Not so loud! He can hear you, Arturo!" But of course my father already knew that; he always expected everyone to listen when he spoke.

So instead of soaking up the sound of applause, my brother carved out a special position for himself, the only desk job in the Family Fortuna—he did the books. Accounting; ticket sales; permits for our acts, which varied depending on the county; venue reservations; purchase of illegal animals from black-market pet shops; wages—Ren handled it all, and it suited him much better than the spotlight ever would have.

My father made him an office from the boards of an old out-house, gutted and cleaned, with wheels slapped on it so the horses could tug it along in our caravan. That was where my brother was happiest—in his upright, coffinlike box, running numbers as he tapped his pencil against his spectacles, sitting on stacks of books that he devoured quicker than my father was willing to buy them. Pulp paperbacks were two for a dime at every general store we encountered, and Ren ate them up like raisins.

Yes, Papa was disappointed to lose the chance to announce one of his own kiddos in the ring, but he cheered up as soon as I was born.

We knew nothing but the Family Fortuna, my siblings and I—we were nursed on talcum powder and sawdust, raised with spiels on our tongues and grime from five different states under our fingernails. We belonged to the circus first and foremost and to our parents second. Children of the road, children of starlight and tumbleweeds. Children of this odd world made of waxed canvas and spun sugar. Each of us a treasure to anyone with an eye for profit, and my father saw me as his crown jewel.

"One day, you'll be your very own attraction," he vowed as I grew. "You'll have your own tent, your own dressing room—"

"My own costumes?" I cut in.

"Racks of costumes," was his honey-dipped assurance, "and adoring fans."

"Fans," I repeated in a faraway voice. "I can really have my own show, Papa?" I pictured satin and sequins, yards of fabric sewn into a slinky dress that barely covered me. I pictured music that rose and fell like the ocean, and lights propped along the edge of the stage like cockleshells, and an idolizing storm of applause.

My father looked at me and pictured screaming.

"Not until you're ready, my dove. Then you'll be famous from Texas to Tacoma." He smiled like the devil, dollar signs in his eyes.

"From Texas to Tacoma," I chanted, and scrambled into his arms.

"My million-dollar gal," he cooed, happy to let me tuck my head beneath his chin. "They won't believe their eyes."

In moments like these, he wasn't Arturo Fortuna, grand architect of the tents. He was my old man, the same person who had wiped my rump clean and spoon-fed me pears mashed in milk. The same one who still humored me with smooches for my skinned knees and sang me to sleep with the queerest of lullabies. How could I be blamed for trusting him?

The greatest showman on earth—how could I not believe him?

If only I had known what kind of ring he was cooking up for me.

The Aviary Extravaganza

"**L**ADIES AND GENTLEMEN!**"

A ringmaster's instrument is his voice, and oh, how my father delighted in playing his instrument. He began bellowing announcements and pronouncements before he'd even rubbed his eyes clean of sleep crust in the hazy dawn, and he didn't stop talking until he was hoarse as a soprano in menopause. His opening lines boomed through the tent, touching every flap and tuck of the canvas with a gentleman's stroke.

"Bienvenidos! Bienvenue! Willkommen! Benvenuto! And any other greetings you desire! I welcome you to the most marvelous sight a human can behold, a flabbergasting feast for your eyes! Welcome to the Family Fortuna's Spectacular Aviary Extravaganza!"

I took a deep breath and rolled it out of me, long and lazy, like a spent lover trying to cool down her loins. Almost showtime.

The best time.

Papa twisted his mustache, which he smeared with pig lard to keep it as pointy as nails. The brim of his hat was perfectly slanted to show just a hint of the scarlet lining. A pop of color—enough to entice, enough to dazzle.

And his coat, his relished funereal black tailcoat with the gold piping along the sleeves and breast, it performed as passionately as Arturo did, the only clothing he owned that didn't seem intimidated to be worn by him. Once my father slipped while hiking and cut open his shin on a rock; he was measurably less careful about repairing his own flesh than he was about sewing up a torn seam in his worshipful tailcoat.

"But this is no ordinary bird show, and this is no ordinary bird!"

The audience was many-headed, and when it inhaled, I could hear the bristling of excitement in its lungs. They were nestled right in the palm of Papa's greed-slicked hand, and by God, he knew it.

My father had introduced me in the ring hundreds of times, and yet even I was not totally immune to the crests and valleys of his tone, the way he wove gold into his phrases. Sometimes I found myself lulled, resting the crown of my head against the steel bars of my cage as if I were just another dusty slack-jaw undone by the magic of the ring.

With a showing every weeknight and two on Saturdays, I had his pitch memorized. I knew when he tired of his speech, when it got soggy and overchewed in his mouth, and he would dip into one of Ren's dictionaries, spinning his sonic kaleidoscope and changing *spectacular* to *magnificent* or *glorious* or any number of words he'd collected over the years like loose change beneath the bleachers.

I knew when he could feel the crowd slipping away from

him like wriggling fish on the run, so he upped the stakes, baiting them with variations on the usual act, which I would then improvise at the last minute. I knew when he was simply in a flashy, boasty mood, adding extra polish to his consonants to make sure the people knew they were about to witness a goddamn miracle.

He was always as excited as they were to see the curtain lift.

We were partners in the ring, he and I; the audience was a rubber ball, and we batted it between his flowery words and my gratuitous performance before we jointly released the people back into the circus grounds, their heads dizzy with fearful exhilaration, my face already haunting the subterranean halls of their minds.

It was a full house tonight, the screws in the bleachers earning their keep. We hit standing room only less than five minutes after the tent flaps opened—always a point of pride for me, to know my crowds would rather make themselves a fire hazard than miss the spectacle of my performance.

People packed in, asses nestled nice and cozy, munching food from the midway. Men gnawed on turkey legs greased with chipotle paste and cloves, sucking the bones clean of gristle. Women shoveled handfuls of spiced popped corn into their mouths as if a famine was coming. Sticky children nibbled their spun sugar on paper sticks.

Mama always shook her head at our patrons, marveling at how the circus turned otherwise decent, mild-mannered prairie folk into feral dogs, and Papa would grin. "That's why they love us. We let them be themselves."

I slid a finger between the drapes of the velvet slipcover that hid my cage from the audience and pulled it back ever so slightly so I could peek out at the crowd.

"I caught her in the wet, sultry jungles down south"—Papa's lies came out as rainbow-spun yarns, as glistening as shouted poetry—"where she made her home in the blackest of caves, feasting on unsuspecting songbirds with her terrible fangs."

The audience tittered.

"Females of a delicate nature, avert your eyes! And keep your children quiet, no matter how frightened they are—screams only drive the creature further into a frenzy!" Another lie—we wanted them to scream. Papa loved to hear his money make noise.

Happy, screaming customers.

"She feeds off your fears, my dear ladies and gentlemen, but her favorite food is warm meat!"

This was the part of the show when Papa pointed to his left with a dramatic thrust of his hand, making a bat's wing with his tailcoat.

Pedro the spotlight boy illuminated the chicken coop at the far side of the ring. A few hens clucked, flapping their feathers at the rude upset.

The audience gasped, and I practically salivated at the sound of their mounting hysteria.

They'd paid their two bits to see a spot of violence—to see brains splattered, to see something alive be torn apart, to see a creature bruised and ugly and possibly naked, a thing that deserved to be feared—and it was my job to show it to them.

"Shall we give her some bait?" Papa unlatched the coop; hens fell gracelessly to the dirt and ran in circles.

I saw only the silhouette of my father through the slipcover, but I knew he was glowing. Made of stars.

"Are you ready to see her?"

A good show is like a poker game, he was fond of saying to anyone who would listen—or anyone who was not a rock—and this was the moment when he showed his hand.

"Brace yourselves!" Each of his words was deliberate now, dipped in caramel and brightened with cinnamon. "Don't get too close . . . to the incredible, the legendary, the bloodthirsty . . . Bird Girl!"

The audience's roar was deafening, almost as loud as Papa's pomposity. He loved cash, but his true currency was applause.

In the detonation of their cheers, I thought of Papa's lecture to all his performers, which came every morning after breakfast in the grub tent, right before the band started its prelude fanfares. "You are all mirrors when you are in that ring. Whatever the audience gives you—their love, their dreams, their devotion—you must give it back to them and then some. Give it back double, triple. A hundredfold."

And then he always dropped his voice to a whisper, as if this were a Family Fortuna secret, as if there weren't dozens of these alleged secrets, a new one invented by him every day: "What they are really doing, you lot, is they are giving it to themselves. They know exactly what they want to see. So show it to them. Be their mirror. That's all you have to do."

In my tent, a drum roll ended; I didn't remember hearing it begin.

Cymbals crashed.

I readied my snarl, every part of me tense, every muscle rigid. I let loose with the growl I'd made in the tent a thousand times. It took little effort to sound vicious, since my voice had calloused into a permanent screech after so many performances.

I pretended to be enraged by the drums, enraged by my captivity, rattling my bars.

Behind my grimace was a hidden smile. I would give them all exactly what they'd come for.

Papa yanked the slipcover from my cage. Pedro the spotlight boy aimed his weapon at my face.

I was as good a mirror as I was a monster.

First came the gasps, the shrieks. A crowd pushed to the very brink of their apprehension, and at their first sight of me, their mouths flew open before their brains even caught up with their eyes.

Papa fluffed them, then I jolted the breath right out of them.

I was just over five feet tall, but I knew better than anyone that sometimes even the smallest things can frighten us into quivers.

Where did they look first? At the long, angular slope of my nose, which curved from my wide cheeks down into the ideal bird beak, monopolizing my face with its skinless strangeness, its keratin abomination?

At the obsidian of my teeth, their razor sharpness inflaming a primordial instinct to flee? I was caged, and only in the safety of this knowledge did the crowd keep their butts in the bleachers.

At the less obvious but no less chilling features: my dark, round, blinking eyes, alive as a raptor's as it swooped from the sky to seize a mouse in its talons?

At the crest of black feathers that grew from my back and shoulders, rankled like a vulture's, giving a fiendish bulk to my frame?

I reached through the cage and grabbed a passing chicken. The audience shrieked in delicious, horrified delight. Their gazes bored holes into me, traveling up and down my teenaged body, inspecting everything. No part of me was off-limits—they'd paid their money to stare, after all. I was not human, I was exhibit.

Now let's hear how much you love to fear me. I drew the chicken, clucking and scratching, to my open mouth.

"You are the mirror when you are in that ring, so don't be self-ish. Don't keep all that glory for yourself." The exclamation point of Papa's lecture, carved into my heart. "They give it to you, and you must give it back to them. Give it back to them a hundredfold. They came to give it to themselves."

People did not come to my tent for the glory.

They came to my tent for the nightmare. To see their worst fears reflected back at them, to know that I was only a mirror.

They came for the mirror.

I placed the chicken's head between my teeth and murmured a quick, half-assed prayer for my fellow fowl.

Bite. Crunch. Rip.

You're welcome, I told it. *I've just made you a star.*

And then the screams.

Chicken blood dripped from my chin, the taste dirty and gritty with poof and fluff, and I commanded myself not to gag as I spat the still-wriggling head onto the ground. The crowd cried out, screeching with glee.

This was what they wanted—to be frightened to the core. To be reminded that there was horror in the world, but that it was safely jailed in the ring, available to gawk at for pocket change but unable to follow them home . . .

Except for their dreams. I would be in their dreams tonight. I would be in their dreams forever.

"From Texas to Tacoma," my father had promised, and he had delivered over and over, week after week, gig after gig, year after year. "They won't believe their eyes."

Droplets of the chicken's inner marinade fell into my cleavage. The noise of the audience morphed into the roar of a wave; all other sound disappeared into the vortex of their hollering.

I locked eyes with Papa. It projected from him in rays brighter than sunlight, his face the clouds and the heavens to me—

His pride in me, too large to fit into the tent, greater than the long shadow cast by our caravan.

Suddenly I was a child again, atop his knee. Suddenly he was brushing my dark hair back from my eyes, the only object of his gaze. The priceless jewel in his glittering crown.

I would have ripped off my own head to have him look at me this way always.

When the music ended and the curtain fell, the audience

exited, twittering and gossiping. Women fanned themselves back to more prudent temperaments. Some children whimpered, some sobbed, some emerged from the canvas silent, lily-faced, my exhibition aging them beyond their years in a single evening. My cage was dragged backstage, and I was released from my steel prison.

There was fire in my limbs, a rhythm pulsing through me, a frenzy in my veins.

I could've worn out a brand-new pair of dancing shoes right then.

I could've never again touched food and survived on just this energy, the zip of screams and applause and noise.

I never felt more alive than in those moments immediately postshow. It was as if I did not exist until my audience saw me.

A sweat-glazed Papa barked commands to the grunts, and then he turned to me, held my chin in his hands. He was the only person in the world willing to touch this face at this moment, to caress this skin, all smeared with hen's blood and the grimy thistle of feathers.

My world pinholed to his beetle eyes, the brilliance inside his head radiating so brightly it could light the ring itself.

He kissed my forehead, and "Beautiful show, my sweet. Simply beautiful!" slipped out the side of his mouth before he dashed away to present his next act.

Partners, my father and I—partners in spells, partners in dreams. He was the god of our circus paradise, and I was the resident archfiend, the darkness incarnate. The devil in juxtaposition, and I was plenty jubilant to play this role for as long as he would have me, so long as he would look at me that way.

It was the role I was born to play. The role this face had secured for me.

My fortune. My fate.

What was the difference?

San Antonio

JULY 1889

"**L**ET'S GIVE HER SOME MEAT!"

Our second night of three in San Antonio, and the hens were being particularly chicken tonight. Papa had to stomp his heels in the dirt behind them so they'd flutter close enough for me to grab, and when I finally got hold of a fat-breasted biddy, I paused.

My tooth was sore.

Last time I'd had a sore tooth like this, I'd ended up cracking it, a big split from fangtip to gums. Those chickens were always tender and juicy once Socorro, our cook, got her hands on them, but for me to decapitate them with only the strength of my jaw . . . it was a miracle I had any chompers left.

I held up the chicken in triumph, a vainglorious hunter showing off her trophy, and pushed against the inflamed tooth with my tongue, testing it.

Beyond my cage, the audience squirmed, just like the hen in my grip squirmed.

Just like my heart squirmed, jolted, and thumped with purpose.

A full house, all of them watching, all of them waiting, all of them wiggling in terror before me—

Except one.

I squinted to get a better look.

A figure at the very farthest corner of the cheap seats, a place out of the spotlight's range but illuminated by the glare off the steel of my cage.

A young man, a year or two shy of actual manhood. He had terracotta skin and black hair as fine as corn silk, grown to his shoulders. His eyes were the crescent-moon shape that came from barely suppressed joy, dark as bitter chocolate, though his lips were a neutral line.

Every other face in the crowd was grimacing or slack with a black-mouthed scream . . . but this boy seemed more bemused than thrilled. Curious. Tickled.

With a snarl that rumbled out of my mouth like a regurgitated train, I took firmer hold of the chicken, sore tooth be damned, and with unusual ferocity, I chomped the bird dead within an instant.

Hot blood poured down my chin.

There. That should do it.

That should shock some proper fear into him.

The air grew fragrant with terror: sour gasps, that ammonia scent of frightened sweat, the curdling of dairy from the fried cheese sticks dropped beneath the benches out of shock.

I let my chicken fall into the dirt and peered at the boy, smug. But he did not budge.

No scream, no shriek. Not even a sharp intake of air.

Pedro the spotlight boy pressed a switch, and as my ring plunged into darkness, I lost sight of the boy. A jagged blade of blunder pierced me through—why hadn't he screamed? Was he truly so unimpressed by beak, feathers, blood?

"What a beautiful show, my kitten." After I rinsed my mouth and caught my breath, Papa pecked my forehead and plucked a crooked feather from my crest. "I've never heard such screams."

I scowled at the memory of my one stubborn onlooker, but when Papa cocked his head at me, concerned, I spared him my angst. "My tooth. It's hurting again."

He tilted my head back, examining the incisor. "It's split. Just a hair. I'll fetch the glue—oh! There's the mayor!" He licked his thumb and spun it around his mustache. "The fiddlehead's playing hard to get with next season's permits, thinks some other show will outbid us, ha! Not when he sees our numbers. We're packed to the gills! You'll be all right, my sweetness?"

My smile brought hot air to my broken tooth, making it ache. "Yes, Papa. I'll be fine."

Off he trotted through the canvas flaps. The drone of ambient circus clamor was audible for half a second, and then the tent was silent as the seafloor, and I was alone.

As soon as the Aviary Extravaganza came to a close, I crept into my wagon and removed the tattered strips of muslin I wore as Bird Girl—a bandeau around my breasts, a loincloth wrapped betwixt my legs. Both needed the sweat and the Texas dust scrubbed out of them, so I left them piled near the door for the washers to take.

The summer breeze was soft as I slipped into a dressing robe, blowing the scent of the peaty soil and the black prairie clover into my parked bedroom. Papa had instructed the grunts to set up near the pastures facing the west side of town so our horses could relax near the lake; if I strained my ears, I could hear the katydids chirping their leaf-hopping opera.

After my last showing, the evening was my own to do with as I pleased. A stroll near the water sounded like just the ticket for me tonight—watch the ripples, toss in some pebbles. Breathe the fresh air.

But first, dinner.

A tray had been delivered for me: fried rosemary potatoes, Socorro's famous lime-marinated rutabaga with stewed fruit, cornbread drenched in frothy cinnamon honey butter, all of it piping hot. Tea steeped in a ceramic pot on top of my nightstand.

I knelt on the floor with my meal, and as I ate, I thought again about the boy in the cheap seats, the way he'd locked his gaze on me in the ring, how the world's orbit had slowed into stillness. He hadn't gawked or stared—he'd just looked. As if I didn't frighten him at all.

Luna's vanity mirror was directly across from me; I glanced in it as I chewed.

Avian beak. Razor teeth. Dark, bottomless pits for eyes. An apex of glossy black feathers.

A monster.

I would've been offended if it weren't so laughable. How could that boy look at me and not see a spectacle? How could he endure this face without his very soul screeching in scaly-eyed fear?

Perhaps he didn't see well, I thought as I tongued a trickle of butter from my wrist. Perhaps he needed eyeglasses. Perhaps he'd thought he was witnessing a very blurry and plain-faced acrobat contort around her steel bars to the percussive stylings of a hen-house frenzy.

I drained the last of my tea and set the dirty tray on the wagon's back stoop.

"That face costs twenty-five cents to look at, my angel," Papa loved to remind me, and so I wrapped a rose-tinted scarf around my head, flattening it beneath my eyes so I looked ready to rob the caboose of a Western Pacific train. A pale blue calico dress buttoned to its seams kept my crest of feathers tucked in.

All my ugly bits covered and out of sight.

My beak protruded under the fabric in a bulge that suggested a larger-than-usual sneezer, but nothing else was suspicious about my muffled appearance; plenty of cake-eating dames roamed our grounds with scarves over their average-size schnozzes, not wishing to filter prairie dust through their fine nose hairs. Nothing applause-worthy. The wonders of the circus would camouflage me—but I always tied an extra knot in the scarf, just in case.

A face as hideous as this one was always onstage.

I plopped on a raggedy hat left at the racetrack by some gambler last fall. Its brim bent down, casting shade over my features—an extra precaution against anyone standing a little too close or staring a little too hard. There was nothing I could do about my eyes except keep my peepers down and hope no one fell into their darkness.

Out of my wagon I slipped like a skulking cat, fluid and

mindful, gravitating toward the shadows. Each tent in the Family Fortuna was buzzing and alive, its own tiny world, and its spectators were glued to their seats. All the better for me to become the invisible girl; no one was aware that the person with the hat and scarf and the long dark braid was the walking, waking nightmare they'd paid two bits to see just minutes ago.

I nodded at a cluster of grunts, the employees who impossibly packed our circus into crates for transport from booking to booking. They stood outside the periphery of Bart the Bull's-Eye's Knife-Throwing Whirligig Riot, sipping beers. Inside Bart's tent, a leggy blond volunteer was bound by her wrists and ankles, spinning, spread-eagle, on the giant wooden target. Men half watching groused to one other as he prepped his blades: "He's gonna get her this time, right through the gullet. Nah, he's gonna miss." But Bart's knives had never once needed a cleaning.

Our iron stomach had her tent flaps open—she was a six-foot-tall Austrian woman who took a cannonball to the gut while she ate a schnitzel. Every night, three seconds after the explosion, the crowd cried a panicked "Ohhhhh!" followed by a joyous "Hurrah!" as she licked her fingers, unaffected, a melody that made my lungs squeeze.

Not everyone performed under canvas. The ribbon fliers were preparing for their last leap of the evening, multicolored spotlights blazing on their poles, shooting rainbows down into the grass beneath the onlookers' boots. The fliers' silhouettes were barely visible against the constellations as they made their death-defying jumps, plummeting to the ground only to catch themselves last-minute with their sparkling ribbons. Their audience reverently muted its gasps so as not to overpower their music, tinkling starlight made by a group of harpists, timpani drummers, and bell ringers.

Beyond the tents, if you wanted to look that far, the gleam of the circus ended abruptly at the beginning of the real world, desert and stars—but the real world had never been a place that held my interest. I was interested only in our stars, the stars we made, the stars we were. How proud I was to be such a heavenly body.

The Family Fortuna: even when it was a young sapling of a show, it had always been the greatest traveling circus this side of the Mississippi. We rolled all year long, hitting every city that would have us in the parts of the country where dust blew red and land stretched all the way to the salty ocean.

Shiny new shows shot down into our territory from the North by railroad, more and more of them every year, circuses that hailed from the fancy European traditions of entertainment: sad clowns with melting faces; white-bearded men on stilts; animals in glittering costumes stacking themselves into pyramids, one on top of the other.

"All silver, all smoke." Papa dismissed anyone who dared compete with his beloved kingdom—but we knew he was secretly jealous of their private railcars.

"Maybe if you didn't spend like an emperor, you could afford more than old chuck wagons," Ren would say under his breath whenever Papa complained about money, which ebbed and flowed like a river of steaming molasses in and out of our strongbox.

Some seasons we feasted; others it seemed like the folks in Kansas dealing with grasshopper blights were eating better than we were.

In 1889 I was sixteen. It was a good year for us. We'd circled the mountains and prairies long enough to see the West change— our crowds used to be exclusively cattlemen and claim jumpers, men who had gotten rich by suckling from the mines until there was barely anything left for the bats, men who wanted to pass the heat with some high-wire distractions.

Now even the itty-bitty towns had their own breweries. Insurance salesmen. Electric streetlamps. Some man in Phoenix made his living by selling ice.

Some of those prospectors who panned the rivers clean of their precious metals didn't head back to where they came from. They stayed. Opened shops or bought sheep or otherwise tied loose ends together to make new homes. This was the firmament upon which we built our own little world—this fizzling, hustling expanse of cowboys and troops and schoolteachers and farm families and bored Mormons with their half dozen wives in tow.

Mama worried about the sauciness of the Southwest. She fretted over the bloomer-style dresses the women donned as well as the tangy language of the ranchers and rustlers who came to our shows after draining their gut-warmers at the saloons. (She needn't have feared; we Fortuna babies had learned all our dirtiest words from her, and the ass-waggling in the kootchie tent had worn down our sensitivities, so no prairie wife's bare shins could have made us blush.)

Our mother fretted all the same, biting her nails over the

effects this wilderness might have on her virtuous young daughters. She loved to pretend the circus life had corrupted her, and to pretend that we could ever turn out any different.

But Mama had always been one of us, even before the circus, even before Papa.

Back in Bozeman, when my father was nineteen, he met my mother, a poor pig farmer's daughter. She was a thrilling combination of pious and daring, a girl of few words—but they were the right ones.

Papa was, well, Papa. Working as a stable hand for the rodeo. Full of dreams, full of hot air. He bought Mama a shot of smoky mescal with his last coin and promised her that someday he'd get them both out of the manure.

He wasn't Arturo Fortuna back then. He wouldn't become that shiny, slick version of himself until he fixed up the new moniker. He was born John Fitzpatrick, a laughably plain name, obviously too standard-issue for the man who would one day produce a show in which his oldest daughter wore only tarantulas to cover her naughty bits as she cha-chaed across a stage.

As for my mother? She remained Quinn through it all, never growing attached to her parents' last name or to whatever last name my father eventually decided for the two of them. I always suspected part of her had been waiting all her life for a husband to tell her who she would be.

Fortuna, he chose, for the way it sounded at once vaguely Italian ("but not in a threatening way," a handler once informed us) and like the very cadence of magic.

Fortuna. Fortune. Your destiny in his hands.

Papa wanted to ride the broncos, but the big boss at the rodeo wouldn't let him. Said behind his back that nobody wanted to see a foulmouthed little cuss get thrown from his mount and be trampled to death. Papa caught wind of this and thought it sounded like a fantastic way to make money. Turned out it was exactly what people wanted to see.

Turned out my father had a knack for putting on a killer show.

He traded for a broken-down dun mare, a sore old gal who wouldn't buck if a horsefly were chewing off her ass. But the way he rode her outside the rodeo grounds, hollering and whooping until he tumbled to the dirt in a suicide leap . . . it didn't matter that she had one hoof in the glue factory. Papa knew how to work a stage. He enticed passersby to purchase tickets to the rodeo, and his ballyhoo morphed into an official and paid opening act in front of hundreds of people at a time. Mama shot guns at a target while on horseback, and Papa trained primped-up ponies to dance in a line, ribbons in their manes, curls in their tails.

When they finally got hitched, instead of buying his new bride a house, Papa bought the Family Fortuna's first wagon, and he and Mama took their show on the road, a sort of working honeymoon. Three babies, a big top, and a buttload of different acts later, their honeymoon still hadn't ever really ended.

Kootchie-Kootchie-Koo

THE TENT OF WONDER WAS ALREADY FILLED with men thirsty for beautiful girls. Female company was often rare for the ranchers who worked between the towns we visited. After long days in the cruel sun, to see a pretty lady who wasn't clipped from a dirty magazine but was real, flesh and blood, dancing before your eyes . . . well, that was why Papa charged twelve and a half cents a head for the kootchie tent. Twelve and a half cents to quench your loneliness and lust for the evening.

Most of our rings were set up for bench acts, our performers doing their shows right down in the dirt while the audience watched from raked bleachers all around, but not the kootchie tent. Here the girls were elevated on risers, and the men stood below the stage, where they could hoot and scratch and unleash their inner coyotes when the all-girl buffet began strutting.

The night's performance was about to begin. Steam-powered lights amped up along the stage, and strains of music started—the opening notes of a sultry tango, the guitarist's hand already strumming a blur in the corner. The audience quieted, the air scorching and humid.

I stood in the very back and to the side, deep in a shadow near one of the canvas flaps. Both my covered face and my slumped posture rendered me unnoticeable among these starving hyenas, and my scarf filtered out most of the undeniable smells of country men—perspiration, sweet dirt under the collar, beef stew.

Music flourished. The house lights darkened, and a round white spot focused on the scalloped red curtains. A single leg in a nude thigh-high stocking poked out between the velvet, a smooth tan calf coming to a spiky end in a glass heel.

The men were drooling. Someone wolf-whistled.

"Let's see the rest of ya, sweetheart!" another man cried, throaty with desperation, and I snickered. How I loved to watch the men be bamboozled, the swivel of expectations, the rug pulled out from under their collective unsuspecting feet.

How I was indeed my father's daughter.

The person attached to the leg shimmied out from behind the curtains and onto the stage, clad in a deep plum strapless gown with a slit cut dangerously high, nearly to the hip bone, shocking red gloves, and a headdress of silk flowers, every color of sunrise, piled high in a crown.

Not a dancing girl at all, but our dearest, darlingest Fernando.

"Oh, hello, boys!" he boomed. My best friend had no use for microphones; the boy had proven to my father that he could handle a stage part when he'd hollered loud enough to scare a grackle from its garbage.

"Welcome to the Tent of Wonder! I am your host for this

evening!" He winked at the men in the front row, his false eye-lashes as thick as tablecloth fringe.

From my place in the corner, I snorted. What a flirt.

"Don't you worry!" he went on before the confused crowd of panting males started to riot. "I'm only the ugly stepsister—but are you ready to see our lovely Cinderellas?"

The men thundered their approval. Their host clapped his gloved hands and put them beneath his chin delicately, as if he were posing for a cheesecake photo, his lips glistening with fuchsia gloss. It took a certain kind of person to hold the attention of a hundred hard-as-hickory cowboys, but Fernando could charm the feet off a rattler—and do it in stilettos, no less.

Years ago, when I was still just a winkling, we played a three-day streak in Elko, and somehow a little boy made it past the gates without a ticket, sneaking into the dressing room behind the kootchie tent.

By the time the dancing girls found him, he'd already dipped into their makeup palettes and fastened himself into a gown with a long, shimmering mermaid train. The grunts were about to toss him out on his scrawny brown ass when one of the girls said, "Wait! Look at his liner—a perfect cat-eye!"

And so, after some convincing, my father let him stay. Fernando was a runaway from La Tia Juana, a street-smart kid who had been sweeping floors for barbershops in exchange for his chuck. Not glamorous work, but better than heading into the mines. We paid him to straighten the dressing rooms and stitch up hems, then promoted him to painting the girls' faces and setting their hair for their acts. Now he was in charge of all the costuming for the Tent of Wonder, and the dancing girls adored him, adopting him as their collective baby brother. His presence onstage was all champagne bubbles and shades of pink and capes made of glitter, which made him the perfect host for the kootchie show. Effervescent. Welcoming.

Fortuna blood ran thick and sludgy with the need to put on a show, but Fernando's love for the stage was pure pleasure.

Tonight's Tent of Wonder show began with a line of heart-lipped girls in jade ruffled skirts. They used to dance their numbers with men in matching suits, but Papa had slashed all the partnered numbers in half for the kootchie tent. *"They* are your partners," he told them, waving his hand at the audience. "You must make them all believe they could have you."

The girls twirled and kicked, every flip of their skirts exposing a flash of white petticoat or an inch of upper thigh above their stockings that in any other situation would be considered too obscene to abide. But here in the church of Fortuna, such peeka-boos were sacraments.

I let my eyes wander.

A typical crowd for the kootchie tent—plenty of boys hovering on the brink of adulthood, here without their mothers' knowledge, eager to get their first views of the female form. By the end of the show, one of them, too liquored up to reason, would dare another of his drunken friends to hop onto the risers and try to get a handful of something—anything—and the grunts would carry them out and dip their heads in buckets of ice water to restore their good sense, if they were born with any. Happened at least once almost every weekend. To some, the dancing girls were specimens in a jar—available to examine, to touch, to handle.

The ones who weren't boys were typically old enough to have daughters in the show. It should have turned my stomach, perhaps, but I'd watched my own father coach Luna too many times to be scandalized. "Less in the hips," he'd instruct, while Mama gave her own input from the nosebleeds. "Tease them. Make them salivate for it. That's what keeps them coming back for more."

The first number ended. Fernando worked the crowd for cheers and coins, and the dancing girls scooped up what they could with damp hands before clearing the stage for the next performers—a pair of conjoined twins Papa had hired six months ago. The Grand sisters, hailing from Santa Fe, both of their heads chestnut-locked, both of their bodies top-heavy. Their goddess-of-love proportions were not hindered by the fact that they were attached at the hip, literally.

Dolores and Delilah. Rare finds for any circus man—but of course Papa had already struck gold when I'd been born. Luck seemed to trail behind him no matter what shithole gig he booked.

The twins held each other's waists and sang a sad cowboy ballad in fringed vests and a single pair of four-legged chaps, unfastened so their shapely stems could be ogled. Slim doll-like faces, sweet high sopranos—the men in the audience were easily taken with the Grands, eyes tracing up and down the twins' four arms, four tits, four legs.

Not flawless performers, not by a long shot—Delilah went slightly sharp whenever she remembered her nerves, and Dolores, on the left, was sensitive to the lights, so her red eyes leaked tears, smudging her mascara despite her best efforts to remain regal and confident.

Still the audience loved them. No one cared that their harmonies were only slightly less grating than a stagecoach with busted-up brakes. No one cared that they were both singular and plural at the same time.

When it came to watching other acts in our circus, I couldn't help but see through my father's eyes, catching only the rare missed steps, the lazy rhythms, the bum notes. Protective, always, of the integrity of the show and of the unstated promise we made to our patrons when we took their hard-earned cash: to dazzle, always.

Papa and I, partners in dreams.

The song ended. Someone shrouded the limes. A sconce was placed over the spotlight, bathing the empty stage in a warm, last-round-of-whiskey glow. The tent hummed with dark excitement, the men straightening, listening, anticipating.

"And now," Fernando purred, crossing the stage with his arms wide, "the one you've been waiting for."

My sister's renown preceded her. The ones who only knew of her by reputation clapped respectfully, not blinking for fear of missing even a millisecond of her presence; the ones who remembered her from our last roll through town went wild with their cheers. Boys who were getting their very first taste of the duchess were reverent as a church choir.

"She trained with the concubines of Persia," Fernando went on, "where the holy men sobbed to witness her dance, their vows to God wasted after seeing her figure. When she performed for the crowned heads of Europe, every last king and queen begged her to stay but a single night so they could forever remember the time they'd housed an angel. Gentlemen, please welcome the scintillating, the glorious . . . your beloved Duchess of Wonder!"

A hand-painted banner of Luna hung outside the kootchie tent, but mere brushes couldn't capture the gleam in her eyes, the silvery glaze of her hair, the luminous moon of her skin, the way currents of glamour and sex now blew through the very air in the tent.

Out she slunk from the backstage shadows like some classical deity too alive to be captured in sculptors' marble. The tent was silent, the men's tongues hanging out of their mouths, turning to leather.

I may have been the Medusa, but she was the one who turned them all to stone.

An elaborate candelabra rested on her head, a crown of dancing flames. Each hand waved an additional orange flame, all of them subservient to her purposes. She moved around the stage in time to the sultry music, draped in a simple modest dress the color of a comet's tail, and five hundred eyes followed her, though not even a knee skimmed from beneath the edge of her skirt—she showed no flesh but a bared shoulder where the neckline of the dress slipped below her collarbone.

For now.

A single shoulder, hardening a couple hundred pricks.

Most of the men were staring with their tongues, but some of them went weepy; one even cried out, "Marry me, Luna! Marry me and be my duchess!" or something equally daffy. Those who were situated in what we called the snake pit, the area directly in front of the stage where the rowdiest, most inebriated men pushed to get as close to our girls as possible, were stoic, spellbound—

But wait.

Dear Lord, it was him.

Right in the center of the snake pit.

The boy from the cheap seats peered up at my sister, and I held my breath, watching from the sidelines for the golden sheen of lust to reflect in his crescent-shaped gawkers, but he revealed nothing.

No cheering when Luna set her blazing candelabra down on the stage. No biting his own cheek when she turned away and slipped both her shoulders from the dress, curling it down to reveal her naked back, which arched so gracefully any man would kill to put his hands on her curves and play her like a violin.

But the boy might as well have been watching weeds grow.

Resentment rolled itself into a lump in my gut. Luna and I worked our crowds in different ways—I preyed on their fear, inciting them to scream, to leave their very skins, while Luna preyed on their more carnal cravings and had them scratching head to toe. But every performer hoped to move their audience. To haunt. To exhilarate. To thrill.

Yet that boy just stood there as if he were passing time in a train station, waiting for the 4:05 to Sacramento.

As if Luna were not a glory to witness. The rest of her onlookers were glowing with piety for their duchess. He, too, should be on fire to behold her.

And he should have been horror-struck to witness the Spectacular Aviary Extravaganza.

I myself burned with ire, my sore tooth aching with the annoyed clench of my jaw.

Luna turned again to face the audience as she slowly blew out her candles one by one, dimming the light. By the song's final strain, one last candle flickered with life, and her dress was down around her waist; her hands, spread like starfish, covered the holiest parts of her chest.

The men were pushy now, my sister's near nudity turning them into pups, wriggling and licking their chops, and still the boy watched, unimpressed, unmoved—

"Avita!" someone said quietly, cutting through the manic noise. "Vee!"

I turned around. Fernando leaned through the tent flaps, his black hair slicked into a lace wig cap, his fancy gown traded for a fur-trimmed pink robe.

"I need you!" he whispered with fierce urgency, then gestured for me to follow him to the dressing room.

Onstage, my sister blew out the last candle and flung her arms out like wings as the tent plunged into darkness. Her naked, perfect breasts there for a flash—and then gone.

The men cheered, calling for more—more Luna, more tits, more of the merciless teasing they had paid for—and even though

I had heard it dozens of times, even though I had seen all of Luna's acts often enough to memorize her every move, my skin still broke out in goose bumps.

Every hair on my body, cocked and upright with Fortuna pride—how could anybody be so unmoved by the duchess?

The lights came on. Luna was gone, and the music for the next dance was ramping up. I shuffled toward the tent flaps, rubbing the shivers off my arms, arching around to glimpse the boy from the cheap seats and chew him out for his apathy, but he, too, had vanished in the blackout.

The night air hit my scarf, and I made for the dressing room behind the kootchie tent, trying to drop my irritation like a plug of dried-out dip. Our grunts would never kick someone out of the circus for not reacting, but perhaps they should. It was worse than heckling, somehow. You came to the circus, and you cheered for the show.

You clapped for the horses, and you balked at the might of the strongmen, and you went all gooey for the pretty ladies when they danced for you.

You came to the circus, and you screamed at the monster.

Fernando

"**T**ELL ME YOU SAW HIM." FERNANDO'S PURPLE gown lay crumpled and hollow on the back of a chair as he changed from one pretty version of himself to the next. The rest of the dressing room was empty for now, the other dancing girls either onstage, tapping and twirling for the horny hordes in the audience, or waiting in the wings for their turn to do the same.

"Oh, I saw him all right." I cracked my knuckles to give my hands something to do; my vexation had me antsy as a worm on a hook. "He pulled the same horseshit at my show. Don't worry, if I catch him snoozing like a lobotomy patient in one of our tents again, I'll have a word with him." A word or two, or a dozen, all of them sharp as steer horns—or perhaps I'd simply give him an up-close peek of my monstrous mug, see if that scared him into submission. "There won't be enough left of him to snore—"

Fernando cut me off cold. "Vee, darling, what on earth are you talking about?"

"The stiff with the long dark hair," I clarified. "The one staring and yawning like he's already been to heaven, so nothing on this earth can possibly impress him?"

Fernando scoffed. "You know not to believe a single man in that crowd. It's all poker faces up and down the line until the right tit pops out."

Leave it to Fernando to ignore such an unimpressionable silent snob; his range of view was much more selective than my own. Still, dissatisfaction itched me raw. If it wasn't tits he wanted, and the horrors of Bird Girl also left him cold and unmoved, then what the hell was he after?

"Besides, I was referring to a different stiff entirely." Fernando untied his robe, locking eyes with me for one urgent, pointed moment.

Ah. I loosened my shoulders, forcing the worst of my annoyances to wane. I knew my anticipated line and delivered it with aplomb: "Is that so? Who?"

Fernando clutched his heart with both hands. "The most gorgeous slab of meat. A happily-ever-after waiting to unfold."

He shimmied into a gold sheath dress covered in about ten thousand sequins, each catching its own spectrum of light. The effect was a wearable, walkable chest of pirate's booty.

"That looks heavy." I sat at a vanity and lifted someone's Belle Epoque to sniff beneath my scarf—floral hints, notes of powdered lady bits.

"So was Christ's cross; we all make our sacrifices." His false lashes amplified his eye roll. "I look too good in this dress not to wear it."

"Well, before you run away with your own reflection, here." I dug into my pocket, then tossed a small parcel into his hands.

"It's wrinkle cream. On account of you getting so old. Happy birthday."

"Don't even tease." Fernando slit open the wrapping paper, serious as a nun. "One of the girls plucked a gray hair from her temple earlier, and it has me suddenly too aware of my years—oh my god, Dos Amigos! Where did you get these?"

The fragrant cigars were rare and expensive, but they were Fernando's favorites. "A girl has her ways," I answered coyly. (My way: an older brother who handled all circus ordering and folded far too easily when I played pesky little sister.)

"Thank you, thank you, thank you!" Fernando lifted the carton to his nose and inhaled. "Now I have almost everything I want. Only one more thing could make my birthday perfect." He sighed with manufactured melodrama.

Fernando had two great loves: show business and beautiful men. His drive for each could tow our entire caravan. "Go on," I encouraged, as a special birthday mercy, knowing that once Fernando set his sights on game, the hunt was swift and unrelenting.

"Tall. White. Clean-cut. Brown hat." He leaned his head back against the rack of capelets. "Broad shoulders and an ass like two scoops of ice cream—wait, you were there. You must have seen him. Down in the snake pit? Oh Lord, don't you love blonds?" He squared his frame in the mirror, the scaly dress throwing feathery reflections of light along the lean muscles of his arms.

"Is this what you need me for? A trap?" It wouldn't be the first time Fernando had requested my help in seducing a cowpoke, though he rarely needed it. No matter where we went, no matter what sleepy little town the Family Fortuna rolled into, if my best friend wanted a boyfriend for the night, he could have one.

"No, no. Nothing so sinister." He preened his eyebrows into two works of satin art on his forehead. "Just a little reconnaissance. Is he ogling me back? Is he here alone, or does he have a wife and kids stashed somewhere in the midway?"

"The usual," I said. Such information was required before Fernando sidled up to any would-be admirer; some stops along the Family Fortuna's route were more welcoming to our troupe's particular deviations than others.

Fernando went on. "Bree and Suzette were supposed to do the Hitch 'n' Slide, but Bree's in the weeds blowing chunks, so I'm filling in."

The Hitch 'n' Slide—a Family Fortuna staple, incepted one fateful evening in the kootchie tent when a couple of grinder girls tried to outdo a row of one-legged ballerinas. Add a raunchy fiddle and a bottle of Red Eye, and the Hitch 'n' Slide became the stuff of kootchie legend. But the ol' Hitch was a tricky son of a bitch to nail. The dancing girls practiced it until their toes bled in their kitten heels—

And Fernando would be far too busy kicking up his covetous toes to spy on his cowboy.

"You hitch and slide your ass off," I proclaimed. "I'll watch your buckaroo."

Fernando pressed his forehead against mine, a gesture we'd

shared since we were children, as if he hoped to transfer the depths of his affection through our skin. "Thank you, Vee."

I was one of the last people to meet Fernando back in the day. The new boy who'd moved into the kootchie tent was mere myth for at least a week before he was sent to my wagon to fetch Luna for rehearsal. He barged in without knocking, and before I could scramble beneath my bedsheets, he saw me.

"Who did your makeup?" he gasped, circling me so he could see my features from every angle.

"No one. God," I added defiantly.

He analyzed me, then reached for one of my pigtails. "You have so much hair. Could I practice finger curls on you?"

We settled into a comfortable friendship right away, our roles finding us and fitting like his favorite pearl-trimmed satin elbow-length gloves. I was dark to his light, matte to his glitter. In the dressing room now, our inhales and exhales matched as we waited for his next call.

"Was San Antonio like this last year? I can't remember." Fernando cinched his cap before donning a brassy ginger Marcel-waved wig that tickled the tops of his sculpted shoulders.

"Not this big," I responded, lifting a tube of something glittery from a drawer of cosmetics. "All of Bexar County's here."

He lengthened his false lashes with fresh mascara. "Maybe you'll get lucky."

I snorted. "I thought I was helping *you* get lucky."

"I'm always lucky," Fernando said. "That cowboy is going

to do naked push-ups in my bunk tonight, and he doesn't even know it yet." He blinked, letting the black goo dry, then nudged me. "What about you? Did anyone strike your fancy? A soldier smudged with soot? A farmer's oldest daughter? A bowlegged mail-boy? You can have them all if you want. The night is young. We'll line them up outside your wagon—"

"Oh, to have your stamina." I took the cap off a pearly pink lipstick and held it up against the top half of my face. "I'm not in the mood for company."

Fernando huffed in disbelief, but I spoke the gin-soaked truth.

The circus was my heart, my core, my lungs. It was the center of my spinning world, and it was worth a dozen sideburned cowboys or prairie gals with soft hair and wind-chapped lips. The circus was worth every stunning person I passed in the midway, every fantasy hatched alone under my quilt.

I needed nothing beyond it.

In these lonely towns we played, anyone could dress themself up, catch a dick for the night. Even a monster.

"Nope. That'll wash you out." Fernando plucked the pink lipstick from me and took up a red orange, the color of persimmons. He lifted my scarf and dabbed that lipstick onto my bottom lip.

A pointless gesture, not only because of my scarf but because my beak protruded so far over my mouth that any color there would be overshadowed. Lost. Outshone.

I reminded Fernando of these facts, but he pressed blotting paper between my lips. "Think of it as a secret." He showed me the lid of the lipstick tube: Scarlet Woman, the shade was called.

"No one will see this bold red pucker beneath your scarf. But you'll know."

I would know.

"Fernando, darling!" Pepper stuck her head into the dressing room and trilled, "They're ready for you!"

Fernando puffed up, his shingled dress straining against his chest. "My public awaits." He smeared a streak of highlighter between his pectorals and fussed with his wig one last time.

"Every show you become more of a diva," I told him.

"That's because every show I become more fabulous," he answered, and together we exited the dressing room and headed backstage.

Showtime. Again.

Birthday Boy

HE WAS MARVELOUS.

Of course he was. Fernando was as good a Cinderella as he was a master of ceremonies. Anything he lacked in technical proficiency he made up for with charm.

When the Hitch brought the two performers arcing in symmetrical zigzags across the stage, Fernando caught my eye and grinned, then nodded toward someone in the snake pit below— a sheepish white cowboy a little older than us. He was exactly Fernando's favorite flavor: blond, brawny, and brooding.

No wedding ring, I noted. Not that it guaranteed a goldarn thing. But I wanted my friend's pathway to birthday bliss to be as straightforward as possible.

With a flirtatious air, Fernando pecked his palm and threw a kiss with a flourish—aiming, of course, right for the hunky blond, who pretended not to go hammer-hard at the gesture.

I huddled behind the curtain, watching Fernando's flawlessly presented Hitch 'n' Slide—and his flawless quarry.

Occasionally my eyes darted across the swelling crowd, gauging the men's reactions, searching for a certain bizarrely serious patron who wouldn't know a decent show if it pecked him in the ass and jiggled its goods in his face.

But the Tent of Wonder was alive with yelps and whistles, the audience spellbound by Suzette and Fernando and the whirlwind footwork of the Hitch.

Neither hide nor hair of the boy from the cheap seats and his fossilized, indifferent gaze.

Good. I hoped he'd left and found something more his speed. Like watching a bathtub fill up with water.

Exhaling with relief, no longer keeping vigil, I relaxed against a tent pole and watched the show sideways.

I'd known every step of the Hitch since I was old enough to stand upright, just as I knew every leap and twist of our ribbon fliers, every trick and tumble of our pony riders, every wrist flick of Bart's whirling knife act. Not that I had any need for this knowledge in my own tent, of course. But I was raised by a circus; some things were absorbed into my consciousness like smoke into upholstery.

In fact, I could feel my own feet tensing now, my toes gripping the insides of my boots, phantom-dancing the steps as the Hitch wound to a triumphant close. When Fernando and Suzette took their curtain call to the roars of an ovation, my own legs trembled as if I'd been out there tapping alongside them.

What a rush it was to feel the fervor of the applause flooding the tent. That sonic wave, powerful enough to make my ribs vibrate in their meat casing—

"Oh, dear stepsister!" Pepper shouted from the opposite wing, cutting into my reverie. "Don't start an encore just yet!"

A trio of dancing girls dressed as haloed angels wheeled a

cascading five-layer cake onto the risers. Eighteen white candles were lit and sparkling, and the crowd whooped; the cake was worthy of its own fanfare. Socorro must have gotten up at the crack of dawn to bake it in addition to her already strenuous task of prepping concessions and feeding the Family Fortuna army twice a day.

But no one could resist spoiling Fernando.

"Our host turns eighteen today," Pepper called to the audience. "Who will give him a birthday cheer?"

The tent chorused with joyful noise.

Fernando blew out his candles, then brought a dollop of frosting to his mouth, making fiercely covetous eye contact with the bashful cowboy as he sucked the sugar from his fingernail. The cowboy's poker face couldn't withstand Fernando's passes; he was absolutely enamored of our kootchie tent host, unable to look away from Fernando for even a second.

Happy birthday indeed, dear Fernando—may your lustiest wishes come true.

"Cake on the green!" Pepper directed. "Everyone gets a slice!"

A tent flap was hoisted up and tied on one side so any patron who wanted a taste of something sweet could stroll outside and have a bite. Inside the tent, the kootchie show would continue for those who preferred something savory.

"A stunning performance," I told Fernando as he crossed to me in the wings. "Enough to hold the undivided attention of at least one stud in the audience."

"Is that so?" Fernando wrapped an arm around my waist, leading me toward the open flap of the tent.

"Oh yes," came my assurance. "And from what I can tell, he's here alone."

He pursed his lips. "Perhaps he'll be interested in a tour of the behind-the-scenes action after the show?"

I nodded as if wrapping up a business meeting with a colleague. "With you? They almost always do."

Fernando affectionately squeezed my middle, and I released him into the current of birthday well-wishers.

Outside the Tent of Wonder, a courtyard of sorts was set up on the lush grass of the civic field. White helium balloons dunked in gold paint, which dripped down their roundness like honey. A tower of glass champagne flutes, their contents rosy to the nose and sticky to the touch. The dancing girls wore golden skirts of an almost metallic fabric, ruffled petticoats visible as they shifted. Each of them donned a tiara, and they brought a hulking, glittering gold crown for the birthday boy to wear atop his wig.

A queenly gold, head to toe.

"Thank you, thank you!" Fernando waved to his admirers, still in master of ceremonies mode. "Now, how about a game to liven up the festivities?" From a pile of party paraphernalia on the cake table, he took a deck of gilded playing cards and held the queen of hearts aloft for all to see. "Who dares to go first?"

He pressed the card to his lips, sucking in air so it would stick, then kissed three of the dancing girls through the queen of hearts.

The cowboy was next in the line-up, but when Fernando got to him, the cowboy let Fernando grab his collar, the card "accidentally" dropping before their lips landed, and the whole place erupted in whistles as the two of them exchanged an unbridled smooch.

"Interesting game." A deep male voice spoke from behind me.

I turned, checking first that my scarf was in place.

Remember, this face costs twenty-five cents to look at.

A man stood right on the border of an appropriate distance between an unsupervised gal and any male who wasn't a relative. He was older than me, though not enough to be distasteful, and had donned well-worn jeans and Cuban-heeled boots. His hat was straw—I hazarded a guess that he worked outside, directly with his calves and his colts.

He probably thought he was good at handling animals.

He had no idea.

He held up the four of diamonds. "Do you play?"

Beneath my scarf, I ran my tongue along the tips of my teeth. It was as dangerous as skimming knives; my smile was two interlocking rows of gleaming razors, sharp enough to tear through chicken flesh and bone and feather.

Sharp enough to tear through most parts of a man, I'd wager.

What a surprise he'd get if I were to remove my hat and scarf and hold that four of diamonds to my own mouth—

The showman in me dissolved. "Cards? No. I'm terrible at bluffing."

He flashed me a wry grin, and it went straight to my loins. "Is that why you're all bundled up? So no one can read your face?"

My pulse struck once.

Not in terror—I was terror itself. I knew that with one flick of my scarf, I could send this man shrieking into the night.

No, my heart thumped with the sheer delight of this serendipity, the treacherous scenario this cowboy had found himself in. While other available female forms flitted around us like fireflies, this man was patient, working at the gal who'd wrapped up half her face like a mummy display at a boardwalk dime museum.

But he didn't know. Perhaps he was like many men and put greater stock in what was below a gal's shoulders than what was above it, but he truly thought I was just another girl.

He didn't know he was talking to a nightmare.

"Should I fetch us a slice of cake?" the cowboy asked.

I peered behind him. The cake was being dissected for parts—Socorro had filled its center with oozing vanilla-rum Chantilly and edible golden pearls.

Even as my mouth watered for a bite of that sweetness, I shook my head. Such a decadence I would have to enjoy in the privacy of my wagon.

"Then can I steal a dance?" The cowboy found my clammy hand and brushed his rough lips against it.

Something in me went slick.

I wanted to stay. I wanted to keep pretending.

It takes a special girl to be as ugly as you.

"More champagne!" Fernando announced—my gilded, shouting savior. He uncorked a bottle, and the sticky fizz exploded out like a satisfied man, spraying the crowd.

All heads turned to him, including that of the cowboy searching for the right question that would unlock me for him.

But I made like a cheap magician, slipped through a gap in the crowd, and vanished.

Guilt shot through me like rickets. Here I was, abandoning my best friend on his birthday, but I thrummed with the hilarious panic of a near miss.

Can you imagine it? The cowboy dipping me back, unwrapping my scarf like it was Christmas morning?

His eyes stretching wide, his cheeks pale as milk?

What a spectacle it would make, some poor horny fool bamboozled by a monster in skirts . . .

A hell of a show.

But I'd already been Bird Girl tonight. I'd already made them scream.

I sidestepped until I was back in the shadows—back where I belonged.

Then I gathered up my skirts and bolted.

Fireworks

WHEN I WAS YOUNGER, LUNA AND I LIVED IN the laundry wagon. We breathed in slickstone and that oaty, almost burnt smell of starch. We dreamed in bluing. There was hardly room for anything but the wooden tubs for scorching water and the shelves for flakes and powders and jars of Mama's deodorizing apothecary, and so we shared a single bed or else sprawled on the piles of dirty clothes (provided they weren't too smelly to abide). We pulled the flannel shirts of a cousin over us for blankets, bunched up the canvas of a retired tent as a pillow.

Back then our circus was still a mewling newborn. Still growing. To keep his people fed, Papa gave everything—and everyone—multiple uses. Our cat tamers were also responsible for cleaning out their feline counterparts' cages on Monday mornings, as well as preparing their strips of raw meat at feeding time. Curtains were taken from one tent as the audience clapped for a show's finale and raced across the grounds to become the sweeping velvet cape of our Scottish sleight-of-hand. At breakfast the risers from the pig tracks were dismantled, the plywood laid down to make our family table in the grub tent. Luna was a clown and also held buckets of cool water for the fire-eaters; Ren put leashes on the jumbo snakes and walked them after helping Socorro soak the skewers for the concessions that night.

I'd never had to prove myself versatile.

Not with this face.

I earned my keep as the big-money hot ticket of the Family Fortuna, the star of the only tent that sold out every show, the lifeblood of my father's circus and his ambition. My only role was to give the gapers a display of such fright and oddity, they'd leave our grounds with their heads spinning, their sense of the world thrown off-balance by my grotesque splendidness.

Give the crowd their thrills.

There was nothing else for me to give—not a dance, not a kiss. Just screams and nightmares for two bits apiece.

These days, Papa had grown accustomed to our established lifestyle. He whined like a poor man if he had to reuse so much as a fork. Someone was in charge of every single bolt in our setup. The steel-framed, slick red wagon Luna and I shared was large enough that it glided over even the bumpiest of roads, smooth as a blimp on wheels.

I let the evening's rush and vigor fade from my system as I changed into a nightgown and brushed and braided my hair. The allure of the cowboy outside the Tent of Wonder had mostly worn off; the impression of his scruffy lips no longer tickled my hand.

Just then my wagon door opened. The gleaming hair of my big sister floated up the stairs; she turned on the lamp without a word, and I squinted as the light pained my eyes.

"Oh," I said, startled. "Hi."

Luna said nothing.

A pale pink brassiere covered with iridescent sequins was practically painted on her upper half, ballooning out into a floral skirt just under her rib cage.

Near her bed, she removed her feather boa, her gloves and stockings, and unfastened her brassiere, without modesty and without a word.

Luna owned a hundred more costumes just like this, cut and sewn to mold her form so when she swayed and wiggled onstage, the audience believed she was royalty—even fabric bowed to the will of the duchess.

They worshipped her like a duchess, too. Gifts stacked up on our wagon steps, at her vanity in the dressing tent, on her pillow—baskets of citrus fruits, expensive furs, tokens for her hair, pearls, shockingly luxurious perfumes and powders, hams and smoked meats, cloisonné pens.

"Finished early?" I supplied. The circus grounds were still open for another half an hour, but Fernando's birthday must have derailed Luna's usual scrumptious bang of a finale in the Tent of Wonder.

"Customer," came Luna's refrigerated response. She pulled a sheer apricot caftan from her closet, which she belted around her middle and paired with simple Grecian sandals. In the dim air of the rooms behind the Tent of Wonder, where Luna performed the occasional private dance for men wealthy enough to book her, the gauzy looseness of the caftan would blend seamlessly with her sun-kissed skin.

Luna's beauty made the rest of the kootchie girls look cheap, but Arturo always said that a decent circus offered something for everyone. "The deepest pockets, the rank and file, the grittiest skinflint with but a penny to his name—a taste for the deviant can come from anywhere." The Tent of Wonder, then, a petri dish of diversified provisions.

The Family Fortuna slogan did not discriminate: *You Won't Believe Your Eyes!*

"Good luck," I called.

As a response—or perhaps she did not mean it as anything at all—my sister pinched the lamp's key on her way out the door, and the room twisted back into silent darkness.

Alone in my wagon, alone in the shadows.

I sat on my bed, my bare toes brushing against the floor, and gazed out the window.

The sky put on a different closing number wherever we went. Sunset here in the plains was like a snuffed candle—one minute the sky was blue rimmed in bronze, and then when the heavenly orb dipped below the horizon, nighttime promptly took over with no fanfare.

When we were in the Rockies last month, the sunsets were dramatic, hours-long ceremonies with phases for each color—twenty minutes of peach, of scorching hot pink, of glazy, hazy purple, and finally a slow bow into inevitable darkness.

And along the coast, where we played the soft white shorelines of California and the cobbled gray beaches of Oregon, the sunset was a mirror. Two halves of sky, the sun falling down from one and into the other.

But the moon.

Bright and full, a winking crescent, fogged over and shy—whatever its stage, the moon was the same wherever we went.

Just like me. Luna may have shared a name with the moon, but I was the one with its unchanging reliability. The Spectacular Aviary Extravaganza, the same wherever we went.

The wagon door swung back open, and I straightened. Luna must have left behind a trick she needed to indulge the private clients of San Antonio.

But the slicked and greased head that bounded into the room belonged to someone else.

"My kitten," came my father's voice in the velvety evening.

I waited atop my covers patiently, expectantly. It was entirely routine for Papa to come see his performers at the end of the night; just like a protective clockmaker might make rounds through his shop, polishing cogs, tightening springs, so too did my father visit the precious segments of his circus machinery.

And as I was the most precious, he checked in on me almost nightly to deliver a trinket, to sneak me a sweet, to sing me an old drinking song that had come into his mind, to tell me one of his favorite porky-pie tales (which all starred a younger Arturo, who was always wronged, always right, and always handsome), or simply to tuck me in, as even the most unconventional father is wont to do to his children from time to time.

Tonight as he came toward me, he held up a small silver tube with a white cap.

Ah. Glue. Specifically Grippy-Tru, which Papa always kept on his person. He'd bought it in bulk from a medicine show in California and considered it a miracle solvent for all manner of damages—broken furniture, torn sleeves, split heels.

Cracked teeth.

"Is the pain bearable? Were you able to eat?" he asked.

I realized with some chagrin that I hadn't thought of my tooth since the curtains went down on the Spectacular Aviary Extravaganza; there had been plenty of other things to occupy me. "Yes. I managed."

Papa uncapped his cure-all. "Lie back now, my dove, and let me take a look at you."

"How was tonight?" I asked as I prepared to assume the position for at-home dentistry—sprawled on my back, mouth open wide—and my father pushed up his sleeves as he knelt beside the bed. It was a perfunctory enough question, I suppose, but for Papa, it was among the most generous gifts he could receive—a prompt that could set him blabbing for days. "Did Sasha make it into the sidecar?"

He squeezed the tube in my mouth, delicately dodging the worst of my razored fangs, and I held myself steady, trying not to flinch at the soured flavors, the palatable record of everywhere my father had been tonight, right there on the rough skin of his thumbs.

"Sasha did fantastically!" Papa's eyes blazed like cliffside beacons, and he told me all about tonight's Liondrome, how Sasha had fared in her new sidecar while her handler and costar revved the motorbike's engine and flew them all around the ring. "Oh, my angel, it was staggering! A treasure to behold!"

The glue's fumes hit my beak, burning my throat. Papa pressed the sides of my cracked tooth together, his fingers trembling with the intricate strength that was required to do so without slicing his digits. I rolled my eyes back, glancing at my headboard, the dried flowers and old circus flyers pinned to the wall.

"One more night in San Antonio," he murmured, holding my incisor steady. "One more show. Tomorrow night, you give them what they want. Give them what they came for."

What had the boy with the smiling half-moon eyes come for, hmm? How could I possibly give him what he wanted if he returned to my tent tomorrow night?

Papa's lecture rolled into my mind—

You are a mirror when you are on that stage.

I couldn't fathom what that boy had wanted to see tonight. I didn't know how to be a mirror for someone who wasn't interested in screaming.

A final peek into my barbed gob, and Papa nodded, happy with his work. "You're all set, my rose. Let it dry for a few hours before you try chomping on anything harder than a boiled egg." He capped his Grippy-Tru and stretched up to his feet. With a final pat on my head, he exited my wagon. I kept my jaw unhinged, breathing out the stink of the Grippy-Tru, the air drying my tongue into sandpaper.

On weekends, Papa let off a trunk of fireworks after eleven—
a whole bunch of Zambellis and Paozhuangs and knockoff Black
Cats and Lady Fingers, bought in bulk and at a discount, all
bursting into the night in neon oranges and soft lavenders and
flashing yellow whites, burning strange flowers and spiked clouds
and odd sea urchin stars into my eyes.

I watched the explosions now, resting my head on the comfortable chill of my pillow, hearing the globs of people *oooh* and
aaah—

But behind those fireworks, the moon.

The moon, the moon.

Only one night left in Bexar County. Tomorrow I'd make San
Antonio shake and scream one last time, and then we'd be rolling
through the desert to unload our tents on new fields, and I would
do it again. And again.

More crowds. More screams.

I tongued my tooth, still sore, until I winced. A shock of hot
saliva flooded my mouth, tasting of copper.

More blood.

Last Call

URNED OUT WHATEVER FLU-POO BREE HAD spread as fast as a grease fire. Half a dozen girls from the kootchie tent were throwing up their boots the next morning. Even Luna was queasy. She slept through breakfast, corpselike, pale against her sheets.

Papa stormed into the grub tent at dawn and slammed his tray down so hard his eggs split. "What the hell am I supposed to do without half my dancing girls, huh? Throw some sheep up on the stage, pray they know how to shimmy?"

"You need to buy them a bigger wagon," Mama scolded. "Those germs spread from bunk to bunk, and they're always sharing lipsticks—"

"They don't need a bigger wagon." Papa lifted a drippy sausage to his mouth. "They need to quit tangling tongues with the first wranglers who buy them a beer. Damn girls are dropping like flies."

"So what are you going to do, Arturo?" Mama waved the crust of her bread at her husband. "Open call?"

"I suppose." Papa shoveled in his food. "I'm sure there are a few decent-looking tap dancers around town. There's always someone who wants to run away with the circus. Ren! Open call! Send out bills at once! Quit sipping your coffee like an old granny—pour it down your gullet and go! Now!"

Satisfied by this, Mama leaned over her tea and said through the steam, "And what did you do last night, Avita?"

I swallowed my mouthful of potatoes. "Oh, the usual. Wandered around. Played checkers. Taught myself a new braid. Read some books." I hadn't gone out to the lake last night after all. My visit to the Tent of Wonder had sucked the energy out of me, but there was still tonight.

"Which books?" Mama squinted her good eye, and I answered the question she was really asking.

"Yes, Mama, I read scripture before I went to bed."

"Good girl." She used this compliment to me as admonishment to everyone else at the table, glaring at them as she stabbed her sweetbreads. "God blesses those who make time for worship." The others murmured repentance into their drinks.

"And what did Fernando do for his birthday?" Mama went on.

"Same as every year." There was no need for me to lie about this—Fernando wasn't her son. "Birthday cake. Booze. Boys."

"Boys." Mama spat the word as if she wished she could light it on fire. "Sacks of hormones with their brains in their balls." She tucked my hair behind my ear. "Good girls stay inside. Read their scripture. Work on their penmanship."

I was a dammed river, the retorts stacking up in me like green water. Mama spoke as if I needed protecting, as if I were the type of girl who should have been locked up in a tower, my virginity sold to the highest bidder. But we both knew I was perhaps the only girl in the world whose virtue was safe around a group of rowdy, liquored-up prairie boys.

Mama stood up, grunting when she put weight on her right leg. I took both our trays back to Socorro's counter.

At our table, Susannah, one of the ribbon fliers, bent down next to where I'd sat, picking one of my feathers out of the dirt.

She stood, and her gaze found me.

Papa sold my feathers as souvenirs, a penny apiece.

Circus employees were encouraged to turn in my strays to Arturo like they were lost coins, but this morning I couldn't stop staring at the feather in the ribbon flier's hand.

It felt like she was handling one of my own teeth.

Papa didn't need new dancing girls after all.

Eight Cinderellas had been tossing their cookies before the circus opened, but by the time the curtains went up that night, the sickness had passed through and out of them, and Arturo had himself a full lineup again.

Luna pushed herself out of bed in the late afternoon, still a little green and shaky, and changed into her Lady Godiva getup— all wig, no clothing, the hair tacked to her flesh in a strategic waterfall over her most intimate parts.

I dicked around in my wagon until the sun went down, and then it was time for another Spectacular Aviary Extravaganza. Time to fuss with my hair, make it wild as a mane. Time to rankle my feathers so I looked violent and unhinged.

Time to make them scream.

Last night the audience in the kootchie tent had their noggins tilted back, fixed on the stage in holy bliss, ready to take their sacrament.

Tonight the people in my ring would stare with their tongues, caught up by the holy trifecta of disgust, fear, and bloodlust.

A different kind of salvation.

I crouched in my cage, a passion burning like a coal in my chest. When the slipcover came off, I rattled my bars and growled and swiped my hands like they were claws. I scanned the crowd of yelpers and wailers, intending to give every last one of them the spotlight attention of my terrifying mug.

I found the pair of half-moon eyes right away. The boy's gaze rushed over me from the cheap seats, and goose bumps erupted on my skin like fire.

No fear in that gaze. No amusement, either. Just a penetrating curiosity, and it warmed me from the inside out. Warmed me like a spotlight. He was looking right at me, looking, drinking me up with his eyes. But I still wanted to make him scream.

With a roar, I grabbed the nearest chicken, crunched off its head, and spat a fountain of blood. I could feel my heartbeat in my cemented tooth.

As the boy stared down at me, that warmth burrowed inward, deepening.

And then everything slowed.

I was certain a new light source had been forged between this boy and myself, a white-hot beam with an arrow-true connection.

The screams in the tent warbled to a half-pace, water-distorted tempo, as if I had walked down a beach and into the sea.

His eyes, still on me.

As if I were in a bubble, and the boy were in the bubble with me.

My body was feverish, not with the oppressive, sticky heat of a Texas night, but like I was the sun, and the boy was another sun, and we orbited around each other.

Still he watched me—

I'd stopped growling. I held my breath and straightened, blood streaking off my chin.

The audience grew quiet.

One by one, they shut their mouths.

The longer I stood here, unmoving, the more they were forced to just look at me. Consider me. A single fart would have echoed like thunder.

A question rose in the back of my throat; I nearly spat it out like a thorn at the boy:

What are you looking at?

Screaming was the currency in my tent. What was I supposed to do with a stare?

The snarl that blew out from my chest started somewhere in my curled toes; my faithful audience shrieked in response, shocked by Bird Girl's sudden callous volume shattering the silence. The sounds of their terror worked to soothe me, to soothe my ego.

But not enough.

The spotlight blew out, and I was plunged into darkness. Houselights snapped on, and as my cage was wheeled backstage, I could still see him.

No scream or gasp or even a flinch. None of my brutal enchantments did anything to upset him; once again he merely looked amused, mildly entertained.

More inquisitive than aghast, more fascinated than frightened.

Cold anger crept up my spine like a legless reptile.

I was the monster. When I performed, you were supposed to scream.

What was the point of the monster if she didn't make you scream?

"Beautiful show, my dove, simply beautiful." Backstage, Papa reached his gloved hands toward me, but my instinct tonight was to dodge them.

"They screamed louder last night," I mumbled.

"Your ears need cleaning. They screamed themselves raw," Papa rebutted. "And that pause to let the blood pool at your feet? Genius! You were a regular horror story tonight."

I wanted to keep arguing—it whetted something within me. Something I felt compelled to keep sharp.

Instead I picked a string of raw poultry from my teeth and kept my eyes downturned until he left to tend to other business.

Papa wouldn't pick up on my irascibility; he was a shrewd man, but it required a specific kind of curiosity to be empathetic, and Arturo Fortuna rarely looked past the end of his own nose.

I ate my dinner, dressed in street clothes, and wound my hair back in a long tail. I rolled up my lingering botheration about the shirker in my crowd and horked it down like a warm wad of phlegm. To be swallowed down and forgotten.

It was eight o'clock, and the gaslights were blazing.

And at the Family Fortuna, there was always so much to see.

The midway was packed, lines of people winding and twisting around one another like a tangle of worms at the bottom of an apple barrel.

But I moved only through the shadows, darting between tents, my face hidden, my gaze in the dirt, until I got to the concession stand.

Socorro was at her stovetop, stirring a batch of chocolate so it didn't harden into sludge.

I poked my head through the window.

"Busy night tonight," she said without glancing up. "These cowpokes are hungry."

"So hungry they ate all the churros?" With my scarf on, I could beg only with my eyes, but Socorro was soft as a cow for me always—as was the churro she pulled out from a stash in her booth.

"I need you to take this to Quinn." Along with the churro, she handed me a small and smelly pouch—a fresh sachet of herbs for my mother. Mama's passion for earth-grown remedies had out-grown basic therapeutics years ago. To her there was a leaf for every ailment, a balm for every blasphemy—not even the stink of this skunk cabbage could overpower my mother's insatiable sense of dogma.

"What's this supposed to repel?" I tucked the sachet into my skirt, praying the pungent odor didn't permanently stain my fingers or my frock.

"Miller moths. And the devil," Socorro answered without a whiff of judgment.

She was an old friend of my mother's pig farming family. Mama called her Aunt Socorro, which made my father scoff, but my mother always pointed out that here at the Family Fortuna, more than anywhere else, no one had to be blood to be family.

Socorro was an impressively large woman with strong hands and a broom's spread of dark whiskers lining her upper lip. She kept her hair rolled up in a bun on the top of her head. As a child, if I caught her at the right hour alone in her bunk, I'd get to see her brush it out into a long bolt of black wool. She'd let me run my fingers along the strands, plucking them like I was working a loom.

She wasn't trained as a cook. She was a juggler, and she was good—she could keep ten rings and four wine bottles in the air at a time. But back when our circus was just a few canvas tarps and some stars in the dust, she got pregnant with the twins, Petey and Pip, and grew as husky as the great northern bears, her stomach round enough to block out the horizon.

Naturally my father, his eye ever watchful for anything that would draw a crowd, decided to turn her girth and spread into money. He made plans to build her a swimming tank in a tent and charge a penny a head to see her massive, shapely body suspended in water. "Sea Cow gives birth to two calves," he salivated. "Do either of those winklings feel like they might have an extra arm? Twelve toes? A tail?"

"I have an extra foot for you, Arturo," Socorro grumbled, running her swollen fingers along her cask of a belly. "As if any mother can tell what's kicking her insides. Honestly."

Nobody ever told Papa no—he was our king. But Socorro did one better.

On a morning when her tummy was jumbled with baby-boy limbs, she woke us all up with a full table of breakfast in the grub tent—simmered in thyme tomato sauce, a platter of sweet buns coated in powdered sugar, tripe with greasy buttered potatoes, coffee in our clay pot.

Before the presentation of this divine feast, the women took turns preparing food—some weeks they were understandably too tired to do anything but heat some beans and screw open the spigot on a barrel of beer.

Papa came out of his wagon that morning and found us all licking our fingers, guilty.

He took one bite of the chocolate gruel Socorro had served as an exclamation point on the meal and muttered, "Fuck," because he knew none of us would be satisfied with any other cook from then on. He couldn't drag Socorro away from this stove and stick her back in a ring—not without a revolt.

Tonight my churro was flaky, piping hot, a storm of cinnamon and cloves—but I wouldn't eat it here. I wouldn't risk a patron getting a peep of Bird Girl while I had my scarf down for a nibble.

So I wrapped my churro tight in its paper and held it against the warmth of my body to keep it from drying out until I could eat it in private.

"Stay out of trouble," Socorro called as she minced coriander into green dust for her pickling vinegar.

"I always do." Mama's bundle safely in my care, I went behind the concession stand and strolled down the tunnel of shadows made by the midway's tents, watching the circus from the inside out.

In her square booth, Genevieve made portraits of customers' profiles. A child, maybe seven years old, stood in front of a domed light to cast a silhouette against the canvas. When Genevieve finished tracing the face, she cut the black paper with a sharp blade and pressed it onto a leaf of white lacy paper.

The child studied it, then cried to her father, "My nose! Look! From the side, it turns up like a pig's snout! Why didn't you ever tell me?"

"Don't be silly," the father said. "It's a lovely little snout." He passed Genevieve her coin and thanked her, but the girl couldn't stop fretting about her nose, which was to my eye delicate and buttonlike and, yes, perhaps a bit piggish, but such a detail would only be pointed out by someone desperate to hurt her. I fantasized about darting into the booth just long enough to give her a glimpse of a truly horrendous nose—this horn, this honker, this sharp instrument suitable for pecking corn, this prehistoric nasal organ with its two holes for breathing and smelling.

What a shame, I imagined telling her, *that your nose cannot book a weekend headliner in Virginia City and buy celebratory steak dinners for every single grunt with the proceeds.*

What a shame that your profile will never appear in a horror rag to be glanced at only in the darkest hours of the night when someone's craving a thrill to heat up their blood.

If only you were just a little uglier, I thought, *then you might be special.*

I crept past our acrobats, whose flickering movements through their crimson tent looked like mosquitos flying to sticky, warm honey. I crept past our menagerie, which held every species of dragonlike reptile Papa could get his hands on—sixty different creatures and counting.

I crept past our medium, a woman named Blanca who looked twenty years older than she was. She read the cards or cut open an apple to examine its core for a coin. People loved to have the secrets of their futures told and went through her line over and over until they received a result that resonated with them as true. "The reality is," Blanca always confessed to us after half a glass of prairie fire, "every one of my fortunes is 'true.' But people only listen to what they want to hear."

Coming up in a circus, an environment where anyone and anything could become a show . . . it had turned me into a voyeur. I imagined, with each person I passed, what was happening beneath their clothes, what form their bodies took—if perhaps the puckering pleated dress of a lovely matron was hiding a third nipple somewhere around her middle, or if maybe a hunched granny in a knitted poncho actually had a beautiful playground of a figure, wrinkled by her years but still capable of launching a thousand ships. I wondered if a man walking perfectly straight was actually hiding a twisted leg, mangled from a work injury with his plow, determined not to betray the pain he felt. If the angelic curls of a lusciously sweet baby in a wheely bassinet were in reality a wig, fixed there with a bit of syrup by easily humiliated parents.

Were there false limbs among us? Batterlike concealer painted onto splotchy complexions? Gloves to hide hands as speckled as robins' eggs? Curlicue tails jutting beneath leather belts where spinal columns had continued growing even after a fetus's tadpole stage? Other strangenesses tucked away out of sight?

It would fold up many showcases, certainly, if all of humanity suddenly cleaned themselves of powder and pomade and strolled around in only their flesh suits.

But even amidst a mélange of ordinary human oddities, my tent would still sell out. I knew this the way a hair under your arm knows to curl, and I reflected on it now with a pleased grin. No one could ever be as hideous as I was.

No, my face was one in a million.

And then I was behind the Tent of Wonder, the banner of the duchess hanging above me.

My sister, goddess of sex and moonlight, gazed down at her beholders from over her painted shoulder. A couple of men behind me pointed out her more ample blessings, tongues lolling from their heads, and when they slipped inside the tent, the roar of applause and all-male hoots that emerged was truly impressive.

Inside, Fernando had just waltzed onstage to welcome the audience and usher them on their journey through the kootchie girl playroom. I longed to enter the Tent of Wonder again tonight, to be jostled from all sides by overexcited man-shoulders and sprayed with joyous spit as they let out their lusty hollers and cries.

But I had a delivery to make, and so I turned on my heel, heading for the busiest, noisiest place on the circus grounds—a place so wild you could barely hear your own mind.

Off to the Races

THE TRACK WAS A WIDE OVAL WITH EIGHT gated lanes, dirt packed thick for the racers' cloven hooves. If the Family Fortuna was Papa's province, the tracks were the feudal lands where Mama reigned as vassal supreme. Each night, the gas lamps lighting up the earth like fake suns, Mama warmed up her piggies and started taking bets.

I walked around the bleachers, which were filled with tense gamblers holding drinks in one hand and slips of paper in the other—proof of which racers they had laid their hard-earned money on—and found Mama at the betting window near the starting line, barking at a peach-faced cowboy whose mouth hung sour. "No changing lanes after your ticket is punched!"

"But I didn't get a good look at the other heats," the man said. "What is this, a blind bet?"

"You can see now, can't you?" Mama wiped a sheen of sweat from her forehead. "Take your ticket and go sit before I call for the grunts!" When she saw me, she rumpled her brow and charged toward me. "Avita, what are you wearing?"

I was befuddled, searching my lower half, making sure I hadn't put my skivvies on over my skirts, but her grimace was aimed at my scarf. It was a beautiful lightweight linen thing, hand embroidered with shimmering gold and a curving blue peacock feather—not that I could take any credit for selecting it. All my scarves came from Papa's pocketbook right into a trunk in my wagon.

But peacock feathers, I recalled now, were forbidden, along with a constantly updated assortment of other items. Taboo. Harmful, even, to our hypervigilant mama's mind.

"Arturo knows better than to bring the evil eye onto our grounds," Mama tut-tutted, her expression stern. Peacock feathers resembled eyes, which meant the devil and any other deity of darkness could use them to spy somehow. (I wasn't certain of the mechanics.)

"Don't worry, Mama," I soothed, folding the fabric so the feather was out of her sight. "Our circus is too good; any evil eye that came to glare upon the Family Fortuna would be too distracted to do its dark work."

For every quip Mama threw at me, I had three waiting in the bullpen. Papa would take credit for my sharp wit, but Mama was the one who'd shown me how to use my words to stab.

Behind the gates, the pigs snorted and wiggled their plump, white-haired bodies. The stink of their reward for racing—cracked sunflower seeds and creamy ale—had them sniffing for victory.

Mama spat over my left shoulder, just in case some demon was lurking there near my skirts. "Be careful, Avita," she warned. "And be sure to say your prayers. The Lord is always watching, but even He has to blink every now and then."

I handed over her sachet, which she somehow sniffed without

gagging before tying it to her belt. Together we set the final gate; it closed with a satisfying click.

"Piggies are set!" Mama announced. "Starter, ready your pistol!" The time for placing new bets had dried up. The very sky seemed to lean in, and everything went as silent as the moment right before a good piss.

And then the gun went off.

The gates sprang open with a clanging of bells, the pigs flying forward into the race.

I loved the way they ran, how their bodies bent in half and bounded, moving more like furless bunnies than future pork.

These were not pigs for eating, though—they were the offspring of Mama's prized boar, General, and her favorite sow, Specific, who had been happily coupled for three years. General and Specific's babies sold for top dollar once they retired from the tracks, breeding hundreds of little racers all around the country.

While the oinkers made their way to the first bend of the track, I perused the crowd calmly, casually.

I knew from a lifetime of experience the difference between staring and looking. A look: a skimming of the eyes, as unthreatening as a mouse dashing across a meadow, your gaze lingering just long enough to absorb information before moving along to the next interesting thing.

A stare, though . . . it was a fiery arrow loosed with a deadly precision. The eyes could gape wide as maws, ready to swallow whatever thing held their attention. If I had collected those stares over the years—harsh, serrated stares at my face, my form, my feathers—I'd have enough weapons to arm a revolution.

I suppose I did collect them, in a way—my tent turned them into coins.

As I scanned the people on the bleachers, I neither looked nor stared—I was searching.

For a quiet laughing mouth, a head of black cornsilk hair, a pair of sickle-moon eyes.

The unshakable boy who'd disrupted the give-and-take of my act, who'd shattered the mirror and stared, aloof, throwing my exhibition off its usual magnificent tilt two nights in a row. I didn't know what I wanted of him, exactly. To yank down my scarf in private, hopefully eliciting the scream that was owed to me? Or simply to ask him why?

Why didn't you scream?

Don't you know what you paid for? You paid for me to scare the shit clean out of you.

Why are you not afraid?

Behind me, the beleaguered call of "Ma! Dammit, he did it again!" distracted me from my quest.

"Lorenzo, my son! Come here!" Mama grabbed my brother as soon as he was within reach. She leaned down, held his face in her hands and inspected it. "What's wrong? You could go fishing with that frown." Ren's mouth was a wide upside-down U shape.

He gently pulled out of our mother's reach. "Mama, you just—you have to talk some sense into him!"

His glasses were pushed up, balanced on top of his overgrown red hair, untidy as a poet's, his shirt messily buttoned. I marveled at how my big brother was a demonstration of the fact that to every force, there is an opposite reaction. Papa lived his life as if he were on display; he was always selling himself, slick and polished and stitched together perfectly.

But Ren was always frayed, stammering, unsure of how to stand or even breathe. If you tugged a loose string, the whole of my brother would unravel and spill open, a mess of numbers and lists and anxieties, onto the dirt.

"What is it this time, Lorenzo, my baby?" Mama was the only one allowed to call Ren by his full name or by any nickname that might remind him that he came out an infant, same as the rest of us. She was also the only one allowed to straighten his appearance. She folded down his collar, preening him like a newly hatched chick. "You look terrible—I told you to keep a comb in your pocket."

Ren waited impatiently until Mama was done fussing. "I've told him a dozen times to check with me before he makes a big purchase like this." His cheeks flushed red as a clown's pubic hair as he jabbed a shaky finger at a crumpled receipt. "Look at this nonsense—we can't afford this!"

"Shhhh." Mama beamed at the pigs cruising around the bend, then got back to scolding Ren. "Lower your voice! If people hear that kind of talk, they'll tell their friends we're defunct. They'll say we're selling fritters made of sawdust and our shows are too cheap to make even a hyena laugh."

I angled my head, trying to read the receipt in Ren's hand, but he glared at me and whipped it out of my sight. "Mind your own business," he snapped, and in the same breath continued his tirade: "He asks me to do the numbers, so I do the numbers. Then he waits until I have to take a shit and sneaks into my office and gets the cash out of the safe like a fucking burglar, all to put a down payment on a carousel—"

"Jesus, Lorenzo," Mama cut in. "It's his circus, isn't it? Just put it in the ledger as an expense and let it go."

"Let him burn through all our money, you mean," Ren mumbled. "Would you hand a blank checkbook to a toddler? He's going to bankrupt us with these inane purchases—"

"Your father has been running this show for longer than you've been alive to pick your nose," Mama finally told him, her good eye glinting. "If he wants to buy a carousel, he must know that people will pay to ride it . . . and it's Lady Rapunzel by a nose!" She cried this last part as the winning pig flew across the finish line, and the audience erupted in cheers and groans loud enough to be heard underground. Mama's crew immediately leapt up to distribute winnings and collect double-or-nothings from the losers.

In the hullabaloo, my eyes roamed the bleachers, up and down every level, inspecting every face.

Every pair of eyes.

"There." When Mama looked back at Ren, she was as smug as a rabbit who'd outrun a coyote. "That pig just brought in enough cash to buy two painted horsies. By night's end, we should have enough for the whole damn carousel, okay?"

Ren did not look okay. He rubbed his eyes with the heels of his hands.

My own hands twitched. Our illustrious Papa had a dark side to his genius, and Ren dutifully took the brunt of it. I reached out to touch his shoulder in a gesture of solidarity—

"Hey! You in charge?" A pasty man in a sable cowboy hat and elaborately stitched shitkickers charged at my mother, stopping just short of the edge of her skirts.

Mama had him sized up before his spurs stopped spinning. "No refunds or takesies-backsies! Your pig wins, congratulations. Your pig loses, better luck next time. Ready the next heat!" she called to the crew, who corralled the tired piggies to their pens.

The man stared down at her, anger unfolding his weathered map of a face. "Oh, there's not going to be a next time. I don't play rigged games." He stepped forward, invading about six inches of Mama's personal space.

"I'll call the grunts." Ren started to leave, but Mama held him back by his jacket, her smile warm.

"No grunts." She maintained eye contact with the man like some sort of hypnotizing cobra. "I want to hear him say exactly what he's accusing me of." Her free hand went to the gun on her belt, stroking it with her soft fingertips.

The man took her dare like a passed cigarette. "A whole hour I been watching your hog race, and the house hasn't lost a single bet. I'm calling you out. I say you're a cheat."

A cheat. The ultimate fighting word, and the man dropped it down in front of Mama without delicacy.

"You." Mama grabbed another man who was strolling past. "Did you win anything tonight?"

The second man blinked. "I got lucky once or twice, sure."

"And you?" Mama asked someone else. "Did you lose everything like this coffee boiler here?"

The man accosting Mama steamed from his nose like his whole head was a teakettle, but she kept at it, asking person after person if they had more or less money in their pockets after their heats. No one had made out like a bandit, but plenty had won enough to pay for their ticket to the circus. A few had even earned a turkey leg's worth.

"You see?" Mama opened her arms wide, like everyone in the bleachers was on her side. "The game isn't rigged. You're just a shit player. You couldn't pick a winner if it bit you on the ass."

I caught Ren's eye, and both of us grinned.

Papa loved his circus second to none, but he loved to brag about his wife, too—how she had been the greatest sharpshooter this side of the Mississippi River back when she was Quick-Draw Quinn, the Family Fortuna's original opening act. How she could blast a hole right through the king of diamonds in a pack of playing cards as they rained down onto a stage or shoot out every light on a catwalk and plunge a whole tent into darkness.

How she was pretty enough that the governor of Texas himself asked Papa how much it'd cost to borrow his wife for a private steak dinner. The price Papa named was more than the state's entire budget . . . but still the governor looked Mama up and down, considering.

How Mama once ate a tornado for breakfast just so we wouldn't have to go around it to get to our gig in Oklahoma—this one, I was fairly certain, was pure tall tale, not that my father could always tell the difference.

Some women grew out of their storms when they became mothers, their wombs too crowded from growing babies to keep all that electricity housed inside. Not our mama.

"Would you like to get back in line and place a new straight on the next heat?" Mama coated her voice in burnt sugar. "Or shall I show you out?" At last her gun made its appearance, a much-cherished Stevens Tip-Up. She held its worn cherrywood grip with all the tenderness she'd once given to us winklings as she propped us up to her breast, face beaming with joy.

If the man was a smart one, he would back down now and go make another bet. An apology wouldn't hurt, either.

There were smart men. Few enough that they were spectacles when they appeared, but they did exist.

This was not one of them.

At the sight of Mama's gun, the man whipped both his Peacemakers from their holsters, the barrels gleaming like teeth in the oily light.

The man was fast, but Mama was faster.

My heart didn't even have time to start pumping like a rich man's toilet tank; Mama cocked her gun and shot both revolvers out of the man's hands, then put a hole clear through the crown of his hat. I could see the rising moon through it.

The bleachers and the track were already quiet; the blasts of the gun made it as reverent as the front pew on Easter Sunday.

"I've got a wager for you," Mama said. "I'll bet you're as bad with your guns as you are with your money."

The old glimmer of Quick-Draw Quinn lived in Mama's one good eye. Without meaning to, she struck a pose exactly like the antique posters of her act, faded lithographs that were now tacked up in the family wagon so Papa could, if he was tired of the version of his wife he had now, flick his eyes over the printed tightness of her old fringed button-down dress and her pouting lips as she aimed her gun at the beholder.

Beneath my scarf, I chuckled. Our dear mama—two women wide, with a bosom that had rocked three babies from here to San Diego and back—never seemed fully herself without at least one gun in her hand.

Her point was made. The mopey cowboy picked up his guns from the dirt and slunk away from the tracks, cussing her as he spun his Peacemakers back into their holsters. The crowd grew loud and unruly in their gossipy side talk until Mama shouted, "Who's ready to win?" and then, with a cheer, back they rallied to the line, placing bets, throwing down money.

Mama hung up her sharpshooter act back when Luna was still in diapers, but she beamed now as if she had never stopped. A scar crinkled along her cheek beneath her wonky eye, a bolt of discolored tissue where a bullet had ricocheted into her and nearly taken her eyeball. An infant in the audience had wailed right as she pulled her trigger, ending her career—but that did not end her love for babies, and she went on to get pregnant three more times after Luna. Once with Ren, once with a couple of unnamed beans that she lost in unexpected pools of blood, and once with me.

I'd always loved that scar. As a child it was a comfort, a familiar sight when the lamps were low and the nighttime made a moonlit terrain of my mother's face—and yet it did not define her. A surface ugliness, one she'd earned doing what she loved. It was forever a battle scar.

A memory in her flesh.

I'd done nothing to earn my ugliness. It was my birthright. My inheritance.

My fortune.

A Talk and a Walk

THE PIGS WOULD RACE AROUND THEIR TRACKS until late, then snuffle in hoggy bliss as their handlers gave their sore legs and fat bellies a rubdown. Since Mama refused to armor up and join my brother's battle against Papa, Ren slipped away from the bleachers for a good long pout, cutting through the field where our horses grazed on columbines and scrubby greens. And I, little sister to the core, followed him.

"Is Papa really going to buy a carousel? How will we transport it? All in one piece, or will it have to be taken apart and put back together for every gig?" I aimed my questions at Ren; they hit somewhere on the back of his corduroy jacket.

"I don't know," he said.

"You'd have to train someone on how to operate it, right? Because Papa won't know how. And he won't learn, not unless someone's gonna clap when he works the controls." It was no secret to me that Papa had his fair share of flaws. I was old enough to know that he was a man of many layers, some of them less than polished. That same hubris that sparked Papa to birth the Family Fortuna also made him into his particular flavor of asshole. But Arturo never professed to be perfect.

Ren didn't answer, so I kept going. "And Mama thinks you should just talk to him? Good Lord! Did she forget who this is? You're better off trying to talk to a grackle!"

My brother made a sound somewhere between a scoff and a snort, further fueling me. "You know what we should do?" I said. "We should—"

"We?" Ren practically skidded to a stop in the dirt and shook his head, jabbing his finger into my clavicle. "This has nothing to do with you. You can scamper on back to your tent now." He broke into a fit of coughs, then glowered at me when I didn't vanish at his dismissal.

My chest flourished with self-pity, burning away my earlier compassion. I hated when Ren nudged me out like this. Like closing a door right in my face. "Ren, come on. I only meant—"

Ren did not stop walking to hear the end of my sentence, so I didn't bother finishing it, but it echoed in my mind, unspoken.

I only meant that you shouldn't feel like you have to do things on your own.

I'm willing to help, because . . . because I know what it's like. For us.

Ren was more than just a brother to me; he was the only other one like me.

I had my feathers, my beak, my monstrosity. Ren had a shorter-than-average height and a septum so deviated it was practically asylum-bound.

But a solidarity should have linked us together, a duty.

Luna was too luminous. Mama leaned toward God-fearing, and so her peculiarity was overlooked.

And Papa was . . . well, Papa was Arturo. Slicker than a Texas road after a rainstorm, but beyond that, he was utterly and aggressively commonplace. He wouldn't stand out in a lineup of one.

No, Ren was the only other one who had been cut with God's queerest shears.

The only other one who was like me at all.

And yet we were still worlds apart.

As a family, as a circus, as a business, the Fortunas were as tight-knit as the stars, as steadfast as indoor plumbing.

But most times when it was just the two of us, Ren looked at me like I was a stranger. Like I was some pilgrim act, an odd stick hired on three gigs back, and not his own baby sister.

"I was only trying to help," I finally said in my most pathetic of tones.

My poutiness worked. Ren slowed down, halting in the thicket, the shrieks of circus bliss coming off as obscene against his mulish dissatisfaction. "It's my job, get it? I'm the accountant. I'm the one who has to deal with him, his ridiculous whims, all of it. The whole damn show is right here in my hands." He held his palms out flat, as if a set of encyclopedias were stacked there. "And it's heavy as rocks, but Papa acts like it's made of paper. It's my job to keep him from crumpling it up into a ball." Then he went quiet, staring at the line in the distance where cliff became sky, and his hands came together in a weak pantomime of the discarding of our circus as if it were the rind of an old fruit.

"I could do your tallies," I offered. "I could organize your office or stamp the payroll."

Ren broke from his spell, glancing up at me like I'd just entered a room where he thought he would be alone for an hour. "No, thanks."

That derision, so easily tossed my way.

But a little sister is not so easily deterred.

"I could do more," I pressed. "I have time to spare. I haven't helped you with your files in years. Remember how I used to—"

"I said no!" Ren panted. "Not everyone thinks you're God's gift to the circus, you know."

The sharpness of his sudden volume stunned me. I didn't move, not even to bat away a cocky mosquito.

"Just because you can stand in a cage and people will throw money at you doesn't mean you know anything about running the show," my brother's mouth kept rushing. "While you're out there hotdogging it in your ring, some of us are wearing our fingers down to keep the machinery of the circus going, and we don't get treats for doing it. Not like you, getting a new toy every morning that you wake up alive."

He jogged to put distance between us in the field, and I let him. He was my older brother. It was his right to walk ahead of me if he wanted to.

It was his right to push me out and close the door if he wanted to.

When he reached the fence, he stopped, slamming a hand against a wooden slat, and called back to me. "Look . . . if you really want to help, try to keep expenses down, all right? Papa thinks the books balance themselves, but if he doesn't stop his spending, soon we'll be bleeding too much cash to pay for our permits."

"I could add another showing," I offered. More money into our registers would help stanch the big cash bleed. Ren's eyes went right to my beak, which poked into my scarf like a tent stake, the fabric ruffling when the wind picked up.

But he just shrugged, as if I'd suggested plugging Papa's financial holes by scouring for loose coins beneath our stands.

"I've got to get back," he declared, and hustled back into the bright lights of the circus. Back to the grind, back to lock himself in that outhouse of an office with a heap of contracts taller than he was, back to hold everything together until Papa made another mess for him to clean up.

Of course Ren didn't want my help, I reasoned, even as disappointment clogged my innards. We were not cut from the same cloth, not really. He may have been a few heads shorter than your average accountant, but he was still a garden-variety human. Entirely natural, firmly in the realm of man.

But I tipped the scales into monstrous, and there I was alone.

I was made for one thing and one thing only:

To petrify. To appall. To thrill.

I hung over the slats of the fence, taking in the horse stink of apple and pear and wet hay.

Something nudged the small of my back, and I spun around.

"Be patient," I told the straw-colored horse nuzzling the length of my dress. I split my churro in half, stale by now but no less delicious, and shared it with her. Goldie munched it gratefully, then let me pick the burrs out of her mane, my lips never once stopping their shushing. It was more to soothe my own gurgling mind than for this comfortable, companionable mare, who was plenty used to handling.

She was once a show horse, back in the early days of the Family Fortuna. Papa bought her in a farm auction, and we raised her from a halter—a winkling, just like us. My father wanted her to be a star, just like us, and so she leaped over steers, raced around barrels, danced in her aluminum shoes on her hind legs until Papa pushed her to perform on a torn ligament, ruining her for the spotlight and nearly costing her a leg. Now she plodded around a well-worn circle in the midway, carrying children who wanted to play at being cowboys, letting them believe they were true-blue buckaroos for a dime.

Trafficking in dreams, just like the rest of us.

The lake was just outside the bounds of the pasture. I could smell it in the air—the stagnant pools on the muddy shore, the tang of fish bait caught in the algae along the banks. The ripples were silver, chopping the watery twin of the white moon into a thousand little glass pieces. I glanced around, then removed my hat, loosed my braid, shook my hair in the mellow breeze, and untied my scarf so I could feel the night on my bare face.

My beak, blocking my view, obstructing half the world.

My teeth, tongue running along their sharpness.

My skin, prickling with the barbs of fresh feathers, their tips resting against my collar.

I stopped moving, my scarf in my hand.

Down the bank, where the lake curved out into the fullness of its figure, a person stood, his back to me.

My heart linked the shape to a face before my brain did.

It was him.

The Boy

THERE HE STOOD, SPRINGING UP FROM THE weeds, lit by the blur of the circus, the desert and the lake stretching out behind him. Only ten paces and two exhales separated us.

I was shivers and fever, desert crags and rain drumming onto windowpanes.

I was cleaved in half—my incandescent rage at how this dipstick had just sat there in my tent, blank as a corpse, and a swelling of unexpected warmth, like when we'd locked eyes in the ring.

Incandescence won out. I lifted my skirts, prepared to charge him.

You do not come to see the monster and merely stare. You come to see the monster, and the monster makes you scream. I will make you scream—

I paused, studying him in the moon's generous gleam. He held in one hand a pad of paper and in the other a stick of charcoal, which he rubbed against the page in delicate scratches.

He used his fingers like they were tools themselves—the pad of his pointer to smear, the edge of a nail to make a clean line.

An artist.

I became a fence post, a rock, a reed in the wind. I was fascinated, transfixed. Curious. My confrontation could wait.

But he heard me or sensed me somehow, even though I swear I was silent beneath the *tsk, tsk, tsk* of the lake's waves.

Up the sandy bluff he came, and I tucked myself behind Goldie, using her as a shield, tracking him. My scarf was in my hand, my face naked as it came.

"Hello?" His voice pierced through the night, innocent, and my heart juiced itself like a little lemon.

His voice, the sound of him. The sight of those long artist's fingers, smudged in black—it fired a thrill down my spine, which buried itself somewhere in my undercarriage.

"I'm here," I called, "in the pasture."

"Oh." The boy neared the fence, spotting my skirts. "Hello, there."

I held my place behind Goldie, only my bottom half visible. He thought I was interchangeable with any other prairie dweller; I wasn't ready to show him just how terribly mistaken he was.

"Is this hide-and-seek?" he asked, and I could hear the rustle of his sketchbook, the smile shaping his words. "I believe I've found you."

A heat glimmered in my chest. "And I'm certain you have no idea what you have found," I countered from behind Goldie's fleshy rear.

It was one thing to see this unnerving visage from the safety of your painted bleacher, dozens of other mouth breathers between you and the cage.

It was quite another to behold this entanglement of nature, this work of horror, this hideous form, up close and personal. No bars. No locks. No fellow slack-jaws to pad your escape.

The boy scoffed, but when I stole a glimpse at his face, he was grinning, his teeth like saltwater pearls in a dark sea. "I won't know until you show me, now will I? Are you shy?"

"I might scare you." Oh, I was bubbling with anticipation, absolutely roiling. If I'd had a cork, it would have shot out of me by now.

"Scare me?" the boy repeated, skeptical. "You can't be as scary as all that."

That did it. That popped me off like a meteor.

Pleased as a pup with two tails, I stepped around Goldie and into the moonlight.

No scarf, no shadows.

And I waited for the scream.

It never came.

From this short distance, I could see the pocks on his cheeks, memories of blemishes, and the weathered tops of his knuckles. He was working class, then. Like us.

Like me.

Daggers of annoyance stabbed me, quick and true. "You were right, it seems. Nothing scares you. Tell me, what is it like to be as excitable as a brick?"

"Oh, I'm plenty excitable," he said. He ducked to climb through the fence rails, and then he was beside me, opening his sketchbook to a well-creased page, holding it up for me to see.

There I was.

In swirls of charcoal, in dust-rubbed shadow, was Bird Girl on her haunches. Bird Girl, hands curled around cage bars. Bird Girl in profile, mid-growl, feathers askew.

He'd been studying me during those shows, committing me to memory so he could trace my lines. I thought he'd been bored rigid, unmoved by my act. Disinterested. But no—here was evidence of a deep interest, a deep enthrallment.

Captured in his sketchbook, which was still warm from his touch.

It wasn't just me. I spun the page sideways, following the trail of likenesses along the edges, my surprise overpowering a quill's prick of selfish hurt. There was Bull's-Eye Bart, Sasha in her sidecar, the ribbon fliers unfurling themselves from the stars . . . and Luna, as continentally cold and captivating as she was on her stage. And Fernando in his gloves, and a whole line of kootchie girls, swinging their ruffled skirts . . .

Faces from everywhere in the circus, here on his pages. Each one drawn with proficiency, each one reflecting wonder.

"You're very good," I said, as quietly as I could while still producing sound.

"Thank you." He offered me his hand. "I'm Tomás."

Our palms squelched as they touched, my sweat against his callouses.

"Avita," I told him. My christened name—not Bird Girl.

I hadn't fully made eye contact with him yet, but I was inching toward it, my peepers flicking like lizard tongues at their mark. What would happen if I looked?

Would another beam be forged, like the electric heat that had connected us in my tent only hours before? Would time stop again, the planet's orbit a slow drag through the seasons and stars, if I held his half-moon eyes with my own again?

A snout nosed itself between my arm and my waist—Goldie, come to join the floundering conversation. I smoothed her mane, grateful for something to occupy my hands.

Tomás patted Goldie's rump. "She's a beauty."

He was referring to the horse, but still. The sound of that word coming out of his mouth made all the blood in my body strain against its piping, boiling to the surface.

"So," I proclaimed, "you came to the circus for work, not for pleasure?"

"Everything is pleasure if you love your work." Those words on his lips. *Pleasure. Love.*

He smiled, and then his hands were in Goldie's mane, too, picking out the pokies I'd missed, dropping them into the dirt.

His hands right beside my hands.

He was newly eighteen, I learned, and the son of a California farmer. He missed his mother and wrote to her often but did not want the pastoral life for himself. "They have plenty of help," he explained, "but it's not for me."

He was living like a tumbleweed, blowing from town to town, doing odd jobs for his chuck, saving his pennies so he could make the big passage to Paris before he was too old to remember that he cared.

"I started doing posters last summer. It's not bad work." He passed me his sketchbook again, showing me row after row of elegant little scribbles of cheap clowns, ropewalkers, jugglers, all for other productions we crossed paths with sometimes: the Valentines, Duke McCluck's Hippodrome, Circus Hypno. "Quick gigs, quick cash. And you get to move around a lot, which I like." He leaned against the fence for support, one arm arching across a beam. "The Family Fortuna's good. One of the best I've seen, and I've seen a lot."

He was beautiful and brave, I thought, but did not say it out loud.

"Actually," he went on, "I need to speak to your proprietor. I'm hoping he's in the market for a new set of posters."

New posters, hand-painted by Tomás—his depictions of me tacked up on every lamppost and grocery store window in the tristate area.

Buoyed by the possibility, I turned the page in his sketchbook again and was stymied.

This was no coal-scratched sketch; this was all color—paint and pastel and *life*.

I tilted the sketchbook, catching the faint entrails of the circus gaslights so I could examine it with care. It was a painting of the back of a woman dressed in a white gown, looking at herself in a mirror. A black ribbon choked around her neck, and her gown showed the slope of her shoulder, her skin creamy. It was intimate, like I was spying in a dressing room.

The background was all spring blues against smudges of gray-green, but the quality was blurry, the brushstrokes heavy. Maybe the printer had smeared the ink when it made this copy. Still, it was composed confidently. It had what Papa would have called "bang."

"You made this?" I said in wonder.

"I did," he responded with pride. "I was going for something vaguely Morisot."

I wasn't sure whether he had named an artist, the gal in the painting, or something else entirely until he said, "Berthe Morisot? Haven't you heard of her? She exhibited in Paris with the Impressionists?"

I shook my head. The name sounded like one Papa would bestow upon a new dancing girl—vaguely French, drumming up images of cancan skirts and ivory cigarette holders.

Tomás's eyes widened to harvest moons for half a second at my ignorance, and I wanted to pop him into my mouth like butter. "Tell me about them," I commanded. "About the Impressionists." He could teach me anything—I'd listen.

And so he schooled me. The Impressionists were a group of like-minded artists working in Europe—France, mostly—and they were, as Tomás put it, "leading a revolution."

Europe was a place my father referred to as the Big Waste— "too much pastry, not enough grit"—and in that moment, I was secretly glad of my father's disdain. I didn't want Papa near anything Tomás loved.

"They only paint what they see with their eyes," he explained. "So many artists make these contours and details that just lie flat on the page, but think about it: In real life, things aren't outlined. Things don't have solid black shadows or branches and leaves that are so symmetrical. In real life, things aren't perfect, you know?"

I would have answered, but I was too busy memorizing the way the muscles in his jaw flexed as he spoke.

"Impressionism is all about capturing what the eye really sees instead of what you think it sees. You let your eyes blend the colors instead of mixing them on the palette."

He could not resist; he traced the splotches on the paper I still held in my hand. And as fascinating as it was that these messy globs were meant to be a sweat-glazed girl in a fancy-ass Parisian powder room, I was more interested in tracking his fingertips as they touched her.

I imagined those fingertips doing a similar dance along my own shoulder, my waist, my legs . . .

"I like this idea—that everyone is looking at the same things, but only a few people can truly see them." He took back the sketchbook slowly and closed it up, a well-practiced ritual.

"Sorry," he concluded. "I could go on and on about it—I forget that the search for the perfect shade of blue doesn't stir everyone like it does me."

Oh, I was stirred. I was whipped. He could tell me about blue, green, yellow, any old color—I'd listen to it all.

His captive and willing audience.

He lifted his moon eyes up to my own dark, starless orbs and smiled, pinning me in place. And then it happened.

Time slowed and narrowed until it felt like minutes, not mere seconds, between inhales and exhales.

The breeze blew through us, carrying a strand of his long hair almost close enough to tickle my forehead.

He didn't move it.

I didn't move.

I'd stood in front of a spotlight nearly every night of my life, and yet I'd never been on display like this.

Goldie whinnied, and Tomás glanced away first.

"Well, it's late. I should head over to speak to Mr. Fortuna—you wouldn't happen to know where I might find him, would you?"

"I might."

It was ten o'clock. Papa would be announcing Pele the Fireproof Woman, who withstood burns, gargled boiling lead, and held a pan on her palms while it cooked eggs.

After that, he'd have a six-minute window before he was due to officiate the wedding of Josephina and her polar bear in Big Red.

"Anything I can say to convince him to give me a commission?" Tomás gave Goldie one last hard rub, waiting for my answer.

I grinned, the wind hitting my razor teeth, drying them, making them gleam. "Tell him Bird Girl needs new posters. Tell him Avita said so."

Tomás thanked me with a gentle bow, and then I watched him cross the pasture, tracking his legs and backside as they carried him through the weeds.

All the way back to my wagon, the desert ground beneath my feet did not register. If I tripped over pebbles, I caught myself without fanfare. Through the shadows of the circus I skulked, and yet I walked on light and sky.

He didn't scream.

Before it had bothered me like a weepy scab, but now I couldn't stop repeating it to myself, an inane lyric.

He didn't scream. He saw my face, and he didn't scream.

Diagnosis

WE CAME TO SAN ANTONIO FOR THE FIRST time when I was five.

Mama buzzed her lips with excitement because our setup overlapped with the takedown of Los Loros, the brothers who performed the Danza de los Voladores on a fifty-foot pole. She forced us out into the field to watch their final showing from a distance.

"Stop! This is our heritage!" she scolded Papa, who yawned dramatically as the five men, rippling with graceful muscles, launched themselves backward from the pole with ropes tied around their ankles and swung around and around, making their slow descent to the ground.

"Are we Venezuelan now? I thought we were German this week. I'll have to order new posters," Papa quipped.

Mama shot him a dirty gesture, hidden behind her vest.

"Our heritage as performers, Arturo," she clarified, but he was too distracted by his own joke to listen to anyone but himself.

Besides, he had his own reason for booking a gig in San Antonio—one Dr. Almond Trimble, a general practitioner originally from the Emerald Isle who had recently moved from Galveston to suckle at the new sanatorium craze happening in southern Texas at the time. Doctors who got even a fingernail on that action made a killing.

The chance to have a highfalutin professional ogle his own flesh and blood was, to Papa, a stamp of approval he couldn't resist.

Papa left me in the middle of the parked wagons our first morning there, perched on the edge of a table, my scarf over my face, a tangle of snakes in my tummy. "You wait right here. We have a special visitor."

He escorted the doctor across circus grounds—I was still his biggest secret, his most lucrative coming attraction, and I could tell by the skip in his step that he was raring to show me off. "No photographs, do you understand?" he instructed the doctor. "I'll rip both your arms off if you leak any images or descriptions before she can be properly debuted."

The doctor was a distinguished white man, shriveled with age. A trimmed beard hung from his chin like an icicle. He set a black leather bag beside him and inched toward me.

"Take it off, my rose." Papa gestured to my scarf.

I hesitated. My father's rules were strict: I was not supposed to show my face to anyone outside the Fortuna family. I was supposed to keep my scarf on at all times.

Yet part of me was itching to see what would happen.

I was itching to make a show of myself.

Papa repeated his order louder.

Behind us, Mama stepped out of the wagon and spotted the doctor's bag.

"What's wrong? Is she ill?" She ran to my side, eyes bulging.

"No, no," Papa said. "I just want a real doctor to inspect her."

"What for?" Mama's worry was contagious; my upper lip suddenly dripped with sweat, my scarf sticking to me, my breath hot.

"To see if she is special," Papa said, and Mama made a rude noise. "To see how special she is," he corrected himself. "To see what kind of a medical marvel we have!"

I knew that gleam—Papa was already adding these very words to my future banner with fresh white paint. "Witness the incredible Bird Girl of the Family Fortuna, a modern miracle of science! Doctors rendered speechless!" If he was lucky, I'd be diagnosed with something rare but easily pronounceable.

Whatever the path to fame, I would faithfully tread it. I would skip along in any direction Papa pointed me—I was his dove, his rose, his special girl.

"We talked about this, Arturo." Mama dashed to my table, blocking me from Papa and Dr. Trimble. "What if they want to experiment on her? What if they want to steal her away?"

"Your brain's popping corn, Quinn. I would never let anything happen to our little bird." Papa straightened, and perhaps to show off in front of the doctor, he nudged Mama away like she was a stray dog. "Now, shoo! Shoo, woman! This is my circus."

Mama let him do this, but her scar rippled silver with tension. Even as a child, I understood: Papa would pay for this insubordination later.

I wondered for a moment, and not for the last time, why Mama was so strict with her children—whipping us at every irreverent question or runaway thought, every comment that came dangerously close to blasphemy—and yet she allowed Papa to behave as if he were the biggest child of us all.

At some point, as the construct of their marriage was being cemented, their shared ideology formed, Papa was dubbed king . . . and he retained that crown even when he was acting like a big fucking baby.

With a yank, Papa pulled down my scarf like he had forgotten I was animate.

I don't know what I expected—a standing ovation right then and there? For Dr. Trimble to fall to his knees and cower, as if Papa had presented him not with a sideshow daughter but with some lost chimera deity that demanded worship?

Maybe I should give a little bark, I thought. *Maybe I should jump forward at him, growl, see what happens when I push someone into a scare.* I was ravenous for a reaction. Yet I looked to Mama and found my restraint.

The doctor leaned in.

His own face was a mask of professional restraint—lips pressed together, hands steady—but he couldn't hide his eyes.

There I saw the recoil I'd craved. His eyes told the story of how, up until three seconds ago, he had no intention of believing Papa's wild tales of a half bird, half girl. How he'd taken it all for an exaggeration and had expected to find a gal with a deviated septum, a crooked nose, some other unusual feature that I was sure to grow out of. How he wished he had smuggled in a camera or some other way to document the specificities of my hideousness so he could carry proof of my unique properties out the front gates.

How he also wished he had refused to come, and wished he could wipe away the images he'd just seen, so certain was he that he would have nightmares stitched into his sleep.

I saw all of this in his anemic gray eyes, and a new feather shot out of the skin on my back, a needle's head pushing through fabric.

"Well, go on, inspect her," Papa yapped. "I didn't bring you here for a free show."

"May I?" The doctor reached for my beak.

I would have gladly leaned in myself, but Papa answered for me: "Of course, yes, yes. Be gentle."

Dr. Trimble's fingers were clammy on my skin, weak, so smooth and tiny, like doll's hands. The hands of a man who labored with pens, scalpels, and oaths to do no harm, not hammers or ropes or saws. This man would never know a blister, though he had likely treated dozens.

I did not trust such smooth fingers.

I had not yet discovered that neither God nor my mother could read my mind, and so I lowered my eyes, ashamed of my rude thoughts.

The doctor mistook the source of my shame. "There, there." His voice, too, was as weak and watery as the wind in Walla Walla, and I didn't like it, either. "Nearly finished."

He patted my knee in reassurance. I felt like a holiday meal, arrayed on a table, ready for consumption.

"I'm going to be a star," I bragged. "From Texas to Tacoma." My chin lifted almost automatically, as if my pride had soaked into my spine.

"That's right, my honeybee," Papa purred. "They won't believe their eyes."

Dr. Trimble gave a mere "Mmm" as he inspected my beak, my teeth, shined a light into my eyeballs that I couldn't blink away for hours, and listened to a bunch of my insides, murmuring, "Incredible, simply incredible," over and over again.

And then it was done.

"There are a few tests I'd like to run," he told Papa. "I'll need to draw some blood, and if it's possible . . . would she let me take a feather?"

Papa stroked his chin, the ringmaster about to make a spectacle out of nothing. "Tests? What kinds of tests?"

Trimble rattled off a list of genetic predispositions, rare hormonal imbalances, infections that could root in the heart and cause mutations at the cellular level. Papa absorbed the words— not that the names of these diseases meant anything to an uneducated stable hand from the shittiest part of the backwoods. *Which would be more lucrative*, I could see him debating, *Avita the Bird Girl of the Family Fortuna, or the Girl with Virchow-Seckel Syndrome, one of only three people ever diagnosed? Yale-educated doctors would pay millions for the chance to dissect her!*

Papa's curiosity won—he made Mama peel back my dress and pluck out my longest, cleanest feather.

I gasped when she yanked it from my skin; she was too

consumed with anger at my father to remember to be gentle. She extended the feather to the doctor, but Papa plucked it from her fingers so he could be the one to pass it into the hands of science.

Blood beaded on the top of my shoulder where the feather's hook had been tugged out like a daisy. I went to wipe it away, but then I saw the doctor staring at my shoulder as if he couldn't believe I was real enough to bleed—as if he couldn't believe it was red and liquid, despite all my other abnormalities. He couldn't believe it looked just like his blood.

I beamed.

Shocking him was addictive.

If I had another five minutes with him, I reasoned, I could make his eyes actually pop out of their sockets.

"Two vials should do it," he said to Papa, then took a syringe from his bag. "I'll collect it now. Will you hold her?"

They never did find anything.

Before we left San Antonio for a triple heyday open excursion weekend headliner in Dallas, Dr. Trimble came to Papa's wagon and knocked up a storm.

"Well?" Papa barked when he threw the door open, his grin bordering on lewd.

"I've pored over every medical text in my library," Dr. Trimble stammered. "I've reached out to four colleagues and my former professor for their opinions."

From my spot at the foot of my mother's rocking chair, I took in the raccoon circles around his eyes, which definitely hadn't been there the last time he'd seen me, and I smiled to myself. I'd kept him up nights, then. I'd dazzled him properly.

"She's an anomaly," the doctor went on. "An absolute medical mystery."

"Hooray!" Papa puffed out his chest. "See what I made? An anomaly! A medical mystery! Write that down, half-pint!" he called to Ren, who had neither paper nor ink on hand.

Mama folded her arms. "You're taking credit?"

"Oh, very well." Papa bent over to kiss her scar. "I suppose you should get some credit. You are the one who formed her in your belly—"

"I swear, Arturo, your blasphemy will bring the whole circus down in flames." Mama pointed a finger up, beyond the roof of the wagon. "God. God deserves the credit, yes? He made her in His own . . ." But then Mama trailed off, considering me, unsure.

Luna stifled a laugh.

"He made her in an image like no other," Papa finished for my mother, "and that is why she is going to be a star." He placed his hands on my shoulders; they crunched down on a batch of new feathers that had sprouted only hours earlier.

So their Avita would become the Family Fortuna's Spectacular Aviary Extravaganza. "A tent of my own!" I gloated as I set out the checkers, plotting to coerce one of my siblings into playing with me.

They'd both heard it themselves: I was an anomaly. I would be a star. They wouldn't dare turn down such a sister.

The poor doctor begged to be allowed to photograph me or

write an article about his discovery. "We don't have to use her name! Please, I have to document this!"

"I said no articles," Papa snarled. "No pictures. When you tell people about her and they don't believe you, you send them right to our ticket booth."

Family Wagon
JULY 1889

THE RAIN BEGAN AS SOON AS OUR CARAVAN toddled out of San Antonio. It hit the roof of our family wagon, catlike, with a pitter and a patter that made me miss our old white kitten, Fox. She was the last pet we'd attempted; they didn't fare as well as we did with the vagabond life. No matter; between the snakes, the tigers, and Mama's piggies, there were plenty of things to pet.

Ren removed his glasses and tilted his head back against the rocking chair, looking about eighty years old as he watched the drizzle. "Into each life some rain must fall."

I was the only one who heard him, which was just as well; I'm not sure anyone else would have recognized Longfellow, but he was one of Ren's favorites. I used to practice spotting alphabet letters in his old green poetry collection; even now, I remembered which pages were dog-eared and crinkled with love.

"Lorenzo. Read." Mama arched above us, pointing at the Bible in my brother's lap, its leather casing the opposite of worn: pristine and barely cracked, opened only at Mama's insistence or by a shaking, almost seismic guilt (also Mama's influence; we did not share her devotion or zeal, to her great disappointment).

On Sundays we were inevitably on the road, and after a long week of shows and bustling, Papa had neither the patience nor the will to drag the whole caravan on a hunt for a proper church, so Mama gathered her little lambs for scripture study in the wagon. The four of us—for Papa would have conveniently disappeared if not for Mama's beautifully violent descriptions of the firescapes of hell, which did not themselves scare Arturo, but the prospect of Mama creating a version of that hell on earth just for him certainly did—were forced to put our noses to the pages of the good book in false but convincing study, prepared at all times to be called upon to recite a holy word or two that had particularly enlightened us.

'Round the family wagon we sprawled, made into dedicated parishioners, with Mama at the built-in table. Her Bible was open to her own favorite passage: "I am He who blots out your transgressions, for my sake, and remembers your sins no more." She remained as straight-backed as a schoolmarm so she could supervise us with her good eye, crack the whip, keep us on track.

Our church services were strange ones. Mama was our preacher, since she'd been raised a proper believer, unlike Papa, who'd been raised a proper scamp. His own mother had died when he was an infant; his father had struggled to put food on the table for Arturo and his brothers, working as a grocer. Caring for his sons' spiritual health on top of keeping them alive was understandably akin to asking a dog to wipe its own ass.

To date, Papa had only ever choked on the word of God.

Luna was beside our mother, curled up on the bench with a

knitted blanket around her shoulders, her Bible against her angled knees. Though a delicate scripture page was between her fingers, halfway turned, her gaze was on the outside, on the arching branches of the slender oaks and the tufts of blue-green needles on the Texan pines, on the falling rain. Mama wouldn't chastise my sister for her wandering attention. Luna's contribution to any situation was to be Luna, nothing more.

Ren took the rocking chair, an inheritance from our mama's parents, humble pig farmers who had stayed in Montana with their stock until their peaceful deaths right before Luna was born. The chair's wood was elm, more than a century old, rubbed gentle from Mama nursing her babies there and then from those babies becoming children who climbed on the rocking chair as if it were a horse with no legs.

My brother read his Bible with a dutiful stupor on his face, though I knew Ren well; he had memorized whole passages without meaning to, simply because his brain was wired this way, to remember things, to find permanent homes for them. He looked at the words, but they did not enrich him, as useful as a garden of vegetables behind a wall of glass.

Our poor mama, constantly disappointed by us.

I sat below my brother on the rug, hunched in the center of everything, with my knees bent beneath my skirt. I was nearly too tall to fold up like this now, but old habits die hard.

Papa was the only one of us not required to read; if he owned a copy of the Bible at all, we'd never seen it. Rather than nagging him to partake, Mama let him absorb his scripture like oxygen, taking it in merely by being around it. She still insisted that he join us on Sunday mornings, though, and he was a wonder—pouting and pacing, unable to sit still for a single moment of his captivity. He would make a spectacular exhibit, I sometimes thought: "The Magnificent Man-Child of the Family Fortuna! He bursts into tantrums at the slightest inconveniences! Watch him shrug off familial duty like it's a coat!"

Today his appetite for attention was insatiable; he'd cut bawdy jokes about the Virgin Mother twice, and Mama's reproaches only egged him on. Papa always dialed up his antics whenever we were en route to a new gig, a new city—restless, obnoxious. Everything to prove.

"Read the verse out loud, please," Mama instructed someone. I stretched out on the rug, nudging my scriptures out of my reach, my chin resting on my hands.

Last night, my bed had been lumpy and too hot, like I was trying to get comfortable on a geothermal spring. Snoozing was as stop-and-go as a train low on fuel.

A vision had drowsily formed in my head during the night's sleepless hours:

Me in my ring again.

A pair of half-moon eyes watching me, the shadow of my beak carved out by the spotlight. The only person in my crowd.

Tomás, centered in the front row, sticky with the nectar of my show, unable to take his eyes off my face, my form.

No cage, no hens, no growling—only me, holding still while he captured my likeness.

Not in his sketchbook. In his very soul.

A sound emerging from his lips . . . not a scream, but something close to it—

"Avita!" Mama snapped her fingers inches from my beak. "Your turn to read."

I flinched, my fantasy breaking away, leaving me to the disappointment of this run-of-the-mill reality. I yawned, buried my head in my arms, and muttered, "Make Ren."

I said this without thinking—a whine from a youngest sibling used to getting her own way.

"I just did all the Beatitudes!" Ren adjusted his glasses, fingers quivering with ire.

"Listen to your mother." Our father piped up from his twenty-minute doze to throw this gruff censure into the wagon.

Ren dropped his hands onto his scriptures, exasperated. "Now you pay attention? Now that it's time to scold Ren?"

"I thought I might pay you back for your earful this morning." Papa jutted a thumb toward my brother, his mustache thrashing. "This pecksniff was lecturing me about the damn numbers at the crack of dawn—"

"Please forgive me for trying to keep our accounts in the black. How dare I care if we starve." Ren flipped through the pages of his scriptures, steam practically piping out his nose.

Papa lifted himself from his stool to pace in an irritated circle. "Oh, here it is. Are we going another round?" To the rest of the family, he announced, "Lorenzo's being tight as a nun about our cashbox—"

"Because you keep setting fire to our money!" Ren cried.

"Because I am in charge of our circus!" Papa spat. "Me! Me alone! I make the decisions, I write the checks, I run our show! And if I want to buy us some nice new posters—"

"We're getting new posters?" I burst, forgetting that moments ago, I was too tired to read from Hebrews. All I cared about was this confirmation. He'd convinced my father to hire him. There would be a new poster of the Spectacular Aviary Extravaganza painted by those hands.

"He's a real find, this paint slinger," Papa declared, smug as a hog in a mudhole. "I've got him riding back in the stock cars, dreaming up designs as we speak!"

Tomás was in the caravan. He was coming along to our next gig. Anticipation brewed within me, a fine tea.

"Wait till you see what this boy can do—he'll sell tickets with a single bill. You'll see." My father directed these final brags to Mama, Luna, and me, ignoring his son due to the correct calculation that Ren would never approve, not even if Tomás were Michelangelo himself.

Ren rolled his head back, letting out a weary bleat. "Our posters are fine! More than fine—those posters have given us a stellar year—"

"A stellar year, huh?" Papa spun a wooden chair around and plopped into it backward, draping his arms across the slats. "If we had such a grand year, why won't you stop bitching about margins and budgets?"

"I keep our books balanced with what we have," my brother pushed. "We can't grow cash on trees!"

"If we did, we could charge a penny a head to see them, couldn't we?" came Papa's wet, huffy response. "Why don't you leave the thinking to me, huh? You keep playing with your little adding machine and your ten key, and we'll pretend it matters. The rest of us will do the actual work of running the show."

Ren jutted his chin sideways; I could see a thousand words pile up on his tongue, but he bit them all down. No use in arguing with Arturo. No use in arguing with a mountain. Neither would budge.

My insides, however, churned with remorse.

Last night, when I'd insisted on helping Ren with his circus gripes, he'd told me the one thing I could do was make sure Papa didn't spend any more money. Convince him to keep the checkbook closed. Bring expenses down while Ren plugged up Papa's outflow of funds—

And in that very same night, I'd slid Papa a reason to fork over more cash.

I buried my nose deep into my Bible so I wouldn't have to look at my brother.

Did Ren know it was me? Did he know it was my fault?

Did he know I was the one who provided Tomás with the magic words to procure his commission?

For surely Arturo would have commissioned a nude portrait of Buffalo Bill Cody atop a frothing hippopotamus if his crown jewel, Avita, had been the one asking.

"Lorenzo." Mama poked at his Bible and sat back down. "Continue. Nice and clear. No mumbling God's holy words. Luna, you're next."

My brother swiveled his glare from me down to his scriptures, and he quietly read, "Now faith is the substance of things hoped for, the evidence of things not seen . . ."

And for the next forty verses, I pretended to follow along, but my mind wandered right back to my daydream, back to the lights, alone with Tomás while he took in the sight of me.

What a marvel you are, he would say.

My conscience was murky with guilt, true—I'd all but taken the bills out of the safe and handed them to Tomás myself.

But Tomás was somewhere in our caravan right now, atop a bunk, his sketchbook full of renderings that he'd soon morph into full-color classifieds.

And the dash and vim of my elation swept all my guilt to the corners.

Just as Ren rolled into the semantics of Abel's righteous sacrifice as compared to Cain's vainglorious sins, everything stopped.

Our makeshift Sunday school, Papa's interruptions, the whole dang procession halted.

Because of the only element that proved a decent adversary for Arturo Fortuna's fire:

More fire.

"It's burning up! From Odessa to El Paso—huge, sprawling flames and windstorms hot as the devil's taint! Grandfalls is an ashtray!"

The original report of the wildfires came from a cousin who rode in on a chestnut Morgan with the news, hoping one of us might figure out how to soften the blow when we told Papa. But my father overheard the dispatch and exploded at the person closest to him: Mama.

"It'll be a ghost town by the time we set up! No one's going to come to the circus if they can't even breathe the damn air!" Papa paced the length of the wagon, tugging on his mustache, something he did unconsciously when he was trying to rustle up a new scheme.

"We'll have to cancel." Mama shrugged, her eyes still on the scriptures. Canceling shows did not bruise her the way it did Papa; he saw pulling out as a sign of weakness first and a blow to his pocketbook second.

"We need to find somewhere else to go, then!" he thundered. "We can't afford any dead days in this season—not with the way our books are looking, apparently." He shot this last point in my brother's direction, and Ren clenched his jaw.

Papa flounced onto the family wagon steps, ran a hand through his hair, and barked, "Someone else will take us. They have to. Lorenzo! What's nearby?"

Ren scrounged up a map from his files and pushed his spectacles down until they pinched his nose. "I can't—there's nowhere," he stammered as he scanned. "All these are outposts. Not enough people to fill a bench."

"This is Texas," Papa growled. "You can't spit without hitting a rancher."

"This is cattle country." Ren's face reddened, the child losing patience with the parent. "So unless you'd like us to set up for the tumbleweeds—"

"I'd like for my bookkeeper to quit being a smartass and find us a place to perform." Papa stalked to the window and leaned his forehead against it, watching the still terrain as if he expected a city to pop up out of the dirt.

Mama stayed at her table, reading her Bible. Luna did not seem to have heard any of the heated conversation or noticed that the wagons had stopped; her focus was far away.

Ren, as usual, looked like an overrun rabbit, about to slump over and let the fox have its feast.

I pushed myself to standing and strolled to the rocking chair.

If we didn't find somewhere to perform, the whole show would be recessed. Arturo's greatest enemy was a hiatus, a pause to catch his breath. He was far more unpleasant with a day off than when he had a dozen places to be at once.

But even worse, if we didn't land a new gig soon, we might lose Tomás. Without a city to play, maybe new posters wouldn't feel so urgent to Papa. Maybe he'd cancel on Tomás, or maybe Tomás would decide to traipse away, find another circus to book him, a circus that could run up his posters as soon as the paint was dry.

Maybe he was already grabbing his bags now that the caravan had stopped. Maybe he was getting ready to open the wagon door—

Without asking, I reached around Ren and grabbed for the

map to offer a fresh set of eyes, to peruse the region for possible gigs—and Ren jerked it out of my hands.

The paper sliced my skin right between my thumb and pointer finger. A drop of blood fell to the wagon floor, soaking into the fibers of the rug.

"Ow!" I lifted my hand to my mouth, sucking on the wound. "God, Ren, I was just trying to help!"

"I don't need your help," Ren snapped. "Go sit and play with your toys until your next show!"

"Quiet, both of you!" Papa shouted. "Let a man think!"

While my father thought—loudly, since for Arturo, to think was to speak—and Ren quibbled and Mama split hairs and Luna dreamed with her eyes open, I licked the wound, its taste metallic, and tried to peer down at the map sideways. Ren could be so goddamn touchy sometimes. All I was trying to do was—

There, a dot not far from here.

The name popped out at me, the script rising to the occasion like it had suddenly been embossed.

Without thinking, I said it aloud.

"Peculiar."

I barely muttered it, but everyone except Luna turned to gawk at me.

"What did you say?" Mama squinted with her good eye.

"Peculiar!" Papa hooted with howling eyes, his grin of the *aha!* variety, and rushed over to the map, which he yanked out of Ren's hands. "We've played there before!"

"Not for years." Ren, having lost his map, opened up a ledger, scanning it for information. "Peculiar, Peculiar . . . Desert town, just east of the forts, but it seems to be a decent size. They've got a proper church, a schoolhouse, mines, a saloon."

That essentially sealed the deal.

There were calculations that went into finding potential gigs, Papa's secret formulas, carefully honed through years of trial and error. Towns that were large enough to have a drinking establishment but too small for multiple drinking establishments were the sweet spots for traveling circuses. The locals would be itching for somewhere new to get their kicks, and they wouldn't be too prudish to buy tickets to our show.

But then Mama slammed her Bible shut, and all of us (except Luna) jumped. "Absolutely not. Not Peculiar!"

"Aw, Quinn," Papa tut-tutted, "now's not the time to get all squeamish about saloons. There's nothing in a drink house that we don't offer in our own rings."

"We used to play there quite a bit, by the look of things." Ren flipped through the ledger, back to the pages that were scrawled in Papa's snarled handwriting. "It got knocked out of our regular route for some reason." He was pensive, trying to unscramble our father's notes. "Fifteen years ago. Wonder why."

"Why'd we stop playing there, huh?" Papa nudged his wife, who let out a sigh like a new radiator.

"Peculiar was a shithole," Mama mumbled, flipping back through her scriptures somewhat violently.

"Then we should bring them a circus!" Papa said. "People in shitholes are always hungry for us and grateful when we show up."

Mama may have shoved the Good Word under our noses like feed bags, but in our circus, Papa's word was the final one, and with his word given, he leaned back in his chair and waxed nostalgic. "I remember Peculiar now. Like it was yesterday. I remember we were one sweaty night away from finishing our run there and already scheduling a return for next season."

Whether he had actually retrieved the memory of playing in this town or if he was just painting a pretty, imagined picture for us, we could not tell.

Nor did we much care.

"You were all just winklings, my dears, the last time we came to Peculiar, and back then we only had the one tent: Big Red." Nowadays Big Red held three rings for our aerialists, our animal trots, and our jugglers.

"And Mama was the sharpshooter, and Luna was still the loveliest clown, and you, my flower"—he aimed this at me—"you were still just a twinkle in my eye."

"No, she was here," Ren cut in, flipping through his pages. "Just a baby."

He glanced to Mama for verification, and she said, with seemingly great reluctance, "Yes, she was born. Born and ravenous around the clock."

I tried to give my mother an apologetic look, but she was too distracted by her umbrage.

"Yes, she was a tiny, mewling little kitten, and the Family Fortuna was new and untested, but God, we were good," Papa amended, giving no acknowledgment to Ren for correcting his time line—and indeed, no acknowledgment that Ren, too, had been in Peculiar with the rest of us.

And then Papa went dreamy.

If properly fluffed, my father would talk a stretch a mile long—there was nothing that could stop him and no way to get a word in edgewise. All we could do was listen.

"We fitted the floors with sawdust back then, before we figured out that dirt was better for the horses and didn't give us all that wet rodent smell. And our only musician was Three-Fingered Carl, so everywhere you went on the grounds, you could hear him twanging his guitar with his stubs. But he played it so pretty. Sounded like church bells. Church bells in the blue dark."

Slathered on the wagon wall above the washbasin was a poster, one of Papa's old advertisements—of amateurish design, but still charming enough to entice—showing Mama and Papa leaning against each other. Mama in her fringed vest and dark plaits and turquoise chaps, spinning a gun at the viewer with a wink, and Papa was in his favorite black tailcoat, back when it was fresh from the dressmaker, a mystery crystallized in his eye, a hiss in his smile, and authority in the arms he spread to his sides. *The Family Fortuna*, it said above them. *You Won't Believe Your Eyes!*

I thought of Tomás. A new poster. His hands painting my lines.

Our wagon rattled, the wind boxing our boards.

Papa walked to the poster now. "There was something happening in the world back then, winklings. Something in the air. A need to be on the stage, a need to be clapped at. It was spreading like locusts—everyone wanted to be a star. And with so many stars in the sky, nobody knew where to look." He raised his eyebrows at us as if we didn't already know what he was going to say next. "So we made them look down here, down in the mud and the stink. Showed them things they'd never thought possible. And twenty years later, that's exactly what we're still doing. Giving them the beautiful, the monstrous, and everything in between."

He could praise himself until the second coming; Christ himself would have to tap him on the shoulder and tell him to shut his gob, and even then, Papa would finish his sentence first.

And then came the big finale:

"Send out the permit requests."

Ren wearily prepared the paperwork: penned a letter to the mayor of Peculiar, asking for a last-minute permit; charted the route for our fat, swinging caravan to cut around the scorching desert mountains; and passed all this to two of the cousins, who rode hard toward the hills.

Something inside of me ached to play mail boy, too, and I was relieved when the caravan started moving again.

Peculiar . . . So I had been there once before. Only as a teeny baby, but perhaps that was why I felt tugged along by some invisible umbilical cord that cut through Texas and the wagon wall and Mama's resolve. Perhaps that was why I felt like a dog returning to retrieve a bone he'd buried in the shade of a tree.

Or perhaps I was just blitzed to keep Tomás's job for him.

By early afternoon, the cousins met us with a response from Peculiar.

Permits granted. The show would go on.

Usually Mama nodded in agreement at Papa's grandstanding or else tightened her fists as she endured it, if she was not in the mood for his bragging. But this time she sat rigid, gravity burning in her good eye. "Arturo, I am telling you, we cannot play in Peculiar. We shouldn't even stop there to water down the horses—"

"What are you farting about? This is the perfect venue for us!" Papa jutted a finger at the billows of far-off heat warping the landscape outside. "We either set up in Peculiar, or we head for the blaze! Do you think anyone will even see our tents through the smoke? Of course not, Quinn! We go to Peculiar—that's it!" He snapped this last bit at Mama, who folded her lips between her teeth.

She glanced at each of us in silent succession—her three babies, fully grown. "It's an unholy place, Arturo," was her weak final attempt.

"Then we'll roll into town on our knees." Papa scanned the pages of Ren's ledger and, with a raptor's grin to rival my own, said to Mama, "Look. See here? Last time we were in Peculiar, we had to open a second line for tickets. We ran out of food the first night, and Socorro had to raid the store for cheese and cocoa beans. Every single tent was standing room only—those slack-jaws couldn't get enough of us! We'll go back to Peculiar now, and we'll make another killing. This is a blessing. I would think you of all people would see that." Papa smoothed his mustache, then tilted back in his chair, smug as a raffle winner. Mama looked as if she were going to bring an avalanche down on him, rocks and snow and ice.

"A blessing," she echoed instead, and numbly kissed the tip of her thumb. Then she sat with her scriptures open, but she did not look at the words. She did not look out the window. She did not look anywhere, and it reminded me of Luna so much, I almost couldn't tell who was who.

I nestled onto the tops of my mother's feet, as I hadn't done since I was very little. "I've been there before? When I was a baby?" I wondered if forgotten memories would be triggered and dislodged from her brain as we drove into Peculiar; I wondered if Mama would suddenly remember it as viscerally as Papa had.

I wondered if the memories could soften her, convince her.

But Mama only said, "When you were a baby. Yes." She did not look at me. No coddling. No lullabies.

We rumbled along, and I stayed on the floor, tucked around my mother's feet.

Mama was raised by kind, soft-spoken pig farmers in Bozeman, raised to be quietly devout. But she was born with a rebellious streak that could not be worked out of her. Not even the long, manure-soaked hours on the farm did much to quell her tongue. She found a partner in Arturo, truly—people often thought of him as the incendiary, but young Mama was just as feisty, just as starry-eyed, just as loose a cannon. And when they started the Family Fortuna, it was as such: two pot-stirrers, ready to churn and burn the world.

And this is how they were, with Arturo as ringmaster

extraordinaire and Mama as the fast-talking sharpshooter who'd just as soon shoot her prayers up to heaven from a barrel than get down on her knees . . . and then there were the babies.

Or rather, there weren't.

Mama had Luna, then Mama had Ren, and then Mama had a few little lives who rented out her womb for a matter of weeks and decided to move on to other worlds.

I wasn't just Papa's miracle; I was Mama's as well. She was sure she'd never have another child, but I was stubborn and stuck out whatever carnival ride Mama's insides put me through. I made it to full-term, Mama waddling through the circus like she'd pissed herself, Papa proudly pointing at her stomach, clucking, "Yep, I did that. Takes a real man, boys, to make a woman that pregnant."

They nearly lost me in the birth, and nearly lost Mama, too— lots of blood, lots of scared hands bringing Socorro hot water and towels and beer. And then, chewing on the end of a cigar, Socorro held me up to my parents, crowing, "It's a girl!" as she glanced between my legs, and all was well until she glanced at my face. "It's a . . ."

My very first audience, and I stunned them.

The incident forever changed Mama; not only were her womanly parts done bearing children forever, but she'd almost lost me. All those months taking up residence within her, stealing her food through the cord that attached me to her, kicking her lungs, feeding on her very bones, and still I'd almost slipped away.

Her sense of playfulness slipped away, too, and she threw her-self into a fervent religiosity that never ebbed, never dimmed. So reported Socorro, and so reported anyone else who had known Mama both in the before and the after. Never before had Mama been one for praying, but after my near-death birth, she mandated it circuswide. Never before had Mama been one for scripture reading; now she swallowed those verses like air.

But Mama was a rascal through and through—a reformed rascal now, but she still maintained a fire like no other, apart from natural disasters. So even when Mama snapped at us to say grace, she laced in a cuss or two.

My mama, the walking contradiction.

I was her baby, the monstrous girl, a baby who could kill—but who had lived.

No wonder Mama thought she needed God so much. Only He could help her make sense of a world of nonsense, even as she helped Papa plop that nonsense into the ring and sell tickets to see it.

Valley of the Peculiar

THE DRIZZLE DRIED UP, AND THE REST OF OUR trek across the rugged land was ordinary. We brushed up against the Pecos River, saw the weed-choked flume where its silver water was carried up and over its southern flow. "That's your mama as a river," Papa ribbed. "The only river in the world that crosses itself."

We rattled past the mountain pastures lined with desert shrubs, an army of bovines munching the hairy crabgrass with walleyed stares. And then the land became deep canyon, the vegetation sparse, the dirt red, and sky, sky, sky.

Our wagons skittered like weevils through a gorge, the Gold Flame–brand, double-axle, reinforced wheels running smooth enough on the raw ground.

Ren, Luna, and I abandoned the scriptures to play an old traveling game of ours called Answers—pedantic, but it passed the time. One person thought of a word or a phrase, and the others would ask questions to earn the letters one at a time. Papa never committed to actually joining our rounds, but he did enjoy ruining our game by shouting the answers when he knew them.

Mama remained alone in her Isaiah. Her mouth was tight as a guitar string, but its corners twitched when Ren's winning guess to Luna's round of Answers was "cockthistle."

Bless Mama, I thought, for always nipping at the tails of her little lambs to save our souls, even though we were stubborn as goats.

We began to itch after a straight hour of Answers—leave it to the road to turn even the most hilariously lewd topics into eye-drying swill—but before we could dissolve into squabbling, Papa put his nose to the window and whistled. "There it is! Peculiar Valley! I'd know it anywhere. Look at those mounds!"

We were quiet as rising dough as our caravan climbed up a pebbly path, following a sliver of canyon between two mountains made of limestone reef, which absolutely looked like a peachy pair of breasts. We felt every bump and grind, even with our fancy new wheels, and by the time we hit the top of the trail and started down into the valley proper, Ren and Luna and I were on our feet next to Papa, scanning for signs of the town.

"Exactly how podunk is it?" I asked. Would they at least have a decent grocer? Or would we be eating canned food from our own stash supplemented with locally sourced roots this week? Would they have any real roads, or would people be stomping through mud and fields to get to our tents?

"As long as there are people, my pigeon," Papa answered diplomatically, a greedy gleam in his eye, "we can put on a show."

He didn't remember, in other words. His brain didn't cling to details unless they were attached to cash or clapping.

The rocking of the wagon lulled me, my hands braced against the window, my beak so close to the pane I could feel the sun's heat through the glass. Everything in me clenched, my glued tooth throbbing with painful excitement. I still felt that tugging, that distant rope that had a hold on me and was now reeling me in.

I imagined the crowds we'd meet here, my bleachers creaking with their collective prurience. I ran through the catalog of screams I'd heard over the years: shrill and wispy. Guttural and phlegm-filled. Startled, pained, raspy. How would they scream for me here? Would it be the chicken's twisted neck between my jaws that elicited their horror, or would Peculiar shriek the loudest at its first sight of me? The possibilities stacked up in my mind, the very anticipation of thrilling a crowd making me almost famished—

Mama slammed a basket of food down on the table. "Lunch," she ordered.

Our shares were divvied up, Papa hoarding the last of the tomato jam for himself.

How would Peculiar like the kootchie tent? At some gigs, the Tent of Wonder was filled with upstanding Christian fathers and eldest brothers who boasted that watching the dancing girls was their civic duty, their way of supporting the local economy. In other towns, the men bum-rushed the kootchie tent as if they'd spotted a glistening oasis after roaming the desert for a year. What kind of men would we find in Peculiar?

Would they lap and pant at the feet of the duchess or admire her respectfully, as royalty?

I picked up a fried potato and hissed. Salt burned my paper cut. I tongued my wound.

In my mind's eye, I saw Tomás in the Tent of Wonder. Luna posing in the limes, his fingers sketching her shape. The duchess, slinking through a succession of shapes, poses, those artist's eyes tracing the length of her . . .

Something crumbled within me, some unspoken hope suddenly blinking out like a lighthouse falling into the sea.

I set myself straight at once. Of course he was going to draw Luna, the Duchess of Wonder, the gleaming pearl of the Family Fortuna. Why wouldn't he draw Luna?

He would draw all of us. Every act, every face.

Papa slapped his knee and hooted, mouth full of chewed-up chalky beans. "Horse tits, it's pretty!" We all rushed to the window to see.

Horse tits, indeed.

The canyon spread to a panoramic basin of grasslands and undulating fields, tinted silver in the bright day. There the town of Peculiar sat, nestled between the bluffs.

"Will you look at that," Papa said to Mama with a polecat's grin. "You said it was a shithole. Podunk, even. But would you look at that. Camelot."

Mama huffed and tucked herself into the corner of the wagon, near the bedroom door. She held herself there, sulking, her knitting in her hands.

Papa hadn't been generous with his descriptions of the town, either; between the two of them, they'd had me expecting some crap cluster of homes so small and stark you couldn't tell them from the outhouses. Instead, what our caravan rattled toward as we descended through the mountains was the most beautiful township I'd ever seen.

Peculiar had once been a boomtown—honestly, what town hadn't, if you were west of the Mississippi? Its buildings were all symmetrical, of similar style, built with similar materials: Victorian, narrow and tall, painted pale yellow or soft pink or seafoam green, with bulging bay windows and thick white gingerbread-icing trim. Everything constructed at once, everything constructed to match, which was about right for these towns that had sprung up overnight to accommodate the miners who were yanking rocks out of the ground.

But Peculiar was *still* a boom.

So many of the other towns where the mines had run their courses were empty husks of themselves—yellowed grass, dusty roads laid like old carpets for newcomers who would never show up, houses sporting rotting boards and broken glass. Peculiar had been out of the mining game for a good decade—everywhere around here had—but it seemed at peace with the loss of its glory days.

I spotted several of these ancient mines scattered around the hills, laid to rest with slats of wood crissing and crossing the ground, their strange mouths nailed shut.

The V&T railroad depot looked alive and well; if we squinted, we could see one of its engines arriving in the distance, black against the horizon, a steel horse coughing up smog as it tore up the landscape.

Peculiar's main thoroughfare cut through the flattest part of the valley. From up here in the hills, we could spot an old ore stamp mill, a decent-size district of shops, a group of larger homes that clearly belonged to the wealthy, jutting up the bluff so the rich could look down at the others in that way they enjoyed doing. (We saw the same setup in every town we visited, no matter how humble, so was it the money that made someone truly wealthy, or did they simply need someone else around to be poorer than they were?)

And who had called this town small?

Peculiar did not have the wide sprawl of Denver or Salt Lake City, but it was chock-full of homes. Chock-full of people penned in by the surrounding hills—which was perfect for us. It meant they had nowhere else to turn for entertainment.

I couldn't help feeling like we had stumbled onto a secret. An Eden.

I'd be growling and rattling the bars of my cage for these townies soon enough.

"Not as big as Fort Worth." Ren stood on the ottoman, his glasses bumping against the window.

"So what?" Papa mused. "The poky towns are always starved for fun. And here we are." He sucked air between his teeth, utterly pleased with himself for forgetting this place for fifteen years so he could remember it again.

Mama was in an utterly different world, huddled in that

corner, staring up at the collection of old Family Fortuna posters, all those years of past color. She seemed lost, like she was searching for the right thing to say but was too overwhelmed to stick in her thumb and pull it out properly.

Papa, on the other hand, had a nose for only one thing.

"There's thousands of overworked slack-jaws down there, all of them desperate to dream, and I want a ticket from every one of them." Papa strolled around his wagon, turning his back on that sweet little metropolis of cornballs to survey us—his children, his beetles, his kittens—and his eyes went dewy as he looked at me. "My winklings, let's give them a show they'll never forget."

Papa's gaze, nibbling at my beak.

My Papa, my partner in performance.

My mirror.

And a new poster to match, drawn by a boy with terracotta skin and half-moon eyes, the generous wind blowing his corn-silk hair to tickle my cheek—

"Good God, we're going to make them scream their pennies right into the ring—" Papa started, words dripping with sap.

But then something charged out into the road.

A white blur—a rolling boulder? An animal?

Our wagon lurched, then slowed.

"Fuck!" Papa didn't wait for our ride to fully stop before he swung open the door and leaped out.

Our other parent woke from her daze. "Shit!" Mama typically leaned bodily for her profanities, which we were all supposed to pretend we hadn't heard. She commanded us to stay in the wagon, then followed Papa out the door, limping her crooked rhythm.

Then it was the three Fortuna siblings and the four Bibles, alone in the family wagon.

Ren stretched his arms wide. "Looked like a sheep to me."

"It had antlers," Luna put in sleepily.

I peered out the window. We were halted on a staggering, powdery trail, the dirt rosy enough to fill in the cheeks of the girls in the kootchie tent if the rouge ever ran out.

"All I saw was a flash of something white," I said. Stark white against the red road.

"A sheep," Ren repeated.

My brother and I were obedient children for about ten more seconds, and then curiosity—or impatience—took over, and we headed out to investigate the holdup.

I tied on my scarf.

Luna remained on her bench, horizontal.

Our whole caravan was backed up, all the horses nosing the tail ends of the wagons before them. Juan, our driver, was guzzling down a prescribed beer, wiping away a swamp of sweat from his brow. "That fucker came out of nowhere!" he kept saying.

Papa scoffed and rolled his eyes. "Stop shaking like an old lady." He bent over to inspect the wheel. "You didn't kill anyone."

I moseyed around to the front of the wagon. The panel was dented, ruining the gilded trim that framed the glossy red paint. One of the cherubs on the wagon's facade was twisted, its lips now warbling a silent, grotesque scream.

There was only road and rock and scrubland around us, no sign of anything alive or dying.

"Could be bandits," my brother said quietly so only I could hear, "using a slingshot to take out our tire."

"I definitely saw an animal." I was certain of this but less certain of the specifics. Did the white blur have two legs or four? Was it the size of a rabbit or the size of a coyote?

Ren looked at the busted wheel. "It'll get us there," he assessed, "but there's a crack in the axle. We'll have to replace it when we get to town." He rubbed his eyes beneath his glasses, his signature tic whenever we had to spend money—

A tic Papa could spot across a whole goddamn broken-down circus. He wagged a finger at his son. "And to think you wanted to cheap out with the Schuttlers! If we'd put those china plates on our wagon, we would have slipped right off the fucking trail!"

Ren mumbled something; the breeze carried it away unheard.

I scanned the patterns of the limestone mountains around us—no wounded creature recovering from our wheels, no blood trail.

"Everyone, get moving!" Papa shouted to all the drivers behind us. "We have a show to set up!" As he passed Ren and me, he chortled once more, "Schuttlers." I was close enough to our father that I could taste the old eggs on his breath.

And I was close enough to my brother that I could feel him clench like an earthquake, then tremble with his canned rage.

"I hear other shows send their squadrons a day early to put

up the tents." Luna spoke from above us, leaning out the open shutters. "More time for Papa to play king."

I reflected on her suggestion, on its truth—Papa probably would relish the time alone with his grunts, guiding his great construction without distraction.

Ren snorted. "Nah, he loves this too much—riding into the towns with his cavalcade like a fucking knight back from the Holy Land." Ren kicked a pebble, then went back into the wagon, dejected. Luna rested her forehead against the window frame, wrapping her blanket tighter around her even though it was scorching.

Me, I dawdled, pretending to stretch my neck so I could eye the length of our caravan.

The sun punched down on this cliffside and through the pashmina of my scarf, warming the bridge of my beak until it felt hot enough to bake a pie crust upon. Still I stood, scanning every wagon, watching for a flash of long, black, corn-silk hair—

Then I spotted Mama's face—drained of pink, her good eye wide as a jackrabbit's.

"Mama? Are you sick?" I sidled up next to her, but she didn't even notice me. The trip had really done a number on her. We had woven and rollicked more than usual on this journey; these old outback roads were not kind to anyone's stomachs.

She stared at the road where our wagon sat; another trail intersected our path, parallel to the canyon, disappearing into the horizon.

"No," she muttered. "Jesus, please, no."

"Nice view, isn't it?" Papa came around the wagon and palmed her backside. "I ordered it special, just for you."

"Get us moving," Mama snapped. "Right now."

"We're moving! Juan's nearly recovered—" Papa said, but Mama pushed him into the wagon.

I followed her, and when the door slammed behind me, Mama shrieked, "We leave now! Avita, sit!"

I jumped into the rocking chair, ignoring Ren's glower.

With a jerk, our wheels pulled out of stagnation, and we were back on our route. I peeled off my scarf and breathed, my sweat making everything taste swampy.

"For fuck's sake, what are you screaming for?" Papa barked.

"Crossroads, Arturo. The devil waits at the crossroads." Mama was the only one not seated; she was sturdy, like her boots were stapled to the floorboards, upright as a preacher. "You parked us there in the crotch of two roads and made roosting hens out of us! You must be careful, do you hear me? There are wolves about."

"It's broad daylight, Quinn! You think the devil's going to leap out from behind a rock and stick us up?" Papa set one ankle on his opposite knee, a sprinkle of rusty dirt falling from his heel onto the rug.

Mama took an egg from the pantry and split it open. She caught the insides and washed her hands with the slime and yolk.

When she spun back around to address us, her eyes burned with the steady fury of exploding stars.

"Do you know what I remember from our last gig in Peculiar? I remember the strangest three days of our lives. Coins went missing and turned up in the children's beds. We found tadpoles swimming in sealed barrels of beer. Someone tried milking one of the draft horses and succeeded." She paused, glancing at her husband. "This town is cursed."

Papa was annoyed enough to box a grizzly. "You sound like a damn church wife."

But Mama didn't bother responding; she fixed her offspring with hard-as-glass glances.

"Nothing funny while we're here, do you understand? We do the show, we pack up, we move on to Taos or wherever the hell we're carting off to next. And you will all keep up with your scriptures and say your prayers—I'll be checking. You too, Arturo. You especially."

Mama would get no argument from me. To hear her mention the devil felt like he might actually be summoned here to our own living room, come to roast a sinner in our woodstove while Papa ran numbers with Ren.

Papa got up, measuring himself against her; he was a whole head taller, but she was the one I would fear if I met them in a shadowy alley. Hell, I would fear her if I met her in a well-lit chapel.

Mama stared up at him. "You say your prayers, or I'll wait until you're asleep and wash your coat in egg myself." She wrung her hands, egg whites dripping on the floor.

Papa collected the breath to fight back, but then something

beyond his wife clotheslined his attention. He bent to look out the window. "Fuck!" he cried, grabbing at his hair. "No! Fuck me, no! I don't believe my fucking eyes!"

We rushed to the windows, and then we, too, saw what he saw. Down on the civic field, three white circles on green—not yet erected, but unmistakable.

Three white tents.

Someone already set up in our field, in our town, where we were supposed to play.

Someone else's tents staked in our grounds.

"Holy shit," I whispered as we rattled down the hill and the sunlight hit the gold dust on the tents' round domes. Beside me at the window, Ren echoed my words.

Mama's plea for prayers would have to wait. We had bigger things to worry about than the devil.

Le Cirque Americana

A WORLD WAS BEING CONSTRUCTED ON THE rippling fields of the township below us. A world so far made only of stake and rod and unfurled canvas—but you could still sell tickets to the potential.

The big top, massive enough to house a congress of wonders, was folded on the grass, one hundred feet of white fabric ready to be unfurled. It didn't reflect the daylight, but rather absorbed it. Other canvases for smaller tents lay in a constellation around the big top, promising equally exquisite miracles.

Everything was white, though you could glimpse hints of gold and silver from the corner of your eye. Whether from an illusion or from actual spun thread, I could never tell.

The wooden poles of the tents had been erected, thick as the masts of some great galleon. Roustabouts tied nylon rigging and hung the incandescents, which danced like fireflies even without the backdrop of night.

And then there were the baggage wagons and boxes, shipped but unopened, and chests sent over from the railway station, and booths and curtains and trunks. Every speck of the field was covered with these mysteries. The whole damn thing made me crave a slice of lacy almond wedding cake—all that smooth, scalloped gold and creamy white. Their gaslights switched on, enveloping the Texas heat in their glow. I wanted to dash in and wear that light like a cape.

It looked goddamn magical. I thought this every time I saw their tents, and every time I felt like a traitor for it.

"Lorenzo," Papa said when he was finished cursing and kicking like a foaming badger. "The permit for the field—"

"It's all in order." Ren was already fishing through his satchel for the appropriate file. "See? We have it reserved. Permits signed and dated." The paperwork was only hours old—the ink was still fresh.

"That bastard." Papa didn't even glance at Ren's permit. He didn't have to. "That slick bastard."

The magical setup ended at the edge of the light—at the precise spot where the civic field stopped and the desert resumed its harsh, patchy terrain. And it was there that our Gold Flame wheels came to a stop, in the shadow of the raised banner that told us where we'd arrived: LE CIRQUE AMERICANA: WHERE ALL YOUR DREAMS COME TRUE.

The suited white man who stood in front of the newly pitched circus gate was more trickster woodland elf than human. He was old and almost short enough to draw a crowd. His powdered face was folded with jowls, and his clouded hair was gauzy as thistledown. The smile he gave us Fortunas as we exited our wagons and spread before him was ancient, like he'd been beguiling people out of their money for centuries.

"Arturo." His voice was the opposite of Papa's loud,

authoritative boom—it was slithery, the sound of mouse feet skittering across stone, the rustling of browned leaves in a bone-cold forest.

"Cornelius." Papa licked the salt from his upper lip. "What in the devil's swinging dick are you doing in my field?"

"Your field? Well! I like that!" Cornelius Leon Reve, proprietor and ringmaster of Le Cirque Americana, played at being baffled—doing a piss-poor job, too. "I didn't realize! I thought this field belonged to God himself and to the great town of Peculiar—"

"Cut the bullshit," Papa growled.

"—which has granted us a triple-day permit to set up right here in its very best location." He reached into the pocket of his coat, a beautiful construction of deep turquoise chintz with swallowtails that brushed the backs of his heels and made Papa's own coat look like a dog-chewed rag. Out of this sartorial vision he produced a paper.

"'The ordinances of Peculiar and all the rightful powers,'" he read, "'do hereby grant Cornelius Reve and Le Cirque Americana full entitlement over the north field of Peculiar—'"

"I don't care if you got on your knees and gobbled the mayor to get your damn ordinance signed," Papa said. "We had this place booked. Fair and square."

Ren gently passed our father the rolled-up permit. Papa snatched it from him, wielding it like a club.

"By all means! There's no reason why you shouldn't stay. We've left you plenty of room." Cornelius gestured to the narrow strip of grass at his feet, not even ten inches wide, the last measure of grass before the field dropped off into rock and scrub and dust. "Why the sour face, Arturo? Your sweet little flea show can't possibly need more room than this."

The sorcery of Cornelius Leon Reve was this—his outward appearance was one of a French import, a velveteen gentleman. So well-starched, meticulously seasoned, you expected even his butthole was glossed and primped by its very own butler.

But in the peaks of his eyebrows and the cementing of his jaw, you could see what he truly was: predatory. Territorial. An animal, like the rest of us.

Sometimes when I was younger, I'd catch a glimpse of Cornelius's teeth—one in particular, a sharp snaggletoothed canine partway back—and I'd tongue my own fangs with a dollop of shame. I wanted nothing to do with him, wanted to be sure I was nothing like him.

Of course, now I understood that he was almost as frightening a spectacle as I was—a money-hungry businessman who was just as cutthroat as Papa.

Ren turned toward us, the sheen of Le Cirque Americana's gaslights glowing bronze on the back of his olive corduroy jacket. "El Paso will take us early, I'll bet."

My heart lurched. *Will Tomás follow if we leave?* I wondered. *Or will he stay behind? Get a commission from Cornelius instead?* It spun my guts just to think of it. "If we leave now—"

"We planned for a show in Peculiar, didn't we?" Papa said. "We advertised for a show in Peculiar, didn't we? Didn't our squadron ride ahead and plaster our posters on every surface in Peculiar?"

His fingers tapped against his coat pocket; I knew he was itching for a hit of snuff, but he wouldn't take it. Not in front of Cornelius. Nothing that might give that puckish ass a hint. "The people of Peculiar booked us for a show, so let's give them a show."

Cornelius smiled, amusement agleam in his eyes, and said nothing more.

He spun around, passing through the silver arch of his circus gates, and farted at us, lifting a leg to let it roll down and out of his pants.

Conversation done—if you could call that series of sideways threats and gnash-toothed insults such a thing.

We watched my father, tracking his mood like he was a big cat in heat, but Papa's grin was maggoty with glee. "And what a show it will be."

Luna, Ren, and I—it was our duty to hate Cornelius Leon Reve, to detest everything about Le Cirque Americana, to vomit at its frippery, its Midas-like structures, its enchanting mysteries. We took this task on happily, letting the loathing root black and oily in our hearts. It felt good to hate for such a noble cause.

But our father danced a more complicated routine with Cornelius, one that had been spinning for years—a dance in which both partners stepped and circled with knives drawn, ready to jab and taste blood. Arturo would have hanged Cornelius from his own twinkle lights at the first opportunity, but at the same time, oh, how he loved this dance. How he thrived on its twirls.

Cornelius had made dick moves before, but outright stealing

our spot? Parking on our field? Bribing his way into a permit? That was a knife swing. A swipe and a slide and a cha-cha-cha.

"Arturo." Mama stalked over to her husband and put her face right by his. "Listen to me. These small-town gillies have enough of a time convincing themselves to spend their money on one circus. Do you really want to make them choose between us and that?" She pointed to Le Cirque Americana's lot. The tents were jacked up now, scintillating against the glowering clouds of late afternoon.

Behind my scarf, I balked.

This was the worst thing she could say to Arturo Fortuna. Mama had shared her bed with the man for two decades; she should have known better than to entice him like this.

"But I do want them to choose, Quinn." Papa's mustache flicked with appetite. "I want to see the look on Cornelius's face when our tents are packed like pickle and he can't even pay someone to juggle his balls." He pushed past Mama, leaving her staring, dazed, at the horizon beyond Cornelius's forest of poles and posts.

And then Papa became Arturo became the almighty, unstoppable ruler of his universe.

"All right, I want more lamps." Papa glared at Le Cirque's miles of shimmering orbs. "Take what we have and double it. Grab the lamps out of your own bunks if you have to. And someone string up some tea lights around the entrance—Jesus, they've made their own sky. Lights! Get me lights!"

And away he danced. "Canvasmen! I want tents staked and raised by nightfall! Right here in the dirt and weeds, that's right!

We'll make them forget all about the pebbles under their feet."
He signaled to the caravan to park and whipped open a baggage
wagon. "Where is Socorro? I want something special for opening
tomorrow morning—something no one's heard of before. Tell
her to play God and invent a new food altogether. Something fried
and un-fucking-forgettable. Something worth five cents at least!"
He dripped with sweat, the orders running from his mouth like
some hot, sour shit.

Ren followed behind him with his clipboard, his jotted notes
as frazzled as our father sounded. I was sure that at any moment,
my brother's pants would combust from friction, his legs pumped
so quickly. When Papa noticed his son trailing him like a pigeon,
he spun around and addressed him directly.

"Lorenzo! I want a bonfire. Right here in the center of the
tents. Make it huge! Big enough that the heat and flames draw
your eyes away from all their pussy little sprinkle lights."

Ren already looked like he was drowning—so many scribbles
on his clipboard, so many orders barked in his face. "We can't have
a fire out here," he tried. "The tents are too flammable. One gust
of wind—"

"Then double-wax the canvas!" Not wind nor storm nor
tornado could blow my father away from the certainty of his
genius.

My brother spoke quietly, as if he already knew he should
abort his words. "We can't—"

"Don't tell me I can't! I can do anything I want!" Papa snarled,
his teeth white against the yucca red of his cheeks. "Now, you go

and spend whatever the fuck it takes to make this place shine. I want the Family Fortuna to be seen from the moon!"

I had never stood so close to a firework, but here was one in a black tailcoat, wearing a mustache and a hairline reminiscent of my own.

Off he hurried to jackhammer more commands at his son while I boiled in his secondhand ambition. Yes, such a show we would give them, we would split the world in two for our crowds, a before and after: before they entered the Family Fortuna, and a forever after in which they'd been titillated, tickled, and tantalized to their very entrails.

And the Spectacular Aviary Extravaganza would be the lightning bolt cleaving it all—

"Ren!" I called, breathless. "Tell the grunts to take a row of bleachers out of my tent. We'll cram them like cattle, and then—"

My brother glared at me, so I let my words trickle to dust.

"That way there will be bigger lines outside," I justified to his annoyed demeanor. "And they'll scream louder because they're claustrophobic." *And scarcity creates demand, and we can add another showing of the Aviary Extravaganza or raise ticket prices if there's enough clamor for seating, and audiences will brag more about the show if they think they got prime spots down at the front.*

A dozen more of my father's hard-won lessons pranced through my head, but Papa's requisites drowned out all other conversation.

"I want all hems in the kootchie tent raised by an inch! Two inches! I want every critter in the menagerie to get their spikes and

scales polished! I want every game in the midway rigged special—
let them win early and often so when they plunk down their coins
for the big prizes, it's a lockup! No winners, no payouts, just a
bunch of try-hards emptying their wallets for a yo-yo!"

Ren's clipboard hung limply at his side, kissing the dirt.
"Anything else? Or should I wait for you to take a breath first?" He
lifted his pen.

"Smartass," Papa hissed at his son. "Just make us look good
and make their show look like pig shit, okay? Can you handle
that?" He stomped away into the circle of our wagons.

The second he was out of range, Ren spat a single word with
unexpected pith: "You!" He charged past me to our mother, his
accusing finger out, his neck purple beneath his collar. "Why did
you egg him on like that? We could have convinced him to go, to
set up somewhere else—"

"And now we don't have to. Now Arturo can finally have his
big face-off." Mama fixed Ren with her good eye, and for a second,
I marveled that I had ever thought Papa was the great manipulator
of the Fortuna clan.

"But—but—" Ren made a final attempt to reason with the
unreasonable, and Mama steamrolled right over it.

"And now we have to beat them once and for all, or else
they'll crush him."

A crack in the mountains punctuated Mama's statement—
there between the two tit peaks, a spurt of lightning against the
gunpowder sky. The smell of rain was faint but unmistakable;
a storm approached, slinking along the same trail we'd taken

151 ☙

into the valley of Peculiar, which already felt like such a long time ago.

A time when Cornelius and his fancy-ass circus were just sties in our eyes, when the most threatening thing to our family was a new gig in a town that may or may not have been profitable, or untamed wildfires, or both.

We had set up in the rain before. Our tents were painted with paraffin wax to weatherproof them, but we were usually on grass, which soaked up water like a sponge. This ground we had to build our majestic circus upon now was all rocks and clay, patches of thistly weeds. Rain would turn it all into a grimy, mud-slick shithole.

But this wasn't an ordinary setup. I watched the first droplets hit my brother's spectacles; he didn't even flinch, just let the rain pelt his face as if it were foolishness to dodge the inevitable.

This was war, and Papa's words to me echoed back like a general's command: *Such a show we'll give them, you and I!*

A blessing from my father, and armor for him to wear in this battle.

My jaw clenched as if I were already growling for them. I had a role to play in this circus, and I would play it until every last throat in Peculiar was screamed raw.

Father and daughter, partners in dreams.

And we would be partners in victory, he and I.

Big Red

NE ROSY AFTERNOON ABOUT FIVE YEARS AND eleven hundred gigs ago, I skipped into the family wagon and found Papa on his bed, hunched over, wringing his hair, a pair of boots and abandoned polish on the floor beside him.

Ren stood patiently beside our father, holding a water-warped poster.

"'Le Cirque Americana,'" I read when he handed it to me, "'where all your dreams come true.'"

"Look!" Papa jabbed a nail at the autumn locations—the same ones we were towing, only Le Cirque was playing them a few days behind us. "They're trying to wash us out!"

"Hush, Arturo." Mama took the poster out of my hands and scrunched it into a ball. "We've dealt with others before—Ringlings, Garcias, Hagenbecks. There are more than enough slack-jaws to go around."

But Papa wasn't soothed. "What about this, eh? Right here—'a mastodon menagerie'—what the hell are they pitching?"

"An elephant show," Ren supplied. Papa could speak purple, but he couldn't always translate it.

"Well, then, let's get an elephant!" Papa shouted, as if one would appear by simply wishing it so. As if Ren could pick up an elephant at the drugstore.

We never got an elephant—too expensive and bulky to transport without our own railcar, and anyway, Papa settled instead for a new contortionist, a gal from Japan who was billed as "the Elastic Orchid, who is always able to make ends meet!"

Within a month, Le Cirque Americana, hot on our asses in St. George, debuted "Drake the Snake Man! Coils himself into impossible knots!"

In turn, Papa hired a woman out of Tempe with trained vultures, which wore scaly caps over their bald heads so they could be plunged into water tanks as our "winged monsters of the briny deep."

A week later, Le Cirque Americana billed their "Irish siren" in Mesquite, a pudgy ginger of indeterminate age in a glittering emerald tail who floated in a soundproof tank with floodlights that tinted the water pink.

And so it went.

Slowly at first, Le Cirque Americana took over whole regions and either bought out their smaller competitors or hounded them until they folded their tents and went belly-up like roaches.

Within three years, we could pull into any locale in the bottom half of the states and see two major shows advertised: Le Cirque Americana and the Family Fortuna.

Our posters were classic: big red letters spelling out our name on coppery backgrounds, arching above caricatures of our best acts. They were streaks of bold color, wrapped around poles and trees and hanging enticingly in shop windows and city squares.

Our best customers at our favorite gigs knew these posters well; even a farmer's tiniest shrimp of a child could peer at our paper tacked to a whitewashed fence, spot our illustrated Papa, and cry, "Circus! I want the circus!"

Their posters were clean. LE CIRQUE AMERICANA dashed upon a bare black surface in a glossy, bold, iridescent silver that could be seen only at the right angle—magical letters. Those posters pulled you closer. Made you guess. Made you wonder.

"My god," Papa muttered every time they put out a new design. "The audacity. The audacity of those fuckers."

No wonder the rumors started creeping around our tents that the owner of Le Cirque Americana was a true wizard, sprung from some misty forest back in Europe three centuries ago. That his beard had been harvested from the silvery sheen of a winter's first snow on bare black branches and grew ten feet in a day.

"That's what they use to string up their lights," a dancing girl commented, proving her disloyalty, "and to rig up the tents and sew their costumes and make the curtains. His beard."

The proprietor allegedly made his grand entrance on opening days in a gold-splattered chariot, and any audience members whose hands he touched during his triumphant circuit of the ring would receive bottomless refills of fizzing amethyst star candies for the rest of the night.

"You'd like it if such stories were true, wouldn't you?" Mama scolded Papa when he fumed. "He's not special, Arturo. He's just another man, trying to earn his bread like the rest of us."

But we knew, even if the specifics of the reports were stretched like raw wool, that there was something eerie about Cornelius Leon Reve. This competition was not the same as when we'd battled other shows for dominance in a territory. This was like we were chasing our own tails.

And Arturo wouldn't let anyone take a chomp out of his own behind.

Somehow the grunts got the tents up and staked before dark, even as a vibrant summer rain blew sideways and the ground threatened to slide out from under us; even this far out in the desert, miracles could be found. That's exactly what Papa was scraping for when he called an emergency meeting in Big Red.

A miracle.

"Hurry, hurry," he whined, "get inside, out of the drizzle. And wipe your goddamn feet."

Tracking grit and mud, we huddled on the bottom bleachers beneath the shadowed ceiling of our canvas cathedral. The entire Fortuna family was here, every last ticket taker and midway handler and pig shit collector, those cousins and aunts and uncles related to us not by blood but by sweat. We waited as our ringmaster paced around the ring like a bridegroom the night before his wedding, his eyes reflecting the yellow-white of the single spotlight glowing him up like dawn.

"You already know what I'm going to say." Papa placed a

hand on the stool in the center of the dirt, letting his fingers drop off its edge as he circled it. "A circus-to-circus face-off, our gates less than fifty feet away from each other. We've never done anything like this before. But we will not fail. We cannot fail. The Family Fortuna is the best show in all of God's landscaped creations! Anything Cornelius cooks up, we serve between our teeth with both hands tied behind our backs, rolling along on a motherfucking unicycle while chanting 'La Cucaracha!'" His volume increased with every word, and to my right, Ren snorted.

"Oh, the ringmaster's hope," he muttered, "that if you say it loud enough, it'll be true." The bags beneath my brother's eyes rippled above his cheeks. I wondered if he'd been permitted to stop moving even once since our caravan had pulled into Peculiar. Even his clipboard looked tired in his lap.

Yet Papa's words had the intended effect on me—making my yearning manifest, my boldness incarnate, folding my own aspirations into Arturo's.

"We're going to make Le Cirque Americana look like curdled shit!" Papa cried, and the tent rang with a charitable cheer.

I listened as Papa threw out instructions like needled darts: Everyone must be on point. Every detail must be honed and sharpened and photo-worthy. The lights must be celestial planets, the music as sweet and strange as a dream, the very air our customers breathed while on our circus grounds must be enough to get them drunk with delectation.

As if we did not strive for such a show every day already.

Papa found my brother and barked at him to alter the animals in the menagerie. "Rough up the hyenas! Speckle them with chalk and backcomb their fur. And paint the baboons' snouts and asses bright purple—make them a wonder to behold. Make them so wild a sight, you wish your eyes were cameras! Go!"

Of my sister, who leaned, velvet-eyed and doelike, against the side of the bleachers, Papa demanded new choreography. "Bring a cowboy onstage and draw on him with a tube of lipstick clenched in your cleavage. Extinguish the flames of your candelabra with your farts—I don't care what, just make it different. Make it special!"

And to Mama, he said, "Start your races as soon as the circus opens, and lift all your wager limitations. If people want to bet big and lose big, let them!"

"The piggies can't race early in the day, Arturo," Mama countered. "They'll get sunburned—"

"Then slather them up with mud before you spank their curlicued butts!"

I had seen my father wound up before, but he was so tightly coiled, even Mama ingested her rebuttal and spun out of the tent on her heel.

The others took their commands with dignity, and quickly Big Red started to empty as folks set off with their marching orders to make our sparkling show even shinier.

There were no additional rashly barked instructions for me. Bird Girl drew crowds to her tent like flies to shit—all I had to do was be myself, and in they would pour, and shriek, and scream.

I'd be so magnificent, the cries from my ring would flush

out all of Le Cirque Americana's noises, and their crowds would stream into our tents, and the coins would overflow our cash boxes like a flood. I'd make each show my best, make Peculiar turn out their pockets for Bird Girl.

My heart was an oozing sore as Arturo spoke, bleeding for victory. Victory for the Fortunas, victory for Bird Girl . . . victory for my father.

Arturo's ambitions, contagious as the pox.

I tilted my head, and then, like Big Red had just birthed him herself, there he was, standing in the anemic cast of the work lights.

He of the hair, he of the hands.

He of the half-moon eyes.

Tomás.

My ears tuned out my father's booming orders, so all I could hear was the leftover rain pissing off the roof of the tent, landing with an almost pornographic drip in the puddles below.

"Ah! Here he is! Our new Michelangelo!" Papa announced to the remaining employees in the tent, and when Tomás joined him in the ring, he wrapped an arm around Tomás's shoulders in a proud, confining squeeze. "You've likely already seen him skulking around, making sketches. We're getting new posters of everything. Every act, every game, every dancing girl's powdered orifice."

Tomás bowed his head in acknowledgment. I arched my neck, straining to lean my face into the bouncing rays of the work lights. Any moment he'd glance up, and I wanted him to see me.

"And you make our circus look good, you understand?" Papa couldn't let Tomás go without a quick muscle flex. "I want a new set of prints ready to fly tomorrow morning. We're going to milk this town for every last penny they have."

"I'll do my best, sir." God, the mere sound of his voice had me close to drooling.

Papa dismissed the rest of his worker bees, then wiped his mouth and sprinted over to me, tugging me deeper into the tent, down the aisle between the hot seats at the front of the bleachers. "My goose! We have need of your spectacular face!"

I blushed beak to ankle, my feathers prickling as I kept pace with my father.

Tomás spotted me now; I felt his eyes take in my scarf, the shape of my face beneath it. *Yes, still me*, I wanted to crow—I could wrap this miscreation up, hide it behind cloth or drapery, but it was always just a flick of my wrist away.

Always moments away from putting on a show.

Then the spotlight went cold. Grunts moved it to the side of the ring, the silvered shadows making bizarre creatures of them. Somewhere rain dripped between cracks in the canvas and into a tin bucket. Yet even in the shadows, Tomás kept his eyes on me, his hands clasped in front of his belt buckle—polite, professional.

"I want you to make a poster for the Spectacular Aviary Extravaganza," Papa ordered him. "I want it to be the centerpiece, the main dish. Avita, you'll pose."

My throat closed around my breath.

Papa went on. "Make it terrifying but shining. Make it lush

and rich and real—people should feel like she's popping out of the paper toward them. Draw them in like leeches to blood." He draped his hands on top of my shoulders. "She is everything about what we are and what we're selling. So capture her, and present it with a wink and a fucking tail wag."

There was nothing Arturo loved more than his circus; to hear him call me the patron saint of the Family Fortuna should have made stones skip across my heart. So why did I feel an impulse to crawl under the bleachers and refuse to come out?

Why did my nerves turn over every cell in my body, as if I were about to stand in front of ten thousand onlookers instead of a modest crowd of one?

A single not-so-slack-jaw whose lips, in this light, reminded me of slices of autumn pears.

"You said you were good enough to sell tickets with a single poster," Papa reminded his newly hired artist. "So do it."

My feathers itched. Pears I wanted to nibble on.

Tomás fussed to open his sketchbook. "I've started a rendering—"

"Finish and dry your proof by sunup," were Papa's uncaring, unreasonable instructions. "The printer opens at eight. I want a banner of her large enough to block out the sun. Paint her quickly, but no gawking. It costs two bits to gawk at that face."

Thousands of people paid to gawk at the nitty-gritty points of my mismatched features—it was my role in the circus, bestowed upon me by Papa's deific hand. So why did his comment sting like a wasp out for murder? Why did my stomach cave in, knowing

Tomás was about to study my face until he knew it better than I did?

Tomás had to be aware that Papa was making an exorbitant request—he'd basically been commanded to forfeit his sleep and get these posters made.

But he only nodded, making some note to himself in his sketchbook.

He's saving up for Paris, I reminded myself. *And Arturo Fortuna notoriously pays his artists well to be bullied by him.*

No need for me to fuss over this arrangement between artist and customer—it worked out to be a prize for everyone.

A distant whooping interrupted us.

"Those assholes are getting into my blackstrap." Papa flew across the tent and flapped back the canvas. In a rare afterthought, he turned back to Tomás and me. "Avita, you give him everything he needs."

But before Papa could haul off to the storage tent to rescue his rum, I squawked for him, hustling past Tomás to the exit. "Papa, wait!"

"What is it, my sweet? You're letting flies in." Papa held open the flaps, standing with the posture of a much more patient man as I crossed to him, the Texas heat already turning the mud to powder beneath my boots.

My father's breath was briny, his voice coming into my ear like a swampy breeze. He focused on me, waiting.

"Papa, I . . ."

Fortunas never trailed off into frustrated nothingness.

Fortunas never ended their sentences with silence—they ended their sentences with more sentences. But all my words were on a train heading somewhere else, heading far away.

Papa, I what?

Papa, I'm suddenly shy for the first time in my life, and it feels like a foreign object lodged uncomfortably in some orifice?

Papa, I want this boy to stay here and draw me, and I also want him to go away, because it feels safer to think about him with some mileage between us?

"I'll hold really still," I finally said, to say something. "We have to beat Cornelius. We have to. And we will. Because you're the best showman on earth." My words were as hollow as a rotten beehive. As trite as a child's praise.

The firework looked at me, his youngest, his star, and he extinguished himself with a soothing hiss. "Oh, Avita, Avita." As tenderly as if we were alone backstage after my show, he set his hands on my cheeks, his palms hot enough to blister. "Such a show we'll give them, you and I!"

I peered deep into the astronomy of his eyes, all those burning dreams. The brightest one was where I lived—his wild, feathered trump card.

I couldn't wait for him to play me.

He pulled back, snapped his fingers at me. "I want that poster to be phenomenal. I want it to be so fucking good, Cornelius pisses his pants when he sees it. So you be a good girl and pose for as long as Michelangelo needs. This is a game of chess, and you're going to lead us to victory. You're the queen, the most powerful piece on the board—and once those crowds get a look at you, Le Cirque Americana will be nothing but a fart in the wind."

And then he rushed off to save his precious rum, leaving me alone in the tent with a boy I barely knew (but whom parts of my body wanted to know very badly) to play living statue. I let Papa's pride in me light up my heart like gunpowder, turning back to Tomás with a peacock's strut.

Such a show we would give them, he and I.

A Professional

I AM MADE OF CLAY.

Our new Michelangelo circled me, shuffling his papers, sharpening his charcoal.

I reached up and flattened and burnished and fluffed.

"I need you to—" Tomás bit one of his well-ripened lips, then gestured to his own face.

I knew what he needed. My scarf.

He'd already seen me as Bird Girl. He already knew what I was. No need to be shy, no need to be afraid . . . for him.

I untied the fabric.

He remained professional as I dropped my scarf to the dirt, but I was well versed in the tells people tried to mask, and a twitch in the corner of his mouth betrayed him. *Yes,* I said silently, gleefully, *remember? This face is as frightening close up as it was in the ring. And right now, it's all yours.*

Clay, stone, fire. Capture this face forever.

His eyes went down to his page, up to my face, down to his page, up to my face, the artist greedy to capture my odd lines, my bizarre evolution.

"Can I get you to turn toward me a little more? Just—like this?" Tomás demonstrated with his own head, angling it so, and I complied, my nerves crawling on their bellies whenever he talked to me.

"Sorry about Arturo," I said through tight lips, trying to speak without moving my mouth. "He can be . . ." A thousand ways to describe my father suddenly battled for articulation. A thousand excuses for him, for his sharp edges, a thousand justifications for his brashness, for how it balanced his genius. "He's a lot to handle," I finished weakly.

"As a proprietor, or as a father?" Tomás's knowing smile was so brief I nearly missed it.

"Both," I told him. "He'll hit you with a dozen orders before sunrise tomorrow. You see if I'm wrong."

Tomás shrugged. "He's intense. The best showrunners are."

Bless him for complimenting my father through me—and clearly he thought it was a compliment for me as well. The daughter, the offshoot. Arturo's partner in dreams.

"You've seen a lot of shows, you said?"

"I have." He finished drawing a long, dark line in his sketchbook, then squinted at my feathers. "I've been hopping from show to show for a good eighteen months, taking all the commissions I can get. Seen a lot of interesting things. Met a lot of interesting people."

I watched him rub something on his page with the ball of his knuckle—my feathers, I deciphered. I tracked his hand as he drew their rough outlines, their jagged horizon.

He scratched the side of his nose, leaving a smudge there.

"Hey, do you think I could . . . do you have an extra one of those I could take? So I get the pattern right?"

My feathers.

"Oh. Yes." I reached behind me and plucked one from my shoulder that was hours away from molting—pulled it out clean, made a chicken of myself—and passed it over. It was still warm from being on my body.

He ran his fingers along the down, eliciting a shudder up my back.

I thought of sick puppies and drowning kittens to keep from going crimson.

"Thanks." And then it was quiet enough that we could hear the grunts hollering, their curses even sharper and fouler now that it was fully and undeniably night, and the bustle of metal clinking and rigging being knotted and planks being drilled into bleachers. Beyond the sounds of our caravan clattering itself into a proper circus, we could hear the night fliers—the mockingbirds, the thrashers, the trilling moths—and the moon itself, which shone down a very specific kind of quiet.

"So who have you sketched so far?" I couldn't sit here in this silence with him, not without crawling out of my skin.

"Just about everybody," Tomás said. "I did the contortionists earlier tonight. Round out your left shoulder a little. That's good."

"Coco and Zita," I told him. "People always ask if their limbs are fake, made of rubber. Isn't that funny?"

"They look it," was his concentrated response.

I grinned. "They're the real deal. Ass over ankles with their own flesh and bone and nothing more. No tricks. No cheats. Not in Arturo's show."

Tomás smiled and kept on drawing.

"They used to do their act totally nude," I went on, "but then the animal eroticists complained they were stealing their crowds—" I broke off, horrified by the words *nude* and *eroticists* that had so casually come out of my gutter mouth like a ringmaster's patter.

His eyebrows lifted, and it was so close to open flirting I nearly liquified.

"It's quite a circus, all right."

And that led us back into silence for another long stretch.

I swallowed, my mouth cotton dry, and shifted my gaze to the rippling darkness of the top bleachers. *Do not say anything else about body parts. Do not make any other comments about sex. Do not even speak anymore.* I commanded myself thus fiercely and pledged myself anew to the role of living effigy.

Tomás interpreted my angst as fatigue. "Almost done," he reassured me, then pushed back his hair and brushed a daub of charcoal dust onto his ear. I almost bit through my lip trying to bury my lust.

"Hang on, it's too dim in here." He walked to the pile of spotlights, and a frenzy started whipping up within me, a real clusterfuck of elation and fire and hurry, right at the base of my spine.

"Aha." A click, and a spotlight shuddered to life. "Let me adjust it . . . there."

Tomás angled the shade, blasting the light at me, and I held myself still.

When he looked into the ring at the newly illuminated me, it happened.

The shift. Transformation—

The Spectacular Aviary Extravaganza.

If the Family Fortuna had an altar, I would be on it. Arturo's monster, worth my salt and every penny I brought in.

The boy from the cheap seats was concentrating hard to scratch out the final intimate details of my features, but he lost himself and stared.

He had to. My face had gravity like a planet. It could suck up the Rio Grande.

Look at him, squirming at the might and awe of this unimaginable mug.

Just like I'd dreamed of the whole ride to Peculiar.

An audience of one, basking in the glory of Bird Girl.

But this wasn't my act. There was not a growl, not a sneer, not a bite of something fowl.

This was something else entirely.

Lights on, scarf off.

A new act—the act of wearing the face that belonged to me.

He had shown me the sketchbook where he kept his dream— the painting of the mirrored girl in her dressing room, that guiding light to Paris, where he hoped to find his great meaning. He kept his dream in his drawings, and he kept it in his heart, and I wanted to show him myself like he'd shown me.

I wanted to show him what I kept in my heart, and I wanted it to dazzle him so much it sickened him.

It felt like hours, and at the same time mere moments, but his charcoal once again began moving. A few bold, quick strokes, a rub of his knuckle, and he was done. "Thank you." He sounded so calm as he went back to the spotlight. "I think I have everything I need."

He switched off the light, and it was dark again.

No growls. No screams.

Just two people in the shadows and the quiet.

I was the Spectacular Aviary Extravaganza, and I made my crowds afraid.

In my tent, I was monster.

I was Papa's brightest star, his ambition incarnate.

In the family wagon, I was Mama's baby and pesky little sister.

At the table in the grub tent, I was Arturo's oddly shaped girl, an acquired taste, but not to be feared unless you were seated in her ring.

I was Fernando's dearest friend, and though he saw my features as perfectly suited for a rollick with his cosmetics, our years together meant he'd learned to overlook the shock of my ragged physiognomy.

Here I stood in front of Tomás, and I was none of that.

Not my beak, not my feathers, not my audience's piercing yelps—or I was all of them at once, and much more besides.

I was only Avita.

Tomás closed his sketchbook and, noticing me watching him,

pulled it possessively to his chest. "Ah, I'm going to make you wait. You'll see it tomorrow. It'll be great. Trust me."

Boldness zinging through me, I held out my hand to him. "Of course," I said, but impatience stabbed into me. I wanted to see what he'd made. I wanted to look at the rendering as if it were a mirror.

I wanted to see myself the way he saw me.

Tomás took my hand and shook it. "Good night, Avita."

"Good night, Tomás."

I led him to the exit and held the flaps of the tent open for him, then tracked his silhouette until I lost him in the night. Not once had he glanced at me with fear lubricating his eyes; not once had I prodded him with a grimace or a slash or a roar.

Never in a hundred years would I have imagined putting on a show like this.

Off I floated back to my wagon, a tenderness sinking into me, softening my chest into well-risen dough.

And there was heat, too, an awareness of my lesser-acknowledged body parts, a sense of turning inside out.

Back in San Antonio, I'd told Fernando that I wasn't interested in company—now perhaps an amendment was necessary. Perhaps it depended on whose company I was in.

Screams were the currency of my tent, my favorite sound in all the world . . . but I could learn to love silence, too.

As I reached for the knob, the door to my wagon opened. I stepped aside, making room for my sister as she descended the stairs, more shimmer than weight, more mist than muscle, a specter in the moonlight.

She wore her steel-boned leotard and ruffled skirt from the kootchie tent, but her fishnet stockings were unrolled to the knee, and she wore no shoes.

With one look, she pinned me where I stood.

Her eyes, like Papa's voice and Mama's convictions, were her greatest instruments. Yes, her tits were legendary, but her gaze was a weapon.

Papa once bragged that he'd trained Luna's gaze by spilling pitchers of milk for her to hold, liquid suspended in the air, with only her eyes, a cloud of white hovering two feet above the ground. "If she can hold milk like this," he would say, "then she could hold a whole herd of red-blooded men."

A lovely story with Papa's fingerprints all over it, but the underlying truth was that Luna was a master manipulator, emotions becoming sand in her possession. Her talent, then, was not dance, or striptease, or seduction—it was a special kind of sculpture.

I waited to see if she would speak, aware of the big-sister little-sister hierarchy that dictated she had the right of way, the right to ignore, the right to pass straight by me without a single explanation. She was brilliant in the art of silence.

But the voice that whispered "Lu?" from behind her in the wagon was not my sister's.

Luna tensed, then sighed. "It's safe."

From the door emerged a young man with dark brown skin

and hair curling and fraying an inch above his head. Jonah, I thought his name was. A roustabout. We'd hired him in Virginia City last year. He did his best to appear steady and confident, but there were nerves in his eyes.

"We were just—" Luna began, and then something in her icy eyes shifted, shattered. Maybe it was her usual Saturday night exhaustion, or the fact that she wasn't the only one in a vulnerable state—I was alone, my scarf in my hand, my ugliness exposed for all the world to see for free. She blinked, her eyelids heavy on their way back up. "He was just walking me home."

There was more to this sentence. I knew it. We were both Fortunas, after all—we were born with spiels and stories and purple prose where others have tonsils. But Luna held back, and I wondered if it was because she felt no need to craft lies for her youngest sibling since I was not a threat, or because she thought Bird Girl, who could not possibly relate to the experience of being caught with a boy, was unworthy of the effort.

"Thank you, Jonah," I said, and hoped my monstrous smile appeared kind. "That was courteous of you to walk Luna home, and to check our wagon to make sure there were no ardent fans waiting for an ambush."

Luna studied me for half a moment, her hair draping across one side of her face, then turned to Jonah. "Arturo will be prepping the fire-eaters—"

"He's not," I rushed in. "Nan and Fry were coughing ashes. He's handling slack for the ribbon fliers instead."

"I'll go around," Jonah assured Luna. He was not a Fortuna;

his speech was not like a lace-trimmed work boot. It was deep and clipped. He ran along the pasture's fence, off into the long grass, and around to the far side of circus grounds where the other roustabouts would wait until takedown.

Then it was Luna and me.

She held perfectly still, but it was me who was supremely uncomfortable. Unsure.

You might have suspected Luna, the Duchess of the Tent of Wonder, who was surrounded nightly by her choice of dicks, to take frequent lovers. They swarmed her, flies at the buffet, and at any point she could leash one or all of them and bring them back to her bed for her own enjoyment.

But she'd always been lukewarm about boys. For a while, I'd thought she was like Socorro, who preferred women exclusively. Or like some of the others in our tented family who did not have an appetite for sex or romance and found there were plenty of other things at the buffet of life that would satiate.

Other humans seemed to be animals to Luna, or specters. Bodies with gold coins for heads. When she danced for them, that was all she seemed to see—money flashing in the snake pit, a thousand breaths finding her neck and thighs.

I'd never imagined she'd pair herself with anyone. Not for free. But then, I'd never imagined I'd be paired in easy conversation with a boy who wasn't blood related.

"Luna," I finally said with a heavy exhale, "I won't say anything. I promise."

When Luna's gaze locked on me this time, it was with a frost chilly enough to coat the entire Salt Lake Valley.

Sometimes I wondered if she forgot about me during the day, if it was only when she saw me in the grub tent or across the family wagon during prayer time that she recalled she had a little sister.

Without another word, I moved aside and let her go.

The Unfurling

WE WOKE TO STARLIGHT MUSIC.

The tweeting of a pipe organ, sharp and yet far-away, hitting the highest notes of the scale with a tremor.

When I opened my eyes, it got louder.

"Sweet Jesus, make it stop." In her bed beside me, a wrung-out, gray-cheeked Luna rolled onto her stomach and ducked under her pillow, trying to scrunch away the sound.

Even in that liminal space between awake and asleep, I heard the clap of shutters as Papa threw open the windows of the family wagon. "Cornelius! You ass weasel! Where are you?"

A minute later, he was slapping on our door. "Fortunas! Get out here! Now!"

Luna grumbled, wrapped her sheets around her; I followed, scarf tied in place.

Ren flung himself out of his own wagon, and we stumbled, bleary in the watery morning light, past our quiet, patient tents to the edge of the circus fence where Papa hunched, wild-eyed.

I always wanted to remember my father in that moment—his mustache limp, shaving foam soapy-thick on the bottom half of his mug. He was barely dressed, a stained towel around his neck dripping onto his undershirt, holding up his unfastened pants with one hand. I cataloged away this image of him. It was equal parts frightening and thrilling to see him like this. A king, disheveled. A king, still only a human.

A king, watching his greatest enemy saunter past.

Out of Le Cirque Americana's gates rolled an organ, the most beautiful machine I'd ever peeped at: a box the color of seafoam on wheels with a gaudy starfish-and-conch-shell tableau inlaid on its sides. The tune was a jaunty old sailor's shanty, and clouds of steam puffed out of its pipes as it curved past us and down the field.

Rows of horses came next, their manes tied into bunches like pom-poms down their necks, their saddles lined with purple velvet, all the creatures the exact same shade of frosty white-blue—had Cornelius bleached them, I wondered? And had he bred them specially to make them trot along so perfectly in unison?

Thoughts like these were a betrayal, I knew, but before I could flog myself for my blasphemy, Papa gripped our fence to keep from imploding.

"Mary's bouncing melons," he swore.

Riding atop an elephant decorated with turquoise-blue peacock plumes was Cornelius himself, seated on a fat cushion the color of juiced plums.

Papa may have fancied himself a king, but Cornelius had made himself an emperor.

Tendrils of his goose-down hair floated about his head, freshly washed like a halo of baby's breath. His tailcoat had somehow stretched in length and width so it covered the elephant's leathery ass and draped off its back in a train. Red rose petals piled on its hem along with flecks of white confetti.

He didn't say a word to us, but tossed a handful of something at our feet and blew Papa a kiss.

Pieces of chewy candy, saltwater taffy, and the wrappers were all ads: "Le Cirque Americana—Where All Your Dreams Come True!"

My father stomped one down into the mud. "Fucking bag of shit."

Behind him, Ren and I held a glance, woe shining in my brother's eyes.

We didn't do parades. Papa pretended it was for the good of the circus: "They're pedantic! Baiting children with music and frills? Leading them out of their houses, down the streets like the Pied Piper? It's a cheap ploy for lazy showmen. Our circus sells itself!"

But I didn't crawl out of my mother yesterday. The real reason we didn't introduce ourselves at each new gig with such a procession was because a march like that cost money, and it cost humility, and Papa had neither to spare.

It killed him to see Cornelius flaunting his goods now. He probably would've traded one of his own children for that calliope alone.

Hell, he'd have traded Ren for much less.

The parade passed our fence, and I accounted for the number of sold-out performances of Bird Girl that would be required to buy their tubas, their drums, their bell-like xylophones. Our guitar and mandolin and marimbas were hollow and chintzy compared to the robust flatulence of Cornelius's forty-piece marching band.

And our fabrics were dull and old and simple, I realized as Le Cirque Americana's acrobats ran past in marvelous one-piece white suits that clung close to the body to show off the impossible forms and lines of their limbs, but also billowed out like wings and tails when they stood up straight.

"We've been performing for ranch hands and tumbleweeds for too long," I thought out loud to my sister, and a leech of fear attached itself to my gut and sucked. It was one thing to believe your own father when he boasted that we were the slickest show on earth. It was quite another to be gripped by Cornelius's torch-light procession, to see the evidence to the contrary strolling right past your beak.

To my left, Luna shrugged. "Cornelius is a collector. This is just him polishing up all his fancy little shits to display."

My big sister, dressed in a sheer nightgown, bedsheets now settled around her hips, watched the line of puppeteers with pirouetting marionette ballerinas jaunting past, and she didn't wince. Didn't look impressed. Didn't look threatened.

I gathered the hem of my own nightgown, remembering every time my father had ever called me his jewel, his diamond, his gem. "Papa's a collector, too," I argued, but she shook her head. "Then what is he?"

"A showman."

The sweaty butts of six work mules pulled shimmering signs that advertised Le Cirque Americana, told us its ticket prices (comparable with ours) and its hours (they opened before we did and closed after us), and then it was over—or rather, it turned into a parade of animal haunches, and we Fortunas watched them all disappear onto Peculiar's main street, the calliope music growing murky as it moved down the drag.

We were stunned into silence, and so there was nothing to drown out the far-off noise of cheers, the whistles, the clapping of sticky little-kid hands as Cornelius showered those townies with taffy.

A noise that made Papa grunt and slam his hands on the fence.

"Tell everyone to get ready," he ordered Ren. "I want to open our gates before that parade circles back around."

Mama opened her eyes so wide you could see the pale sheen of her scar tissue, its edge blurring into her lash line. "You want to open two hours ahead of schedule? Come on, Arturo—"

"I am telling them that if they aren't ready to put on the best fucking show the world has ever seen in thirty minutes or less, they can all beg for jobs at the crusty old Manatee Odditorium in Florida!" Papa wiped the melting shaving cream from his face and splashed it onto the ground. "Now!"

It was a ridiculous order. There were people who needed to be in hair and makeup and wardrobe who weren't even awake yet—Fernando usually took a full hour just to pick out his gowns. Big cats needed to be warmed up and cuddled and fed, and with the rush, they would now have to be coaxed with extra meat to behave. Lights needed to be double-checked, the bulletin needed to be posted, everyone needed to eat and digest and have a chance to visit that place—that in-between place that existed in our heads, an almost tangible destination, where we all went before we performed. A place to center ourselves, to reflect on what we would be conveying to our audience today.

Everyone needed time and preparation to give the kinds of shows that would satisfy our king, Arturo, and make him feel competent.

But here at the Family Fortuna, we dealt exclusively in the impossible.

And so, despite all odds and calculations, despite all bad-faith projections, we all knew everything would be ready and everything would be perfect in thirty minutes or less.

When our ticket booth drew up its curtains and our gates flew open, it was with particularly venomous pride that Papa ushered in the first customers of Peculiar. "Welcome, welcome, one and all!" he said, almost sang, tipping his hat to each soul who passed him. "Come right in, come be dazzled! Come be amazed! Come and see things you never could have imagined—you won't believe your eyes!"

And as the people of Peculiar poured in, I marveled at what we'd found here in the desert: a town so hungry for entertainment, they would pay to watch two circuses wrestle to the death in the grass and the mud.

"Well, good." Mama surveyed the crowds around the midway, a cacophony of bells ringing and prize whistles sounding and talkers polluting the air with their pitches for two-for-one games of chance and contests of strength. "Arturo must have been saying his prayers after all."

I looked at her over the edge of my scarf, amused, until she broke. "Oh, all right. I prayed for him. Some for him and some for the circus. I prayed for all of us. Prayed for victory. God will not forsake us." She frowned, peering at the contented customers around us with chilled suspicion in her good eye, fondling the bouquet of stinking herbs tied to her skirts. "Stay in the light, Avita. And keep a prayer in your head at all times. We'll be done with this absurd dick-measuring contest soon enough."

Papa strolled up the midway and joined us, wearing his triumph like a rose in his lapel. "'For the people of Peculiar were hungry, and we gave them meat. They were thirsty, and we gave them drink. They were strange, but we were stranger still, and charged two bits a head to stare at our oblations . . .' Aw, come on, Quinn, don't give me that look! I'm celebrating!"

Mama met his blasphemous biblical plagiarizing with a clench-toothed scowl, shaking her head as she stroked her sachet.

"Look at this!" Papa, ever the ringmaster, spread his arms to show off the throng of patrons—as if we had missed them, as if we needed him to personally show them to us, as if they did not exist until he spoke of them. "Cornelius thought he had us with his fancy-ass parade, but wait till he gets a peek at these crowds, my loves. I know exactly what he's going to do. He's going to lift up the tails of that souped-up coat of his, and he's going to—"

The ear-blasting trumpet of an elephant's trunk stopped Papa cold.

Le Cirque Americana's calliope music, the toots and gilded shrieks of the organ, crept into the background of our circus, and then it was as boisterous as if the pipes were here in the midway.

Cornelius was bringing that tempting procession past our grounds.

Past our people.

Our customers quieted to listen. A few of them leaned over the fence to see the grand parade turning around, then whispered to their friends, their words inaudible, their frenzy unmissable. One by one, they tipped out of our lines to follow Cornelius.

"Son of a bitch," Papa uttered, pushing his way to the gates. Mama and I followed, Mama to extinguish whatever blaze Papa was about to set, and I to fish my father's cockiness out of the manure by reminding him that only a genius could produce a child like myself.

Le Cirque Americana's parade wound past us, bringing with it a multitude of townies, all shiny and smiling, marching under the spell of the procession's glamour.

"Look at all those people." I tried to stop myself from counting heads.

"Those aren't people," Papa muttered, "those are dollars with feet. And if they can follow Cornelius like a bunch of lemmings, we can bait them in here just as easy."

Within our own gates, our customers tilted their heads at the passing herd, their tickets feeling dog-eared and damp in their palms.

"Oh no," Papa suddenly snarled. "Oh no, he wouldn't dare—"

I whipped my head up to see what Papa was bitching about now and gasped.

Atop his elephant steed, the man of myth himself, Cornelius Leon Reve, rode right through our banner, tearing through the length of paper, taking down the tassels that framed it. He ripped right through the Fortuna name. It lingered for a moment across his chest, then fell, and his mammoth's feet pressed it carelessly into the dirt.

Cornelius held up a megaphone. "Ladies and gentlemen! When you are finished taking your tour of America's worst farm, hurry into Le Cirque Americana and see a real show!"

Beside me, Papa tried to shout over Cornelius, but even the power of his voice—his greatest gadget, his instrument—was drowned out by the volume of the megaphone, and so he gaped like a fish, right there on his own circus grounds.

"Fuck you and your hairy mother!" Papa foamed, but Cornelius didn't even look at him as he marched his floppy-eared ride into his exquisite circus, that minimalistic white, black, and metallic aesthetic almost insulted by our smears of color, our patterns, our racket. I wished I could cover Papa's eyes so he didn't have to see the number of people who lined up to buy their tickets at their booth.

But when he turned back to Mama and me, Papa had a

bobcat's grin on his devilish face. "Now, now," he practically giggled, "wait just a minute. They haven't seen it yet."

"Seen what, Arturo?" Poor Mama was exhausted by my father's whiplash of emotions.

Instead of answering his wife, Papa scanned the circus staff around him and ordered, "I want my new banner! You, go find the poster boy and tell him to bring the banner to me! No, I want *all* the posters. Rip them from the lithographer if you must. Bring them to me now!"

One of the cousins ran off to track down Tomás, and my stomach gurgled.

The raging excitement of the parade would be easily outshone by the coming reveal. During the midnight hours, I knew, Tomás had holed himself up somewhere and made a likeness of me with his paints, then laid it out to dry in the dawn.

He'd stared at my face. Traced my features. Mixed colors so his lithograph would match what he'd seen last night in Big Red.

And now here came Michelangelo from the yard behind the wagons. Blue paint smudged his fingers, a dab of white was forgotten on his forehead, and his long, beautiful hair was tied back with a strip of leather. God, his hair . . . I loved when it waterfalled down his shoulders, but now that it was pulled back in a knot, you could see the chisel of his jawbone, the smoothness of his cheeks like clay pots—

My desire for him punched me right in the gut, stealing my breath.

"Well?" Papa shouted at his artist. "Where is it?"

"Here they are," Tomás panted before Papa detonated, passing him a long metal tube. "The banner's with your grunts. They're running it up the flagpole now."

The flagpole . . . We never really flew any flags on it, like Old Glory or the Lone Star, but it jutted straight up from Big Red and fluttered with advertisements to add vertical movement to our horizontal majesty.

That meant the new banner of Bird Girl would tower above the circus, flying high enough on the tarnished staff that even the patrons of Le Cirque Americana could take in the image.

But I almost forgot about all that as Papa unrolled the bundle of posters from the tube and I got my first glimpse of Tomás's finished work.

My stars, it was astonishing.

The first poster: our tattooed women painted in all their glory, their inked biceps looking thick enough to throttle a grizzly, our pony riders atop horses speeding past golden chariots full of clowns.

The second poster, a collage of acts: our ribbon fliers dipping down from the skies, so gracefully rendered you could feel the wind in their hair; our human arrow jetting from her crossbow; a gaggle of sword-swallowers tangled in the scaled muscles of our pythons.

The third poster melted me: Luna, all moonlight and ardor, the ins and outs of her splendid frame composed against the glow of the kootchie tent. The other dancing girls were posed behind her, all of them as lovely as pearls on a necklace, but Tomás had made Luna the diamond of the set, and a swell of deep gratification washed away any pangs of jealousy I might have harbored over her session with him.

"Yes, yes, yes, my God, yes!" Papa's reaction did not disappoint; he shuffled through the silvered papers, eyes bulging like grapes ripe on a vine. "And our pièce de résistance?"

A snag in my chest. A spark of wonder.

That was me they were speaking about. My banner. My rendering.

Tomás said nothing, only pointed in the direction of the flagpole. Up, up the banner went on its ropes, my anticipation building to a burning crescendo within me—

I thought of last night, alone in the tent with Tomás. His hands, the spotlight. The silence of someone simply sitting across from my face, considering it, taking in its lines, its angles, its details, finding the parts of my monstrosity that might even be, if not beautiful, then appealing—

The banner went up, the breeze displaying it proudly . . . and dismay pinched my core.

I sank into shadow. Flat as a cowpie in the sun.

"Look at that," Papa breathed. "Look at that!"

I did. I did look. And it made me want to vomit.

Our posters last year were painted by some chap in Oregon with a prodigious employment record—he'd done all the other big productions, plus some ten-in-ones along boardwalks and a handful of Wild West shows to boot.

The illustrated Bird Girl, as he'd depicted me, was outlined in sharp black strokes, the coloring prismatic, my pose exaggerated, villainous. A stylized take on my visage, to be sure, but that was standard for bills in the circus industry—ornamental conceits, all, so you'd be compelled to fork over your dimes to see what we really looked like.

That's what all our prior advertisements had been—cheap rope to lasso you closer.

And as Ren had pointed out, they'd worked. They drew customers. They drew coin.

But Tomás made my old poster look like a rube had done it with a toothbrush and greasepaint.

I looked, and I saw—

Beak shine. There was nothing about the nose on that painted creature that resembled cartilage or flesh; my beak curved down in a vulture's swoop, its tip sharp enough to tear meat from bones and pluck up maggots to feed nestlings.

Feathers the color of dried dung, not at all the sumptuous, silky black plumes I grew on my back but rugged and unkempt as my depicted hair, the two snarling together in a savage bush that was impressive and fearsome when you considered it grew from a human.

Eyes like spilled black oil, galaxyless and hungry, and, as Tomás had captured them, boiling with anger. This was perhaps the most shocking part of the entire piece: the volcanic rage that was scratching to be released from every rigid muscle, that had me hunched over with fury, preparing to spring out of the painting to chase, to hunt, to kill for sport.

I racked my memory of the previous night, searching for the moment when I had exposed such a temper. Never once had I raised my voice. Never once had I bared my teeth like a scavenger.

He relied upon the memories of your show, I scolded myself. *Of course he did, you clod. The Spectacular Aviary Extravaganza is about fright. Horror. Dazzlement. He watched your show twice—he knows what you become when you growl, when you rattle your cage, when you feast on fowl.*

Our old posters showed me mid-snarl, too—teeth splayed, back arched, my signature pose.

But this was beyond the delightfully frightening. This was . . .

I had to look away, had to put my eyes on something else—Tomás.

He clutched his sketchbook, curling his fingers around the covers.

That painting he had made that he carried with him every-where like a talisman, a beacon to Paris, where he'd join a revolution of color and light and beauty . . . was he as proud of the banner he'd made of me? Did he think it was a beacon, too?

He peered at me, gave me a polite smile.

My insides soured.

And then it hit me. All the posters were exquisite, precise—he had very nearly landed Luna's beauty on paper, something I'd always thought impossible. And the other posters, too—Tomás had taken the Family Fortuna, ground it up into his paints, and made it come to life.

Tomás had captured truth. That was his gift.

Oh, Lord, I was a damn fool. I blinked over and over, trying to wash the flushing pink of my humiliation and stinging regret from my field of vision—but what had I expected?

Truly, what had I expected?

Something indulgent.

Something that took the blatantly humanesque parts of me in good faith and blended them with my malformities in reverent homage, in light-handed strokes, in patinas of unrestrained glory. My glossy hair. My smooth, unfeathered forehead. My hands, which were not claws at all, but graceful and pale.

Something that captured the best of my avian components, gnarled and horrific though they were: the supple sheen of my feathers, the sly curve of my keratin beak, the mirror gleam of my razored teeth, uniform as obsidian in sand.

I wanted to see last night's mood caught on paper. I wanted to see my conversations with Tomás dabbed into the portrait. That warmth I endured whenever he locked eyes with me, and the way he grinned at my banter, and the tremors of desire running through my body like a voltage wire. The moment when I had sat as muse, and Tomás had aimed the spotlight in my direction, and a silence had held us both—

That's what I'd hoped to see on my banner: proof that last night, I'd been more than just Bird Girl.

I'd even hoped—oh, God, the shame nearly shattered me like an icicle—I'd hoped Tomás might paint me like that Paris girl. I'd hoped he had enjoyed stirring me up with his teasing words, his coy glances, and that he'd immortalize me, too, with swirls of color.

But the finished banner was like any other horror rag—

No, it was better. It was better, because Tomás was good, really good.

And that made it so much worse.

It hit everything on Papa's checklist, however—I looked like God had a sadist's imagination and a hellish sense of humor. No, I looked like the devil's own creation, like he had been allowed to make one thing of his very own on the seventh day while the Lord put His feet up, and I was that malignant product.

That was me, up there on that banner.

It was worse than any mirror.

"Look above you, folks! Behold the monster that awaits you after dark! Get your tickets now before you lose your nerve!" Papa's voice was overwarm and husky from a morning of yelling, but its effect on your body was still fantastic. It seized sensory control, working in ripples from the skin down, burrowing in—and it took me over, his trill of "See the creature that has inspired full catatonic shock all the way from Texas to Tacoma, if you dare!"

He directed this last comment to a broad, rough-necked cowboy, who took it as the personal challenge Arturo had intended it to be, spinning his spurs all the way to the ticket booth to prove how brave he was.

Goddammit, Papa was good. We were so good together—partners in dreams, partners in wonder.

Watch as he sells me with the charm of a debutante's mother: a nightmare, a horror, a daughter—peep if you dare!

"If you want anything changed—" Tomás started, but Papa shook his head so hard his lips smacked.

"Don't change anything!" Papa stared at the banner; if he could have, he would have eaten it. "It's perfect. Absolutely horrific." He peeled his gaze away only to watch the customers react to the flagpole, chortling with glee.

There were gasps. There were interested clucks. There were irreverent boasts and frightened laughs.

"Did a woman fuck a bird," someone said, "or did a harpy fuck a lizard?"

"Just a cheap costume," some dissenter said. "There was a boy like that at the Hippodrome, remember? With the rubber fish tail?"

"He itched his legs when he thought we weren't looking." Her companion smirked. "Oh, Lord, I'd rip that face right off, if it were me."

The surge of commentary left me cold, even in the heat of the desert.

It was one thing to hear them scream when I was in my ring.

It was quite another to hear their honest thoughts, their unabashed reports—everything a scream was meant to say.

"No, I saw the Family Fortuna when they came through Durango. It's real," someone else said, and as the group moved away from the fence and back into our wonderland, we heard him finish, "Fucked me up. Every creak of my floorboards had me sweating for weeks!"

In a daze, I moved my hands up and down my dress, like I was patting myself down for loose change, for bucktoothed pride—but I was a cup with no water.

My family peeled off to attend to their circusy duties, my father practically skipping like a drunken goat, so pleased was he with the way the morning had warped in his favor.

Tomás, too, evaporated with the sun.

I stood alone near the fence, a hundred people bustling around me, kicking up dust.

Just as well.

No answers, and no questions, either.

Only a banner with my own face on it, looking me straight in the eye—and a scream of my own lodged under my tongue.

I was a bird with no wings.

I was a girl with no face.

A monster.

And for the first time, I was afraid.

A History

REN

DID I REQUEST THEE, MAKER, FROM MY CLAY
to—

"Keep up, hop-along, or you'll be left here for the seagulls!"

Across the boardwalk, my father, oiled and beet-faced, peered at me with such impatience, you'd think me an untrained beagle, not his only son.

At fourteen years old, I was plenty used to Arturo's inflamed manner of communicating with me, and truthfully it would likely startle me at this point to receive anything but contempt from him. My existence was a bur in his heel, and therefore my purpose was to make the raising of me as painless as possible.

I fumbled with my book, trying to wedge my mark in place before closing it, but I lost the whole thing to the reality of gravity, the hardcover tumbling upside down, crunching onto the salt-rotted slats of the boardwalk. A few passersby chortled at the scene. By the time I'd smoothed the bent pages and pressed my Milton against my chest, Arturo had sounded a gruff, annoyed gurgle and stalked on without me.

We were on the rare holiday. The Family Fortuna didn't have an off-season; my father simply drove our caravan wherever there was sunshine. The sun came out, and wallets followed—and that's where Arturo wanted to be, always, ready to give people a reason to let their coins roll. He'd have opened the gates and worked our crowds every day that ended in y if Mama hadn't insisted on taking Sundays off.

And this year, she'd convinced him to take a proper rest, a week away at the beach. My father hated rest, and he was notoriously suspicious of the ocean and all people who delighted in gulping lungfuls of that fresh sea air. But Santa Cruz was cheap, the kind of place where a single dollar could be stretched to cover accommodations at an inn on the pier, hearty crab platters, and all the lemon ices your kids could gobble.

A real family holiday, all five of the Fortunas together in respite, yet splintered across the boardwalk, left to our own devices.

Mama stood in line to chase down vittles—boiled mutton with oyster sauce, baked trout, cups of clam chowder and stewed prunes—for when Papa got peckish, he became even more like a child.

Luna headed for the beach to watch the cloister of seabirds in the tide pools. Avita, bundled up in hat and veil like a mourning widow, followed Luna.

And Arturo, unable to abandon his inner ham for even a day of restoration, headed into Santa Cruz's most lurid of offerings: Big Burp's Waxworks and Mystifying Exhibition.

A dime museum.

A sideshow.

I was expected to nip at his heels, to jot down his ramblings as they spurted from his mouth, to translate them into something logical on the page. He loved to visit other exhibits, not as a fellow showmaker seeking inspiration to enhance our own acts, but as a god, coming down from the clouds to snicker at the mundane mortals attempting to display a pathetic fraction of his own prowess.

Arturo had already waltzed through the neon-pink lips of Big Burp's open mouth, the painted wood threshold leading to a dark tunnel of tawdry possibilities. Crowds bunched behind him, around my bench, between us.

I could stay here and read, watch for my father's greasy swirl of a noggin emerging from the sideshow, and catch up when he headed to the promenade to heckle the Little Miss Aphrodite Pageant. He might never know the difference, since he so rarely waited for a response or a nudge from conversationalists before barreling on to his next point.

Some clockwork mechanism swooped Big Burp's wild eyes down to look at me. His mouth yawned wide, the ticket seller in a motley patchwork coat bouncing his pitch all over the scale to lure people in.

I knew this type of museum. We all did.

We'd seen them dozens of times, and the whole setup reeked of shoddy work, of chalky makeup and strategically placed dim lights to make the wonders within seem believable. Forged certificates of authenticity that no one would ever be able to verify because there was no such archive to check them against. False second noses attached with plaster. Limbs folded back to create scarcity. Half-decayed invertebrates and developmentally arrested animal fetuses posed in jars as marvels of science, all of them quite ordinary.

It could not have appealed to me less if it were the actual portal to hell.

But I'd lingered alone too long.

Already the stares had begun. Already the gawks, the double-takes, the fingers of children pointing, their mothers hushing them mid-question. A Pekingese on a leash sniffed at me with a snobbish indication: *Well, you're certainly supposed to be taller than that!*

Being raised in a circus had given me a false sense of security, I suppose—a fellow with dwarfism and a bad back was perfectly commonplace when he lived life under a big top . . . and was an exhibition of his own, whether willing or not, when out in the world.

Or maybe I'd merely forgotten that anyone else could make me feel as out of place or as small as he could.

Into the dime museum I went. There were chortles from the ticket takers about my height, but I outran them, weaving past clusters of beachgoing families who'd decided Big Burp's was a decent enough respite from the sun.

Perhaps that was how it should have been advertised. I strolled through the museum's rooms, less than impressed by the rickety exhibitions—the glued whale bones posing as ridiculously proportioned shark skeletons, the collection of hairpieces, jars of floating body parts that allegedly belonged to heads of state, celebrities, criminals. A giant plaster leviathan gaped at patrons, its mouth a cavernous black pit. Even if the signage hadn't been riddled with grammatical errors and basic anachronisms, it would have been unconvincing.

Not that it mattered to the majority of the people who came through institutions such as this. They were not paying to see high-end artifacts or fact-checked oddities. They were only interested in amusement. Tomfoolery. Thrills.

No sign of Papa anywhere. No sound of him, either. I followed the convoys of pointing, hee-hawing spectators through the dim corridors, scanning the perimeters for somewhere I could sit and read my book—

But something else caught my eye.

Tucked back in an alcove, near a window that was too grimy to let in more than a fraction of light, there was a display on scientific curiosities that had me hooked.

A replica of Galvani's experiment in which he'd attempted to resurrect dead frogs by sparking them with varying voltages of electricity.

Models of the creatures called dinosaurs hanging from the ceiling by wires, all reptilian rubber and wing.

Maxwell's flywheels, bits of charcoal presented as pure phlogiston, glass skulls demonstrating a phrenologist's handiwork, and more, all of it somewhat dusty, neglected compared to the other, grabbier attractions in Big Burp's.

I was the slackest of slack-jaws, a total booze for this exhibit. I'd read about all of it, all these men shaping humanity's very knowledge, which in turned shaped what humanity was capable of—and here it was, as if Big Burp himself knew I was coming and slapped it together to be worthy of my coin.

Behind me, while I was busy ogling the resplendence of these scientific minds, a trio of men wandered near, near enough for me to hear their discussions of the displays at hand.

My brain went off like a bottle rocket. I pretended to be studying the mural of Darwinian evolution (as applied to a rather tastelessly drawn and clearly fantastical Caribbean mermaiden), but I wanted to hear it all. Absorb it all.

Their voices were drab and droll, no sense of pageantry in the slightest. But of course I would think such things, I chided myself. The son of Arturo Fortuna, man of a thousand tones. Papa had trained my ear well.

He would think this exhibit was ridiculous, boring, a waste of a decent corner—but he would be wrong.

This was no ordinary circus. This was the circus of nature.

"—that German fellow, the one going on about craniometry," said a man in a gray hat.

"Blumenbach." I spoke without thinking and instantly winced. I'd given an answer when I had not been specifically asked for one. Such an offense would earn me a full dressing down from Arturo, who despised when he struggled for the perfect response only to have someone else beat him to the punch.

The men turned toward me.

And I felt it. The moment when I myself became exhibition.

God, I hated it. I hated it so much.

For a moment, I'd thought I could do it. I'd thought I could be an ordinary person, ready to indulge in a sharing of opinions with fellow-minded readers.

But they stared, taking in the sight of me, and I nearly crawled out of my own skin.

"Well!" one of the men finally said. "Look at this little scholar! He knows his physiologists!"

Meanwhile, the man to whom I'd replied did not look upon me with vengeance but with gratitude, as though tossing a correct citation or a rectified statistic into a conversation was not a call to arms, as my father regarded it, but a kindness, a communion.

"No," I said, emboldened into confessing, "I know my *Frankenstein*."

This made them chuckle, and it was a beautifully pure sound—free of cruelty or mocking.

Their eyes were still on me, yes, but the usual scorch of exhibitionism had faded. They were not looking at me to taunt; they were not using me for their own levity, unwinding the little knot inside me and tugging on my strings. They took in the book under my arm, a gilded Milton, and brows raised all around, mouths closed, gazes expectant.

They were waiting for me to say more.

I mentally unearthed all I'd ever read about German theories of comparative anatomy and wet my lips. A sensation stirred within me, a buzz unlike anything I'd ever felt. Even surrounded by the unimaginable marvels of the circus, I'd never before experienced such euphoria, such rapture—

"There he is! And he found the most humdrum display to cross his eyes with, I see."

My father's voice echoed through the room, rattling every model, every frame, every window. He could have been quieter, but he chose not to be. Every word, every inflection, was all completely in his control, and his boisterousness had the exact reaction he was hoping for.

The other men glanced up, away from me, disrupted. Papa paraded through the room, his mustache wrinkling with aversion.

I wished I could disappear; I wished I could shrink down even smaller, roll under the cabinets, become a dust particle, a flea, a mouse turd. Anything but endure this scene.

Arturo cracked another joke at my expense, brought to laughter by his own drollery, but the men shuffled their feet. This was not their flavor of entertainment. Not their type of show.

This reaction would only rile Papa up—thank God, they turned to go, to find somewhere else to continue their conversation in private. I ached to go with them. If I were a dust particle, I could ride along and listen. But Papa put his hand on my shoulder as the men headed for the exit, as if he sensed I would follow them if I were not kept in place.

"Wait!" he suddenly called, and I died. *Let them go, let them leave!* I wanted to shout. *They want nothing to do with you.* I wanted to protect them from my father, from being roped into his pre-posterousness. But being polite, civilized men, they turned back, though they did not bother to hide their annoyance.

Arturo jutted a finger at the Darwinian mural, at the ugliest version of the mermaid mid-evolution. "What do you think? Do you buy into it?"

Did they buy into it? I cringed at his impresario's intonation, the way he gestured to the display as if he were a farmer hocking wares at market. This was not a decently priced watermelon; this was Charles Darwin's theory of evolution, something the great-est scientists in the world were considering and debating, poking holes into or stitching their own theorems onto. It was not some-thing you bought or fell for wholesale.

The man in the gray hat, who had clearly had enough of this buffoonery, straightened, clearing his throat. "Are you asking if I, a tenured professor of biology, buy into Darwin's theories of transmutation of species and natural selection? Yes. His is the soundest theory of organism development and scientific natural-ism we have. While there may be gaps in its execution, those are challenged and filled daily. It explains so much."

"It explains so much," my father echoed, and for a spare second, I was hopeful. Had the man's sophisticated rejoinder actu-ally left Papa spellbound?

No such luck.

"Does it explain that?" Papa was sticky with mirth; he

yanked a flyer from his coat pocket, and I crumbled with chagrin anew.

Avita was there on the flyer, eyeing the viewer, THE FAMILY FORTUNA emblazoned above her. A caricature of Papa's black top hat was stitched above the *F* in Fortuna, a reminder to all who entered his circus that this domain had a king and the king wore his crown with preening authority.

I stood beside Arturo as he held up his flyer gleefully, pinched between his fingers, waiting for the men to take it like he was handing out cash.

The man in the gray hat slowly shuffled toward him, took the flyer, considered it with consternation. My sister's face was portrayed as straightforwardly as anyone could with ink and paper, but even so, such proportions, such features were automatically dismissed by the eye as invention. Fiction.

Arturo did not skip a beat in his advertisement. "We roll into Fresno the day after tomorrow. You'll want to come and take a gander at her, see if it explains any gaps in the theory. Although I would speculate that not even Darwin himself could have predicted this." And then, to me: "Come on, chum, or I'll throw you headfirst into the leviathan."

My father waltzed past the men, who held the flyer like it was beach trash. I rushed along behind him, burnt with humiliation.

Avita was no fiction, though. She was real, flesh and bone and feather. A doctor had come to see her once, but no diagnosis could explain her weirdness. Even I had searched through my books and requested papers from libraries to pinpoint her particular infirmity, hoping to satisfy my scientific curiosity with a name, but to no avail. Oddities happened, without explanation and at random. It was as simple as that.

But to the Fortunas, it would never be that simple. When you lived in a circus, you were put on display if you had even the slightest of abnormalities . . . unless there was someone stranger than you to pull away your crowds. Though I knew it wasn't fair, the first time I had looked at my baby sister's face on that flyer, I had thought, *Good God, Avita, can't you tone it down? Do you always have to be so good? So magnetic? So thrilling? Can't you leave just a crumb for the rest of us?*

And as I peered at her banner now, waving smugly over the Family Fortuna's lot, I couldn't stop a barrage of equally traitorous ruminations from parading through my mind.

Good God, Avita, do you have to be so extraordinary? I work my ass off for him, not eating, not sleeping, not resting until the circus is precisely as polished and gleaming as he demands, yet he won't even look at me. Not unless he has another order to give.

Won't look at me, won't listen to me, won't think of me. Not when Bird Girl has the stage.

Iron Hot

FERNANDO WAS ALONE IN THE DRESSING ROOM, pressing a length of loud lime-green calico with a fluting iron—some new costume he was stitching together, a skirt to button onto one of the girls so she could twirl around the stage like a desert mermaid. I studied the freshly born ruffles as I perched on the stool beside him, crossing my legs.

"Exciting morning," he commented dryly, sticking the heavy iron back in the stove's radiant coals to reheat. "I've never seen Arturo this bloated. He could charge headfirst into a hurricane and come right out the other side."

"He's finally getting his big face-off. He's wanted this for years." Only after I said it did I recognize the automation of my commentary—the dutiful daughter offering her lines like it was a script.

Was it a script?

"Only because he thinks he'll win." The way Fernando worked the iron was mesmerizing to behold; he clamped the flaccid calico between the V-shaped metal, then released it with a yawn of steam, leaving a trail of perfect folds along the hem.

So whirling was the storm in my own head, I almost missed the stinging honesty of his response. "Wait—you don't think we'll fill our tents?"

Fernando shrugged. "The Family Fortuna is good. You know we're good, Vee. And Le Cirque Americana can be tackier than a pair of men's britches. But come on. It's no contest. Where would you spend your coin if you could only buy one ticket?"

His words weren't meant to be hurtful or flippant, simply the neutral observations of someone with no real skin in the game. Fernando was family, but he was not a Fortuna. His affinity was bought with room and board and a small but steady salary.

Almost as if to prove he was being objective, he added, "Arturo's the better showman by far. Anyone could build Le Cirque Americana if they had enough money—Cornelius bought his way to the top. But he *is* at the top. There's not much else we can do."

I chuckled—as if this relentless competition between the two circuses were a case of simple math.

As if Papa would ever accept that the world was simply stacked against him. As if he wouldn't rearrange hell itself if it meant he could have every advantage.

Fernando suddenly let out a sinful squeal. "Did I tell you about Pepper and the mustachio twins?" As he fluted another layer of ruffles, he spilled every bit of circus gossip he possessed. As the hub of the kootchie tent, all these little tidbits of stories and secrets were laid at Fernando's feet, sometimes unintentionally, and since he was jazzed by the chance to spill this juice to me, I said nothing. I let the prattle of lighter subjects wash over me: who borrowed whose hairbrush and passed along the lice they'd caught from a barkeep; who had stepped on whose tap shoe, and who speculated that it had been deliberate; who had walked in on Bart the Bull's-Eye tangling tongues with Graciela the cake lady.

A dancing girl came inside to grab her cigarettes and locked eyes with me in her mirror; she peered at my scarf, right where my beak was hidden, then turned away, like my mouth had gone rogue and snarled at her of its own accord.

Chagrin congested in my throat.

You are that mirror when you're onstage.

What did the dancing girl see when she looked at me?

Did they all see it?

Had they all seen it all along?

"One more thing." Fernando dropped his volume and kept his lips stiff. "Your sister's been sneaking out of the show early—on multiple occasions. Some of the girls think she's got—"

"Oh. Yes. She's been working with customers." I dropped the lie effortlessly and with minimal guilt. "Arturo's been lining them up."

Fernando merely shrugged and fluffed the skirt, spraying various sticky substances on the fabric to freeze it into perfection.

My sudden loyalty to Luna was a bit perplexing, but before I could reflect on my role as her secret keeper, Fernando spoke. "Doesn't matter anyway. Not even the duchess can beat Cornelius. There's only one act that could spin this all in Arturo's direction, and that's you."

Heat traveled up my neck, and I inhaled.

"I know for a fact that Cornelius doesn't have anything like Bird Girl on his docket, and it could cost him. People think they want that shiny savoir faire he serves up, but eventually everyone's inner philistine comes out and they get hungry for something truly repulsive."

Repulsive.

Me. My monstrous face on that banner.

Tomás in the tent, quietly drawing my features.

The sound of screams echoed between my ears, and I was dried out, a barren lake that would never again feel rain—

"Vee?" Fernando tilted my chin until I was looking at him. "What's wrong?" Even in my scarf, he could read me like a compass.

Answering my best friend, however, would require me to bore directly into the drippy caverns of my soul and put into words that which I had not even begun to explain to myself.

To start, I offered this, which rang out like a confession as I said it: "I know what we're up against with Le Cirque—I know this isn't just a regular headliner weekend in some podunk town—but maybe I could . . ." I picked at a loose thread on my gown, tugging until it gave and wormed around my fingers. "Maybe I could do something else."

"Something else?" Fernando pursed his lips. "You mean—"

"Other than Bird Girl." I was raised by a circus; there was glitz under my fingernails and a tentpole in place of a spine. I could skip into my ring and put on, with glazed proficiency, any kind of show. I could sneeze out a tap house shanty. I could jump and juggle half a dozen eggs or dance the mazurka on stilts . . .

But none of that mattered. I sighed, thoroughly trounced by reality. "I'm Arturo's big trump card," I pronounced. "His grand finale." Bird Girl was supposed to be in her tent tonight, running double showings, rattling her cage and chomping chickens. "There's no way he'll let me do anything else." Fernando had said it himself—there was no way Papa could win without me. Without Bird Girl.

"Oh, Vee." Fernando plunged the iron into a bucket of water and met my eyes, giving me his full attention, a gift that nearly made me well up from gratitude. "I thought you loved it. Being Bird Girl."

Being myself.

A tent of my own.

An act of my own.

All those years. All those butts in bleachers. All those screams.

"What is it you want to do, exactly?" Fernando leaned over to a vanity and dabbed a berry gloss onto his mouth. "You want to dance? Or spin with the aerialists? Do you want to be the bell-in-the-jar? Or sing?"

I considered his question.

Like a dream, the memory came to me: the way the crowds in the Tent of Wonder shifted and blurred in the reflection of the stage lights like a living, moving painting. The sound of them clapping and wailing for the dancing girls, for Luna, for Dolores and Delilah, for Fernando and Suzette, that rhythm, the tambourine jingle of their cheers. Their wanting, something you could feel like warmth from a campfire.

Other memories brimmed to the surface, too: the flap of my newly printed banner, disturbing the breeze with its abhorrence.

Shrill, mewling screams. The understanding that I was detested. And I had chased it! I had longed for it! I had longed for my crowds to cower from me; I had longed for the burden of their fear.

You are a mirror when you are on that stage, Papa always said. *Whatever the audience gives to you, you must give it back tenfold.*

The audiences of the Spectacular Aviary Extravaganza did not give. They always took and took and took.

I'd thought Tomás saw through that mirror.

My painted visage, quivering in the sky, said otherwise.

I found my own reflection in a vanity. "I want the whole world talking about me," I said, staring into my own dark eyes. "I want them watching my every move. I just don't want to make an ass of myself anymore."

And I never wanted to put another chicken's squirming head between my teeth.

Never wanted to frighten a crowd into screams again.

The fluting iron's hiss died out as it cooled. Fernando tapped his finger on his chin as he contemplated the possibilities. "Well, love, there are plenty of places we could use you here. You pick things up fast enough—but you know what you have to do first, right?"

Instantly the prospects flooded me. Get fitted for a new costume. Tell Pedro he could roll his spotlight over to the shallow divers for the rest of the gig. See if the dancing girls wanted to use me in their pineapple dance tonight.

See if Tomás would let me sit for him again. See if he could see me as something other than a monster.

"You need to talk to Arturo."

My gut distended. I knew Fernando was right, but that didn't make it any easier to swallow. Talking to Arturo was always like wrestling with an eight-legged snake.

"Avita." Fernando lifted my chin. "I know he's Arturo, but he's your father, too."

Bless Fernando for knowing exactly how to breathe courage into my bones.

"Just ask," he said. "The worst he can say is no."

I was Papa's million-dollar gal. My wagon was filled with a decade's worth of toys and trinkets, the spoils of his love. And I put on a hell of a performance every night as Bird Girl—there was no reason why Arturo shouldn't let me finagle the Spectacular Aviary Extravaganza into a new show entirely.

I wrapped my scarf tighter around my selling points. I barely felt my boots grind into the dirt as I headed in my father's direction with single-minded purpose.

Just ask.

Ask, and ye shall receive, as the Good Book says.

And not even Mama would argue with scripture.

Ask, and It Shall Be Given You

"**P**APA, I NEED TO TALK TO YOU."

The third time I said it, I was finally able to finish my sentence without my father butting in—to congratulate himself on the marvelous horse-and-rider routine currently happening on the other side of Big Red's curtains, to give orders to the grooms who would rush out and handle the dapple grays as soon as the act was over, to prattle on with the kinds of show notes that were usually snapped at Ren.

My father peeled his eyes away from the rotund rumps of the horses as they galloped around the dirt. He turned to face me, a trough of water between us.

"Make it quick," he said with a parent's waning patience. "As soon as Jo-Jo finishes her tuck and tumble, I'm closing out the show."

I knew every Family Fortuna act like a spider knows flies. The girls would do a few more laps of their tippy-toed choreography before launching into their flips.

I wiped my damp palms against my skirt. I only had a minute, give or take.

Good. If I had more time, I'd be a coward, stretch the minute out, wait for the precise opening—but the moment was now.

Now.

"I want to do something different." My chest thudded, my vision starry with nerves.

He's my father, I reminded myself. *I've tangled my arms around that scruffy neck for sixteen years.* As a child, I'd sobbed on his chest when my cousins wouldn't let me play. I'd looked deep into his eyes and copied his breathing to steady myself as he dabbed away the blood from my pluckings.

But my nerves did not flap away.

My father's mouth split like an oyster beneath his mustache, that old devil's grin I knew as well as my own teeth. "Yes, my kitten. Growl first, then shake your bars. Break out of the whole fucking cage, if you're so inspired. You know where the release is." He granted me the wicked, conspiratorial chuckle of a man who'd squeaked out a fart without anyone catching him. "That new banner of yours is something spectacular. Michelangelo did us proud, my sweet. Those cake eaters know they're in for a scare, but once they see you in the flesh, they won't believe their eyes."

His hand went up to the curtain, wrinkling it back. From the ring, the glow of the lights cut past the horses and backlit Papa's slick head in a halo, making him look like some sort of fiendish saint.

"No." Just saying it out loud infused me with courage, with strength. Made me feel like I'd just ripped a length of canvas in half with my bare hands. "Something different. Something else entirely."

This plucked Papa's attention away from Della's flawless

triple-crag twist in the saddle, and not even the ripples of applause could lure him back. "You're getting at something, Avita. Quit dicking around and just say it." His voice was as dangerously soft and slow as a faraway locomotive.

Just say it.

A flash in my mind, a fantasy gestating within me: the Tent of Wonder, the sounds of an audience worshipping me, the power of a song winding out of my throat.

The thunder of real applause, the generous gift of an audience's adoration.

I couldn't be the girl on the banner again. I couldn't lock myself back in that cage. I wanted something new.

Wanted it so bad, I would've swallowed a whole nest of hornets to get it—but Arturo would never want to hear that.

Arturo would never care that someone near him *wanted*.

I had to make him care.

Speak his language.

And Arturo's language was always, always about money—not just money you could store in a safe and count when you were too jazzed up to sleep, not the money you passed from hand to hand to buy yourself flour or thimbles or a wife for the night.

No, Papa spoke strictly in economics. There were other people's wants, and then there was what he wanted, and one was always worth more.

Boldness sped through me like a comet; I talked before it burned itself out. "I can sing, you know. And I've always been a good dancer. I can keep five clubs in the air, and I'm decent at vaulting. I know every kootchie tent song by heart—"

"I don't need another whore, Avita." Papa's glare could flay a crocodile. "I need you exactly where I have you."

More cheers out in the ring. Jo-Jo was launching herself from horse to horse now, getting ready for the big finale. Any second, Papa's focus would whip away from me, away from my pleading, and back out to his favorite place: the here and now.

Here and now, I was desperate.

I was all afire, blood flowing with purpose. I was my father's daughter. I had to convince him before I forgot that particular magic.

"How do you know you're not missing out on your best dancing girl?" I said. "What if I could bring in even more money in the Tent of Wonder? I could be starring in songs, packing the snake pit shoulder to shoulder. With this face up there, paired with a song and dance . . . just imagine the possibilities!"

A bit of proper training, I assessed, and I could be at least as good as the other gals in the kootchie tent. Of course, I'd never be the duchess, but I could be something else.

This face would be a shock at first, of course—but my audiences could see past it, if I steered them that way.

I could make my audiences love me. Nightmare and all.

An act of my own.

Out in the ring, the two horses synchronized their trotting. Jo-Jo would be rolling through the air any second now.

But I'd snatched Papa's regard away completely. He was too busy falling in love with his favorite creation all over again to notice anything else in his circus.

"Look at yourself," he encouraged. "You're doing exactly what you were born to do—you're a star, my dove. Why would you want to give that up?"

My heart lurched, dangling on a cliff.

"This is your moment," he went on, dropping into storyteller mode, serious and enchanting and impossible to ignore. "Can't you sense it? Electricity in the air? Wonders, hiding around every corner? A feeling that at any moment, you'll go to take a breath, and instead you'll gasp?"

Yes, I could feel it, and I could hear it. Mama had told us all to keep a prayer and a hymn in our heads while we were here in Peculiar, but something stronger blew through the wind here. Possibility, like a magnet, drawing me near.

Pulling me under.

And Papa was already in the deep.

"There's no need for you to spend the day worrying over such intricacies." He put a crooked smooch on my forehead, the exclamation point to end this conversation. "This is a game of chess, remember? You are the queen, and with you on the board, Le Cirque Americana doesn't stand a chance."

Papa's words shaped me like a chisel—why had it never been this obvious before? My father painted pictures for me with his words, as he did with everyone he met . . . only now his manipulation felt as apparent and crude as if I were seeing it happen through a window in broad daylight.

A mirror.

I could feel him flattering me.

All those years of flattery stacking up, and I could finally see how it worked.

Was I so easily pliable?

A jolt and a rippling gasp from the crowd finally turned Papa's head. He rushed to the curtains to spy.

In the ring, Jo-Jo was neither atop her horse nor airborne; she was splayed in the dirt, limbs wriggling like a water bug. Della was already sprinting over to her injured partner, and the grooms ran out to handle the horses.

"She missed." Papa crunched the lapels of his coat as he muttered, "All these people here, for fuck's sake, and she missed."

Beyond him, Jo-Jo arched herself up to a kneel. Even from backstage, we couldn't miss the mess: a peacock's eye of bunched-up flesh on her knee, a busted nose dripping onto the dirt, a shoulder hanging at a sickly angle.

"Good God, she really got tossed," I couldn't help remarking, bowels twisting.

"Get Della back on Rancid, now!" Papa bypassed me completely, shouting at the grooms, spit foaming up into his mustache. "Get her tumbling!"

I'd seen this same thing hundreds of times—Papa's entire world pausing not because a performer was injured but because the delight and applause had stalled. But I gaped at him now like this was my first time seeing the show.

Jo-Jo was coated in more blood than a vampire. She'd wake up tomorrow patched with bruises, possibly with a newly shaped nose, and she was down one working arm. Tonight Papa would tend to her busted limb himself when he had a moment to spare— or when his fuse wasn't so short, whichever happened first.

But right now Papa only heard a lapse in applause. The sight of his equestrienne smeared in the dust? Didn't even itch.

"Don't look at me like that," he barked, like I was an animal he'd caught nosing in the trash bins. "Those riders know they'll get banged up by the end of the season. Jo-Jo will be fine—and if she isn't, we've got plenty of May Firsts to take her place."

Papa justified it so easily. The performers knew the risks. At least once a week, he recited this rationale in the grub tent like it was written into Exodus. And anyway, they were replaceable. The patrons were secretly hoping for a disaster. They secretly wanted to see blood.

And so he pushed his performers to the brink, let them batter themselves until they were crapping out blood and their ribs were bent in half, all so he could give the crowds what they wanted.

Fernando was right. He was my father.

But he was also Arturo.

Seek, and Ye Shall Find

"**I**F YOU'RE GOING TO HIDE IN HERE," SOCORRO said, pointing at me with her straining spoon, "make yourself useful." She flipped the spoon around like she was a king bestowing a knighthood, and I took the handle and dipped into her stockpot, stirring and stirring.

I needed sanctuary.

I needed someone who was the exact opposite of Arturo in every way.

I needed a different kind of mirror.

While Socorro passed churros and fritters and other delicious morsels to the hungry patrons, I listlessly creamed butter, babysat caramel sauce, and wiped spots on the counter that were perfectly clean.

Socorro inspected me, her sweaty eyebrows furrowed. "What's all this about?"

A good question, I mused. What *was* all this about?

Not just about the Spectacular Aviary Extravaganza. Not just about the flutter of Tomás's banner, his silence, Papa's *no* stinging like a slap to my very soul. Not just about my face, the sharpness of my reflection, how the world was full of mirrors all of a sudden and some were harder to look at than others.

It was about all of this at once, and more.

I swallowed down all possible explanations like old vomit and held my breath, staring at her like I was about to confess to eating a baby.

Socorro pursed her lips, her whiskers fanning out as she studied me, searching for some crack in my foundation, some easy way in. Finally she tugged off her apron and threw it onto the flour sacks.

"Boys!" she called to her sons, who were just outside the booth, ladling cider for the masses. "Keep an eye on things while I take a walk." She enveloped my hand in her huge paw like I was a winkling again, accompanying her to the market for Black Jack and beans. "Come on. I can't think with all these lights in my eyes."

Every time I looked at Le Cirque Americana, their tents had grown. Yesterday their white poles had pointed straight up to heaven, steeples as tall as redwoods; in this early evening they shone bright as a cluster of grounded stars.

Socorro led me out the back, away from circus grounds, and I climbed behind her in silence, my steps strong and sure after so many years of walking in the darkness.

After a while, she stopped and whistled. "By ginger, that's quite a view." The residual heat from the scorching day had dried her forehead perspiration into a circular shine; she retwisted her hair into a floppy bun as she rested her haunches against the slope of the hill.

We'd climbed up to a grassy outlook edged by a sharp cliff

of rocks, up to where the two circuses didn't exist anymore, not really—the Family Fortuna and Le Cirque Americana were not as well delineated as they were down on the ground. Cornelius's gleaming fence and box office were intimidating in their glamour, and their angles cut beautifully against Papa's placement of the menagerie, almost like they'd planned it this way.

A tango.

Beyond the mess of lines and stakes and the winding pathways of paid-and-ticketed people searching for their next great wonder, the township of Peculiar was charming and well kept. Even the roof shingles and the horses tied to their posts along the main drag radiated something extraordinary in the evening glow, and I found myself nearly barking with irreverent laughter.

"Good Lord! Mama made such a fuss about this place," I mused, "but look at it. It's the same as any other Friday gig. Nicer than most of them, too." Such a rebellious statement against my mother would never ruffle Socorro's feathers, but when I glanced at her, she held herself extra still, her jaw clenched as if her words were fighting to be said and she was blocking them with her teeth.

Yet there was no hesitation when she finally spoke to me. "You're out of sorts, sweet potato." Socorro sounded so genuine, it was the same as being hugged by her. "What's going on in that head of yours?"

Mama would have told me that mood swings were natural, especially for young girls who neglected their personal scripture study.

Ren would have huffed and straightened his glasses, then

disappeared into a flurry of paperwork with a roll of his eyes and a murmured "I don't have time for this, Avita."

Luna would have been dressed and out the door before I'd even spoken.

And Papa . . . I already knew what happened when I tried to speak with Papa.

Everyone was just an audience to him, even his daughter. No matter what, he'd find a way to twist the spotlight where he wanted it.

"What was it like," I finally said, "when you said no to Arturo?"

A throaty chuckle rolled out of Socorro almost instantly. "Quite a gamble, wasn't it? Odds were in favor of him ripping off my head, sticking it on a post, and charging people five cents to throw eggs at it. He really wanted his Mega Manatee—he had the posters drafted and everything."

Posters already made. An artist waiting for his commission. A banner hanging from the tallest mast, waving its promises to any customer with an extra coin jingling in their pocket.

"He wanted to showcase a live water birth. Probably would have dubbed my boys the Dolphin Babies or some horseshit." Socorro let out a familiar scoff, the same one many others emitted when they remembered that Papa's brilliance came in tandem with his shameless assholery.

"But you got out of it," I said. "And you're still here."

"I nearly wasn't." Socorro reached down to rub a pebble off her calloused heel. "I made damn sure your father knew that my foot was down. He knew I'd rather pack up my boys and leave. Leave the circus life altogether, get my hands on a plot of cheap land somewhere, spend the rest of my days trying to teach hens to cluck." She gave me the conspiratorial grin of a skunk in the bushes. "Lucky for me, my black pudding did a lot of the convincing."

My mind was awhirl, glutted with memories and probabilities and scenarios.

"You want to know the real reason Arturo changed his mind?" Socorro cut into my scheming, her chiding tone ringing with good sense. "Because I was right, but I didn't try to stop your father from insisting that *he'd* been right, that it had been his idea to set me up at the stove. Arturo loves to be right as much as he loves to brag about it. He'll switch from a no to a yes or a yes to a no to follow the changing winds and pretend he'd said it that way all along."

I thought about Socorro's old juggling act, her meaty hands transformed into graceful springs, catching and tossing any item that would be recognizable to your average shitkicker from their place in the nosebleeds. No argument about it—Socorro had been incredible in the ring. A real star.

But she was incredible where she was now, burning sugar to drizzle onto popped corn, rolling up dough and using her pinkie fingers to get it to pucker, pinching the perfect amount of spice into her chili so the prairie folk would feel alive with the heat but wouldn't bitch that she'd scorched their tongues. Socorro could have kept juggling. She was brilliant at it—but she was brilliant at cooking, too.

She'd just needed to give everyone a taste of what she was capable of.

"How do I know if he's right or if he just . . . needs the winds to change?" I spoke sheepishly, but I was hot with genuine curiosity. Socorro alone would give me the truth.

She hooted, slapping a knee. "Arturo gets it right about as often as a cat buries its own turds—that is to say, it happens every so often, usually by accident. Your father's not God, as much as he'd like to believe he is." The setting sun shrugged out from behind a cloud just then, piercing Socorro's wrinkled eyes so I could see the ochre in them, the same color as tarnished brass. "Now, when it comes to his circus? Be careful, sweet potato. Oh yes, Arturo's had some fizzlers over the years. But one way or another, whether he's actually as good as he advertises or whether the universe rearranges itself in his favor just to have a decent laugh at the rest of us, your old man knows how to put on a hell of a show. I'd advise you to let him do just that. Especially when the stakes are so high."

My lunch withered in my stomach.

I didn't know what exactly I'd been fishing for, but this was not it.

And then my aunt made it even worse.

"I don't know what's chapping your hide, Avita, but I do know that your papa openly adores only two things in his life: the Family Fortuna and you. He's a real pain in the ass, yes, but whatever he's doing that's got you sore, he's only doing what he thinks is best. As your proprietor, but also as your father. He'd never lead his daughter astray."

That's funny, I wanted to spit back, *I didn't think Arturo had any daughters, just two rivers to pan until the gold ran dry.*

"Thanks, Socorro," I intoned in a saccharine, overripe voice, the kind a child uses to get out of some well-earned trouble. But I was hollow as a split drum.

"Ah, well." Socorro lifted up her sniffer and inhaled. "Time to head back down to the land of chewed cigarettes and crotch rot. Not nearly as sweet-smelling as up here. Hopefully the boys kept the booth standing. Come along. Your mother will be wanting you back down inside the grounds."

"Back to the safety of the flock," I snorted, but Socorro shook her head, a stern look in her eye.

"Your mother doesn't have the fondest memories of our last visit here." Her gaze went faraway, beyond the horizon and into some past I could never be a part of. "Let her keep her special prayers and her trinkets and sachets. It's her only defense against such memories."

She reached out an arm and sucked me into her side, patting me with a comfort that ordinarily would have put all my worries and angers out to pasture. But right now, her touch made me feel like I'd stepped on an anthill, little pieces of me bitten off and carried away.

"Arturo's a tough nut," Socorro said into my scalp, "but as his daughter, you're on his good side. Best stay there as long as you can."

Through the crowds of cake eaters I walked in my scarf, behind the midway, past the rows of tents, their flaps still rolled open for the daytime acts.

The Romanian gymnasts, who hopped along balance beams and cartwheeled across bars and split like shards of dancing light.

Isabel the strongwoman, who lifted a pallet of iron weights with only her pubic hair.

Bungo the wild man, who ate an entire barrel of flour and coughed out puffy clouds, his eyeballs shifting, rolling yellow in their sockets.

The Tent of Wonder was closed, but a brand-new life-size cutout of Luna was propped against the flaps, chin tucked, her one visible eye ablaze, peeking over her shoulder while her ass, juicy as a summer nectarine, threatened to drag the moon out of its orbit.

Tomás had made this. I recognized his style at once, his unique perception of the world.

From a safe distance, I watched the boys and men approach the paper Luna. I watched them point and gape as if they were unsure if it was real or not—as if they were trying to work out if she would still be paper later tonight when the kootchie tent opened, because such a perfect being could not possibly exist in corporeal form.

Some of them touched the cutout, groping the flat likeness of her rump, and then some of them got very daring and vulgar with the false version of my sister.

I thought about Tomás back in the weeds, Goldie standing between us.

The world had stopped when Tomás had looked at me then. Time had stopped.

Everything else had grown hazy, but me, I'd been sharpened. Parts of me that were usually soft and flexible had been fired and molded and held their form.

Like I was being seen for the first time—

And then he'd seen me again under the spotlight in Big Red.

I had thought he'd glimpsed the Paris girl in me. I had thought he'd paint me as he saw me—my unusual features captured by the strokes of his brush, made soft and light—like his beloved Impressionists. I had thought he'd paint me a revolution.

But the banner. He, too, had been seduced by the nightmare. Instead of a face of noble contradictions—a bird, yes, but also a girl—he'd drawn one that looked like someone had taken a file to a felled log and scraped it into a monstrous masterpiece.

The truth.

That banner was his mirror. My mirror. It showed me exactly how Tomás saw me.

He was wrong, I recited as the teenage boys humped the Luna cutout, growing louder and more irreverent every second. *They are all wrong. Let me show them. Let Tomás look at me again and see me. Let them all look at me and see more than just Bird Girl.*

Let me look at myself that way as well.

As for Arturo, he was a showman, wasn't he? Luna had said so.

But so was I.

Every inch my father's daughter—so I would have to show him.

First I needed a dress.

Something gorgeous, something showstopping.

Something that would convince the crowds I was more than just an exhibition. If the crowds were convinced, Papa could be convinced.

I scanned Luna's side of the closet in our wagon, breathless, bewitched by what I was about to do.

I eyed dresses mottled with glitter and jungle-bold colors, Luna's special gowns, stored here as overflow from the kootchie tent's dressing room—marvelous, every one of them, but any of these would earn applause even without a human body to cling to.

I needed to wear the dress, not the other way around.

And then I found it, scrunched back behind the other scaled and sumptuous garments—Jesus, there were so many dresses—

A white corseted sleeveless bodice embellished with tiny jewels that caught the light, stole it, held it.

A skirt of layered white netting rested on the waist, hemmed higher in the front and cascading long over the butt in a tulle tail, which then dripped into feathers.

I pulled it out, carried it across the room the way a bride carries her wedding gown, held it up against myself in the mirror. I tugged off my scarf and buried my face in it; the dress carried a scent of citrus and musk.

This one.

This was the dress I'd wear when I—

Something fell from its folds. A small scrap of paper rolled tight as a cigarette.

I picked it up and opened it. On it was written, in messy handwriting, a single line of poetry:

Skin like the moon, a heart wasted on its shores—

A noise behind me.

I was on the tips of my toes in seconds, one hand gripping my scarf.

An unknown voice, an intruder—and my only thought was to protect them from the weapon of my face.

But it was Luna, on the floor beside her bed, leaning against the wall, limbs buckled and bent around her. Instead of her usual curvaceous, billowy self, she looked angular, a puppet with its strings cut. Her head lolled, hair matted. She moaned, a basin in her lap.

"Luna?" I touched her hand—it was cold as glass.

"Is it time to go on?" she whispered without opening her eyes, then retched.

I peered at her nightstand clock. "Tent of Wonder opens in half an hour." Which meant I was due at my own tent in just a few minutes. My heart kicked like a jackrabbit.

She wobbled to her feet and reached for water to rinse out her mouth. I lit the lamp for her since she seemed so unsteady and caught a glimpse of her sallow skin, her cheeks tinged with sea green instead of her usual rouge.

I blinked. "You look awful."

She sat at her vanity and started tonguing a mint, and her

stoicism returned like a wave to the shore. "Don't you go on soon?" She opened her pot of foundation and loaded up her sponge with a trembling hand.

"Don't you?" I fired back. I was never this bold with my sister, but tonight I was too drained of patience to hold back.

And since I'd already loosed the catapult of my composure—

"Here. I found this in your dress." I thrust the piece of paper toward her.

Luna took it and read it.

"It's yours," I pushed before she could deny it. "It sure as hell isn't mine."

I didn't think my sister could blush.

"From Jonah?" Merely holding on to this white dress made me ballsy.

I didn't think she was going to answer me at all, but then she said, "Yes." She drew a streak of highlighter down her already-perfect nose and blended its edges away.

A portrait of a girl looking into a mirror, seeing her gorgeous self reflected back at her.

Tomás's hands streaked with browns from his portrait of a monster.

"He—he's a poet. He leaves them for me sometimes," she said. "I must have dropped this one."

My breathing grew shallow.

Someone loved my sister so much that he wrote her snippets of poetry and hid them for her to find, tiny delights. The star of the kootchie tent, more beautiful than Venus herself, and did she understand any of it? Did she understand how lucky she was?

"So what's your plan?" Luna asked, changing the topic, her eyes in the mirror fixed on the dress in my arms. "He pulls the cover off, and surprise, you're a swan?"

I clenched the dress until the sequins dug into my skin. I should have wrapped it in a quilt to hide it, but I managed a shrug and a lighthearted laugh. "Pretty much." We both knew it was the only way. If I asked Papa for permission, he'd play priest and tell me it was simply against the laws of God—and in this circus, Papa *was* God.

Luna eyed her old dress in my grip. Maybe she would finally play older sister, show some possessiveness. Maybe she'd demand that I put it back so it could hang on a cold wire for another five years.

I held her gaze, held up my head as if she were my audience.

She merely said, "He'll never allow it," and went back to painting herself bushy-tailed.

All my fingers tightened, nails slicing into the meat of my palms.

I would not lapse into brooding.

"Then what else am I supposed to do?"

Not all of us had gorgeous faces to fall back on. Not all of us could inspire people to love us into poetry.

Some of us had to give in to dark instincts. To trickery, to defiance.

Luna was about to respond, but she turned back to her basin and gagged up a slime of yellow-green bile.

I rushed forward to tuck back her hair. "Should I get Mama?"

"No!" Her refusal was so forceful it caused another retch. "No. I just need . . . a minute."

My sister was never sick. Never weak. Not unless she was on the rag, which collapsed her for at least a day, but I'd never seen her cycle make her this nauseated.

She hadn't been bedridden with cramps in some time, I realized. Not in Wichita. Not in months. This illness was such a rare sight because it had been so long since I'd seen her anything but radiant.

Three days ago, the other girls in the kootchie tent had had their stew coming out both ends, but that had been a quick in-and-out bug, and Luna was still sick—

And then I understood.

The retching, the fogginess, the way she twitched like a coyote in the crosshairs whenever I mentioned Jonah—

My sister was pregnant.

"Luna." I put my hand on her back and hunched over to look at her—not in the mirror, but her real face, pale flesh and weakened blood. "How long?"

She paused. I saw her considering me—she could clam up, keep things shut up inside, treat me like one of her men in the snake pit, only allowed to see a part of her, to know a part of her.

If I were nude in the spotlight every night, I'd probably want to keep some things to myself, too. Keep my heart my own, even when the world had access to all my cracks and both my nipples.

But somehow, I passed her test.

"Since Easter," she confided.

Almost five months. Good Lord. I sneaked a peek at her waist—she was seated, so it was difficult to tell, but perhaps she was softer around the middle. Her tits were always bulging out of her costumes like dinner rolls, but perhaps they were plusher than usual.

"Oh God, he's going to shit a brick when he finds out," I said without thinking.

Luna pounced on that word. "When?"

I was starting to learn what fear smelled like. I was starting to learn that fear liked to dress up in furs and pearls, disguised itself as elegant or confident or aspirational, but it always smelled the same. I was learning to recognize its stink.

Luna thought I'd rush off to Papa and spill. She thought I was relishing the destruction it would cause. Christ, everyone truly saw me as a monster, didn't they?

"Luna, I didn't mean—I won't be the one to tell him. I promise. I won't say a word."

My sister's expression remained frosty. What reason did she have to believe me? We'd never been each other's keepers. Hell, we'd only ever been playmates by default.

I watched her now, confronting her own reflection, spiking her lashes with mascara, and searched through my words with a Fortuna's craftiness to find the right thing to say to convince her—

But Luna spoke first. "He'll never let you. He'll never let you be anything else."

"No," I said firmly. "I am going to make him see."

I'm going to make the world see.

I'm going to break the mirror.

Closing her makeup box, Luna changed into her gown for her first act—a silvery one-piece, which she would wear as she emerged from a giant clamshell, a regular birth of Aphrodite, enough to make the patrons of Peculiar hard as steel. The fabric clung to her chest and hips, draping perfectly to hide her swollen middle.

"We are who we are." Luna turned to me one last time, fastening her headdress onto her moonlight hair. She was beauty itself. So stunning it hurt to look at her. "No one knows that better than Arturo."

But before she floated down the stairs, she studied me carefully as I gripped her old costume to my chest like it was armor, and she almost smiled. "It'll suit you."

"You're pissed," Fernando diagnosed as soon as I found him, polishing shoes in the kootchie tent dressing room. Two dancing girls glanced up at me, then slunk out of the room, exchanging worried looks; when the daughter of the circus owner came in looking like a storm, you gave her space, lickety-split.

"You've got that little crinkle between your eyebrows," he went on, "same one your mother gets when Arturo—"

"I need a favor." I opened my duster, which I'd clutched tight around me as I ran from my wagon, and Fernando's eyes boggled at the sight of the white crystals along my bodice.

"Look at you," he breathed. "You finally have the boobs for it. Wait . . . does this mean—did you talk to Arturo?"

"Yes," I answered honestly. I did talk to my father. I did tell him what I wanted.

And Arturo couldn't see it—

He couldn't see me as anything but Bird Girl.

So I'd have to show him.

I swirled my hand in front of my face. With some reservation, I said, "Make me look pretty."

Fernando swooned toward me, his chest warm against mine, his heart beating at my lungs. "I never thought this day would come," he sighed.

I pushed him off me, chortling, called him a jackass, but I sat in his chair, scarf in my lap, ready to be painted into something else.

A History

LUNA

"**S**O, IT FINALLY HAPPENED, DID IT."

It did not come out like a question.

Papa was not squeamish as I confirmed to him that yes, my monthly bleedings had started.

I was fourteen, perhaps on the older side. Mama seemed surprised that it hadn't happened yet—how strange, she must have been thinking, that I should be onstage in the kootchie tent, dancing as the duchess, but not yet a woman in the strictest sense.

Avita noticed first. "Holy Christ!" she shrieked, a phrase we weren't supposed to use or else Mama would scrub our tongues clean of the little demon that had made us say it. "Luna, what happened?"

The blood was so bright, so slippery on my legs. The smear on my bed was the size and shape of an egg, cracked and spilled.

"Are you—are you—" my sister stammered.

I shushed her. I pulled off my nightgown and piled it on the floor along with my sheets. I carried little sentiment about this mythical crossroads of the female persuasion—it was inevitable, after all, that I should make this journey. Other girls in the Tent of Wonder griped about the inconveniences, the discomforts, the pains.

I did not feel tugged in either direction, nettled or elated.

Today was a day like any other.

"Go tell Mama," I directed my sister. "And fetch cold water."

While my bed dressings soaked in a tub, the three of us went into town. I needed supplies. Mama held an arm around my waist, and I understood myself to be fragile now in her mind. Avita traipsed along behind us, wrapped in her scarf. The years between us had never felt so vast.

As we waited for traffic to slow so we could cross the main drag, Mama smoothed a strand of my hair with calloused fingers. "I remember when it was me. When I was picking out my rags. I bled through my only dress, so my mama made me sit naked on the back porch while it dried." She laughed good-naturedly, just enough for us to catch sight of the gap between her front teeth. "I didn't feel much like a woman, my only sandals all caked in pig shit and my dress patched with pieces of my father's old coveralls." She shook her head. "Oh well. That's the dress I was wearing when I met Arturo, and it didn't scare him off. Neither did my scabby nose or this hair of mine—I never knew what to do with it, so I just rolled it into two knobs on my head, like raccoon ears. And Arturo still picked me out of the crowd."

It was a gentle lie that she tucked into my hair, the idea that she had ever been the ugly duckling she'd just described.

We had one old, peeling photograph of Mama and Papa when they met, taken against the whitewashed fence of the rodeo, and perhaps she did have a peeling sunburn and square horse teeth that she hadn't yet grown into. Childbearing hadn't yet softened her hips or boosted her bustline. But to describe herself as a late bloomer was deceitful. She had always been beautiful.

"It's an awkward time, that space between girlishness and womanhood," Mama finished, "but we all get to the other side of it eventually."

Avita was the one to catch Mama's second lie. "Luna's never been awkward," she pointed out.

Our mother chuckled and squeezed Avita's shoulder. My own mind swirled into a chasm of suspicions.

I didn't hear jealousy in Avita's tone, merely the urge to set the record straight. But my sister's ugliness was not just a phase, not an unfortunate side effect of her impending adolescence. Once her own flailing hormones settled like stirred-up silt in a riverbed, she would not grow out of her hideousness and into a swan.

Avita peered at me, and I knew she understood: you never grow out of your own face.

Inside the boxy little general store, Mama steered me toward the fabric and directed me to select some cotton and flannel from the fat quarters to strip into rags. She sat on a bench nearby, resting her bum leg, and Avita knelt at her feet, nestling into the folds of Mama's calico skirt, its threads housing dirt from every road in the tristate area.

I touched nothing, but made my way along the shelf, shopping with my eyes. I could hear Mama's sighs growing impatient;

she would say I moved at a tortoise's pace, that I acted like I was onstage, waiting for a cue.

I could only say that I knew what I liked and did not like.

I made my selections, took a bundle to Mama and my sister.

And then I felt the shift.

Someone was watching me.

The store's owner, a thin man with a hungry air, stared at me from the opposite end of the aisle. From the corner of my eye, I tracked his gaze, which shifted away from me and onto the cluster of advertisements tacked to the front window.

Our poster, the Family Fortuna poster, hung in the center—a painted duchess peeked over one shoulder next to the dates and times of our gig, shushing the viewer, as if I had already told you a secret before you'd even purchased a ticket.

My place in the kootchie tent was still new, but I'd done enough shows to carve out a reputation among the men of the southwestern territories. Those who hadn't seen me in person had heard about my magic over foaming ale at saloon counters.

The other dancing girls would have found it a real rib-tickler: the duchess, all silvery moonlight and pheromones and summer butterflies on the poster, here in this store, bleeding through a makeshift wad of cheesecloth in her bloomers.

To the man, it made no difference. He had tongues hanging out of his eyes. "You're . . ."

He didn't need to finish, and I didn't need to respond.

Like a lamp, I switched it on.

Opened my mouth slightly, as if in a pant, eyes hooded, darted to the side like a cat's. Somewhere in my expression, a smirk hid, though exactly where was difficult to pinpoint—it was in the apples of my cheeks and the corners of my lips and even the arch of my back, and it was coiled, ready to spring.

Papa would have been thrilled—his Luna, his duchess, out in public, a walking lithograph. Lovely enough that men would pay to see me again and again, to verify the exact heft of my young, still-growing breasts, the exact sheen of my sun-bronzed upper legs.

Mama unfolded a flyer and set it atop her dollar. "Her show starts at eight."

Flesh and bone, flat lithography in a window, dripping blood—it didn't matter. I was only an advertisement.

"Eight o'clock," the man confirmed, and I spotted a familiar twinkle in Mama's eye—a proud gleam similar to Papa's: the ringing of a cash register, the crispness of a buck transferred from hand to hand. Mama was just as satisfied to have made a sale. Proud of this creation of hers, proud of her Luna, her commodified Luna.

Proud that this grown, perspiring man had his eyes plastered to my ass.

Everywhere I went, it was just another performance for me.

Avita knew, and would have been the first to remind me: you never outgrew your face.

"So. It finally happened, did it."

Mama fluffed my clean sheets onto my bed, and Papa inspected me from the doorway, arms folded. Like a farmer tallying the hens that had laid the night before.

Yes, it finally happened.

Just like that—the switch of a lamp.

Now I could grow a baby if I wanted.

Papa's instructions were unusual for a father to bestow upon his newly menstruating daughter but perfectly normal for a proprietor to say to his lucrative hireling.

"You go see Socorro right away for contraception," he said. "You start growing a baby up the stick, and the duchess is finished. Done, do you hear? No one's paying money to see Mother Goose in the kootchie tent."

He was delighted, no doubt about that. His Luna, his silver dollar, at last a proper woman. It opened all sorts of doors.

Once Papa left the wagon, Mama showed me how to keep myself clean, how to stuff the rags into my underthings to catch the blood, how to wash them discreetly, how to count down the days from my last cycle to predict the next one's arrival. "Tell no one that you're bleeding," she warned. "You must restrain yourself around boys and men. No flirting, no sitting on laps. No being alone with them, unless it's a customer."

Off she swept to request a special meal from Socorro—something simple, heavy on the meat, laced with turmeric to help with inflammation.

Alone in our wagon, Avita spoke from her corner, her dolls in haphazard piles. "Are you excited? Now that you are a woman?"

But my insides had begun to ache.

As if I were baking something—as if I were an oven.

The pain was slow. Burning, radiating from my center, just below my navel.

Something wringing itself out.

Something unsettling.

I stared at the ceiling.

Excited? You don't want any of this, Avita. Boys unable to meet your eye because they're too fascinated by the two hills of fat on your chest. Grown men asking your age, asking to buy you drinks, things you don't even like. Your own father plugging you up with preventatives so he can trumpet you as ripe for the plucking. And then there are the ones like that man in the store, who—

The world went hazy. I closed my eyes. "I'm not growing into a woman," I finally told her. "I'm becoming less of a person."

Ugly Duckling

LUNA HAD MADE A TERRIBLE CLOWN.

Papa tried to help her get some laughs and wrote down lines she could deliver in her dry, unenthusiastic tone, but not only was she genuinely unfunny, she was genuinely disinterested in this role.

Dutifully she donned the baggy pants and red yarn wigs, but somehow, even before adolescence fully claimed her body, her goofy costume flattered her frame.

When adulthood did come knocking, her breasts swelled against the buttons of her clown suit. The pants flopped above her ankles as her legs stretched into long stems. Not even the heavy white powder could hide the sharpening of her jaw. The soft chub of youth was melting away. New bones poked out, paving the way for a woman's face.

One night in the clown tent during the mutton toss, Luna's sheep crashed with her atop its wool. Her wig flew off, and all that silvery hair spilled out, running down her shoulders like a flooded reservoir. She wore it long back then, and the effect of that hair against the garishness of the limes and the crude flannel of her clown shirt? It was like a beam of moonlight had sprouted from her head. A pouring, a magic. A bit of wonder.

Men noticed my sister that night. One man in particular—
Papa.

Back then, the kootchie tent wasn't ruled by a duchess or a
queen or even a leading lady; it was a true variety show of tits and
glitter. A dozen or so girls danced nightly, switching in and out of
lingerie, gowns, cosmetics, headdresses. They cycled through a list
of songs our band could play. "Give them things they've never seen
before," was Papa's only instruction.

The dancing girls, as I remembered them, were very pretty,
every one of them—but details beyond that were lost on me.
Despite differences in skin tones and hair textures and the sizes
of chests and butts, they were interchangeable to me. All square
white teeth and drapes of waving skirts, faces like Byzantine
dreams, a blandness of lips and limbs.

They needed a leader, and when Luna began to sprout and
caused adverse reactions in the clown tent, Papa knew he had
found one.

"You see," he told Luna as they studied the aimless hip
shaking and sloppy grapevines in the Tent of Wonder, "each of
these lovely girls is a pearl of polished beauty—but when there
are so many on a necklace, you don't notice the individual pearls
anymore. You don't really see any of them. What these girls need
is a diamond to offset them. They need someone whose sparkle
will make them all shine."

Luna said nothing.

And so the very next morning, Papa began to shape her, and

since I was a nosy child, left to my own devices on circus grounds as long as I was in my scarf, I followed them.

In the daylight, the empty Tent of Wonder was a very different place. The sun chased away all its sultry magic, filling it instead with velvet-blue shadows.

I sat in one such patch of darkness in the back, half hidden by a stray flap of canvas, practically glowing with the poison of envy.

Luna got to be in a new act, and I was still shuffled into my wagon at night, locked inside with my toys and my swing and my imagined future. Someday that would be me, I reassured myself.

Someday, when I was ready. From Texas to Tacoma. Papa had promised me.

But for Luna to move ahead into a new tent while I was still waiting . . . it filled me with rancid jealousy.

Papa led her past the tea lights and up to the stage. When it was uninhabited, it was huge, large enough to swallow a fourteen-year-old, or make her invisible. But Luna stood perfectly still, glancing out at the ghost audience, and her nonchalance filled up the room. It was the exact opposite of what was expected in the kootchie tent—instead of passion, Luna presented boredom; instead of white-hot temptation, Luna offered coldness.

The contrast was exhilarating, and Papa, he knew it. He was jittery as a sinner in church.

"Carmen!" He clapped his hands like he was calling for a puppy.

Carmen was the oldest of the Tent of Wonder dancing girls

and the most vivacious. Fernando and I sometimes mocked the way she hung her lips open when she shimmied, trying to be suggestive; to our young sensibilities, she looked like a frog catching flies.

Papa ordered her to teach Luna the ways of the kootchie tent. "Learn the steps as best you can," he told my sister. "You'll start as a chorus girl next month—that gives you plenty of time."

He planned to slowly acclimate her to the moves, to the bone spurs caused by spinning in heels, to the sunless nocturnal shift of the nightlife, to the economy of the space, the other girls beside you, the boundaries of the stage, the heat of the limes on top of tightly laced costumes, the men below, pressing closer and closer like mangy lions stalking the weakest of the prey . . .

Instead, what happened was this.

Carmen took an obvious and instant dislike to Luna. That was the way it was with my sister. Women even twice her age felt like Luna had taken something away from them just by being beautiful.

She got men hot, but she scorched the women as well.

"I'll show you a basic two-step." Carmen flipped her boa tighter around her neck. "Try to keep up."

Someone sidled up beside me in my hiding place—Ren, who was supposed to be getting Papa's signature authorizing Socorro's supply list but saw my backside poking out of the tent flaps and came to investigate.

"Is she any good?" he whispered.

I shrugged. "Don't know yet."

Papa turned on the gramophone. A sultry, brassy tune blew out the flaring horn, filling the tent. Carmen began moving her hips in small waves, enough to rock a boat without capsizing it.

Luna watched from the corner of the stage, silent.

Carmen amped up into grinding and shuffling her feet, and I flinched with secondhand embarrassment; I'd seen her in rehearsals before and remembered her being much more commanding than this. The way she shimmied her body and slid the boa around her shoulders was more amateurish than alluring—graceless, even. She finished with a heavy-footed thud and a pose that would have been a fall—I would've bet money on it—had she not saved herself at the last second.

Poor Carmen. Normally she was very good, but as we would soon learn, everyone turned into flopping walruses when Luna was nearby.

I glanced at my big brother to gauge what he thought of her. He pursed his lips. "She's all right."

Papa lifted the needle, pausing the music. "Now, my Luna, I want you to try to do what she did."

Carmen, her forehead shining, threw the boa at Luna's feet. *So there*, the smug fold of her arms seemed to say.

But Luna didn't pick up the boa.

Without a word, she strode to the middle of the stage, and then she did exactly what Luna still does—she created magic, somehow, out of nowhere, using only her eyes and her lips and her body. Your brain knows she is dancing, swaying, but you only barely register the movement. She is a specter, a silhouette, a song, and she is sex itself.

She was all of those things even at the tender blooming age of fourteen.

Next to me, Ren shifted, demonstrably uncomfortable as our sister removed her boots and stockings, an act she had done in front of him dozens of times in the family wagon, albeit in a more domestic fashion than this. Her creamy legs extended, toes pointed, as if it brought her great pleasure just to do this, just to remove a sock.

"Uh, I'll get Papa's signature later." Ren cleared his throat and skedaddled, taking his papers with him.

When the music ended, Luna was in her underthings, though it seemed like she should have been a lot more naked than that. It felt like Luna had shown us her very soul, all her private parts. In the wings, Carmen withered like a plucked rose, and her jealous glare could have ignited wood.

Papa and I were a pair of slack-jaws, trying to unwind my sister's magic. Somehow she had danced and teased and spun but not budged from her spot on the stage. She'd stolen our hearts clean out of our bodies but stayed in the very same square foot she'd started in.

I wanted to hold an audience captive like that someday.

I wanted to clutch a crowd in my hands like that someday.

My father was many things, but a lecher he was not. The gleam in his eye was for the massive amounts of cash he saw when he looked at his gyrating daughter.

Carmen spoke first. "It was sloppy. You need to—"

"No," Papa cut in. "It was perfect. You're our diamond. A swan among ducklings."

Carmen was moved to the back row after that, but she didn't make it to Luna's debut. She quit and hauled ass back to Fort Bend County, where we'd found her. Last we heard, she was selling cat dances in saloons at two cents a pop. She took the boa with her.

When we hit Reno, Papa surprised his new swan with a custom-made sparkling white costume for her first show. Luna nearly sold out the tent. Scores of sweaty men pressed in tight to see whatever she was willing to show them, and she brought in a river of tips to boot. And then, as she progressed and grew into her role as the duchess, that old swan costume was retired. Shoved to the back of the rack, hidden behind more colorful, more mature, more tantalizing selections.

It was likely that neither Papa nor Luna had even thought of the white swan costume in years.

But it was this very costume, which Luna had wearied of long ago, that I had wiggled into, searching for my every breath as I'd angled my elbows to adjust the lacings on the back.

My black feathers blended with the swan costume's white ones. I could inspire some new good vs. evil tableau. In this getup, I could play an angel plagued with devilish doubts.

Not too far off.

Fernando worked on me silently and confidently, but when I forced myself to root around in my own body, I found only fear, flapping in my stomach like bats. "Maybe I shouldn't do this. He's going to blow a fuse."

Fernando shook his head. "Don't think about how he'll feel. How will *you* feel if you *don't* do this?"

I considered his query. If I chickened out, I knew I'd never forget this moment, this night, hovering so close to this precipice. I'd be forever haunted by every song-and-dance number ringing through the circus. Music would provoke resentment in me; my bitterness would bloat me like gas whenever I caught the sound of sprinkling applause. A door would slam closed before I ever got to tiptoe through it, and I'd never stop wondering what was beyond its threshold.

"There. That's it," Fernando said suddenly. "You're ready."

At his gesture, I gingerly edged off the chair and stood, hands splayed out in an awkward pose. "Well?"

He nodded, didn't stop nodding, his smile buttoned up over a fizzing pride that oozed from his radiant eyes. "Perfect," he said, "absolutely perfect. Now look at yourself."

I turned to the mirror.

I looked, and I saw—

It was everything I'd hoped for.

Without my scarf to shield my grin, my razor teeth were on display like a rack of knives, and my nose would never be anything but an eyesore . . . but it didn't matter. It all worked together, an amalgamation of the appalling and the divine.

Just the sort of strangeness the Family Fortuna prided itself in showcasing.

And I shone.

"You're a magician," I told him. "I owe you for this."

"Just make good use of it. That's all I ask." He arced around to peck my cheek, squeezing my shoulders. "Give them hell, Vee."

I came into my tent through the back. I crept into my cage and pulled my slipcover into place.

Papa's silhouette was impossible to miss through the red fabric. I drew the cover back so I could spy on him. He paused to speak to Pedro the spotlight boy, fussing with the buttons on the cuffs of his tailcoat.

There had been a glimmer of compassion in my father earlier that day, but it had since been shaken from him. He narrowed his eyes as he strode toward my cage and seemed to be made of iron as he said, "Are you ready to put on a show, Avita?"

No *my pet, my dove, my sweet.*

Only the name he and Mama had given me, to keep me on a certain leash.

"Yes," I told him.

"Make it your best," he instructed, and the lights went dark.

My cage was rolled forward, and the curtain opened. My skin prickled as if before a storm.

Showtime.

Crucified

"**L**ADIES AND GENTLEMEN!"

There was a velvet slipcover and a row of steel bars between us, but I could still hear the strain in Papa's voice. It was subtle, nothing an untrained ear would pick up, but I recognized it instantly—a shredding of his cords at the ends of his words, an extra sharpness and grit in his syllables. He was bushed. He was blood-hungry. He was wishing Le Cirque Americana were a bug so he could crush it beneath the heel of his boot and drink himself into a restorative stupor.

"I found her in the sultry jungles down south . . ."

Papa never got fatigued, not the way most people did. The more worn out his body, the more alive his mind became, jolting him with half-aborted ideas and soggy whimsies. Almost as if his ego, independent of the rest of the man, believed itself capable of propping up a human beyond his physical need for rest. But right now, my father sounded plain fucking tired.

I, on the other hand, had never been more awake. Aware of every pump of my ventricles, every change in temperature from moment to moment.

I'd let Fernando take his brushes and puffs to my face. And as soon as the cymbals crashed, I'd be ready. I wouldn't growl inside this cage, blinded by a spotlight as the crowd made a zoo animal of me.

No, I was going to sway like a cobra dancing for coins. I was going to gulp down air and croon out a song. I wasn't going to alarm them; I was going to charm them.

They were going to love me.

I would make them love me.

"Screams only drive the creature further into a frenzy!"

Good God, the ring was gigantic. From behind the bars, the space had become so familiar to me, I'd always imagined I could hock a glob of spit at whatever bristly-haired church wife hunched in the front row.

Now, peering with fresh eyes, I saw how much room there was—enough to cha-cha a partner all across the dirt. Room enough for me to dance around on my own.

I was not daunted; I was inspired. Yes, yes, this could work, I calculated. The Spectacular Aviary Extravaganza could be reordered, molded into a new act with music and glitter and the marvel of a monster with a voice. I just had to let the audience convince my father that it could work.

I was starving for it. Already I anticipated how loudly the applause would rumble in my tent once I finished my surprise number.

Applause and cries and blessings.

A proposition or two would be welcomed—every once in a gig, there would be someone in the crowd with unusual romantic leanings. I'd take anything. I was here to be adored, watched, worshipped—to be heard. To be seen.

And what about Tomás? What would he think?

Was he sitting in my audience tonight?

Would he march right out and paint over his banner once he got a load of this performance of mine? Would he demand I sit for him again?

"She feeds off your fears, folks, but her favorite food is warm meat!"

My whole life was the circus. My first steps, toddled past the golden tigers. My first playthings, tubes of greasepaint and ropes of burnt-out twinkle lights. My first words, all dirty ones, because that's what got me the most attention, the most chortles, the most encores.

I *was* the circus.

And it was time for me to show my audience what I was. More than feathers and teeth. More than bird and beak.

More than monster.

"Yes, hear those biddies cluck with panic! For they know the creature is waiting nearby—they can smell her, the predator!"

Papa loved me.

He loved me now, and he would love me even more when he saw what I was truly capable of.

More than he'd ever imagined. More than *I* had ever imagined.

From Texas to Tacoma.

The audience tittered in all the right places during Papa's final words, and I shifted. In this costume, I felt delicate as an icicle, which was an awkward state. White swan feathers poked out above my tailbone, fanning out over my ass, and in order to keep from crushing or breaking them, I stayed hunched over, squatting like a little rabbit in its hutch. The sequins, too, dug into my thighs and the insides of my arms, leaving marks like scales. But these discomforts were small prices to pay.

My father reached the end of his introduction, and my heart spiked as the cymbals hissed.

Avita, my wonder! he would coo tonight after my encore, *you had a song in you all this time? Well, any old jackass can shake out a musical hoo-ha to pass the time. But you, my angel—you're more than special. You're unstoppable.*

I pursed my lips, giddy with expectation. I may have looked the part of an aberration, but I was made for more than mere frightening. I had the heart of a showman. A songbird. An artist.

"Here's your monster!" Papa pulled off my slipcover.

The air was thick with unspent breath—the audience held back their screams for me like they were Mama's piggies, gated and baited and ready to fly.

Silence.

Everything was still as I looked out at them. The steel bars threw black lines of shadow on me, but I knew they could see what I was—I knew they could see my beak, my feathers, my black-hole eyes. I knew they could see my white getup, odd against my darkness.

I could taste their bewilderment. I could taste their incredulity as I unfolded myself from the corner of the cage and released the trick lock.

Tonight the monster emerged from behind her bars, not with a rattle and growl, but replicating the grace and allure of the Tent of Wonder, each step slinky and intentional, posture steely, a tantalizing mystery in my gaze.

Out of my cage, unfurled to my full height, my full glory, I embodied the very slogan of the Family Fortuna: *You won't believe your eyes!*

All the audience's expectations thrown down into the ring and shattered like fine china—

Just like Arturo would want.

My showman's ears picked up the crackling chatter of their confusion. The mirror between performer and onlooker was foggy. They'd arrived in their seats hungry for something bloody and ugly, but instead they'd been served a more delicate confection.

They were surprised, but I wouldn't let them leave unfulfilled.

Pedro the spotlight boy shined his white orb directly on me. The guitarist, Rosalita, plucked an opening refrain—I'd paid her a nice bribe to strum me some accompaniment. There had never been any joyous music in my tent; every rippling note seemed a good omen.

I'd picked a hurdy-gurdy hall standard. Every slack-jaw would know it well, which meant they could bestow upon Bird Girl their undivided attention while I gave them my heart.

Time to give it to them.

I opened my mouth to sing.

But I didn't make a peep before someone screamed.

That first scream, crisp and shrill—it rolled out of someone like a fire alarm.

My heart throbbed like a juicy wound.

It was contagious. More screams, shrieks, cries.

Me, a songbird, and they shot me in the wing with every screech they made. I didn't get a single note out.

Rosalita stopped her strumming—or perhaps I couldn't hear it anymore over the clamor of uninterrupted fear, the catharsis of communal terror.

The intensity of my humiliation was so thick it clouded my vision. And as a reflex—an instinct so ingrained within me, it would be the last thing to fade from my bones when I was dead and buried—I looked to the person who captained this ship.

The person who raised me to love the ring.

The very person who plunked me into this cage and fed me to the throngs every night.

The audience's screams biting at my neck, and my song, my offering, clawed into shreds—

But Papa was nowhere to be seen.

And then all the lights went out.

Caged

MY SPOTLIGHT GONE. THE WHOLE TENT doused of any gleam.

The crowd bellowed in a panic, their seats creaking forlornly as they waited, uncomfortable, in the darkness. This wasn't a stagehand's mishap or an issue of faulty wiring—this was deliberate. There was only one switch that could kill all the lights like this: the master switch in the back of the house, right next to the spotlight.

And there was only one person who could command such darkness in the middle of a show.

One person who would want to keep my expensive face out of any glow that wasn't spotlighting my atrocity, keep my voice from spinning out a song rather than rolling out a growl.

Papa had done it. He'd signaled for the grunts to shut me down. Luna was right: he would shut down anything I tried unless it ended with me dripping in dead chicken. Unless it was the Spectacular Aviary Extrava-fucking-ganza, he'd hunt me down and sink it.

He wanted my audiences to be disgusted by me, to be proud of the generous measure of their own bravado, the guts it took to sit in my bleachers and watch me in the ring, safely behind bars.

He wanted to turn them all against me.

Like he'd been doing my whole life.

From Texas to Tacoma. An act of my own, he'd promised.

An act of my own, I'd dreamed—but we were not partners in dreams. We were partners in profit.

I made it backstage, and there I caught my breath, letting the volcano rise within me, its embers in my middle, the heat rising up my throat. Out in the ring, the lights flickered back on. The audience's screams tampered down to guttural, surprised chuckles.

I inhaled courage.

I exhaled and tasted fire.

The moment Papa charged backstage, he unscrewed his smile. "What the hell are you doing?" He curled above me, his swallowed rage making his cheeks match the red satin lining of his hat, which he ripped off his head and hurled at my feet. "Are you trying to ruin me?"

"I'm trying to show you what I can do!" I hurled right back. "I told you, I want to do something else! A new act! Sing! Dance! I could learn the high wires, if you want. Bird Girl stands there while they stare at me like I'm not even alive! I want to do more—"

"You're already our best-selling act! This is more than anyone else could ever hope for, and you want to throw it in the shitter?" He paced around and around me. "They worship you!"

"They scream at me!" I moved into his pathway, Luna's old swan costume straining as I stood, tight in all the wrong places. Had I really thought it would fit me like a second skin? "I'm a nightmare to them, Papa! No performer wants to be screamed at—"

"Every performer wants to be a star!" His eyebrows went up in what appeared to be genuine pity. "A tent of your own, my diamond. It's all the rest of them dream of—and you have it here, right in your hands—"

"No!" I was never a particularly defiant child, not in the way youngest siblings are often mythologized; I never had to be, not with Papa handing me sweets and playthings on a silver platter. Not with Mama letting me shirk my scripture-reading duties at a single whine.

But I could feel sticky stubbornness coming on like a fever. "This is *your* tent, *your* dream, not mine! Not anymore." I wiped away the sweat collecting on my lip with the back of my wrist. "I can give them a new kind of show, if only you'd let me! You killed the lights before I had the chance! I could make them love me—"

"They were screaming from the moment they laid their peepers on you!" Papa's delivery was smooth as tarp, metered and calm, a rattler about to pounce. "You gave them the chance to hear you sing. They didn't want it."

My throat nearly collapsed on me with my grief.

Goddamn it, he was right.

Arturo was right.

I tried to give them a song. They didn't want it.

I thought that if I performed something sincere, something as real as the first flakes of gold in the Santa Maria, it would be enough.

I thought that if I performed from my heart, they would forgive me my face—but these features were too great a sin to be canceled out by some slick choreography or earnest vocalizing, or even by Fernando's deft hands with his makeup brushes and glitter. There was no prayer for a face like this.

There was only this face. My face as fact.

My face as fate.

Of course they screamed. To look at me was to require catharsis.

I turned my head, because if I watched my father perform his pity act for another second, I'd combust. My reflection burned back at me from a dead spare spotlight bulb.

The sphere of the bulb warped the world, elongating lines and shapes as if everything had sunk to the bottom of a fish tank.

But warped or no, it couldn't be more obvious.

Ugly. Monstrous. A spectacle.

The steel-barred contraption behind me was not my cage, nor was the red canvas of my tent. The ticket-holding, merciless patrons were not my jailers, nor was the sullen man with the rubbery hair and the tailcoat and the lips itching to go back out and jabber and pitch until the crowd was sated—

Arturo was not my jailer, nor was he my cage.

Even though I wanted him to be, desperately. Everything is easier when there's a villain.

But there were no villains here.

Only a monster.

And a face that had caged me since the moment I tasted life.

My face, my fate.

My fortune.

Soured and trembling with rage, eaten alive by the unfairness of it all, I ignored a sob spasming in my chest.

"Oh, my sweet, my sweet, my sweet." Papa's words found me through the worst of my angered heat.

My feathers rankled around me. I couldn't take another round with my father. His words would sparkle and sting at the same time, and he'd expect me to take it all like a spoiled, broken-in colt.

If he spoke another one of his tricks, if he reached out to stroke my face or cup my chin as he always did after my shows, I would snap my teeth at his fingertips. I would push him away, if he dared to touch me—

So I ran.

Out from under the work lights, bolting like a chicken who'd seen the ax, desperate to outrun the cage—

And I crashed right into him.

Dreamy Tomás of the corn-silk hair and the radiant brown skin and the artist's hands.

Bing, bang, boom, right into him—

And the noise that came out of him . . .

I could never forget it.

Worse than a whole tent of slack-jaws.

His scream was the ugliest sound I'd ever heard.

My throat bobbing around my own withheld scream, I rushed off into the night, knowing I could never outrun my own face, my own fate, but hoping to at least find somewhere without tents, without rings, without crowds.

Without mirrors.

Favors

LUNA

TONIGHT AFTER MY SHOW, I RETURN TO THE wagon I share with my sister and find a pile of gifts on my bed.

It's a common occurrence for a man in the crowd of the kootchie tent to watch me perform and decide he should send a tangible appreciation to the duchess.

An appreciation, or perhaps the gifts are meant to be invitations. There are men like that, who attach invisible strings to their tokens so I might feel like I owe them something in return. I sit at my vanity, wiping away my makeup.

Then I begin to sort.

Sifting through my gifts means cataloging the parts of my act that made impressions.

And since my act is essentially an offering of my body, I catalog the parts of myself.

There is always a ring. Tonight it is a diamond, princess cut, flanked by clusters of smaller gems. "I ask that you keep it upon your glorious, delicate finger always," says the accompanying note, "and I promise that someday I'll return to see you again and will bring a ring for each of your remaining digits." I know the jewelry from Tiffany & Co. well—I think I've been gifted something from every page of their blue book by now.

A selection of Dupont brushes are here, made of the finest hog bristles. "For your moonlit locks!" says their tag. "Would that I were the one running my fingers through those strands!" I am always slightly curious about the men who know what an investment a Dupont is for a woman. I suspect many a luxury brush I have in my possession was meant to go to a rich trophy wife who originally ordered them, but was intercepted when her husband scrambled to find an appropriate offering for the duchess, who eclipses his wife in every possible way.

There are glosses and paints for my lips. There are perfumes for my neck and wrists. There are Pears' Otto of Rose soaps, and Little Fairy suds, and tonics for my skin. "Not because a goddess such as yourself needs any aid to make her glow," reads one nervous note sent with a lavender lotion that was eight dollars an ounce in *McClure's* magazine, "but because such a goddess deserves the finest of all things."

There are gowns and robes and slippers. A cape that supposedly belonged to Empress Eugénie de Montijo of France. Beaded, laced, frilled, silken—I am gifted clothing for all possible occasions. And these are the tokens that come with the most obvious suggestions: "If you're in need of an event where you can show off such a gown, my valet is standing by to make arrangements." "I'd love to attend my bank's holiday soiree with you on my arm, sparkling in this." "This robe has a matching peignoir. It hangs in my closet, hoping you will say yes."

I keep what I like, discard what I do not, and let the oppression of such arm-twisting blow away like powder.

There are men who want to feed me, always, for some incomprehensible reason. Tonight's feast includes extract of barley malt, a sack of Gold Medal flour, several baskets of mints and pastries and chocolates, and a Swift Premium ham.

There's always a ham.

Men thinking of my mouth, my appetite, my throat, my stomach, all at once.

Men picturing me devouring these indulgences, hoping one day I will devour them as well.

An admirer, thinking of my arms, sent tennis rackets.

An admirer, thinking of my lungs and my constitution, sent tickets to ride on a motorboat called *The Dutchman* in San Francisco.

An admirer, thinking of my form, offered to purchase an insurance policy for my legs, guaranteeing them for one thousand dollars with Prudential.

Many, many admirers, thinking of my nose, sent flowers.

Many, many admirers, thinking of my nether regions, sent lingerie, usually with a letter that they likely considered to be tantalizing in its sordid confessions, but that I threw out without even opening.

And portraits, many portraits. Some masterfully done, some laughably poor.

Men become artists when they leave my audience, inspired to capture my likeness no matter how little experience they have with pen or paint.

A rare surprise here and there, but the haul is always much the same.

Tonight the men gawked at my hips, my feet, my smoky eyes. They drank in the feminine jut of my breasts, the pout of my lips, the draping of my hair. They were rendered lightning-struck by the leanness of my calves, the grace of my clavicles, the bend of my elbows—a thousand details that would never, ever be spotlighted as sensual, but on me, on their duchess . . .

A mere fart would have them clambering to mail me every one of their earthly possessions, because to be male and stand in my audience is to believe you can buy your way into a chance.

There is only one offering here that does not dissect me into segmented body parts like I am cattle.

A tiny scroll of scrap paper, almost too ordinary to notice. If you didn't know to look for it, you'd toss it into the trash—

But I reach past all the favors, all the gifts meant to court me like an empress, and I take up the scroll.

I unroll it.

Its words knock me over, then float me to the stars.

A gift not for my eyes alone, or my heart, or my brain or senses.

But for all of me.

Parts of me that I will never show onstage.

Parts of me I thought no one would ever want—but I give them now to Jonah.

My own favors.

Appreciations, invitations.

From all of me.

I pull my covers around me, still holding my poem, and lie on my side, ready to breathe myself to sleep.

It is only then that I realize Avita's bed is empty.

Out of the Nest

THE NIGHT WAS FULL OF STRANGE SOUNDS, the scamperings of creatures winged and clawed. The wind blew across my ears like they were seashells as I trudged through the scrub, no aim at all except to put as much distance as possible between the two circuses and myself.

They glittered behind me—the polished, deep white sparkle of Le Cirque Americana's restrained halcyons and the golden, organic, gritty glow of the Family Fortuna's rusty old gaslights.

Somewhere under those lights, I knew Arturo was clamoring his lungs out, barking at anyone unfortunate enough to cross paths with him, refusing to admit he'd let his best-selling exhibit run right out from under his nose but griping at everything all the same.

The carnival of thoughts in my own head sputtered to a halt—not that I had finally found peace, but my legs and body were so worn and aching by the long hike up the hills and the late hour, I'd made myself too exhausted to feel anything but stagnant.

I was a wandering stray, a dropped coin. I was alone.

I tried to rub warmth into my arms and thought of my feathers dropped in my ring as I raced away from Arturo. It had been years since I'd had bald patches like this, years since Mama had plucked me this naked. I shuddered at the memory of my mother's hands, so quick and biting as she cleaned me like poultry. Papa, too, had pulled out many, his enthusiasm sometimes leaving sore patches of gooseflesh. Touching those spots was like touching the softest parts of a baby's head.

I wished I could be a baby again, stupidly cooing and clacking my beak, covered in the ungodly fuzzy down of a chick, unaware that no matter how tantalizing the setup, how big the arena, how sweet my voice or stunning my getup, no one would ever be able to look past my gnarled form, my attraction for a face.

Something darkened the moon, and in a single breath, it was bright again. An owl traveled the sky, flapping back into the night, searching the ground for its next feast.

I tracked its flight, discarding all concern for where I was heading, where I would sleep tonight, what mercies I might possibly find in the wide expanse of desert that awaited me should I keep going. The only thing that mattered to me now was this particular dance, one foot in front of the other, away, away from my wretched failures, away from my downed dreams—

And then I saw it. The crossroads.

The very spot where Mama had hissed at all of us to say our prayers, where we'd hit some unknown animal before glimpsing Cornelius's treacherous takeover of our fields.

The devil was at the crossroads, Mama would say if she were here with me, standing on the incline.

Mama said a lot of things.

Creeping forward, I watched the moon's sheen on the roadside pebbles, took in the stars ahead, glinting in curving lines, mimicking my path.

When at last I stood upon the dirt trails where so many wheels had rumbled past, I braced myself for fear—for the dark adversary himself to slink out from the shadows, to feel the chill of God's abandonment.

Instead I felt my heart permanently scar.

Here at the crossroads, I did find myself looking into hell:

The gates of the Family Fortuna in the distance, cedar and iron, easily deconstructed, easily hewn. But instead of leading to fire and brimstone, they would lead me back to my father.

They would lead me to scoldings and thrashings, pitying looks that would cut deep enough to bleed.

What were you thinking, Avita?

You abandoned your audience. You abandoned your show.

You don't know how lucky you are to have your own tent, your own little kingdom, even if you can view it only from behind steel bars.

Perhaps if you growl twice as loud, they will forgive you.

Perhaps if you fill up the cheap seats and pack the front rows and cram people into the aisles three times a day, I will forgive you, too.

I knew Papa's lines better than anyone, even before he'd scripted them himself.

And I was tempted to crawl into one of these abandoned mine shafts and disappear forever rather than to return and expose myself to Arturo's triumphant *there, there* and his unsubtle *I told you so.*

My eyes grew watery with the scorch of ungracious tears, and it all blurred—the haze of two circuses trying to outshine each other, the gleam of Peculiar's streetlamps, the flicker of the bonfire, that ridiculous measure Papa had ordered, hoping it would outblaze the lights next door.

I tried to stand as tall as a water tower—as tall as my pride—to avoid the colloquial tail dragging between my legs.

But eventually the sun would rise again. My feet would not carry me forever; Bird Girl had to feed, had to drink, had to sleep.

It would burn me up to return to my father—to see his lips curl up in a sneer, the inevitability of the Spectacular Aviary Extravaganza. My audience had proven it to Arturo tonight, and to me. What more could I do?

What more could I be than a monster?

"Avita?"

Mama stood not far off, her hands running along her arms, chilly in the bone-dry nip of a Texan summer's eve. It was dark, but I could make out the streaks of old tears down her cheeks, her jaw gritted with some wild worry.

She bridged the gap between us, steering the situation right away, taking my shoulders and holding me at a distance while she inspected Luna's old costume on my body. "Avita, what are you wearing?"

God, it had never fit right, had it? The costume hung loose where Luna's chest had filled it and stretched uncomfortably tight around my hips, the sequins hanging on for dear life. Seeing myself through Mama's good eye, all justification for this glorious getup, made for someone far more suitable than I, was gone.

"Mama, I—" And then out it flooded, my lachrymose confession:

My apparently one-sided dalliance with Tomás. My humiliation at seeing my new banner. The fissure inside me that split wider and wider with the desire to be more than the monster in the cage. My boldness as I'd pulled on Luna's old costume and tried to glean some of her allure from the sequins.

My sincerest attempt at dazzlement.

My shock as Papa snapped the lights off on me, a tender mercy from a ringmaster trying to kill a fumbled show.

My humiliation as I realized the audience in my tent did not care if I sang, did not care if I wore every diamond in the kootchie tent's wardrobe, did not care if I was Arturo's brightest star, his crown jewel, his perfect dove.

They would never let me be anything but a monster.

She patted my back, nodded quietly when cued to do so. She comforted me as doggedly as only a mother could—not denying the reality of my situation, not downplaying the severity of my features.

And then she said, "It's not the calamity it might seem, Avita. It'll be a fair blow at first, but we'll manage. And there's plenty of other things you can do. You can help Socorro in her booth, or you can work the piggies with me—"

"I—what?" I peered at my mother. "What are you talking about?"

"Giving up the act, of course. Giving up Bird Girl. Listen, I have to tell you . . ." A fearful glint shone in Mama's good eye as another cloud passed over the face of the moon. "I never thought you should do it. I was against it from the start, but Arturo . . . Arturo insisted. It's better that you're not onstage anymore. You can find something else to do, like Ren."

I leaned away from her and sucked in a lungful of air, ruminating on her words. Not perform? The very thought was like pushing a knife's point into my belly. "I want to perform, Mama. I want to be onstage—of course I do. But I want to do something else, something new."

"You already have an act, Avita," Mama spat, "and now you want another one? You're spoiled. You don't know how lucky you are. How many people would kill for the chance to do what you do?"

An image flashed before me—ancient, elderly Avita, sagging skin around her beak, world-weary in her black eyes, hands shaking as she brought a thrashing chicken up to her decaying, broken-off teeth, her face scarred from a lifetime of being pecked and scratched and screamed at.

Were these truly my choices?

Rile up the crowds to shake and scream until I keeled over, or surrender the stage forever?

That felt akin to choosing between my hands and my feet. My eyes and my ears. There was no lesser of the two struggles; there was only pain and a different pain.

"No," I insisted, dead still, my feet sinking into the soil beneath me. "No. Papa could dream his way straight out of hell— he can come up with something new for me to do. Something that won't make them scream. I know he can. He's just being stubborn."

"He won't listen to you." Mama clenched her jaw.

"He won't listen to anyone, you mean—not even you!"

I'd let it fly, a single arrow of truth, and it caught Mama right where I'd aimed—in the chest. I watched her sink with it, her eyes widening.

"You didn't want to come back to Peculiar," I went on. "You told him in the wagon over and over that we should roll right past this town, but he paid as much attention to you as he would a mosquito."

Mama's nostrils flared, and she switched her hips, a common motion when her leg was troubling her. "I won't have you explaining my own marriage to me, Avita. There were—are—other considerations. It isn't what you think—"

"It's exactly what I think! Papa would shovel his own family into the coal bin to keep this circus going. Even you!" The wind rippled through me, but I was blazing, a bonfire. "Don't pretend I'm the only one he's milking. Look at you. You've given an eye and a leg to his circus, and every day he asks for more."

"Most circuses go belly-up after only a few years," Mama tossed back. "The Family Fortuna is what it is because we're all willing to sacrifice." Her maternal sternness flared, but it was a winter breeze compared to how hotly I burned. "And because of Arturo. He's a smart man, Avita—he's never had a flop, not ever—"

"Because everyone treats him like God!" My chest lurched.

"All your prayers, all your scriptures, your devotion—you give it all to Arturo, and he laps it up."

"Avita!" Mama was quick as a rattler's strike, seizing my wrist with one hand, slapping my sacrilege away with the other. But it was like a fly biting at a wildfire. Nothing could stop my surge of unclean candor.

"It's true! We all worship him! You, Socorro, every last asshole in the Family Fortuna! You do exactly what he demands every time. Oh, you might think you're tricking him, swerving around the exact details of his orders, but we all eventually jump through his hoops. You'll do anything to avoid the eye of his wrath—that's your real Lord and Savior!"

Even Luna—her quiet, ambivalent reverence.

Even Ren—his fear of Arturo striking him down to the spine. And me.

I'd believed Papa like his words were commandments. Sweet Lord, I was more gullible than a campaign donor.

I'd trusted him more than I'd ever trusted God.

"I'm not saying any more prayers," I told Mama, a new conviction pushing through me like feathers nosing up through flesh. "Not to Papa. I belong in that ring. And if Arturo can't dream up something magnificent for me to do, even with this face, then he's not the showman he says he is."

Away from the crossroads I strode, away from my mother. Away from the slew of muddy, sticky despondency that had coated me since I'd left my ring—

"Avita!"

I ignored my mother's cry. I wouldn't be so easily halted; a comet doesn't easily bend its streak through space and time, not until it's been burned down cold.

But just before I took the descending path back to the Family Fortuna, I turned around.

My mother, who bore the scars of times when circumstance had picked a fight but she'd triumphed. Mama, who loved to reach down and touch her darling Tip-Ups as a reminder that whatever came at her, she could shoot it down faster than it could fly.

Mama, who fought off malevolence like a sheriff had given her jurisdiction. No mirrors facing each other. No sharing combs. No lighting cigars with candle flames. No kissing redheads after dark. I had no idea where Mama had collected all these fanatical notions or when she'd decided that scripture and prayer were not enough to keep her family safe. But long ago, she'd assigned herself the task of watching for the devil and his cohorts in every wormy fruit, every black kitten, every glob of spit that cleaved itself in two before it landed.

Yet a life spent dodging all fearful things meant a life guided by fear.

And a life spent chasing applause meant a life guided by an audience.

My whole life, I'd been chasing applause from an audience of one.

It was time to chase a new audience.

It was time to throw away all mirrors.

"You're remembering wrong," I called to my mother before

I left her alone at the crossroads. "We both are. Arturo wasn't the one who made me Bird Girl. I was."

The memory came at once, swilling my mind in a sodden, hazy rush: my first time in the ring, and I was the one who had chased the screams. It was me.

I was the one who had put my act together.

And I'd made myself a star.

I'd done it once. I could damn well do it again.

A Ringmaster's Wife

MAMA

ARTURO'S HEAD IS HARDER THAN ROCK.

When he asked me to marry him all those years ago, back when he was as twiggy as straw and I still slept with a rose under my pillow, I looked him straight in his starry eyes. "What if I say no?"

And he smiled like a weasel. "If you want to test me, test me. I'll affix myself to your porch like a damn mailbox and wait you out. You won't slink away from me—I'll keep asking until you say yes. You are supposed to be my wife. And we are supposed to do great things together."

I loved his resolve back then. I thought it was romantic. I'd swooned at the idea of him hearing no a thousand times, no every day for a year or longer, and still coming back to my door and my window and my garden. I pictured him following me around in the fields, proposing with one knee in pig manure, wearing himself down like the loamy edge of a great riverbank. I loved the idea of him begging—but I decided to spare both of us the trouble and said, "What the hell. All right. Might as well."

As our nuptials approached, I twirled in my farmhouse bedroom every night, holding my hair up off my neck and shoulders, imagining yards of chiffon and a rhinestone gown that I knew we couldn't afford. *No matter*, I told myself. *I'll wear his dreams for my wedding gown, and then someday they will clothe our children.*

Now I am not so sure his head is good for anything but cracking open geodes. His stubbornness is an anchor, and it will sink this family.

"No, no, no!" he calls out now, and swipes his arm across the table in front of him, sending his papers cascading across the ring. Something inside of me dries and shrivels. Honestly, none of our babies ever made such a racket.

The girl who is juggling in the spotlight trembles, her neon balls falling into the dirt.

"It's all wrong!" Arturo thunders. "I already have jugglers—jugglers ten times better than you, and with twice the tits! What makes you special? What makes you think you should be here at all?" Without waiting for her reply, he spins on his heel and marches to the tent flaps. "Lorenzo! Get in here!"

The juggler scampers out into the steamy morning, a sob catching in her throat as she goes.

I shake my head from where I stand in the back of the tent, leaning into the blue bleachers. Life as a performer is hard enough—you must hear no a thousand times just to get one yes so you can then be paid less than a quarter of what you deserve. Otherwise someone will offer to do the same job for free, for the exposure, for the joy of standing in the lights, collecting applause, as if that thrill alone can nourish you like a warm meal. And all the while you're searching for other odd jobs that will actually pay money you can spend on food and housing and, well . . . Arturo doesn't make it any easier.

The real audition is not just the two minutes you spend selling your act. The real audition is your determination and your survival before and after.

"Hey." I let my voice echo from my place in the shadows— Arturo is not the only one who knows how to change the temperature with only his voice.

Arturo sees me, and his face crumbles like a wet cobbler.

"Don't you do that," I warn him. "Don't you act like the devil himself just walked into the room. I'm your wife."

He rolls his eyes, the closest thing to an apology Arturo Fortuna ever gives. "Oh, now what, Quinn? I'm busy!"

"Take a break, Arturo," I say, picking up his scattered papers from the ring. "Stop making poor girls cry, by Jim. There's no need for open call today. Wait until you've cooled down—"

"No!" He glares at me like I'm a barking animal, out of line. "I've waited this long to drown Cornelius in his own golden spit. I want something new in our tents today. Now!"

My own father was not an explosive man. He was quiet as a rooted tree, married less to my mother and more to his routine: up at dawn to slop the pigs, driving piglets to market in the arid heat of Montana's afternoons, evenings devoted to scripture and prayer. Most days I barely heard him speak twenty words.

So three weeks into my own marriage, when Arturo began

blowing up at the smallest things—I had cooked his meat too tough, or he was frustrated by something in the circus that was beyond his ability to manage—it frightened me. I scrambled to make things right, to chase the storm clouds from our shared sky.

Now I ignore his tantrums just as I ignored the children when they grew out of babyhood and clawed at my skirts while I did chores, begging to be held just because they were bored.

"You're certainly not going to find someone if you keep exploding like that," I tell him, bridging the gap between us, dragging my leg along. It didn't hurt when I woke up this morning, but Arturo's bickering makes the old slug wound ache. "No one wants to work with you when you scream."

"Then I don't want them!" Arturo shrieks. "I can scream as loud as I like—they should all feel grateful to even be given a shot to work for the Family Fortuna. Lorenzo! Now!"

My son comes into the tent, exhausted and harried. He is a jumble of red tape, shuffling pages on his clipboard, trying to straighten them.

"What the hell are you sending me?" Arturo says. "I asked you for the cream of the crop. I can't charge a rat's ass to see any of these bums. Patrons will revolt!"

Lorenzo is already small, but next to his father he always shrinks so far down I am worried he will collapse in on himself.

I stare at Arturo, my thoughts spinning as fast as a Hotchkiss barrel.

Is this what I wanted? Is this what any woman wants? We want a man who will raise our babies, bring them up like fragile violets, a man who will help them bloom—and Arturo has always done this for Luna and Avita. He has always treated his daughters like they are the most precious petunias—but my Lorenzo he treats like a weed.

"I asked you if I should prescreen them," Lorenzo manages to croak, "but you said no, that you wanted to see them all yourself."

"Because I can't trust you to send me proper performers!" Arturo throws his head back and pinches the bridge of his nose as if his own son is a thorn in his big toe. "Just—fuck off, then. Make yourself useful to someone else. Go polish a goat's balls, for all I care. I'll do this myself."

The rage burns liquid in my lungs, but I have spent so many years swallowing it down, it doesn't make it far. My tongue stays cold.

And my son, my dear Lorenzo, leaves the tent before I can apologize with my eyes for what I married. I know without seeing it that his face is like a drawstring purse—cheeks slack, mouth pulled tight.

Arturo runs his hands over his face, tweaking the ends of his mustache. Holy shit, he looks old. He's hoping his ringmaster's authority makes up for the wear and tear, but in this light, the years don't lie—and they're plain as balls on my own face, too.

"I am never going to find someone," he moans with exaggerated trauma now that we are alone.

But I'll have none of it. I'll breathe flames if he forces me to play along with his invented disasters. "Listen to me. Of course you're not going to replace her with a new act overnight—"

"I never said anything about replacing her," he snarls. "We've been overdue for a new act for months. Cornelius is breathing down my neck—"

"Horseshit," I burst. "Cornelius doesn't have to do anything but wait until you light your own ass on fire. He's more patient than you could ever be. Just find her and apologize."

There it goes again—a dull spurt of pain in my thigh. Too many bullet fragments for the doctor to fish out, and so now they are part of me. They did not choose to marry Arturo, so all they can do is ache like dull nails against my bone when he speaks.

"What are you even—you're so—" He stops, and I barely hold back my chuckle. Arturo is out of words so rarely, it feels like a holiday whenever it happens.

"Why the sputtering? Did a fly buzz down your throat? If you'd put all this attention toward dealing with your daughter . . ." I hope he interprets the quivering of my chin as fury and not despair. "You only have three children, you know?" Fury and not worry. Fury and not all the emotions swimming through me that kept my feet cold all last night.

Avita had not yet returned.

My motherly instinct told me she was crouched in some hidey-hole, balled up in adolescent resentment in the kootchie tent wagons or in the grub tent or behind Bart's Whirligig target. Arturo could either wait out her angst, or he could bait her with that rarest of all sights: an admission of regret, a plea for forgiveness from the most stubborn man ever molded for this earth.

283 ☙

Yet another instinct, deep rooted and darkly distraught, feared for Avita, feared her being out of our sight.

She did not know what things could happen in the shadows of Peculiar. None of them did.

Lorenzo sticks his head back into the tent. "Do you want to see the rest of them or not?"

Arturo swills the last of his coffee. "Yes, yes! Send one in already!"

And to me, he folds his arms and says, "I'm busy, Quinn, all right? There's another dozen of these hacks out there and a tent to fill before twilight. Go cluck at someone else."

I nearly wobble, my heart thumping loud as gunshot. "Maybe you can hire someone to apologize to your second child, too, Arturo, before he walks out on us as well."

I stalk away, punching through the flaps, my limp heavy. As angry as I am, I make sure to look three times angrier.

"Aw, Quinn—" But the canvas smothers the end of his plea.

This I have learned after twenty years of marriage: There is no sense lingering in an argument. There is no sense staking a tent in a muddy, smelly swamp. Arturo could stand in such a bog for a week straight, weaving sentences out of starshine and algae, and he would always think he had won, even if he were just gabbing at shadows.

I want to speak to Lorenzo, but he is managing a lineup, organizing the crooked crowd of would-be performers outside the tent.

My sweet son. He was not born with any of his father's charisma; he is missing that particular rib. Even now it is a struggle for him to keep the attention of this group—he holds their futures in his palm, and yet he still cannot persuade them to listen when he speaks.

I will check on him later. I've seen him more upset than this, closer to the edge.

But still, the sharpness in my leg warns—Arturo is wearing him out, too. It's only a matter of time before Lorenzo has had enough, and then he will fly. Just like Avita.

Just like I wish I could do most days. But first I'd need my love for that asshole carved out of me, my devotion. A doctor can't do it.

Like the bullets from my last performance as Quick-Draw Quinn, that love is a part of me. Embedded.

I wait until the wagon door shuts behind me and I'm near my bed before I release my breath and let the tears sting. My leg hurts, but I find my way to my knees, and through clenched teeth and a tongue that is already practicing comebacks for when Arturo drags me back into his swamp, I pray.

I pray for Avita, for her return.

I pray for Lorenzo, that his patience will never run dry.

I pray for Luna—for what, I don't yet know. Though I see so much of myself in her, I know so little about my oldest child. That is how I know she is likely in need of a prayer just for her.

I pray for Arturo, even, for heaven to soften his head and pull it out of his ass before it's too late.

And for myself, I pray for the same thing I've prayed for since the last time we came to Peculiar.

Forgiveness.

"For what I did," I beg, "please, please, please forgive me. Forgive me."

Forgive me.

This prayer, it is a part of me.

Embedded.

Old Boot

REN

I KNOW IT'S A CLICHÉ OF EPIC AND HISTORICAL proportions to hate your own father.

I could thumb through the books of any town's library and find at least a dozen characters whose stories are about pushing back against their old men. Oedipus is banished by his own dad. Hamlet is practically suicidal when the late king drops that plea for vengeance on his head like a crown. Isaac is nearly stabbed by Abraham, and even though the angel of the Lord stays Abraham's hand before the blade goes in, I'm sure nothing is the same between the two of them after that.

The world is full of despicable fathers.

But mine takes the cake.

Last night when I went to bed, I was overlooking a cliff, but my feet were still on the ground. Yesterday he yelled at me for more than an hour about the parade I couldn't have predicted; the thousand-dollar publicity we hadn't booked or paid for; the tigers, who were too sick from bad meat to perform, as if that were something I should have anticipated and prevented.

And this morning he barked at me for the shitty local talent who turned up for our open call. When I asked about Avita, who did not show up for breakfast after her botched show, Arturo flicked my ear and told me to keep my nose to my clipboard, mind my own business—as if the Spectacular Aviary Extravaganza, the most important, most lucrative act of the Family Fortuna, were not my business.

And then he stepped backward and knocked me over, and looked down at me as if I were not his only son, but a runny pile of pig shit, before stomping away without a single apology or offer to help me up.

Yesterday I was staring over the cliff's edge.

Today I am dangling off the side.

I'm gripping the rocks, a chasm of black ocean crashing beneath me, and he won't lift a finger to help me up. Instead, as I kick to save myself, to crawl back to safety, he barks at me to get the orders from Socorro signed and oversee the ticket booth and *why are you such a twit, why haven't you thought of this impossible thing before it even popped into my own mind, why are you never enough?*

He may as well shove his boot into my face and watch me tumble.

Before I fall, before I drown again in his demands, I haul my pathetic self away for a respite.

I can't find a quiet place to hole up on circus grounds, not without Arturo sniffing me out like a wolfhound so he can castigate me until his voice is raw. Still no Avita, and Arturo will make me pay for whatever transgressions sent her running.

So I make for the nearest spot where a man can slap down a penny in exchange for a place to sit unbothered.

It's late afternoon when I arrive at the Old Boot. Located on the bottom floor of the Macintosh Hotel on Peculiar's main drag, the red bricks bleached by the sun to a pale brown, the front door grand and ornately carved into a biblical tableau, the Old Boot is at first sight a standard-issue saloon. Some of the polish comes off onto my hand in a greasy swipe as I push my way in, and the scent of raw alcohol and burnt sugar stings my nose.

Once inside, I can see the charm of the place. The striped wallpaper is old but clean, the paintings on the wall are of tasteful Rubenesque nudes, women with their rounded parts carefully hidden by fig leaves and boas and other cheats, framed in fake gold scallops.

Tables abound with the drinkers and punters of Peculiar flooding the local economy with their proclivities. The bar is packed with men making use of the sour towels that hang near their stools to wipe the beer foam off their mustaches. Saloon gals jump like fleas from patron to patron, all apple-cheeked smiles, collecting tips as the cheap ale flows like the Rio Grande.

With a nervous churn in my stomach, I peer around, looking for a space to call my own for a spell while I catch my breath. There in the farthest corner, an empty counter stretches in front of a window, the sunlight infiltrating at its gloaming angle . . . but if it's not coming from a spotlight, I don't mind such harshness. If it's coming from the mere sun, it'll be a reprieve, comparatively.

I weave between packed chairs, dodging kicked-out spurs and spittoons, until I finally claim my spot.

"What can I bring you?" The gal taking my order eyes me up and down but says nothing of my unconventional height. Either she's already casting about for a decent tip from me or she's seen stranger things perched atop her stools.

"Just a beer, thanks." I plunk down a coin and spread my ledger in front of me, scratch paper at the ready.

She brings me back a whiskey instead. "Beer's bad today," she explains. "Real horse piss."

"Oh. All right." I don't usually take to the hard stuff, but she lingers while I sip and chuckles when I cough the fire from my pipes.

"Burns a bit," she says, "but there's a nice woodsy aftertaste waiting for you . . . if you can handle it."

"It should do the trick," I tell her, and she leaves me to my numbers. The pulpy wood flavor of the drink finds me, and my head starts warming up. I take another sip.

Numbers. All these numbers.

The thing about numbers is they're so simple. They always add up. They don't obscure, they don't fabricate, they don't bamboozle.

They either match up or they don't.

And these numbers don't.

There's a discrepancy in our books wide enough to drive our caravan through. Arturo sprang for the new posters, the bills, the banner, and flipped all our numbers sideways like he'd played a bad hand at a high-low table.

He's too absorbed in his little face-off with Cornelius and his conniption over Avita to understand what I can see right here in our ledgers: if we can't pull away from Peculiar in the black, there won't be a Family Fortuna. Not anymore.

And it will be his fault. I'll know it, Mama will know it, every person who has ever encountered Arturo and his big, leaky head will know it—but my father will still be convinced that the failure is mine alone.

I balance the ledger in half a whiskey.

I make a list of things I need to do to achieve this balance on time, either by persuading my father that the ideas are his or by accomplishing them behind Arturo's back entirely.

Extensions of credit. Cutting costs where we can: ordering the second-best coffee beans, reusing costumes from prior seasons, halting all new hires. Returning goods we haven't used yet, pawning goods we had no business purchasing in the first place.

Calling off the deal for that ludicrous carousel. Arturo will pop his spleen with rage when he finds out, but if he'd rather auction off his kootchie girls for petty cash to buy his carousel, I'll hang the horsies on the brass hangers myself.

The second half of the whiskey I sink into like a hot spring.

I think I understand now why some reach for the bottle— without meaning to, I've unhanded my heaviest burdens. Simply dropped them at will, let them melt from my spine, away to some unknowable hole in the universe. All that is left in my head is this warmth, this wool.

The great spread of apathy covers me like a quilt, cozy, congenial.

Money troubles? Why worry? If Arturo isn't going to swirl his brains over the dams in his cash flow, why should I? Permits? Contracts? Infrastructure? Busywork! My father would make a show out of a couple of moldy boards and a jar of fireflies? Let him!

He's Arturo Fortuna, he loves to boast—so let him be. Let him be all of it: ringmaster, dictator, monarch, and God. I certainly never get to be God. God gets all the credit and none of the blame, and I've been sneered at for a snowstorm pulling down our tents in Lubbock.

"Another?" The girl handling my drinks has a fresh pour in front of me before I can think to answer. I don't lift it to my lips right away; I want to savor this—this buoyancy, this disillusionment that has me so at ease. One more drink, and I could tip out of weightlessness and into inebriated wrath. But every minute that passes brings me closer to sobriety, and to the patrimonial gauntlet in which I spend my torturous days.

Here, I am stuck.

Here, I am weightless.

I wish I'd brought a book.

Piercing through the window, the sun spears its golden rays across the valley, across my face, blinding me to everything but its glow—

Until a silhouette blocks out the light.

A soldier, young, silver-buttoned, and blue-eyed, scoots out the stool beside me. "Do you mind?" he asks. "I hate to drink alone."

His name is Stewart. He's an infantryman in Company C. He is chatty.

He's on leave for the week, and while the rest of his company get their boots resoled and shop for women, he's been ordering steaks on the government's dime, nursing good liquor before it's back to the bucket-made grog he'll have at the fort.

He was previously located across the frontier in the Dakotas, but he's marching to a new assignment in West Texas.

"A promotion?" I say when he dances around the word.

He grins like a weasel in a henhouse and points to his lapel. "Got a spot for that brass right here. And my brother David's the one who will pin it on. He's all decorated himself. Sergeant major for two years now."

A regular family affair. I take another sip of my red-hot. "A pair of soldiers wearing the brass. I'll bet your old man's proud."

"Proud?" Stewart scoffs good-naturedly. "He recruited us himself. My father's Lieutenant Colonel Woods, fourth brigade, first division—but I know what you're thinking. I earned my rank fair and square. No favoritism, I guarantee it."

But you are favored, I nearly mutter. *You can talk about your father without a whiskey to loosen you up first. You can say your father's name without cowering small enough to be the cow shit he thinks you are. The very fact that you are defensive about it means you're favored enough to have never needed it.*

"What do you do?" Stewart glances at the papers sprawled in front of me on the counter. "You're a numbers guy?"

He locks eyes with me, and his smile is like an autumn night. "I'm a numbers guy," I affirm, "but I'm actually much more of a words guy. Do you read?"

The light shifts just then, and I assume the sun has banked into the horizon.

But there is a head on the other side of the Old Boot's window, a face glaring at me through the pane. Arturo's glower could split a cabbage.

My conversation, over.

My spirits wilted, my body drying itself out as I gather up my papers and toss a bill on the counter.

Stewart might be addressing me as I hop down from the stool, but I don't hear him. My limbs have their own priority: to get me to Arturo, front and center, and to take in his demands before he starts thumping at me for dawdling.

"We're in the fight of our life, and this is where I find you?" Arturo spews as I scramble out onto the saloon's porch. "Bending elbows with the rabble while we're wearing ourselves to shadows?"

Mouth still tinged with the peaty fire of the whiskey, I take in a breath. "I *was* working. I was balancing our books." I lift up the ledger as proof, all my numbers in tidy rows and columns. "We're still in the red from the art commissions—"

"Horseshit!" His shout makes the door rattle. "We needed new rags to lure the crowds in! It takes money to make money, Lorenzo, and you're a goddamn skinflint! You'd clench every last one of our coins until the embalmers took 'em and plopped them on our cold dead eyes!"

Apathy, yanked off me, leaving me exposed.

All my warmth, my floating weightlessness, splashed frigid again by Arturo's freight train temper.

"There won't be any money left if you spend, spend, spend!" I burst. "God, how many times do I have to tell you? You're driving our show right into the dirt because no one else dares to reel you in!"

And I'm here every day, trimming the fat, making miracles happen in our accounts, pulling the strings so he can pretend to be the one running the show, and this is how he repays me?

Snapping at me in front of whatever crowd he can muster, all so he can make an exhibit out of being a father?

Arturo grinds his back teeth, assessing me with those jaybird eyes. "You're pissed," he chokes out. "Sloshed as a wet dog."

Not as pissed as you are every day on your own ego, I nearly spit.

"Find a barrel to dunk your head in," he snaps, "and get back to the circus. Get back to work before that boghole Cornelius rolls right over us. Now, before the crowds thin out!"

My father is the greatest ringmaster west of the Mississippi.

He could recite the dullest verses of Deuteronomy, and people would stop to listen.

He is slicker than Texas oil, tougher than jerky.

He never enters a room without knowing exactly where and how he will stand, who he will look at, and what he will say.

He can drum up a buttload of people and lasso their money out of their hands and into our vault, over and over, like waves.

But he can't convince me to buy his bullshit anymore.

My throat is dry as kitchen sherry. Alone outside the Old Boot, I swallow, then swallow again.

My father's words echo in my head, but they fade to quiet when I peer at Le Cirque Americana, and a wild thought crosses my noggin. Their lights bounce off my spectacles, and it suddenly seems as obvious as a fifth ace in a deck of cards.

Papa is the ringmaster; he knows this better than anyone: "If you bring out a turd, but you tell them it's a rare diamond, they'll be on their feet clapping and *ooh*ing and *aah*ing before they ever notice it came from a pig's ass."

I've let Papa make a turd of me.

But not anymore.

I'm going to make myself a diamond.

The Family Fortuna is only a stretch of dust away from Le Cirque Americana's gates, and our big top glows red as a drunkard's nose in the impending shadows. It looks absolutely patchwork compared to the grandness of Le Cirque Americana. I search my innards for pity for my father and cannot find a shred of it. Then I slip away from the saloon, still tiddly with drink, and let my feet carry me toward the beacon.

Moon

LUNA

I AM GROWING A MOON IN MY BELLY.

It is late in the evening.

Avita's bed was still empty this morning, and her place at the grub tent was vacant.

Whispers roll through the circus about how she went vicious during her act, demanding something more than mere chicken meat. About how she broke loose from her cage and charged the crowd. About how Arturo's behests finally drove her into that pure monstrosity that was always simmering just below her feathered skin.

I have sorted through the rumors and strained them for wisps of truth: that my sister, after a lifetime of supping on Papa's fawning and coddling, finally choked on his demands.

So she has flown.

And she has persuaded me that it is time for me to fly as well.

I have spent most of the day lying in my wagon, partly because to be upright in the world makes me nauseated, almost like gravity no longer exists for me—but also because I can't keep my hands off of myself. The little moon pushes out my hips, rounds my stomach, and makes me soft as a dumpling, makes me quiet, makes me patient.

Our sweet little moon

I have always looked down at myself and wondered if I was truly alive—the thing that is supposed to be me feels like a prop. An ornament, a product for sale.

Now my skirts are too tight and none of my stockings can contain my thighs. Now I finally feel like I am home inside my own body.

I do not know much. I don't have Papa's raw brains or Mama's sharpness. I don't devour books like Ren, and Avita's burning passion has always seemed like it would be an inconvenience. But I know this: with every passing day, I am becoming more and more Luna. I think I could know love.

I would circle the Earth for you and still

The moon in my belly makes me hungry like I have never been before. Instead of surviving on water and reeds, Socorro brings me rich stews and sourdough bread, and I eat her pastel de tres leches late into the night. Cinnamon and chocolate gather in the crevices of my fingernails; I lie on bedsheets sticky with powdered sugar.

I don't worry about the duchess maintaining her figure. I don't worry about the men in the kootchie tent, what they will think of my new pumpkin shape and dimpled ass.

I want my little moon to grow and grow until it blocks out the sun.

A thousand moonrises and sunshadows

Socorro knows. We haven't spoken about it, but she started brewing me ginger tea when I was retching up even the air I ingested. She knows.

Avita knows. She promised not to tell anyone, and I believe she meant it . . . at least, in that moment she did.

Ren knows—of course he does. He hasn't made full eye contact with me in days.

I suspect Mama knows, though she hasn't outright asked me. I suspect she has noticed that I haven't brought my bleeding rags to the laundry in months. She says nothing, but I see that glimmer in her eye when she studies me. Mama is cold-blooded. She is a mountain—she prefers to remain distant and silent while the people around her reveal themselves to be fools and pigs. I am like this, too. That's how I know she knows.

Papa doesn't know.

And I am leaving before he finds out.

Another moon for the moon, my love, for you

I have dozens of these, his love for me scrawled on paper and cut into pieces so I may spread it out over my day. Sometimes I go into my dressing tent before my show and find one folded under my lipstick. Sometimes I come to my wagon at night and there is a rolled-up scrap of paper tucked beside my doorknob. Sometimes he passes them to me as we kiss, and I open them later to find lingering evidence of his adoration for me.

I won't be able to hide it much longer. It was difficult enough to get past those first months of sickness and exhaustion. The simple task of leaving my bed wrung me out like a dishcloth, and summoning the energy to be the duchess, to be a goddess for the men and boys in the audience—it was like swimming in a lake of sand.

When my little moon began to fill out, I spoke to Fernando about my costumes. I told him that my appetite had been insatiable lately and that Socorro had insisted I follow its promptings for my health, and so he would have to dress me in things that would drape over my middle and hide my plumpness.

But now no amount of strategic curtaining can hide my secret.

If Papa weren't so obtuse, he'd have seen it by now . . . but he isn't stupid. I want to be gone before he finds out why my songs have been so breathy lately, why I've made excuses instead of indulging our high-paying clients.

The door to my wagon is opened by someone gentle with the wood, someone who has crept stealthily into this wagon a hundred times.

A hundred times at least, and yet my body still tingles when I know his touch is forthcoming. Jonah whispers the door closed and sinks onto the bed behind me, and then it's me, and him curled around me, his hands smoothing over the growing expanse of my torso where deep inside, our moon sleeps.

He's been busy making plans and paving the way for us to go—working extra hours, skipping lunch, saving every bit of his money for our railway tickets, and I've been pawning jewelry, hiding away everything gifted to me by the men I dance for. Those things belong to me, no matter how Papa wants to rearrange reality. He would say they are the property of the circus, but he would also declare me property of the circus, and Avita, too.

A rough year for Papa—he is losing so many of his things.

It's not just Papa who has things. Ren has his books, and Avita has her dreams, and Mama has her pigs. Papa has all of us—he has this circus, and what do I have?

For a long time, nothing.

Now I have this.

I have something real. Something tangible. These calloused young hands in mine, this celestial orb in my womb, the heavenly light of a body radiating within.

I'll run far in order to protect what is mine.

We've been planning for weeks. Once I realized I was with child, Jonah and I took a midnight stroll in the dark hours after the Family Fortuna closed, and we both knew we didn't want this life for our little moonlet; we wanted more.

"I want to cook for you," I told him that night. "I want to be a proper wife." I meant it. I would learn to grow a garden from scratch and make him dinner every evening and learn to sew and darn his socks and keep his house. I would do it all for him, I promised. I would become everything I was not, anything to make him happy.

He tucked my hair behind my ear.

"It won't be as easy as that," he warned, and then he spoke to me about budgeting and bills and our insignificant means, all concepts that made me dizzy and bored.

Mama and Papa have always shielded their duchess from such practical matters—or did they starve me of them?

All I know of the world beyond my stage is what I've gleaned from the men who pay to watch me. When I twirl for them, they offer up their sadnesses—*my wife left me, my farm burned down, it's hard out there, honey, but your sweet ass waggling to the beat of the music makes it all better.*

So this is the true costume I wear: a skirt woven of their worries, a top made of their greatest fears, which I remove and fling into the crowd, and to them it is like I have thrown their fears away. This is all I know.

But Jonah hasn't always been a citizen of the circus. Jonah knows how it is out there, knows that we will have to scrape and gather to make it. It will be a new dance, a new hustle, one I'll be able to do only as long as I have him by my side.

Outside, the land glows purple. The circus is loud, but I learned to tune it out years ago.

Jonah props his head up on one hand, looks at me. "Will you miss it?"

I think.

Some things I will miss. The smell of the gaslights. My costumes—they are all cut to my exact proportions, made of such rich, soft fabrics, such decadence. Socorro's chili, the smell of the wood-burning stove in the family wagon, and of course I will miss the sound of them chanting my name. But I am breathless at the thought of a single new, tiny voice calling for me.

Ever since I started growing my little moon, I've looked at

my own mother, at her softness and her wrinkles, and I know my body will be the sacrifice. My waist may once again become slim, and my breasts may once again become buoyant, but no one will pay to see a woman adorned in the skin stripes of childbearing.

Papa warned me all those years ago.

So I must say goodbye to the duchess. She will be as good as dead as soon as we leave.

"Yes, I will miss it." I don't have to explain the complexity of what I mean: yes, I'll miss it, but it's time to leave.

Jonah reads it on my face, then lies back down and closes his eyes, as if he is bearing the pain of my loss for me. "I would carry it for a while, if I could," he said to me in the early weeks, when only nibbling on a raw clove of garlic eased my misery. And I know he thinks the same of my heartaches now.

I carry our moon for him. I would do anything if it meant being with such a person.

Like porcelain you are

Like porcelain you make me

Easy to shatter—just keep the moon whole and in my sky

When the pillows on my bed shine like ghosts in the darkness and the night is deep enough to mask our silhouettes, I squeeze my Jonah's arm. "Let's go."

His eyes move beneath their closed lids, a faint smile on his lips. I wonder, not for the first time, what the blending of our faces will look like. When the baby is born, will it have Jonah's serious brow, my sharp jaw? When it grows, will it have Jonah's muscular limbs or my gracile ones?

And then, to chase those dreams, we lift ourselves off the bed, and out of the wagon we go.

The Family Fortuna is alive, its ticket buyers running loose like startled chickens into tents awaiting their crowds. We plan to sneak along the perimeter, to become shadows—but when we walk down the porch steps to the weeds below, Papa is waiting.

"So," he says, "you got yourself knocked up."

Jonah carries my bag down from the wagon and sets it in front of us—a barrier, a shield. Papa eyes it with amusement.

"You think you can just go? Go act normal? Just have a normal life? You'll never be normal. You can't leave."

Dealing with Arturo means running out his clock. I don't have to respond; I only have to wait for him to talk himself into circles.

I lean forward and kiss his cheek, his mustache stabbing me.

"I won't hold your spot," he says. "I'll replace you." He thinks this is a threat.

"Replace me," I tell him, and when I bend down to pick up my bag, I let my coat spread open so he can see the full girth of my belly, the ways in which my body has already morphed. I stopped being his duchess a long time ago.

He stares for three whole breaths. "When—" is all he says; this little moon eclipses my father's golden words, and I am already proud of it.

"In the winter," I say. "It'll come in the new year."

It's still months away, but the roundness of my middle makes it real to him.

"If you're hoping for my blessing—" he starts.

I laugh. His blessing? What would I even do with such a ridiculous thing as that?

There's nothing like laughing at a man to make him feel two inches tall—and at that height, Papa puffs himself up like a cobra. "You think the world is going to accept you? You're a whore," is the venom he spits.

Beside me, Jonah rustles like storm-blown canvas. I find his fingers in the wide sleeve of his shirt and hang on to them, pulse them. I won't argue—by the Bible, I certainly fit the definition—but I did not come out of my mother that way. And I will not let Papa forget that he has shaped me into this. He has turned me into this thing that he now finds reason to despise.

"You're the one who sold me," I say. "You've sold your own children to get the whole world off."

It's more than I've said to him directly since I was very small, back before I knew to keep my mouth closed around Arturo Fortuna. I learned early that it was best not to give him too much, or he'd take it and sell it for pocket change.

As I lead Jonah away from the wagons, away from the circus, away from the lights and into the wide-open darkness, I know I am right to do this.

I was right not to let my father know me, not to let him see me.

He will stand there in the yard, watching me leave, watching my bowlegged steps and the bulge of my moon belly until our figures melt into the night, and I will not look back.

There is one moment, as we reach the edge of the field and

must make a final step onto Peculiar's thoroughfare to the train station, which will take us west through every town until we hit ocean, when I realize this will be the last view I ever have of the Family Fortuna.

I soak it in, the gas lamps gleaming against scarlet tents, turning them into great, pounding, bleeding organs on the horizon.

My heart.

It is harder to walk away from than I ever imagined it would be. Not from the show. From my heart.

My family.

But when my feet land on the metal steps of the train, my gait is steady, and I pull ahead of Jonah, even with the extra passenger inside of me. I want to get to our new future as quickly as we can.

A new moon.

A new moon.

Stranger in a Strange Land

REN

THE LIGHTS SHINE SO BRIGHT, IF YOU STEP *inside their gates, you'll think you're among the stars.*

I still recall the opening lines of the damning newspaper article about the then up-and-coming Le Cirque Americana. Even as a winkling, I understood what it forecast: a deluge, a downpour. An uproar unlike any other from my father, who had chased headlines for years and would have given his left nut for a journalistic rave like this. When I read it out loud to Mama, she tossed aside her knitting and scrunched up the whole paper in the fireplace. "Do not let Arturo see it," she ordered us, and we were able to keep him insulated from the rumors for a good while.

Rumors that inside the grounds of Le Cirque Americana, it never rained and the wind never blew; it was always a perfectly balmy, delightful, early autumn day or a made-to-order, barely chilly evening, no matter the climate. Cornelius had his own weather machine, the whisper networks boasted, while we dug trenches around our tents anytime Arturo got even a whiff of a storm.

Rumors that all the big cats in Le Cirque Americana, when they finished their acts, shrank down to little striped and spotted kittens that wandered the crowds, allowing people to stroke their fur and appreciatively feed them morsels of greasy chicken.

Rumors that the food they sold was bottomless, that as long as you stayed on circus grounds, you could munch and munch, and your carton of popcorn would always have at least one handful left, that your taffy roll would keep on unrolling.

Rumors that Cornelius's beasts all understood orders in English, French, and German; that his men were strong enough to crush melons between their thighs; that his women were so scintillating that they'd be visited by Zeus in various showers and animal visages if the horny old god were still around.

And of course, there were the rumors about the acts themselves.

Tents of horse shows, of beautiful riders tied to galloping grays, riders who untied themselves as the crowds cheered and dismounted with the grace of arachnids on their webs.

Tents with men doing strong teeth on zip lines, tents with a trio of polar bears waltzing with a veteran animal trainer in a ball gown. Tents with tricky donkeys and high-wire contortionists, whippet hounds and leapers flying over rows of camels, alligators, hippos.

One tent in particular, where patrons paid five cents to step inside and whisper their secrets—to whom or what, no one knew, but people were rumored to leave that tent feeling measurably lighter. Buoyant.

Now I stand inside Le Cirque Americana, and the grounds before me are littered with the truth.

One truth about Le Cirque Americana that you'd never guess unless you had a ticket in hand:

Their tents are not really tents.

Yards of canvas draped over staked poles and rigging always conjure up visions of sweating roustabouts with chiming hammers and ambitious hands counting every stitch, industrious as pioneers. But these smooth, rounded walls are some other fabrication entirely, more solid than canvas, more ethereal than metal. The conical ceilings come to perfect points like the Great Pyramids, and slim flags are mounted on top, all of them uniformly black—but out of the corner of my eye, I swear they shimmer gold.

Soft white fabric forms doors, so patrons can still experience that all-important sensation of pushing through into another dimension. If the tents contain magical worlds, there must be doors. Thresholds. Entries.

When I am sure no one is watching too carefully, I put my hands all over the outside of one of those tents. It is slick as rubber, my fingers sliding along the surface like a skater on ice—it's not weatherproofed with paraffin wax, but something better. So this is how Cornelius can sell tickets even during windstorms and violent rain. The velour, as I pass through a doorway, ripples like a pond in Kentucky. Material of the highest quality. Material of the most expensive.

Arturo could never afford it. He could never stop his frivolous spending to save for it.

And so he loses out on the chance to sell more, more, more.

The concession booths are not tucked back in the midway, stationary, like ours in the Family Fortuna, but seem to appear every twenty paces or anytime you are craving a bite, whichever is closer. They serve the usual fare, but consummate versions— the Adam and Eve of shaved ice with rainbow syrup, and baked parmesan pretzels the size of my head, and spun sugar on sticks— fairy floss, they call it, which immediately and magically makes me crave a bite even though I've consumed so much of the fluffy sugar over the years, my teeth ache at the mere idea.

But Cornelius's own inventions are otherworldly—marbled coffees that swirl in mugs with edible straws, potato chips soaked in vinegar and parsley that somehow still crunch, roasted walnuts dusted with nutmeg, fluffy marshmallows shaped like clouds, drizzled in lightning bolts of dark chocolate.

I fork over half a penny for what they call sweet nachos— a pile of bruised Ambrosia apple slices slathered in hot caramel and sprinkled with vanilla-ginger pumpkin seeds and toffee. My guilt over handing money to the enemy is gone the minute I take a nibble—treachery never tasted so good. These are worth diving into hell for.

"Well! That's the magic touch of money." I can hear my father's snide assessment even from here; I can feel the itchy heat of his discomfort to be standing among such regal banners and bunting. "Spend a couple thousand of Daddy's trust on this much satin, and of course the cowpunchers will come a-running. It's simple math."

No, I push back in my mind. *You're jealous. You're so jealous, you're pissing green. This isn't about money. Cornelius is a merrymaker, just like you, and he's good. He's really fucking good.*

It would shred Arturo up to see just how good Cornelius is.

It's soul-stirring to chide my father with the backhand of truth, even if he isn't here to take it.

I am here.

Skipping happy as a cricket, I head farther into the veritable wonderland, winding through the circus, my mind set into a kaleidoscopic whirl.

I could belong here.

I could make myself belong here.

Arturo treats me like a dirty stray, even though I roll over and fetch without fail, but I am worth hundreds.

And I am going to prove it.

Synchronized daredevil diving, half a penny for the cheap seats! Watch the Swann Sisters twist and soar, then land in the pool with nary a splash! Don't miss these bathing beauties—spots for you, your wife, your sons!

Sword-swallowers from Slovenia! Stilt-walkers from Norway! Foot-fiddlers from Panama! See it all, hurry, hurry, right this way!

The rattle of the drumline, the unanimous gasp at the swinging trapeze, the quiet buzz of the lights, all electric, all steady compared to the oily flicker of our own gas lamps back in the dirt—

And the good people of Peculiar, strolling alongside me, a grateful bunch.

But every circus comes to an end eventually; every circus has a row of tents that is, to the unsuspecting patron, the cliff at the edge of the known world. Beyond those tents is the yard, where performers escape to smoke roll-your-own bogies, touch up their powder, let their bellies hang out, and otherwise be their less-than-polished selves without any cake eaters gawking at them. Not even Cornelius can make a gig stretch around the whole world.

I find that edge here at Le Cirque Americana, and as I march up to an usher, fully caparisoned in the richest of white-tailed habiliments, his smile tightens and he says, "I'm afraid it's employees only past this point. I do believe the orangutans are about to start their polkas in the easternmost tent, if it interests you."

I plant my feet and sing out, "I'd like to see your proprietor, please."

The usher snorts. "Mr. Reve is very busy. Now, move along, and have a splendid evening."

But I remove my spectacles to polish them on my hem, and I smile with my eyes, serpent sly—and I do not feel ashamed to tell you I learned this from Arturo. The circus is the only school I ever had, and I have always been a dedicated student.

"Oh, a thousand pardons for the intrusion. But you see, it's regarding your neighbors here in Peculiar. The ones across the way? I'm sure Mr. Reve is discriminating with his time, but I'm also sure he'll want to see me—and he'll certainly want to hear what I have to say about the Fortunas."

It does the trick.

"Right behind the tableau wagon, you'll find the stable tents. Ask for Miss Cline. She's Mr. Reve's assistant—if you want to see him, you have to go through her."

His words have a tinge of warning to them, but I walk away from him without even a smidgen of uncertainty.

Sweet-talking is never an obstacle for a Fortuna.

Good Lord, I chuckle, *if only Arturo could see me now. Maybe this would finally shut him up.*

An Offer

REN

FIND THE PROPRIETOR'S TENT BEFORE I FIND Cornelius's Miss Cline—I know my way around a circus, after all, even if Le Cirque Americana's backstage setup makes the Family Fortuna's look like a junkyard.

His tent stands out at once, the only splash of color among all the other snow-white domes, a golden silky thing that looks like it should have two camels and a gold-coined harem flanking its flaps.

No assistant to be seen, and no one is paying attention to the bookish young man hovering outside the owner's tent, adjusting his glasses, smoothing his corduroy jacket, as suspicious as a possum.

No one there to ask for permission.

What is the worst that can happen? I challenge myself. *You might be asked to leave? Well, fine.*

I have already endured much more than that.

I have already endured Arturo.

So I roll back my shoulders and barge into the tent, smile blazing like an asshole.

Smiling like Arturo.

Inside, the tent is luxurious and bedazzled, hung with brocade tapestries in silver and gold, the floor softened with fur rugs. The whole construct is held up by a single gilded pole right in the center, which means this is a small enough space that only one person can be in here at a time—aside from Cornelius, that is.

A powerful maneuver, to make your guests feel cramped and intrusive in your space. Arturo always tries to go big, cavernous, impressing with audaciousness and volume. But Cornelius seems to understand the surprising power of understatement.

And the legend himself is seated behind a mahogany desk, inking his John Hancock onto a stack of paperwork. A cabinet towers behind him, every drawer chock-full of files—a magnificent backdrop for a proprietor who clearly likes to handle his own red tape. I can't remember the last time I saw Arturo willingly touch anything made of paper—except for his money, of course. Every bill carried his fingerprints when it passed back into circulation.

So Cornelius bunks like a king, but he does not lounge like one.

Arturo is a sizzling stick of dynamite, but Cornelius is more like a clockmaker: steady, measured, in control. All suddenly feels right with the world.

I hold myself steady, my hands numbly hanging at my sides.

Cornelius Leon Reve is much older than I expected him to be, almost powdered, and slighter. Fragile. Has he always had such somber eyes? Like nothing on earth could entertain or dazzle him?

And finally he notices me. A quick flick of his eyes up and down my presence, lingering for a moment as he registers my less-than-average height. He picks up his tea, a pungent, rich-smelling liquid that carries a hint of something citrusy, like it's trying to make up for its sludgier parts; he sips at it medicinally, and I almost wonder if he is allergic to pleasure. But then I recall his twinkling countenance when he crashed through our banner, balanced atop one of nature's more preposterous creatures.

So, then, he is capable of devilish delight.

Good. I am here to bring him one such joy.

Taking me for a local sniffing for a way out of Dodge, he utters, "No open calls."

His voice is a door shutting, lock turned, key pocketed.

No questions. Not a smidgen of curiosity about why I am here or what it would take to get me to leave.

Nothing but the scratch of his pen and the faint shouts of the roustabouts closing down the circus for the night.

Luckily I am becoming very practiced at squeezing through locked doors.

"You'll want to know who you're turning away, at least."

He finishes writing his sentence and jabs out his punctuation before glancing up at me again with a faint, suffering smile. "And who are you?"

"I'm Arturo's head accountant, his manager, booker, handler, and only son. Or rather, I was until twenty minutes ago."

Cornelius is not like my father; he does not relish reactions.

He wants facts, plain and simple, so he can process and calculate the exact rational output of appropriate emotions.

But even so, I catch a whiff of his true response—a balk, a skipped heartbeat, his wrinkled throat bobbing up and down in surprise—before he coolly says, "Ah. The birthright in the flesh. Interesting. To what do I owe this visitation?" His scrutiny hits me like arctic waters as he asks, "Are you here to spy?"

"Not at all." I keep my hands laced neatly in front of me, my posture unfailing, my proud jaw indicating my confidence. "I'm here for a job."

Cornelius leans back into the leather of his chair. "I'm not sure I believe you. I know the kind of devotion his people have."

And I can't help it—I laugh. Shatter whatever poise I've been attempting to demonstrate and let my snort echo in the tent.

"He's bleeding. Not just money, not just customers, but performers. His own children are flying the coop—how's that for devotion?" The hairs stir on my arms, riled up without a prompt, but now that I have a captive audience, I go on. "I know everything about Arturo. I know how he runs his shows—his schedule, his routines, his overhead. He's an absolute visionary, one of a kind . . . but vision doesn't do shit if you're a complete dickhead."

Jesus Christ, it feels good to preach aloud, to say such things knowing the other conversationalist will agree, already agrees, already smells what I've stepped in and dragged through the door. I feel loosed, too, to speak in the muckety-muck vernacular of circus folk—not that I am prudish about such expressions, but

I have always prided myself on choosing the most enlightened words I can reach, recreating sentences and metaphors from my shelves of literature.

But there are times when a four-letter word has no cerebral substitute.

I beam at my candidness, but at the same time, an ache forms in my chest.

God, things could have been so different.

I could be sitting across from Arturo at the bonfire, the last customers trickling out of the gates. Drinks passed around, along with whatever concessions Socorro had left over. Mama could excuse herself to bed, kissing my forehead, straightening my collar, nagging at my father to dip into his Matthew and Mark before dawn.

My father could bark orders at a few errant grunts, then turn back to me and say, his mustache curling with smug self-importance, "What a show we had tonight, my son, what a miracle!"

"Yes, they were licking it up out of our palms tonight," I'd agree, then tilt back onto the bench, letting the stars overtake my vision.

I gave it all to my father, and yet I would have given more.

But he is an ingrate and a bastard.

And any final speck of compassion for him goes *kerplunk!* Right down into my guts, to be shat out in a hole somewhere. Buried forever.

Cornelius tut-tuts. "Arturo. Terrible at holding on to things, even after he's chased them—too much want greasing those fingers. Desperation. It's a shame, really." He holds his saucer as he drinks his tea. "So you want me to hire you as one final fuck-off to Arturo, is that it?"

"No." I swallowed, slicking my tongue. "I want you to hire me, and we'll end him." My leg muscles tremble with my hidden rage. I will tap dance for the devil himself before I ever work for my father again. "You'll hand me the knife," I finish, "and I'll stick it in his back."

My father's precious circus, stripped from him like a sweet stolen from a spoiled child.

The Family Fortuna, Arturo calls it. Because if we're a family, we won't ever push back. We won't ever leave. But we're not a family.

Mama, my sisters, Socorro, all the migrant workers who break their backs to pack and unpack our caravans, all our performers who survive Arturo's emotional fireworks so they can dazzle the masses—

We've always only been Arturo's piggy bank, his bottom line.

My home for twenty years, and in my head, it is already no better than ash and wind.

Cornelius runs a delicate finger around the edge of his tea-cup, a possessive, contemplative motion, as he considers me. He's searching for any excuse, any reason not to put me on the payroll for Le Cirque Americana, and he's coming up dry. All of Arturo's systems, his contacts, his every practice, right here on a silver platter. My brain, too valuable to pass up.

Cornelius and Arturo, they are not so different, but the places where they diverge are more vital than molars.

The only thing that could improve upon this situation would be a telescope so I could watch my father when he hears the news.

It's too much to hope that he might feel remorse, but I might be satisfied if he is so angry he yanks all his glorious hair out by the roots.

A single betrayal for a million tiny cuts.

"I'm terribly sorry, Mr. Fortuna," comes Cornelius's plush, patient response, "but I'm not in the market for any new staff members. Best of luck to you."

Something turns over within me. My smile stretches a tick wider, then falls. "I—what?"

Cornelius has already drained the last of his tea and purses his lips to see me still standing there. "You might write to Professor Noel's Radiant Prism in Albuquerque. Last I heard, he was looking for a decent stable hand for his ponies."

I feel like I've been kicked. "But I'm bringing you all Arturo's inner workings. His connections—everything you need to smash him—"

"I don't need to smash him," Cornelius counters. "Nor do I need whatever intelligence you think you're gifting me by coming here. I know enough about your operations over there. I know they're quaint, they're unpolished, and they're outmoded. Arturo himself sets plenty of fires. He'll burn himself down in time. I needn't wait much longer."

My head, plunged into a cold lake at twilight. My heart, stuck through with needles at every angle.

I waltzed in here so smug, so cocksure, so *Arturo*—

But I am the same here as I am there.

Nothing.

"Now, there is one asset I'd be willing to take from Arturo's clutch, if you're offering me my pick of the bunch." Cornelius's face suddenly splits into a wolfish grin, and pain ripples through me, fresh and searing.

No. Please, no. Not—

"That Bird Girl of his. Your sister, isn't it? The Spectacular Aviary Extravaganza? Arturo loves that act. So do the people— every showing is sold out. We don't typically peddle such . . . unusual performances, but perhaps you might negotiate a meeting for me with your father's beloved showpiece?"

He wants Avita.

Avita, the crown jewel, the feather for his cap. The face that launched a thousand standing ovations.

Suddenly I am back in Big Burp's dime museum, outshone by Avita's face on a flyer.

And I understand.

I will never be seen as long as I am standing next to her. Not by my father, not by Cornelius, not by any of this world I am a part of.

I drag myself out of Cornelius's tent without another word. I can be silent as well as invisible. No one calls after me.

Did I request thee, Maker, from my clay to mould me man? Did I solicit thee from darkness to promote me?

Milton scrolls through my mind unbidden.

I never asked anything of my father—only to love me and be loved by me.

I did not ask to be born to this family. I did not ask to be part of this world.

And since this world does not ring out with supplication for me to stay, please, stay . . .

I turn to a new horizon. A new world.

A History

ONE SCORCHING MORNING WHEN I WAS YOUNG, Papa woke me at sunrise.

"Breakfast now?" I muttered, dazed with sleep, and tried to pull my quilt over my face.

"Get dressed." Papa's hot, sharp breath blended with the remnants of my morning dreams. "Today's the day." And my toes jittered, gleeful enough to rise up into the air as vapor.

We'd just arrived in Cody, and the blue of the skies suggested God himself wanted us here. It was bold to set up a gig in this place. We'd be competing against the nearby medicine shows, the rodeos, the stampedes, the opening of elk season—but Arturo Fortuna was not known for his timidity.

Papa led me into a newly staked tent, the bleachers cobbled into their stairlike structure, fresh dirt in the aisles.

Nerves raced through my system, accelerating me toward a horizon I'd been looking toward for years now:

Getting in the ring. Getting under the spotlights.

Other children of the circus were thrust out in front of the crowds as young as six days old. Luna had performed as a clown for as long as I could remember. But thus far I'd been restrained, held back until Papa deemed me ripe enough to peddle.

He'd promised me.

An act of your own.

Into the center of the ring I skipped, taking in the cavernous space. Without all the butts in the seats, the tent seemed massive, its own continent.

My father nestled himself onto the front bleacher, leaning back into the old wood. "Now, go ahead. Dazzle me." Papa wasted no time with niceties; even the earliest hours of the day were money.

All this space, all this room—I was minuscule in the ring, and with Papa's quibbling eyes tagging my every move, I went rigid with apprehension, that old flop sweat stopping up all my good thoughts. "I'm really ready?" I sought assurance.

"Of course you are, my dove," Papa soothed. "You were born for this—born to be hand-fed to those crowds. They'll guzzle you down and ask for seconds—you simply must choose what you're going to feed them."

"I thought I could dance," I said. "I've been practicing a song—"

"Avita, my sweet." He dropped his voice to a whisper, and chills erupted along my arms. God, how he could flex his words and move worlds with a single syllable. "You've been waiting for this your whole life. A little ditty? A hornpipe they could see at any hurdy-gurdy hall? No! You're special, my kitten. One of a kind. Now, do something that will truly dazzle me."

In the center of the ring, there was an empty cage. I recognized it immediately as one of the cages for the big cats—Betsy the Bengal tiger had just "retired" on a farm upstate. It must have been hers, not yet hauled off to its proper jurisdiction.

I eyed the cage, its cold steel bars. The cats made me sneezy, and I could tell there was something about my beak they didn't trust.

Dazzle me.

There was plenty of room for me—Betsy had been ginormous. I crawled into the cage and buckled my limbs. *Fans from Texas to Tacoma*, I chanted in my head. My first time in the ring, and it was nothing like I imagined.

On the other hand, Papa practically drooled when he saw me, my beak nose poking through the bars. "My sweet, you are going to be a star. But a girl in a cage is a starting point, not an act." Inspired to lecture, Papa jolted up to standing and paced the ring. "In every act, there is one important ingredient—"

"You say that like it's a recipe," I said.

"It is a recipe," he said, "and without the proper ingredient, no one will eat it. Now shut up."

My knees hurt. "So what is this big important ingredient?"

Papa rolled his mustache between two fingers, as if coaxing the answer to my query out of his mouth like it was a fine instrument. "Ah, the ingredient is my secret, and it's the reason the Family Fortuna has bookings fifty weeks out of the year while other circuses only sell tickets when their baby elephants are born."

I forgot I was crammed inside a cage for beasts and smiled, pride running through me.

Every few years, a new circus family popped up and hounded our trail. They took our gigs, one-upped our acts, poached our customers. But they all washed up in the end. They all closed their canvases, sold their costumes, went back to normal life. Back to being ranchers, or bakers, or beggars.

We could never be normal. We were Fortunas.

And Fortunas did not dish out commonplace songs or dances. I would amaze my crowd with a different sound.

I let out a growl, a pathetic, hollow noise. Even I was underwhelmed.

"No, no," Papa coached. "If you're going to growl, make it big. Terrify me. Make me piss in my boots." He came closer, clapped in my face, and in response to that sharp, violating clatter, I summoned a noise from my depths. Curled my fingers into claws. Bared my strange, mirrored lizard teeth and filled the tent top to bottom with my growl.

"Yes!" Papa nearly wept with excitement. "Very good, very, very good! Now, let's see it."

I shifted, waiting for instructions that didn't come.

"You want your own ring, your own fans?" Papa said. "Then convince me. You have a cage. You have a growl. You have that glorious, wondrous face! Show me you can cook up an act."

"But you didn't tell me the secret ingredient!" I complained.

"And if you figure it out," he said, "then I'll know you're ready."

He plopped himself back on the bench, and I pouted. We both knew Papa could have just tossed me into the ring and cranked on the spotlight. People would have come. People would have paid to stare—he knew this. But showmanship ran thicker through his veins than even greed.

My heart pounded—not stage fright, but Papa fright. This was my chance to impress him, to prove I was the star he'd always wanted me to be. But what was he expecting me to do? Choreograph my entire act alone in sixty seconds? My very Fortuna blood was at stake.

I thought. The performance I wanted wasn't titillating or violent; it was simple and honest. I wasn't easy to look at—I knew this—but I had always thought I'd dance, moving around the stage so gracefully and quickly, an audience wouldn't have a chance to fixate on my face. I wanted to stop looking like a bird and start moving like one.

But the desire to please my father decayed my insides, rotting away every other thought. His dreams for me washed away my dreams for myself.

I closed my eyes.

They won't believe their eyes.

I shifted onto all fours like an animal. Three breaths, in and out, and I transformed, in mind and in essence. Another growl surged from me until my chest rumbled, and I shook the bars of the cage so they rattled a jangled tune.

Frustrated, caged beast, I tried to project.

Papa's face was blank.

I froze. It was palpable—with every second I spent in this cage, I could feel Papa's attention draining, slipping from me like sand. I'd heard about this, about this darkness when an act lost its audience. I wasn't prepared for how devastating it felt. How personal.

A dying performance had a corpselike stink to it, and with every tick of Papa's pocket watch, it made my nose burn, choking me.

In a panic, I glanced around me for something, anything, to save me.

One of Socorro's chickens, a plump white hen, strutted across the ring. The damn birds were always escaping their coops, walking in and out of the tents and leaving slimy smears of shit for the customers to track all over the circus grounds.

My fear melted like ice in vomit.

A secret ingredient.

I attacked the chicken, grabbing it through the bars of the cage, channeling the power of the huge scary desert hawks that carried away water snakes for dinner. It squawked and fluttered and kicked at me with its sharp black claws.

Bird grabbing bird.

Then it didn't matter anymore what Papa was doing or thinking—all that mattered to me was that someone was watching.

An audience.

My breathing changed—heaving, turning hot inside me. I wondered if I was as red as I felt, burning up with adrenaline.

Mama didn't perform. Not anymore. She gave up her act to raise her babies, then raised pigs when her babies were grown. But some nights, if it was stormy, she'd wax nostalgic and tell us about the circus's early days.

"There's a moment where everything else melts away, and it's just you and the lights and the stage." Her eyes would go soft, rain pitter-pattering on the wagon's roof. "That's the moment we all live for," she'd whisper.

Pay was feast or famine for a circus worker, even for a headlining performer. We all lived out of suitcases and bunks, rolled through the world in wagons. We never stayed in a place long enough to put down roots. But that moment, the one Mama was talking about—the moment I was feeling now, with the chicken in my hands—made it all worth it. It was the reason why everyone stayed.

I was transformed. I really was a hawk; I was every hawk that had ever lived. I was old as the hills, a starving dog staking out a piece of meat, predator and phantom, nightmare incarnate.

Tightening my grip on the hen, I could feel her heart, the life flowing through her.

Papa wanted a show? I'd give him a show.

With an inhuman roar, I bit the chicken's head clean off. Sinews stretched, flesh pierced under my teeth, and the neck snapped. For a second I paused, warm blood drizzling down my chin.

Papa didn't move, but I got a good look at his face—pale, mouth opening and closing like a landed trout.

The spell broke. I spat out the chicken's head, watched it roll in the dirt. The taste of dirty fowl blood permeated my tongue. I was shaky, adrenaline leaving my body in waves.

"Unexpected," Papa finally managed to say. "The secret ingredient is the unexpected."

My grin stretched so wide my cheeks ached. I had done it—I had shocked the man who had seen everything.

"Does this mean I'm ready to be a star?" I said.

Papa picked up the chicken's head, inspecting the carcass where I'd ripped it loose. "It means you're a chip off the old block," he said. "Instincts of a showman. Yes, my rose, you're going to be a star."

It was me. My show. Always mine.

Always me, reaching for a scream. Always me, giving them a thrill.

It would have been so easy to wish away this face.

To despise it, to fantasize about my own features matching my siblings':

Luna's smooth cheekbones.

Ren's wide mouth and square white teeth.

A nose, slim and turned up, a cleft at its end, like Papa's.

Hazel eyes, clever like Mama's.

The feathers on my body shrinking and falling off. Nothing but young skin, untested, utterly human.

It was too easy to look at this face, this gloriously hideous form, and decide that I'd been duped. Defecated on by fate.

But it was never just about my face.

It was always, always about the whole act—

The curtains, the ringmaster's introduction, the drum roll, the name of my show on the ticket, the secret ingredient. All of it worked in harmony with my face.

A face that could never be obscured by glittering costumes or swift dancing. A face that could never be softened by hurdy-gurdy standards or unflinchingly musical vocalizing.

No, this face was made for grabbing people by the throat. This face gave the gift of jamming your senses, of making you forget everything you'd ever seen before, everything you thought you understood about the world.

And I couldn't wish away something as special as that.

Last night, I'd left the crossroads sometime after midnight, still burning, my thoughts running amok.

Mama's words had done little to comfort me. Instead they'd drawn me through time, hurled me back to my very first performance.

Me in the ring with my audience of one.

I'd wandered along the desert road, following it down Peculiar's main drag, letting my ire and my bewilderment keep me awake. When I came back to our circus grounds, it was nearly morning. I did not want to go back to my wagon, where I'd lie on my own bed surrounded by the trifles and indulgences my father had dispensed for my unyielding submission. That felt too much like returning to Arturo himself, and I was not yet ready to confront him.

Not until I had confronted myself.

So I hid.

Socorro would have had me, but Papa would have scoured her wagon first.

Fernando, too, would have let me hide in his bunk—even if

he'd had other plans for it—but Papa would have yanked me out of there by my big toe and rebuked me upside down.

I considered every nook in our grounds—the clown tent, the hollow beneath the ribbon fliers' platform, the pastures, the space behind the big cat enclosure.

My aim: Anywhere I could sit in darkness. Anywhere I could hold my fire. Anywhere I could go where Arturo would not find me.

In the final hour before dawn, when the ticket booths were still closed and the spotlight on my banner was pinched shut and the Family Fortuna was a-snooze until the opening hour, I tucked myself into the one place I knew would remain unsearched:

My cage.

Wrapped in my slipcover, wrapped in every show I'd ever performed, my back against the cold iron bars, I hid, and I slept through the rest of the morning and the coming day.

I awoke sober.

I awoke clear of mind, my heart drumming evenly, my feathers soothed and lustrous, my purpose as plain as the beak on my face.

It was a beautiful evening, the weather made to order. I wove through the tents and the midway, swiping a glistening hot churro from Socorro's booth, lifting the bottom of my scarf to eat it, savoring every sugary bite.

Arturo was a difficult man to challenge, but I was difficult, too.

How I was my father's daughter.

My yearning was tight as a kernel inside of me, and as I got closer and closer to the family wagon, where Papa would be dusting off his tailcoat from the afternoon horsie games and regreasing his mustache for the evening shows, I could picture it like it was yesterday—

Those boys climbing up on one another to see inside my window.

My father tallying up the lifetime of tickets his Bird Girl would peddle. "My million-dollar gal," he loved to trill, the magnificence of the possibilities filling him like a holiday ham. "They won't believe their eyes."

I'd surprised him once. I could do it again.

But when I walked into the family wagon, juiced up for a wrangle, I was the one who was surprised.

Drinks with the Devil

I STOOD IN THE FAMILY WAGON, MY TENDERIZED heart ready for the grilling.

But so far, no flames—only my father seated in the rocking chair, his mustache frizzled, his tailcoat in a heap on the floor, absolutely silent.

Papa's bed was unmade, yet by the look of his pillow, he hadn't gone horizontal last night for very long. The bed jutted out from my parents' room in the family wagon at an angle like a spoke from a wheel, facing both the door and the window. Plenty of room for my father to pace and twitch his nights away, the kingly bed meeting anyone who entered the royal chambers with its messy authority.

Mama's bed was tucked into the dim corner near the wash table, the quilts neatly smoothed and folded and pillows punched and fluffed until they held their shape.

Her only view to carry her off to sleep (besides the view of her manic, scheming husband) was a wall of old circus posters, a copy of every one Papa had ever commissioned. We'd printed, stacked, tucked, and stapled these all over the Southwest, on fences and lampposts, in barbershop windows and on saloon mirrors, slapped on the backs of farmers' carts and coal cabooses. At least one of our posters had hung on the swinging door of every shitter in the tristate area, and here were the remains of that great collection—age-warped, wrinkled, fading in the crosshairs of sunlight and lantern blaze.

You could recount the years by those posters, and that's exactly what I did, recalling how the timbre of my audiences' shrieks changed depending on how dry the air was, remembering how fast my bleachers filled up in Albuquerque last year, when the summer storms turned the main drag into a red dust river and I'd taken it upon myself to turn any skeptics who had begrudgingly purchased tickets just to get out of the rain into full-blown Fortuna devotees.

In the future, when our posters for this Peculiar gig hung on the wall, I would remember the time I'd fished for golden applause with an honest song straight from my heart . . . and gotten an earful of screams instead.

I'd remember the gig where I changed everything.

"Papa, I—"

I stayed where I was, eyeing my father, taking in the strangeness of his muted, draggle-tailed presence.

It felt like the scales of the universe had tipped completely vertical, sending everything toppling into its opposite. The sea hanging overhead. Snow sizzling as it fell. Children complaining of old age and babies sprouting beards. Feet grasping at pens and hands shoved into boots.

Arturo without words.

"Papa, I'm sorry," I said, earnest as a fever. "I'm sorry for leaving, and I'm sorry for upsetting the show." If he was waiting for me to say I was sorry for trying something new in my tent, he could go ahead and dig his own grave—he'd be waiting forever.

He finally spoke.

"Sit." Papa clinked two glasses on top of his dresser and gestured behind me. "Mama keeps a bottle of whiskey behind her Bible there. See if she's got any left."

Yes, right in Mama's nightstand, a half-drained bottle of Southern Comfort. My father poured us each an inch, immediately sucked his down with an audible lip smack, and poured himself a second.

I cupped my hand around my glass but did not drink. It was enough just to hold the amber liquid, to imagine it burning down my pipes. My thoughts were banging around in all directions, a galaxy of aimless comets, hell-bent on collision, and I wasn't convinced that booze would do anything except hasten the crash.

"You know Katsuki had a bum show last night?" Papa said, cutting through the quiet. "Nearly lost her thumb. Not because of Sasha, though. The damn cage door jammed, and she got impatient. She's lucky she can still count to ten."

I could picture it—Katsuki, our tiger mistress, rushing to yank her appendage free of the cage's metal teeth while the crowds chanted for Sasha to bare her glorious fangs again, which looked so gleaming and deadly against the soft velvet pink of her tongue.

"You've never bungled a show before," my father went on. "It's a record to be proud of, my dove—a long stretch of perfect performances." Only a half truth. Back in San Antonio, Tomás had been a pair of eyes and a silent, screamless butt in a seat. "But you were bound to louse up a showing sooner or later." He paused, sucking air through his teeth. "I just wish you'd done it when the stakes weren't quite so damn high."

I thought of Tomás again. I understood exactly how it felt to watch your audience skedaddle out of your tent knowing they were not sated, to know that you as a performer had not twisted to your full flexibility. To miss that connection.

But I wasn't going to let Papa twist this into a simple scuff-up when it was clearly a fully orchestrated rebellion.

"I didn't bungle anything," I insisted. "I would've hit every note if they'd let me sing. Every step, every twirl, on the money."

"Oh, my sweet." Papa reached to stroke my cheek; I let myself be comforted by his touch. "Yes. Yes, I wish you could do those things, too. I wish you could do more. But let's not forget . . ." As smoothly as a weasel, Papa took something from his breast pocket.

A mirror.

The round mirror fit perfectly in the grip of his palm. "If only things were different," he murmured. "If only you were different."

He held it up to my face, naked as the day I shot out of my mother—

But I pushed it away.

"No. No, I know what I look like. I don't need to be different. I need to get back in that ring."

I prepared myself for Papa to fling his fevered arguments back in my direction, but I was bamboozled by his demeanor.

My father sighed and leaned back in his chair like an arthritic old farmer. Arturo's words—where were they? Where had he stored them, and at what point would they come bounding back out of him like a goddamn jack-in-the-box?

I was ready for them. Ready to swat them away from me like killer bees aiming to wound—

But Papa merely reached into his coat pocket.

He produced a faded ticket, yellowing along the edges, and passed it to me without a word.

"Frederickson," I read dutifully, "July fourteenth, 1883." THE FAMILY FORTUNA, announced the bold type along the length of the ticket, a much plainer iteration of the tickets we printed now. "So what?"

"That," Papa said with a minuscule flourish, "is from your very first show."

Swept off my feet again.

Papa, sentimental? I'd never have believed it. But there it was, pinched between my trembling fingers: a ticket he'd kept in his precious coat pocket through wagon rides over rickety bridges, takedowns in blistering-hot rodeo grounds, show after show after show.

And he kept a piece of *this* show.

My first.

Away my mind wandered, traversing the rocky terrain of years, searching for that first time I ever performed in front of a paying crowd, searching for the details. Which row of bleachers was filled the highest, the blue or the green? What kind of chicken did I bite that night, a Jersey Giant or a Rhode Island Red?

Did I laugh after the show, or did I beam, or cry, or all three?

The worn ticket in my hand unlocked it—

I remembered the moment the curtain dropped, the noise of the audience fading along with the spotlight's warmth. I remembered the long tails of my father's black coat swooping around me as he lifted me up on his shoulders. I remembered riding through the city of emptying tents at closing time, Papa kicking littered white bags still sticky with cling-on pepitas out of our way, my stubby little-girl fingers gripping my mount by his astounding hair as we passed. "Our little sparrow did her first show tonight!" Papa had hooted to every worker who would listen. "She's a natural! Blew the house down!"

That voice, thick as uncured honey, heavy as satin, boasting about his peach of a daughter even though she had a face for an arranged marriage. That voice, rumbling around my dangling legs like the first tremors of an earthquake.

And here was that same voice now. Papa could make his tone gentle enough to pet, gentle enough that even a baby might be fooled into sleep, and the old desire was still in me, the need to make him proud of me. Proud of his sparrow, his kitten, his dove.

"When they gasped and screamed, and you stood there in your cage, just taking it in . . ." Papa tilted his head back, lounging in the triumph of this memory, of the night his own loin fruit became his greatest business resource, and I readied myself to feel invaluable and cheap at the same time—

"I was so relieved."

Again my insides clenched. Such a twist in my father's sentences I could not have predicted—but his bright eyes, focused on my face, were brimming with a patriarch's sincerity, not dollar bill signs.

"Do you have any idea what they'd do to you out in that ring?" Papa wiped a sheen of liquor-induced sweat from his upper lip. "Do you know what those crowds would do if I didn't tell them they were allowed to be afraid of you?" And then his exclamation point: "They would eat you alive. They would skin you and stuff you and pluck your feathers to take back home, just to prove to their friends that the monster from their stories is real." He took another quick dash of Mama's whiskey right from the bottle. "But I present you to them on a platter, and so they worship you."

A tent of your own.

From Texas to Tacoma.

All those tickets, all those shows.

All those screams.

My father was a greedy man, yes—but a father who loved his daughter.

A father who wanted to keep me safe, to transform me into an asset so no one would see me as a threat.

I'd thought it was a cage—my life, my act.

I'd thought my father's love was a cage.

"We were lucky last night," he concluded, his words gentle as the hum of a faraway train. "Lucky they didn't rip you apart."

His love, ironclad and bottomless, even deeper than his

theatricality, his charisma. He loved me more than he loved my face, my moneymaker.

I would trade everything in my wagon—every toy, every trinket, every spoil—to make this moment last for the rest of time.

Yet he was wrong.

My father was wrong.

Arturo Romero Fortuna, the finest grandstander on land and sea, and he was wrong.

And I would have to show him he was wrong, because my father loved to be right—and so I'd lead him to those pastures as patiently as he'd held my hands as a baby while I learned to toddle. I'd show him how to be right.

"If you tell them I'm a monster, they'll believe you." My knees turned to water, my honesty lighting up every one of my nerves. "You told me I was a monster, and I believed you."

Papa took in a prickled breath. "You tried, my goose," came his reply, right on schedule. "You tried to sing, and they screamed right over you. If those slack-jaws would only let you be anything but a horror—"

"No." A heart could get used to saying that word over and over—it awakened something in me every time I spoke it, the winds of a tropical evening stirring me to glory. "Did you stay upright on the first horse you ever rode? How much time did you spend in the dirt?" Those tales of Papa as a young cuss showboating for the rodeo crowds—they were emblazoned in me, as close to my soul as scripture. Our family stories, our origins, and I could recite the verses by heart.

Of course Papa was flung from those horses. Of course the crowds laughed and jeered.

And he shaped his act around those tumbles.

Every performer fell in the dirt at least once. The ones who became great were the ones who rolled around in it. Made the grimy bits the best part of the show.

Arturo had said it himself—he handed me to the crowds on a platter and told them exactly what I was.

It was time for me to reintroduce myself.

"But . . . *monster!*" Arturo's case was weakening; had he not been slightly boozed up by Mama's secret juice, he might have clapped this conversation closed long ago. Perhaps it was merely the juice, or perhaps it was the fatigue of our arduous rivalry in Peculiar, but Papa was soft right now, pliable as India rubber. I would keep kneading him until he flattened his own quarrels. "That word draws a thousand people in a hot minute! What can you possibly give them that will match it?"

"I know exactly what I'll give them." Even with my avian face, even with my strange beak and distorted proportions, the smile I flashed at my father now was a mirror image of his own devilish grin. A scoundrel's smile. "Something unexpected."

Arturo's mustache rippled. "The secret ingredient." His tone was rascally, full of sauce, and a needle pulled itself free from my heart. There my father was at last, that same circus moxie that he'd bred into me, and the sight of it shining sprightly and potent from his gaze had me nearly inside out with relief.

But then—

"Bullshit," Papa murmured. He leaned to the side, reaching for another nip of Mama's whiskey. "It's all bullshit, Avita. It always was. There is no Fortuna family recipe. There is no secret ingredient. There's only Cornelius and the rest of us pathetic clunkers who were dense enough to think we had a chance against him."

My father, full of stars, and yet here he came, crashing all the way down to the gutter.

Immediately I summoned a preacher's exuberance. "Don't be a sop! We just need to hold out a little longer—"

"We won't hold out! Do you understand me? It's over!" Papa grabbed his glorious black hair and tugged. "He had Peculiar the minute he pulled up and plopped his golden butt on our field. He's just letting us dangle for his own sick jollies until he rolls over us—"

"So let him." Righteous exuberance gave way to brazen confidence, the kind of pluck I'd learned from Arturo himself. "Let him roll over us. Let him spank us from here to Mexico. It doesn't mean we won't sell tickets to our own tents—we will. A metric fuck ton, like we always do."

Papa let his hands fall from his face, watching me.

"Because even if he makes enough money to gild his own ass, we'll always have one thing he doesn't have and never, ever will."

Bird Girl, my father thought—I could see the words twitching his lips, but I said something else that brought a quiver to his chin:

"We've got Arturo Fortuna, the greatest showman on God's green earth."

Arturo Fortuna leashed and collared every audience that strolled past his ticket booth. His showcases were so unmatched in wonder and shock, the Pope himself had condemned them as heresy. As a ringmaster, he brought his crowds so far up his ass, they made him into a sock puppet.

And I was goddamn proud to be his dove. His gleaming jewel. His daughter.

My father's exhibition of candor was done. He stood, smoothing the ticket from my first night in the ring. He pulled on his tailcoat and looked down at me, twisting his mustache.

"Your curtain goes up at sundown. Dry your eyes. I expect you there and ready to put on a show."

And I rose up like Lazarus, ready to remake myself with the rarest of gems in my possession: my father's trust.

You are the mirror when you are in that ring, he always told us. Tonight in my tent, I'd be ready for Arturo to look into the mirror.

And whatever it was he hoped to see, I would give it back to him.

Give it back to him tenfold—but what I really wanted to do was give it to myself.

A New World

REN

I T IS SURPRISINGLY EASY TO LEAVE.

I'd always waited for the tipping point, expected it would come like a cheap firework, a greasy explosion that singed my eyebrows and scared half my remaining years out of my nerves. Instead it turned out to be more like a kettle boiling, a hundred little shifts in temperature.

Avita ran out, and when I came home to pack, I learned Luna had also left, and then I added up every time Papa had spoken to me like I was hired help and not his flesh-and-blood child, and then Cornelius didn't want me—and now that I have sobered up, I see it for the mercy it is.

Now I can get out of this business altogether. No more orchestrating the unloading of the stake wagons, roaring myself hoarse to direct the boiler, the horses, the sledge drivers, the pole riggers. No more passing out the alfalfa when Arturo forgets to sign the checks, no more staying up to send off the night riders with the bills, no more waking at the crack of dawn to update the route book and set us rolling. No more arm wrestling with my father over every little detail, no more saving him from himself and going loony trying to make sure it always looks like his idea.

How could I do any of that for another show without constantly hearing Arturo's voice in my head, a snatch of every cruelty he's ever yelled at me, a catalog of his worst accusations?

No. I walk away now, and I walk away forever.

At the train station I buy a ticket: first to El Paso for a transfer, then to Philadelphia, and then a final switch up to the biggest city I know. If I am going to feel small, I'd like to do it in a place where everyone else feels small, too. It will take me nearly a week to get there, which seems like a torturously long time to stew over the uncertainty of my future. I don't have a job waiting for me. I don't have housing. I don't have security or anybody there to take me in and show me around. I will be completely and utterly alone.

And the trains will sequentially take me farther and farther from the Family Fortuna's territory—into new territory. I am jumping out of my skin with elation and simultaneously shaking like a newbie on the high wire.

"Hey." A frizzball of an attendant leans her head out of the train and addresses me where I stand on the platform. "Last call. Train's got to keep a schedule. You on or off?"

I am on.

I bought myself a first-class ticket, and I did it with Papa's money—money I slipped right out of the register. If he can blow a whole wad of cash on a moldy green tank that once held the mollusks at the South Point Aquarium, he can fund his only son's quest for self-actualization.

As a final fuck-you to him, I chose the most expensive ticket possible, and up until the moment I actually saw the seat, I thought that might have been a mistake. I thought maybe I was a fool for not saving that money for my new life in New York City, a fool to not stretch every dollar as far as it could possibly go without snapping. But the puffy pale blue seat is twice as wide as I am and soft as goose down beneath my tired ass, and all my regrets fly into the engine to be eaten with the coal as fuel.

All my life, Papa has fought to make the Family Fortuna as fancy and luxurious as his taste allowed while spending dimes instead of dollars, but I have always known he was tacky as hell.

Now I have confirmation.

The decor of this single train compartment has more class than every Fortuna put together. I nearly lose my head and ask for a downgrade to a worn-out standing-room-only coach, convinced that I, too, am too tacky to belong here, but a young man in a black suit looks up from his book, catches my eye across the aisle, and smiles.

Moby-Dick, he's reading.

I've not yet read it, though *Typee* caught enough of my fancy to entice me into a second Melville.

And it is as easy as that: a smile, a book, and I decide that this is where I belong.

There is a word in German, which I've never known how to properly pronounce, but I think of its definition now: the guilt that nibbles at you when you are in the throes of pleasure.

No such guilt nibbles at me now.

My office has been an outhouse. Now I make up my mind: in New York City, I'll settle for nothing less than a desk with a view, preferably overlooking water. I will find myself an employer who sees my brain as the marvel it is, pays me for it, speaks to me with the dignity owed to one's fellow man, and never sees my less-than-average size as any indication that I myself am less than average.

The train lets out steam and jolts forward, and before I can suppress it, I startle.

The man in the suit chuckles warmly. "Too fast for you?"

"Takes some getting used to," I answer honestly.

Thankfully the man and I have something else in common—we prefer silence. Silence is what I need as we roll through the country, through terrain I have traversed with the circus, but always in the mud-splattered wagons—a view that is never beautiful because it is too zoomed in, too close to the shit and the scabs and the split ends. To ride through the state in a train is the equivalent of removing your glasses. In this haze, this soft aspect, the world is at its loveliest.

I press my face against the window, but not too hard—I don't want to strain the bubble, the dream, this moment I've imagined a thousand times but never actually thought would happen.

I will miss my books.

I will miss my family—my sisters, my mother.

I will miss my desk—I'd finally arranged it all just so, all my papers perfectly organized, and now I am heading far away from anything resembling organization.

But I am also leaving behind my fears. The cruel words of that greedy bastard, who gave me my name and my jawline and every insecurity a person can have. He will never yell at me again.

I make eye contact with the man across from me again as I pull out one of the few novels I packed, a much-loved first edition of *Great Expectations*, and I nod.

Nothing is certain, except for one thing:

I am free.

And I am going to be fine.

There's another German word, and its pronunciation is also a difficult one, but its meaning is simple: the feeling that you have finally arrived.

The train is still running through Texas, but I feel as if I have finally arrived.

Commission

I KNOCKED ON THE CROOKED DOOR SAGGING IN its frame. The woman running reception for the Old Boot eyed my scarf with suspicion but gave me the information I sought with little begging. Perhaps she chose not to push odd-looking strangers too hard when the circus was in town.

Tomás opened his door and didn't work fast enough to hide the surprise on his face. "Avita. Hi. Sorry, I was just napping."

I took in the sight of him—the sleep crusting his eyes, his rumpled hair and shirt. A little less extraordinary here in the harshness of morning in a pay-by-the-day hotel, but you could say that about many things in our industry. The circus had a way of casting a glamour over everything in its wake.

I was nervous as a newly shorn sheep, but I gulped down my fright. "I'm here to ask for a favor."

"A favor?" He tilted his head.

I held up a fistful of bills. "Well, now, does it count as a favor if you're paid handsomely for it?"

Tomás frowned, and for a moment I regretted seeking out our Michelangelo—but then his mouth split into that wry smirk of a smile. There he was. There was that lighthearted, kindly boy I'd met in the pastures of San Antonio. "Come on in."

I peered around the room. It was tidy enough, aside from a damp towel hanging near a washbasin and a few crumbs on the nightstand.

"You're leaving soon," I assessed, catching a glimpse of the traveling bag on the bed.

Tomás busied himself with a coffee tray, splitting the remainder of his brewed joe into two cups—a gentlemanly gesture. "That's right. I'm off to chase Baron McKinney's Cirque Aeon—do you know it? Apparently they're due in El Paso tomorrow, and their posters are looking a little shabby. Or they will be, once I show them what I'm capable of." He passed a mug to me.

I studied it, swirling its contents. "You know," I said after a moment, "Le Cirque Americana must pay well. Cornelius is always looking for ways to stomp out any other showman who dares to breathe. I'll bet if you told him you'd just left Arturo's—"

Tomás laughed. "You've always got an angle for me, don't you? Thanks very much for the tip, but I've heard too many things about Cornelius. A real pain in the ass to his freelancers—he lures you in with an ironclad contract, then lowballs the snot out of you once you've already started the work. That's the reason he sends out for those fancy New Yorker printers—no one out here will work with him anymore."

I had to chuckle at this for Papa's sake; it appeared the Family Fortuna had a couple of things Cornelius would never get his silver mitts on. Those posters Tomás had painted for us? Those were now valuable originals to be hailed in the Family Fortuna archives as concession prizes forever.

"So." Tomás took a seat in a chair near the window. "What kind of favor are you here for? Another poster?"

I nodded. "Yes. A new banner."

He scratched the back of his neck, trying to hide his worry. "Uh-oh. Does Arturo not like the other one?"

"No, no. He loves it. It's a splendid banner." I spoke the truth—Tomás's depiction of the Spectacular Aviary Extravaganza was a marvel, a masterpiece, even if his portrayal had devastated me. I set my shoulders, my nerves jumping so hard they nearly made my ears flop. "This is for a new act." I handed him the money, politely looking away while he counted it. "Is that enough?"

He balked as if he'd been slapped. "This is more than enough—this is triple my usual rate—"

"Good," I cut in. "Because I need it in triple the time. This has to be ready to fly as soon as you set your brushes down."

Tomás frowned. "But the lithographers—"

"No lithographers," I commanded. "No need for them. It doesn't have to be on paper. I'll take whatever you can paint it on—do it on wood if you have to. But I need it ready to be hoisted in an hour. Can you do it?"

Tomás clenched the cash, peering around his room. In a corner I spotted his supplies; this would take a fair amount of his paint to complete, but with the money I'd passed him, he could restock with enough tubes to last him until the next century. "Will a bedsheet do?"

I watched him prepare his workspace, mesmerized. It was akin to watching Socorro fix up our grub tent for a decent meal—mixing his paints on his palette, sharpening his coal, preparing his drop cloths. With a chill, I realized I was privy to the sacred rituals of his craft; I tried to maintain reverence as I waited. It was possibly the most intimate thing I'd ever witnessed.

A gift, to be able to watch someone who truly loved their work.

"All right," he said at last. "I'm set. You just tell me what I'm doing. Another Bird Girl poster?"

"No. Well, in a fashion." I summoned bravado from my very bones, even as I trembled in my boots. "I want you to paint me. All of me. My face, my feathers, everything." I gave him a beat to digest my instructions. "*All* of me. And only me. Do you understand?"

Tomás did not hesitate. "I do." As a tender mercy, there was a chivalry reflected in his eyes. I basked in the warmth of safety, of knowing I could trust him to handle this delicate request with courtesy.

When I was ready, I stood in front of his easel, the sheet stretched taut along its frame. Only me, standing before him. My boots, my dress, my scarf, my underthings were tucked into a tidy pile at the end of his bed.

It couldn't have been a more sordid-looking scene. If someone were to walk in right then, they'd have accused us of all manner of sins. But the ways in which Tomás looked at me, scrunching up his brow, studying the lines and angles of my form, and the way

I held my pose steady, muscles stiff and unyielding, was anything but sensual.

I stood tall, my feathers in a crest around my neck. A pose that would've been at home in the Tent of Wonder—but not even Luna stripped herself this bare. I folded my arms across my chest and angled one leg in front of the other, arching sideways to hide my more confidential features. Otherwise it was all on display. The curve of my back. The half-moons of my ass. My legs, my ribs, my naked ankles . . . and my face.

I looked right at Tomás, imagining he was a tent full of spectators. Imagining he was a field full of ticket-holding patrons, and I looked at him the way I wanted to look at them.

Unapologetic. Vulnerable. Unafraid.

"Yesterday when I bumped into you outside my tent," I said after a moment, "I didn't mean to scare you."

"You didn't," he said. "Just startled me."

But I wasn't so easily convinced. I pushed back, savvy to the polite fibs of the world. "You certainly sounded scared . . . which is understandable. I know what I look like." This face scurrying through the circus grounds in the darkness—the sight would have coaxed a yelp out of Wild Bill.

Tomás lowered his hand from the easel. "There's a difference," he replied, eyeing me with patience, "between being truly afraid of something and a quick, cheap thrill."

He went back to his rendering, and I meditated on his words.

The scream that had come out of him last night—its noise had slapped me, cracked me right in the gullet. Right in the soul.

It had echoed through the meat of my brain ever since . . . but now when my memory played it for me, I could hear it. That difference.

Not the scream of someone facing a terrifying creature of night and fearing for his life, but the short, sharp squawk of someone briefly shaken up. I'd scared the bejesus out of him; he hadn't been praying to Jesus for rescue.

A scream could be innocent. A scream could mean revulsion, but a scream could also mean sheer delight.

The symphony of cries I'd heard in my tent during every gig I'd ever played—they washed over me now, and I listened for every note: tones of merriment, of alarm, of foreboding and of dread, of exhilaration and nausea and abhorrence.

I was more than just my face, and a scream could mean more than just fear.

Still, it could be that Tomás was lying to me, sparing my feelings. Perhaps I really had frightened the piss out of him, and he didn't want to admit it now.

The notion that Tomás might tend to my feelings with sensitivity was also pleasant to consider.

He worked diligently, running his gaze along the parts of me that I had never imagined I'd showcase this openly—

And yet it was my face, out of every square inch of me, that felt the most exposed.

My beak.

My mouth.

My bottomless eyes.

When he had the shape of me down, Tomás told me I could sit. I dressed slowly, then took a seat in a chair near the window.

There I waited as if frozen in a tableau until he finally announced, "All right. Finished. It really should dry before it's moved at all—"

"No time," I said. "It needs to be hung right away."

He held out the sheet, taking in his handiwork with a pleased air. "Well, come take a peek, then."

I crept around the easel, careful not to step on the damp globs of paint dotting the drop cloth.

I looked, and I saw—

"Splendid," I pronounced. "Absolutely perfect. Just one more thing: Help me get it flying before you leave?"

Tomás carried the banner gingerly across the circus grounds, with promises to take it to the grunts and supervise them as they strung it up the flagpole.

"What about the old banner?" he asked, studying the way it currently rippled between the tents.

"Leave it," I said. After all, I couldn't deny the truth of this physiognomy—I was monstrous through and through.

I was a great many things.

I would not hang around to see it raised; I had other tasks to attend to in preparation for my new debut. And Tomás, as soon as he'd handed off his work, would head for the train.

"Thank you," I told him, and when his gaze locked upon mine, the world spun around us. I fizzed with affection, warm as goose down. "You'll make it to Paris. I know you will. You're talented enough."

"And you'll make it . . ." Tomás paused, considering me with some amusement. "No, you've already made it."

I smiled, showing all my glassy razor teeth. "No. I'm only getting started."

Birds of a Feather

A LONG WHITE GOWN WITH A PEARL HEADDRESS. A military getup: short navy pleated skirt and brass buttons.

Something lacy with bloomers and a parasol.

A full-body stocking of transparent black nylon.

Capes of velvet, flower halos, fur-lined singlets.

Fernando and I scoured the costumes in the dressing room. I had a hell of a performance to give tonight, and I was buzzing for it with every cell in my body.

We just had to find the perfect gimmick.

"What about . . ." Fernando held up a zebra-striped catastrophe, and I nearly shook my head off my shoulders.

Back to the racks, then.

Back to the dozens and dozens of versions of myself I could be.

My silence might have been interpreted as nerves or as subterrestrial thoughtfulness; in truth it was nothing more than frozen concentration, dedication to this colossal task: to prove myself worthy of more than just screams.

My fingers brushed it first.

I knew it by feel, by the soft satin of the bodice, the minky liquid of the skirt, and by the flutter of memory in my guts.

"Christ," Fernando whispered as I tugged it out into the light. "Do you think it'll—"

"Yes." I didn't need measurements, didn't need a fitting. "It'll work."

Another dress of Luna's, something she'd worn from time to time when she needed to make a bang of a spectacle. Last time I'd put on one of her old garments, it had sagged, clearly wrong for my frame, but this one would fit. I knew it would, because this time I wasn't counting on the costume to upstage my hideousness.

This time I'd be dressing to match my own face.

Luna had left all her costumes behind, most of her shoes, as well as the brushes and perfumes and assorted tokens from her scores of loyal fans.

And she'd left this gorgeous piece, this slinky black corseted singlet with the half skirt that trailed out in a train wide enough to be staked and used to house a show of its own.

I knew Luna would be pleased to see it in my hands. I'd show this old getup a hell of a good time.

When I locked eyes with Fernando, we did not need full sentences.

"With the—" he started.

"Exactly," I confirmed. "And what do you say you—"

"Brilliant. All that color." Fernando scanned my hair, face, neck, hands, every part of me that could be further ornamented.

I trusted him—trusted him to blow up this surprise, make a firework out of me.

"Do you know what you're going to do yet?" he asked, reaching out to fluff my hair, dreaming up something fabulous.

I shook my head. Specifics of my act were still piecing themselves together. All I knew was that I would make them love it. If I danced, I would make them stomp their feet. If I sang, I would make it their favorite song.

I was my father's daughter, after all. I knew how to put on a hell of an act.

"Whatever it is," Fernando assured me, "it'll be spectacular. Now, we've got a lot of work to do before your curtain goes up." He hung the costume on a full-length mirror, determined that it needed a steam, and took the pressing iron to the coals.

When he returned, he plopped me in front of a vanity and started sectioning my hair, using clip after clip to divide the locks so he could work his magic.

"So. A bit of dish," he started.

I was thrumming with the impatient joy of preshow perturbations and also desperate for a distraction before I worried myself to shreds. "Spill," I encouraged.

"That cowboy from San Antonio? The one I was—" He paused, momentarily prudish as he searched for the right words.

I provided them swiftly and without judgment. "Tangling tongues with? Yes, go on."

"Charlie. His name's Charlie." Fernando glanced at me briefly in the mirror before adding, "Sullivan."

I absorbed this utterance like a pie to the face. "As in—Sullivan Hall?"

My best friend nodded, taking a comb to the crown of my head.

Sullivan Hall, grandest and most renowned of the hurdy-gurdy halls in California, was the golden-palaced dream of many a dancing girl who worked in our kootchie tent. Their stag events attracted the wealthiest beaus of the West Coast, many of whom were searching for sweet little slices to spoil and support while they dallied behind their too-tired wives' backs. Sullivan paid his dancers more than fairly, treated them like royalty, and dressed them in finery from his costume shop the size of a barn—

And I had a hunch, even before Fernando confirmed it, that this last detail was a key ingredient in this particular dish.

"Sullivan Hall is looking for a costumer," Fernando said, laying it out, "and Charlie offered to introduce me to his uncle."

I watched as he volumized my hair, clamped it with hot tongs, rolling it into perfect barrel waves. This entire dressing tent, these racks of frippery, this metric of aesthetic that the Tent of Wonder had become famous for . . . Fernando had built it up from scratch. Starting from nothing when he'd scampered into our circus, he'd turned a line of wannabe cancan girls into the duchess's own consorts, bejeweled beauties, a resplendent pageant to behold.

And now he had an invitation to go work his magic somewhere else—somewhere he could truly glitter and shine.

"Vee, what should I do?" I heard no hints or breaks in his

voice, no clues that he already knew what he wanted and was simply fishing for a confirmation.

"I would miss you," I told him instantly, truthfully. "If you left, I would miss you every single day."

He knew me too well to let this statement stand alone; he could hear the *but* in my words. In the vanity, his reflection cocked one eyebrow.

But how could I possibly tell you to stay? How could I encourage you to turn down this opportunity, possibly the biggest chance of your life, to stay here in the dirt with a megalomaniac for a ringmaster and a kootchie tent with no duchess?

"What would you tell me," I finally said, "if I had this chance? What would you say? Because that's what I want you to do. I want you to do exactly what you'd want for me." My heart shattered as I said it, and I refused to picture the possibility—the Tent of Wonder without its soul, the costumes hanging solemnly on their racks, forlorn without their maker.

But things change.

For better or worse, things change.

"This is my family here. You are my family. This job, this show . . ." Fernando peered around us, and I followed suit.

All of these girls sitting in tights and petticoats and half-buttoned shirts, preparing for a showcase to twist our audience's necks, give them shivers and stars.

"But maybe you were made for more." My chest brimmed with tenderness. There it was, that welling of tears, that sniffle of beak as I said the thing I wished my father had said to me.

"Well. None of that matters tonight. Tonight the world revolves around one thing and one thing only." Fernando fluffed, plumped, laced, and polished until he pronounced me perfect.

A glance in the mirror, and I rippled as if underwater.

As if in a dream.

I clung to his shoulders, a strange tremble in my muscles. "I feel weird. Like I'm about to fall over a wave."

Like I'm on the cusp of something.

A cliff, a hill, a road.

About to slam off the edge of the world.

Fernando's smile for me was untiring. "I believe that's what all stars say before they shoot themselves across the night sky."

There it was.

My commission, waving above the circus.

The sun had not yet drowned in the horizon, but it had started its eventide descent, and it cast its golden bloom in a perfect frame around my banner.

Pausing outside the kootchie tent, scarf tied tight around my wares, I looked, and I saw—

My hair, rivulets of gleaming black, streaming down my shoulders.

My frame, inviting and strong and proud, though not without modesty; Tomás's brushstrokes were celebratory, my limbs shapely, my curves generously depicted.

My gaze unflinching.

Those black eyes stared out at the circus crowds with

unmistakable invincibility. *Say what you will,* they encouraged, *but never can you say I am afraid.*

And my face, this simply staggering face—

Tomás had captured in his portrait everything I loved best about my face. Its gruesome bits, its unheralded charms.

I could have outpranced a pony. I could have set a cauldron to boiling with only my piping hot glee.

A banner I had commissioned of myself, by myself.

I could not believe my eyes.

Behind me, I heard snatches of commentary:

"What in the blue blazes is that supposed to be? A new show-girl in the kootchie?"

"Jesus, that's quite the mug on that gal, isn't it? Quite the bump, too."

"You could always stick a bag over the top, couldn't you?"

"Looks daft. Looks like a Fortuna."

"I'm getting my ticket, are you?"

"Avita."

The last speaker sounded hoarse with despondency, the word nearly splitting apart with exhaustion. When I turned to peer at my mother, her appearance matched right up; her good eye had the red starbursts of someone who hadn't had a decent night's sleep in days.

My whole being seized up, recalling our last exchange up at the crossroads. "Mama—"

But she shook her head. As her hair shifted, I caught glimpses of a few gray strands piercing through her scalp like icicles.

She looked at the new poster as if it were winged and breathing fire, diving down to gobble her up. Pain wrenched her mouth into a pucker.

When she locked her gaze on me again, it was there, unmistakable: fear, shining like a flame.

Fear of her daughter. Fear for her daughter.

Part of me longed to run to her, to let her fold me into her arms, to feel the beat of her heart steady against mine. Part of me longed to promise her I would go back to my cage, keep myself safe, so she would never again have to gawk at me with such trepidation.

But no daughter can cage herself forever.

I kept my chin high as I turned on my heel, heading into the dressing room to prepare for my show.

If she wanted to keep watch over me, to keep me safe, she could take a seat on the bleachers and watch me fly.

All of them would watch while I took to the sky.

Winged Things

MAMA

THE FIRST LIFE, I LOST BEFORE I KNEW I WAS with child. I'd barely noticed my monthly bleeding was late, and then the bleeding came, and I understood.

The second life, I lost in South Bend. The pine trees stood watch as I washed out my sheets. I did not let myself cry, though Arturo wouldn't have minded; I kept looking at Luna and Ren and hissed at myself to be grateful.

On the third loss, Arturo had questions: Were there any remnants? Anything to show at all?

I knew what he was thinking. God help me, I had already thought of the same thing.

We'd seen so many things in jars: stagnated piglets and crocodiles and, yes, human fetuses, all displayed in sideshows on the road. The idea of displaying our own creation was tempting.

"No," I told him. "No, there's nothing. Unless you want to rinse out my skirts for weeks and wring out the blood."

He left it alone after that.

When another little life burrowed itself in my guts, Socorro fed me chicken soup with carrots and piping hot atole. "Not for the baby," she informed me. "For you. For your strength." When my belly swelled and warped my shadow, Arturo insisted I hand over the pig races to someone else and spend the time resting, but the ritual of the gates, the bets, the rush of the winning snout, all of it was too soothing for me to give up. My internal tenant jumped with every pistol shot, and I delighted in the proof that it was still growing, still thriving.

I was round as the sun and ready to burst when Arturo added a new gig to our route.

"Peculiar?" I echoed when he told me our heading. "What the hell kind of name is that for a town?"

"The perfect name for a town about to host the likes of us! They'll know peculiar when we roll into their fields!" Arturo jigged around the wagon, believing himself to be the king of cleverness for his flourishing business practices, and I, his wife, did my part to polish that crown of his. The Family Fortuna was galloping up a ramp of success with no signs of slowing. If Peculiar would bring us the next plank to add to that ramp, I thought, so be it.

But the trek through the valley was rocky, the wheels hitting every bump. A bubble of nausea nestled under my ribs; my passenger thrashed and rolled, kicking my lungs, stealing my breath. Socorro felt my tightening belly and instructed me to lie down. Soon, she pronounced. Soon it would be time to deliver.

I'd survived two deliveries already and recalled the sensations of those labors—all my muscles stiffening, my bones straightening, my mind clearing and shrinking down to this one impossible task: to push a baby out into the world and live to see it afterward.

All my parts coordinating, a mounting certainty thrumming through me, some primordial door in my brain unlocking to guide the mother in me through this ordeal—

And this was different. The closer we rode to Peculiar, the dizzier I grew, and the more unsettled. I paced our wagon, Luna and Ren underfoot, Arturo speaking a long trail of loud nonsense to everyone and no one. My breaths were shallow, and the air tasted strange—coppery, metallic, with a tang of blood.

"Something's not right," was my muttered chant in every corner of the wagon, with every turn of my heel, every jostle of the road.

"Everything's splendid!" Arturo kept shouting. "We're about to deliver the show of a lifetime to the good people of Peculiar—they won't know what hit them! They'll never be the same!" He did not understand that I was not seeking a reply or an assurance; he did not understand that a conversation could exist without need of his voice barging in.

Shadows grew as the sun sank, long and sinister out the windows. We rolled closer. Every nerve of mine fluttered, a thousand insects beneath my skin. My heart thudded into my chest; I feared it would explode through bone and plop onto the rug.

"Relax, my flower!" Arturo took me by the elbow and tried to guide me to the rocking chair. "We'll pull in soon and post bills and stake tents, and—"

The thump that jolted our wagon was large enough that it shut even Arturo up. Everything in our wagon shook, and an axle squealed before we shuddered to a stop.

"What in the devil's blue balls was that?" Arturo thundered, that mustache of his cutting across his lips at perturbed angles.

"Don't look at me!" I barked. "Go outside and see what happened." Honestly, sometimes I peered at the man I'd married and wondered how he managed to pull his own pants on.

Luna and Ren rushed to the window, gazing out at the pale blue twilight. Our wagon balanced on a winding mountain road, just beyond the peak. If I squinted with my good eye, I could make out the glitter of a township below—our heading, Peculiar. Arturo's latest Shambala.

The baby pummeled me in the lungs. I gasped and found the space inside of me lacking, too cramped, too seized to properly get a deep breath.

"I'm stepping outside for air," I told my littles. "Stay in the wagon. Watch for Papa."

Outside, the evening ran its chilly bite along my hands and neck and face. The ground was uneven beneath my boots. I inhaled again, seeking fullness, seeking buoyancy, but there was no room within me; I could only sip at the air.

Kick, kick, kick . . . The body within my body set a rhythm for itself, and I wondered if it would be a dancer. I wondered if I would look back on this moment with fondness, a sneak reveal of my child's future proclivities. Right now, I only felt vexed. I only had room for one emotion. No breath, just baby.

The wagon's wheels were askew in the weeds from our graceless braking. No sign of what had caused the hubbub—a crooked tire from lurching past a sharp rock, perhaps? Or had our driver dodged an unknown shadow, steering us into the dirt?

And then, as if answering my silent inquiries, the light shifted, and I saw it—

Beneath my boots, near the tires, a bird.

Black feathers. Small black feet curled up in pain. Black beak shining silver in the dusk. Eyes closed forever.

Its wings were stiff, flattened against the sides of its body.

Dead.

Crunched by our wheels or stunned lifeless as it flew into the wagon, I didn't know.

But it was dead at my feet.

A sensation crescendoed within me, a rising tide. The wrongness of it coated my tongue—the wrongness of this bird, this halt on the hillside, this town.

I gagged, unable to look away from the bird. Hot spittle ran between my teeth.

Black feathers sleek in the dirt.

Wrong, wrong, something is wrong—

"Quinn!" Arturo stomped around the wagon, then popped his head out the door. "What are you—" He paused, seeing my face, seeing me half bent, hands on my knees, that impossibly huge belly impeding my own gravity. "You're pale as milk. Are you sick?"

"I—" The world spun. I glanced down at the bird again.

Wrong, wrong, wrong.

Something was wrong.

"Socorro!" Arturo called, hurtling down the wagon steps. "Get Socorro, you fuckers! Hurry!"

He rubbed a hand up and down my spine, but I could not concentrate on it.

Couldn't concentrate on anything but this rotting, churling sensation gripping my every cell—

Wrong, wrong, wrong.

Something split.

Something wet, warm. A trickle.

A surge—

"Quinn." Arturo's voice was muted, sending a barb of fear through me. Arturo wouldn't lower his voice for a funeral march.

And then I heard myself, heard the noises that were issuing from me like the blaring grunts of a twisted trumpet.

"Quinn." Socorro this time, leaning over so she could read my face. My vision went white as pipe clay, all except that bird, *the bird, we killed the bird*—

"My water broke," I managed to tell her. "It's starting."

It was starting, and it was wrong.

Something rotten, something wrong.

I surged with Avita for the rest of the night.

Arturo ploughed the caravan ahead and ordered that the setup begin. "A decorated mother," he chortled, "and she didn't even know she was laboring! Thought she was seasick!" Once Socorro assured him that his wife was not dwindling but merely in the early throes of childbirth, he found it easy to laugh.

"Everything is ready, my love," he boasted when he returned to the wagon after midnight, reeking of drink. "Tomorrow morning, we'll open our gates to Peculiar and let them into our world of wonders!"

He collapsed in his bed, and even his snores were resonant enough to announce a tent.

Socorro stayed with me, breathing with me through the pain, checking my body for ripeness, enduring the lonely hours of blackest night.

Something felt wrong. Socorro asserted that the delivery was going well and that every baby was different.

But every time I closed my eyes, I saw that bird, and a slime of guilt began to creep through my innards.

Something wrong. We did something wrong.

I did something wrong.

After the better part of a year spent growing another life, the belly ripe, cheeks purple, veins and bones and lungs all straining and pushing, every drop of blood pushing—

Out she came.

A muffle, a cry, and a head.

The rest of her slipped out, and there was a gasp.

"Quinn," murmured Socorro. I could not decipher her tone.

I took my mewling pink baby, who rooted at my breast for comfort, and then I saw.

Fingers and toes were counted—ten of each. (But that face.)

Limbs were tested—two arms, two legs, healthy and strong. (But that face.)

A straight spine, clear airways, and a snarl of wet, swirling black hair. (But that face.)

It is every mother's hope that her child bears the pressures of delivery, that they come out like bruised fruit but slowly unfold and brighten, letting the sky and sun and world ripen them.

But this was beyond hope. Beyond expectation.

"Your daughter," Socorro said, and her pronouncement shook me from my awe. She passed me a blanket, and I wrapped my child and warmed her, letting her suckle.

I patted her hair, patted her soft, fluffy down, felt it dry under my fingers.

Socorro had no answers. I did not even know what questions to ask.

And after my initial hesitation, I tumbled headfirst into love with my daughter, who was sturdy like I am and rascally like Arturo is, who fed well and slept little but seemed content to stay awake and watch the world.

Arturo will be thrilled, I thought as I studied her strangenesses. *He'll believe his own panache brought her this unlikely form.*

But as she bloomed, healthy and flourishing aside from that face (that face!), I did not lose that sense of wrongness.

My mind cataloged everything I'd done during my pregnancy, everything I'd eaten, everything I'd said. The skipped prayers. The forgotten scriptures. The heedless way in which I'd moved through the world—a world that had rules, laws, boundaries.

It was plain as that, you see?

I had neglected worship, and I'd bled out our offspring. Our wagon had slaughtered a bird, and our daughter was born with a beak and feathers.

And then it was impossible not to see it everywhere.

A splinter on the table in the grub tent? A dancing girl would trip onstage that night.

A roof shingle on the wagon that warped in the rain? A drought was on its way.

A stray cat came to collect gossip.

A potato in the pocket guarded against achy bones.

Things should break in thirds. Do not rock an empty cradle. Clothing should never be mended while you wear it—

A thousand little rules, and as long as I followed them, nothing could happen.

As long as I followed them, we would be safe.

Arturo convinced me to let her perform, and I allowed it, as long as he was nearby. As long as Avita stayed in her cage, where our crowds could not rush at her with the proverbial pitchforks and torches, she would be safe. But here's the rub, as Arturo would call it:

All those years, all those rules, running myself ragged to make everything right for everyone in the circus—and it never once made it go away. That sensation, that sticky panic, that oppressive wrongness.

It never went away. It only got worse.

I cannot know if we hit the bird. I cannot know if Avita looks the way she looks because of something impious I did.

But today, right now, as I take my seat in her tent and reflect on the pose of my Avita on her new banner—still vigorous, still powerful, still as resplendent as a heaven-sent miracle—that sense of desecration lifts a little. A fog clearing.

This is right. Everything about Avita is right.

And when she finishes her act, whatever it may be, I will try my best to clap.

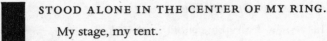 Knock, and It Shall Be Opened Unto You

I STOOD ALONE IN THE CENTER OF MY RING.

My stage, my tent.

My act.

Right now, waiting in the darkness, the whole world was mine.

My dress had been worn by my sister, but I was not trying to become the duchess. I was simply part of her line. Fortuna blood ran through me, ran into the seams and stitches of this costume and back out again.

I could sense them out there, my audience. Tittering, uncertain of what awaited them when the spotlights switched on.

They'd been drawn into my tent by a banner too exquisitely strange to be ignored: a young woman cutting a sensual figure, a horrifically carved face that unsettled the soul, a divinely unapologetic glance daring onlookers to come see more, come look closer, come find out.

And here they were, packed to the gills.

Wormed on my hook.

Pedro snapped the spot on, aimed it in my direction, and I was ready for them.

Ready for the screams.

As soon as the light hit my mug, there they were—

High-pitched, hairy, curdling my guts.

Screams.

I could hear their fear, the vibrato in their shrieks. Mouths frozen in horrified smiles—but screaming through their smiles at the wonder of it. The wonder of me.

I expected them to scream. I waited for it.

Chin lifted, mouth closed, peering right past the lights.

No cage, no chickens. Only me.

I waited, and I looked.

Time warps when you're onstage; a minute stretches out to feel like a torturous hour. Your body buzzes at you to hurry up, move, say something, anything to fill these blank, empty seconds—

But I waited.

And slowly, the screams stopped.

It was quiet enough to hear crickets fucking.

Nothing else. Only me.

A whole tent of onlookers clutched in my claws—

There was fire in my lungs. I cleared my throat and watched my crowd.

They waited.

Waited to see what I would do next.

The band swept us into the music, the lights dimmed, and a haze of amber limelights sparked up around the ring, finding the subtle glitter in my black gown.

I sang.

I sang, and they listened.

I had them spellbound, if not a little unsettled by this unusual interpretation of a monstrous curiosity. *Not to fret, not at all*, I tried to impart to them through my notes. *Be unsettled. Be enchanted. Be thrilled in every possible way.*

Right in front of me, just beyond the ring where the light dropped off into shadow, Tomás stood.

A sweet ache rushed through me. He'd put off his train to come to my show.

Hands in pockets, head tilted back, eyes glazed and unblinking like he was staring at the face of God—I could have blown him a silent kiss, and he would have toppled over.

A wink might have shot clean through his heart like a bullet.

He'd seen me all along. In his own way. With his charcoals, with his paints, with his extraordinary eye, he'd seen me. Seen how spectacular I was as Bird Girl. Seen how spectacular I was as Avita. Seen that I was so much more.

I looked toward the back of the house, overwhelmed by the way this audience let me hold them, let me caress them with my strangeness and my song—

And there he was.

My father.

He suppressed his reaction like a stifled cough, throat bulging, mustache fidgeting. Well? Had I convinced him?

I sent out my notes, *bing-bang*, into the ring. No warbling like a canary. No coquettish tone for the men in the crowd who wanted to pop me into their mouths like a sugar cube. I was here to ruffle feathers.

My song was not sung; it was preached. Flung out at its target, a perfect bull's-eye.

My father's gaze was running along the benches, taking stock of my audience. The aura of a grunt wafted off him as he surveyed every onlooker, and my heart pooled in buttery affection. He was watching for taunters. Watching for mockers. Watching for hecklers or needlers or screamers.

Watching for anyone who might ruin my show.

Look here, not at them! I wanted to shout. *Who gives a fuck about those walking tickets with ears? Look up here, look at the ring, look—*

My breath came in heaves, my hands balled into fists.

This was my act now. An act all of my own.

And my audience looked where I wanted them to look.

I took it, all that they were offering—unbridled want and love and fear. I arched my back, letting my voice hit the ceiling and dig down into the earth beneath us—

And I felt it.

My dress, the long half train of my dress . . . it no longer swept around the stage like a dark cape.

No, it was feathers.

My arms stretched out to either side—great black wings unfurling, my magnificent feathers sheening like velvet against the golden luster of my tent.

Papa stopped dead still, staring right at me.

The audience gasped, and I devoured it—the most delicious thing in all the world.

The music played, and I flapped my wings, lifted my beak, sang on.

Some screamed, some cheered. Whatever they wanted to take from me, I was here for them.

For my audience.

Here to dazzle them in all ways.

At the song's zenith, just as the strings ramped up into a staccato rhythm and the thirds became fifths and the melody arched up, up the scale for a big finish, it happened.

More feathers flushing down my torso. My wings gaining air.

My feet lifting off the ground.

I could not tell if I was more frightening or more exquisite, but I was surely both. I could not tell if my face suddenly tilted more human, now that my body had burst forth into feather and wing, or if the whole of me was now more bird than girl.

The only mirror I had was my audience, and they were silent as I ascended into the air, high enough to touch the tarp.

My final note grew like a branch born of my throat; it anchored itself somewhere in the soil of my chest. I sang the lights bright, everything else in the world flaking away into stars.

Satisfied, I landed in the dirt and folded my arms at my sides. Arms again, not wings. My feathers splayed all around me in the ring, molted, as the music died.

I braced myself for whatever would greet me: more screams, peals of laughter, graveyard silence. But the applause was thunderous. Enough to pierce an eardrum, enough for Cornelius to hear in his fancy-schmancy tents next door and wonder what on earth had been set loose on our grounds.

Applause, and my whole world pinholed to Arturo's brimming eyes, his stunned mouth agape, like he was just another slack-jaw with a ticket in his grasp, delight emanating from his glorious head like a halo.

There, Papa, you see?

You see what I was capable of all along?

"Beautiful show, my sweet," he murmured, his heart unraveling in the light, "simply beautiful."

A History
(Sixteen years ago)

PAPA

I HAVE NEVER BEEN A PATIENT MAN.

Who can wait on the world when you're burning up inside? Every second of my time means money, money walking past our gates instead of landing in our cashbox, flooding our midway, rolling into our rings after we've charmed it out of purses and pockets.

Peculiar's proved to be a golden goose. Customers walk the grounds with grins plastered on their mugs, like we've brought them a slice of heaven smuggled between our tentpoles and our concession booths.

Quinn went into labor on the road. She and the baby are all bundled up in the family wagon, and Socorro brings her teas, meals, other concoctions for females in such circumstances. "Mother and baby are doing well enough," she reports to me, arms full of fresh towels and rice bags for the coal stove.

"Well enough? When do I get my wagon back, huh? My bed?" Behind me, a bell and a whistle sound; somewhere in the midway, a cake eater's hit the milk bottle jackpot.

Socorro tightens her grip on her towels, her jaw stern. "Soon" is her infuriating response, and then she's gone, back to the family wagon to tend to Quinn. To sleep in my bed until Quinn's healed enough for company.

Meanwhile, the people of Peculiar charge through our gates at sunup, and they fork over coin for circus chow and try-your-luck games until we corral them from our grounds at midnight. Every minute here is a triumph. I witness our daily tallies, and they make my head spin—so many tickets, so much cash. More than we have ever made. I can only suppose that our newest little rug rat is some sort of lucky charm. A bringer of fortune.

Finally, after my third night of snoozing with the clowns, Socorro opens up my own wagon to me. I bound up the steps at twilight, the master of my domain once again.

Quinn sits up in her bed, babe in arms, noticeably tired but lovelier than ever. I tell her as much and kiss her cheek, but when I move to peek at the latest of my loin fruit, Quinn pulls her out of my reach.

"Let her sleep," she instructs. "You'll see her soon enough." She tucks the blankets around the babe, and I think little of it.

I think little of anything except sprawling out on my own mattress, not because I am particularly tired but because a man belongs in his own space with his own things.

A man in his own bed.

Quinn asks after the circus's operations, and I tell her the week's best stories: the sea captain who caught the garter in the Tent of Wonder and earned his pick of dancing partners for the hoochie coochie; the trapezists nailing their catch-and-releases; the cigar-smoking suit who requested a luncheon with me tomorrow to discuss taking the Family Fortuna for a run on his showboat, the *Floating Palace*.

She listens, asks few questions (I answer as if she has, anyway), then nods off while I oil my mustache, the babe in her arms.

I let her doze, leaving to finish the evening's ringmaster duties, and return to my bed after the grounds are empty of patrons. Quinn's left the lantern burning low for me, the soft honey glow hitting her face as she sleeps, lighting her up like an angel.

A woman to be proud of—she'd delivered me three babies, and yet I'd be fibbing if I said she hadn't helped bring the circus to term as well.

The baby rests, tucked in Quinn's arms. Although she has been alive now for nearly four days and I have still not introduced myself, only a muttonhead would wake a sleeping infant. I've raised two children from nurslings like this. Surely the third Fortuna model will follow suit.

After a nip of blackstrap and a brushing of my coat, I, too, slip into slumber, a senseless smile upon my lips. I am utterly pleased with myself for nailing the gig and propagating all that money. I am utterly pleased with myself for nailing my wife and propagating another Fortuna.

Tomorrow, who knows what I might spawn? What brilliant conceits I might pull forth from my brain? What schemes I might shit out to bring the good people of Peculiar more dazzle, more flash, more grandeur? What fortune might bring?

I am not a man who requires much sleep. Usually my mind buzzes like the noisiest pub in Texas, alive with ideas for acts and whispering new spiels and chatter, chatter, chatter.

But the baby cries and cries. My first night back in my own wagon, and she is robbing me of my sleep, and for that I am not sure I will forgive her, not even if she's been a good luck charm for our Peculiar showings.

"Quinn," I groan, "you must get her to stop! Use those fantastic breasts of yours and just shove it—"

"Arturo, I am trying." There is a seriousness in her voice that makes me pause.

Marry a woman who is calm and steady, my father used to tell me, *and you'll live a calm, steady, metered life.* He'd beam at the woman he'd replaced my own mother with—she was less woman than lamb, and true to his word, my father never went without a hot meal on the table or a warm spot in his bed.

But I never wanted a lamb. I wanted a storm cloud. Someone electric. Someone with a brain and a heart and legs to run alongside me.

So whenever Quinn went soft like this, quiet, clearly holding back more words than she said, I knew something was wrong.

She turns the key on the lamp, making the wagon too bright to abide. I tear out of my bed with a grunt and stand above her bed, rubbing sleep from my eyes.

The baby pierces the night again with her yowl.

"Does she need clean rags? Rum for teething? What?" I am groggy and trying to remember the catalog of things that can plague infants in these early days. They are such helpless rats in the beginning, just balls of fur and milk sweat and tears.

But Quinn shakes her head.

"Arturo," she says. Weariness cracks her voice like dry earth. She stops bouncing the bundle in her arms, goes slack, lets it rest on the bed before her. The babe cranks up her volume, offended.

"Good God, woman! Don't just abandon the thing!" I hunch to take a turn with the squealer.

But Quinn reaches for me with both arms, blocking me. She clings to my long johns with trembling hands like a parishioner pleading with her priest. "Arturo, forgive me! I have to tell you—"

The baby lurches out with her tears, a primal cry that is more monstrous than human. My temper flares; it is useless to scream back at a baby, of course, but I've yelled at rocks that have dared to trip me.

"Enough!" I bark. "We hear you, we all hear you—the man on the moon hears you, with all your racket. You're hot? You're cold? You're gassy? What?"

I pick her up, my hands gentle even if my voice is not, and I hold her up to the lamp's gleam.

Beside me, Quinn clenches my nightclothes, taking in a sharp inhale.

I peer down at my new child for the first time, and I see—

A beak for a nose.

Two glassy black eyes.

A mouth of tiny obsidian teeth.

The down of future feathers.

My knees buckle. I do not blink, do not breathe. I have been struck speechless.

No words . . . I have no words . . . but as soon as I can, I will find them, and then—

"She is—" Quinn starts, then breaks into a sob. "Look at her. She's—"

But even she can't finish.

What is she? Cursed? Deformed? Taking after a long-ago ancestor with absurdly dominant genes? An affront to everything human? Yes, all those things, possibly, but there is something else, something else she is, and I haven't landed on it yet.

"How?" I whisper, still stunned like I've been smacked in the noggin with a frying pan. "How could it—" I pause, watching my daughter in my hands. She's stopped her screeching now. She's settled, staring up at me.

Quinn lets out a sob, and I can ignore her no longer. I finally turn my attention to my wife, who is blubbering like I have never seen before; not even when she lost her other pregnancies did she look so despondent, so torn. "Quinn? What is it?"

"Look at her!" Quinn bursts. "Look what I've done to her!"

"You?" I chuckle. "How? Did you chisel away at her while she was in your stomach? Carve her up when she was born and plant her feathers, water them to make them grow? No, this was not your doing, Quinn. This is something else."

The word tickles the tip of my tongue, forming, nearly ready to fall out. My daughter peers up at me, studying.

Something in me flutters, deep and ancient.

Something in me melts.

Quinn will not be comforted.

"There were signs—I should have heeded them, Arturo. I should have known." She looks so despondent, it knocks me on my ass—I have never seen my wife look this lost, this sorrowful. And for what? A healthy baby girl whose lungs are strong enough to belt out her angry song, whose black eyes shine with life?

My wife's hands are covering her face, and she's shaking her head as she cries violently. Her milk spills out of her, soaking her nightdress in wet round patches. "Forgive me, Arturo," she says, "forgive me. I'm so sorry. Forgive me."

I instruct her to move aside and climb into bed next to her, the babe in my arms.

"Quinn, my love," I soothe. "There is nothing to forgive! You've done it again—you've made me another, and you're alive to raise it. That's more than I could ask for. Now rest. Rest!"

My wife chews her lip nervously, some dark thoughts brewing that I cannot begin to understand—some postpartum nonsense, some black hysteria leaving her body. It happens sometimes; mothers' brains get all crossed up during pregnancy, and it takes some time for them to unwind. But eventually she calms herself and falls into a deep sleep, lying flat at last on her pillow.

I hold on to our girl, tilting her so the lamplight catches her astonishing features—

And I feel it. That ache within, the one every father gets when he looks upon his own kin.

My heart cleaved in two when Luna was born. I will never forget holding her, all silver, all beauty, a wisp of a flower who ate and slept like a dream.

My heart split again when Lorenzo was born—my guts seized up in pride and adoration at my son, my son who cooed at me from his cradle, my son who fit so neatly in the crook of my elbow, my son, my son, my son.

And now, just when I think there is no room left in my heart for anything else, another daughter—and a spectacular one. A miracle.

"My darling," I tell her, and she listens, those big bird eyes looking at me, taking me in. I drop my voice low, make it as soft as the rushing waves on a lake's shore. "My star. The newest star in my sky. My darling, my daughter."

And I love her more than a circus, more than a performer. My world pinholes small, to this moment only—a father holding his most precious jewel, something worth more than all the money in the Southwest.

A daughter.